SARAH MASON

Hell of a Ride

First edition

ISBN: 979-8-9992950-1-9

Cover art by Evgeniia Gurcheva
Editing by Evelyn Summers

This book was professionally typeset on Reedsy.
Find out more at reedsy.com

Foreword

For the ones who wrestled their demons and still found reasons to dance.

For those who've loved and lost, fallen apart, and stitched themselves back together with trembling hands.

You don't have to be unbroken to be worthy.
You are not damaged, too loud, or too much—you are exactly enough.

For the women who aren't there yet, who are still finding their footing, still learning to forgive themselves, still trying to believe they deserve the good things coming—you are healing, even when it doesn't feel like it.

This story is for the beautiful work in progress you are.

May you find peace, joy, and the kind of love that starts within.

Preface

<u>Reader Advisory</u>

This isn't the kind of love story that stays tidy.

This book includes themes of addiction, recovery, PTSD, grief, references to past abuse (both physical and sexual), strong language, teen pregnancy, and open-door intimacy. The characters stumble. They regress. They hurt each other before they learn how not to.

There are no easy fixes here—only hard-earned ones.

If any of these topics feel too close to home, please take care of yourself first.

And no, the author still cannot be held responsible for emotional damage— but she is rooting for you.

Happy(ish) reading!

I stumbled up the stairs blindly, my stomach in my throat and my heart pounding against my rib cage like a wild animal trying to break free. Swallowing the rising bile, I paused at the top, swaying like I couldn't feel the ground under me. My ears were ringing, I couldn't breathe. I heard my mother yelling for me, but her voice was distant, like it was traveling through water. "Holly, baby, wait! Please! Oh, David…what are we going to do now?"

That last bit was directed at my dad, who had remained frozen in front of the TV at the verdict. Not guilty. The words echoed around the room like a curse. How had they found him not guilty?

Almost on autopilot, I made my way down the hall to the trophy room. My mom loved this room. I had too, once upon a time. Now, standing in the doorway, all I felt was horror. Rage. Disgust. I shuddered at the feel of ghost hands on me, taking what wasn't theirs. Greedy, vile, wrong.

His hands.

Scott Lauren.

I was a child, and I hadn't been the only one.

A sob broke through, my eyes taking in the endless photos and awards. Pictures of me throughout the years, owning the stage like I'd been born to it. Pretty dresses. Big smiles. Bright hazel eyes. I didn't have to look in a mirror to know they weren't so bright anymore.

The last stage I stood on wasn't for a crown—it was for a courtroom. One hand on a Bible, the other clinging to what little strength I had left. I had felt so embarrassed, so ashamed, despite everyone telling me it wasn't my fault.

It was never the victim's fault.

I hated that word. Victim. But I sat there and told the truth anyway.

Not guilty? After what he did?

"This is our home, David!"

"It was our home. How can you sit here and say you want to stay after what that bastard did?"

I tuned them out, and my eyes landed on the Miss Jr High School USA trophy, my last and biggest. Tears blurred my vision, and I was moving towards it before I could even process what I was doing. I screamed as I threw it at the nearest trophy case with all the strength my sixteen-year-old body possessed. The glass shattered—sharp and violent, like the pieces of me I couldn't put back together. As the whole thing came crashing down, my parents went quiet. But the silence just made everything worse. I screamed again as I grabbed another trophy, throwing it at another case. Glass shredded my bare feet, but I barely noticed. It was nothing compared to the pain inside.

My father made it up the stairs and to me within minutes, but it felt like years. By the time he burst into the room, glass carpeted the floor and blood slicked my palms, threaded through my hair, and welled between my toes where I'd stepped without feeling it. He came up behind me, wrapping his arms around me. I kicked and screamed until my voice was hoarse. "It's ok, baby. It's ok, I'm here. Daddy's here. It's ok."

He didn't let go, no matter how I thrashed, until finally, I went slack, completely spent.

As I turned and buried my face in his chest, sobs wracking my body, I caught sight of my mother in the doorway, hand over her mouth as she took in the destruction. Her eyes, just like my own, were wide, and tears left tracks through her carefully applied makeup. My father ran soothing hands up and down my back, not the least bit bothered by the blood. I felt him look over at her. "We're leaving, Ruth. That's final. This town has nothing left for us."

His tone left no room for argument.

Chapter One

❧

The Board of Directors at Children's Healthcare of Atlanta practically swooned when my father accepted their offer as head of pediatric neurosurgery. My mother moaned about the heat and humidity, the lack of beaches, and pretty much everything else, but she preferred it to the position in Missouri, which, to her, was a social and economic death trap. Not that anyone asked me. I honestly couldn't have cared less where we moved. Alaska or Timbuktu, just somewhere they wouldn't know me. My father chose to drive the almost 2500 miles from California to Atlanta. I spent most of the ride curled up in the back seat, staring at the bandages on my hands and legs. The clean white cloth hiding the slices of skin the glass had torn away.

My father, the type who couldn't stand silence, tried endlessly to make conversation, talking about the new job, how much he thought I would like our new house, and the fun things we could do. His efforts to pull me into a conversation were fruitless, so he switched to my mother.

For three days, I did my best to ignore their conversation, their voices like the buzzing of a bee. A really, really annoying bee. They were trying so hard to make this feel like a normal move, even though we all knew what it was.

We were running away.

As we passed the "Welcome to Atlanta" sign, I rolled down the window so I could take in the city skyline. I was immediately hit with air so thick and hot that it clung to my skin like it was alive. My mother started fretting over her hair, which "simply wouldn't survive in this climate."

I rolled my eyes and stuck my head a bit farther out the window as my dad hushed her. "We're about 20 minutes away now. You ready?" I cast him a disinterested glance and he frowned sadly, "Come on now, bug. I know it's hard, but a fresh start will be good for all of us, don't you think?"

They still tried hard to treat me like I was their perfect little girl with an unfettered smile and curly pigtails. Like I hadn't become someone else that day. The day society let a monster win.

As we pulled up to a wrought iron gate that swung forward quietly at the press of a button from my dad, I got my first real look at the new place. I stared at the white columns lining the huge porch, perfectly spaced and gleaming in the Georgia sun—a stark contrast to the brown stucco framing back home. Bougainvillea had wrapped itself around the fence there, but here everything was pristine. From the long driveway that ended in a grand circle, like it was waiting for a horse and carriage to pull up, to the perfectly trimmed rose bushes along the front of the house.

When I climbed out of the car, instead of being hit with the salty, comforting smell of a nearby ocean, I smelled nothing. No brine, no humidity, no familiar rot of sea grass. The air was sterile, like it had been cleaned before I arrived. Like it hadn't decided whether I belonged in it.

We had about an hour before the move-in team would arrive, so Dad ushered me inside, encouraging me to find my room. Mom walked through the foyer like she was starring in some real estate show, touching the walls and murmuring things like, "Oh, this molding is to die for." Who even says stuff like that? But despite her bright smile, I could see the tremble of uncertainty in her hands as she made her way down the marble-floored hallway. My dad stood next to me, and he pulled me into his side.

"What do you think, bug? Gorgeous, right?"

I nodded mutely and didn't point out that it felt more like a movie set than it did a home. Our old house had been warm browns and rich blues, the sunlight reaching into every corner of every room through the open windows. A breeze flowing in off the water carried every little trouble away. This was all whites and blacks and emptiness. Which, I suppose, made it just like me.

I ducked away from my father and headed up the winding staircase that looked like someone had pulled it away from Heaven's gate. It was beautiful, in a cold and holier-than-thou way. The hallway at the top was lined with rooms. I went all the way to the back, then chose the one on the right at random. It was indeed a bedroom, not a bathroom or linen closet. Standing in the doorway, I eyed the emptiness like it had secrets of its own. There was a massive bay window that opened to a private balcony and two doors, one of which was open and showing off a walk-in closet. Neither my clothes nor my furniture were here yet, but I stepped inside and tossed my backpack on the floor, approximately where my bed would go.

I opened the door to the balcony, which overlooked our expansive backyard. There was an outdoor kitchen, which my dad would just love, and a white-stone basin, water rippling in obedient little waves—like the ocean, only housebroken. The faint rippling sound coming off it made me feel just a bit better. I pulled my phone out to take a picture, but stopped. Who would I send it to? All my so-called friends had abandoned me. I had stopped using social media during the trial, and the thought of reopening my old profiles made me feel ill. Like a grave robber. My hands started to tremble, and I clenched my bandaged fists before closing my eyes and forcing myself to take a breath. In, out. Just breathe. What was that thing Elsa had said? Conceal, don't feel?

I plopped down on the ground and sat staring at the pool for I don't know how long. A knock on the balcony door had me turning to find my dad, who gave me a smile that didn't overshadow the sadness in his eyes. "You good, bug?"

I opened my mouth to tell him I was fine, but surprised myself by saying, "I was gonna show my friends the new house. But then I remembered I don't have any friends. So, that's great."

He sighed and slowly lowered himself to the ground, years of bending over a surgery table making him stiff. "You'll make new friends here. This will be a fresh start for all of us, you'll see." He caught sight of the outdoor kitchen and elbowed me before pointing at it. "Oo look! Not a thing in the world that fire-grilled pizza can't fix!" He grinned at me before taking my hand gently in his. "It'll be ok, bug. We're in it together, yeah?" I nodded, and he pulled us both up off the ground.

"Ok, I hate to run, but I have to get over to the hospital—leaving you with your mother. Try not to kill each other, ok?. Moving crew will be here soon." I gave him a look and he laughed, the sound only mildly forced.

My mother appeared in the doorway of my bedroom and clapped her hands together when she saw us. "Oh, goodie. Found you!" Like we had been hiding or something. Dad walked over, kissing her before disappearing and leaving the two of us alone. Mom looked over at me, her overly bright smile wavering for a minute before she plastered it back on. "I don't know about you, but I think this place could use a woman's touch! Want to come shopping?"

I, in fact, most definitely did not want to go shopping with her, but I knew that if I said no, not only would she act like a kicked puppy, but I would be stuck here in the way of everyone moving our things.

That's how I found myself sulking behind her at some place called *Restoration Hardware*. A name like that, you would think cute. Thrifted. Charming. Oh, no. Not here. The furniture looked like it had been made by cherubs, blessed by monks, and cost more than most cars. My mom cheerfully introduced herself to the sales associate who had the unfortunate luck of being there that day. When the girl looked at me as my mom droned on about the stress of the move and any other random thought that crossed her mind, I shrugged helplessly.

"Don't you think this dove gray would look positively lovely in the entryway, Holly? Maybe have someone reupholster those two old chairs that sat in the main hallway?"

The old chairs in question were two blue velvet wingbacks she had bought not even a year ago, but I nodded in agreement whilst staring at a lamp priced at $1,200 and wondered if it granted wishes. Once upon a time, I would've loved this. I would've bounced along behind my mother, helping her pick out matching candles and begging her to let me design the foyer myself. I used to get excited over seasonal throw pillows and other pretty things. Like my mother, I had been bright and vivid and always smiling. I knew the names of famous designers and thought that mattered. Back when I thought I mattered.

Now, I listened to my mother insist that the sales girl call her Ruth and not Mrs. McCarthy while staying silent. I tried to make myself smaller in my black hoodie and faded skinny jeans, shrinking under the bright lights, frowning at the shiny gold lamp, which seemed to mock my discomfort. My mother pulled me from the depths of my misery, and I turned to her with a frown. "What, Mother?"

She flinched, just barely, at my harsh tone. Ever the dramatic prima donna. But she recovered quickly and held out two gray swaths of color to me. "I was calling your name forever, silly. Which one do you think?" I eyed her, then the cloth she held out before me, and glanced from them to her. Her bright, eager smile made the shining lights all the more overwhelming, and I suddenly wanted to be literally anywhere else but there. "Well?" she pushed, shaking the fabrics like I hadn't noticed them.

Finally, I snapped, "For the love of God, Mom, does it really freaking matter? They're gray. They are both gray, Mom. God forbid you put a bit of color in the room. Like, oh, I don't know—blue? Like the so-called old chairs you literally just bought?"

The sales girl's eyebrows disappeared into her bangs, and my mom's bottom lip trembled as she dropped her hands like she was holding rocks. I couldn't find it in me to care. I held out my hand. "Give me the keys, I'll be in the car." She handed them to me wordlessly, and I turned without another word. Tears threatened to spill from my eyes, a part of me feeling bad for going off on her. But, as I swiped at them angrily, I shoved my feelings down where they belonged.

I didn't even have to look behind me to know she wasn't following. Even now, she was oblivious to the way I was falling apart. All the times I had flinched when he adjusted my costume or refused to look him in the eyes, she had cheered the loudest for me. She had been so focused on winning, on being perfect. She never saw it, or maybe she just didn't want to see. Just like now, she never really looked at me. Never really saw me. I wasn't about to stand in some overly pretentious store with her and pretend everything was ok. Not anymore.

I was so lost in thought, marching towards the car with my head down, that I didn't even hear the motorcycles flying through the parking lot. At the last second, I heard the tires squeal on the pavement and jumped to the side. The rider managed to control his bike despite the abrupt stop, and three other bikes pulled up next to his. I let loose a string of Italian curses I had learned from an exchange student we had hosted a couple of years ago and spun towards the idiot.

"Oh, I'm sorry! I must have missed the part where the parking lot became a racetrack!" I glared at him because it was definitely a him based on the way he filled out his jacket, and I only got angrier when he pulled off his helmet and saw that not only was the ass-hat good looking, but he was *laughing.*

"Geez, princess, too busy planning your next party to pay attention?"

Now, usually, I would walk away. The old me would've. A flippant toss of hair, rolling eyes, and a decided sway to my hips to make sure he was watching. The new me? The new me had just walked away from picking a fight with her mother and was ready to rip him a new one. "Princess?" I seethed, "Fine. If you want to play the nickname game, I can do that. How about…pool boy? No, that joke may go over your head. Oh, I know! Idiotic man-child with small dick syndrome! Or is that too long for you?" I batted my eyes at him.

For a minute, the four guys across from me just stared. Then one of them, a tall blonde, burst out laughing. "Oh fuck, Jackson. She's reading you dead to rights."

Jackson, the idiot in question, glared at his friend. "Shut up, Dalton." Dalton was not the least bit fazed and made a show of wiping a tear from his eye.

Jackson turned back to me and took a step closer. "What the hell is your deal?"

I scoffed, "Oh, I don't know. Maybe tread marks just don't go with my aesthetic." Dalton snorted another laugh, but another glare from Jackson had him quiet.

"Maybe watch where you're walking? You don't own the town, *princess*." His tone was biting, his gray eyes cold.

I gestured to the pavement. "I was walking in the walkway. What part of the *walkway* did you not get?" Jackson opened his mouth to say something, but another one of his friends stepped forward. This guy had blue eyes like Dalton's, and they looked similar enough that they could've been brothers, but his hair was dark and he was at least a year or two older.

He put a hand on Jackson's shoulder. "Come on, man. Let's go. No harm, no foul."

Jackson looked like he wanted to argue, but instead said, "Yeah, sure, Mac. This chick ain't worth my time." I flipped him off as they got back on their bikes and rode away.

When I climbed into the car to wait for my mom, I braced for the inevitable feelings that being alone somewhere quiet would bring. Oddly enough, I had started to welcome them. At least they were something, compared to the usual emptiness. But this time, they didn't come. I thought about Jackson and his friends, how he met me tit for tat instead of tiptoeing around me. I could appreciate that. I was so tired of being handled like I was going to break, like I wasn't already broken. That little argument had felt like therapy. I should know I had been to plenty of sessions.

Except, somehow, my mind wasn't replaying every word looking for landmines. There was no spiral, no shame, no script I needed to rewrite. Just... quiet. Because someone had actually pushed back instead of treating me like a fractured, porcelain doll. Pretty and delicate, and in need of repairs.

About thirty minutes later, my mom appeared out of the store. "That girl was so nice! She helped me pick out a bunch of things and even arranged for it all to be delivered. Must be those Southern manners I hear so much about." She hummed a tune under her breath, reaching for the radio. "Where should we go for dinner? Your dad said he was going to be a bit longer at the hospital."

I sighed, resisting the urge to get out of the car and just run. She wasn't just dismissing our earlier spat. She was acting as if it hadn't even happened. It was so typical of her, I really should have been used to it by now, instead of the disappointment creeping through my chest. I wanted her to see me, to speak to me, not at me. But I just said. "Whatever's good, Mom."

Mom wanted to "get a taste for local cuisine," so we found ourselves at a little rinky-dink spot called Laverne's. The booths were all faded, the tables stained, and the floor was kind of sticky. When we walked in, she made a face like she was fixing to tuck tail and find somewhere else. But a big, loud woman hollered from somewhere in the back, "Hiya, folks! Be right with ya!"

Mom grimaced at me. "I guess we just seat ourselves?" She took approximately ten years picking a booth in the mostly empty restaurant. My guess? She was trying to find the cleanest one. Finally, we slid into a booth covered with local advertisements, and I tried to fight back a smile at the sight of my uppity mother clutching her purse in front of her like a shield.

A few minutes later, the lady came over and greeted us with a wide smile that showed off a couple of missing teeth, her brown eyes warm and friendly yet incredibly sharp. She was wearing a rather hideous, cheap tracksuit, a giant fake diamond pendant, and her wig looked like two balls of yarn had gotten into a fight with a curling iron. I instantly liked her. My mom looked at her with what could be described as wide-eyed horror. She handed us two menus, which, unsurprisingly, were faded and old.

"Welcome to Laverne's, y'all. I haven't seen you around before! I'm Momma Laverne, though everyone just calls me Momma. What can I do for ya today? My chicken fried steak is on special, if you're feeling hungry."

My mother was still staring at Momma Laverne like she wasn't sure if the woman was even real. Momma Laverne, for her part, didn't seem to mind in the least. She had the kind of energy that said, "Go on and stare. I'm a lot to take in, and I'm ok with that. Love me or leave me."

I glanced between her and my mother for a minute then cleared my throat, "Umm, yeah, actually. We just moved from California. Mom wanted to find a spot for authentic Southern food. I googled it and found this place."

Had I noticed how worn down the place looked in the Google pictures? Absolutely. Had I mentioned it to my mother? Definitely not. And her reaction was even better than I could've imagined. "I will happily take your chicken fried steak." I was genuinely confused on how chicken and steak could be in the same sentence, or how you were supposed to fry a steak. But it couldn't be that bad if it was on special…I hoped.

Momma Laverne switched her attention to me. "And what sides would you like with that, honey?"

I blinked at her. "The usual?" Her laugh was as big and loud as she was, and my mom jolted like she had been physically shocked.

The woman winked at me, "The usual. You got it, honey." I suddenly wondered what I had gotten myself into.

My mom finally found her voice, "Could I please have a cobb salad, with kale?"

Laverne tilted her head, "Doll, the closest thing I have to kale is collards, and I can promise you that won't taste good in a salad. How about romaine?"

My mom looked at me like she wanted to make sure I wasn't recording this as an elaborate joke. I grinned at her, and she chirped back, "Sure!" Laverne turned back towards her kitchen, hollering that she would have someone bring over drinks. My mom looked at me again, "But she didn't even ask what we wanted to drink?"

I shrugged at her and looked towards the rest of the restaurant, taking everything in. There were old records nailed to the wall, a broken guitar hung up over a frayed and yellowed picture of a band, and newspaper clippings all over the place. I couldn't smell much over the cloud of slightly overwhelming floral perfume Laverne had left behind, but, looking at the chipped flooring that can't have seen a mop since before I was born, maybe that wasn't a bad thing. God, I hoped my attempt to give my mother a heart attack didn't end up killing us both with salmonella or some crap.

A girl about my age made her way over to us with a tray of drinks, and when she stopped at our table, my mom told her she had the wrong one, because no way that was all for us. The girl shook her head. "Nope, Momma said you guys wanted the real Southern experience. Welcome to Atlanta, by the way. I'm Maria."

Maria set down two glasses of water and two glasses of a brown liquid, plus a little sugar caddy. My mom eyed it distrustfully. Maria was wearing a jacket despite the summer heat. I was dying in my sweatshirt, but my mom had told me that it wasn't necessary as we left the house, and now, I was going to keep the thing on even if I melted.

Mom seemed to gather herself and smiled at the girl, who smiled back. "Thank you for the drinks, Maria. I'm Ruth, and this is my daughter, Holly. You guys look about the same age! She could use someone to show her around."

I groaned and slumped in my seat. "Mom, please do not force me off onto some hapless girl like a lost puppy."

Maria's lip twitched, like she wanted to laugh. "You would be a very unusual puppy. I heard you're from Cali? Maybe I could call you Sunny?" I gaped at her, then reached for my straw like I had suddenly become very interested in trying the drink she had brought over. Of course, I dropped the stupid thing, and Maria bent over to grab it for me. I bent over at the same time, and that was when I saw it.

A familiar blue-purple. Another spot of fading yellow.

Her eyes met mine, and she practically threw the straw down and said. "Enjoy your tea!" before disappearing into the back of the restaurant.

I stared after her, trying to process what I had just seen. Someone had hurt her, like really hurt her. That one bruise had been fresh, too. No wonder she was wearing the jacket. What else was she hiding? I was pulled from my racing thoughts by my mother coughing and spluttering like she was a victim of waterboarding.

I looked over at her as she set the glass of tea down on the table and raised an eyebrow in question. She gestured at the glass. "That is positively foul. That girl said it was tea, and I took a big sip, thinking it would be a nice bit of refreshment from this heat. I think I'll just stick with the water." She pushed it away from her like it might bite and took a hesitant sip of the water before smiling at me.

I tried the tea myself, still thinking of Maria, and found myself agreeing with my mother. It wasn't as bad as she had made it out to be, but I could practically feel the sugar gathering on my tongue. Hard pass. A little tea with your sugar, anyone? She pulled out her phone while we waited for our food, leaving me alone with my thoughts. A few minutes later, Maria came back out with a massive tray carefully balanced on her shoulder. This time, I was sure she had the wrong table. She didn't speak much, just naming the dishes as she set them down.

Mom's salad. My chicken fried steak. A bowl of collards, whatever that was. Mashed potatoes. Corn on the cob. Yams, which looked like a suspicious pile of orange covered in marshmallows. And pinto beans. Momma Laverne appeared behind her with a plate of something she called cornbread. My mother stared at the food, which was easily enough to feed ten people. I stared at Maria, who seemed very determined to pretend like I wasn't there.

Momma Laverne ushered Maria back to the kitchen, leaving us alone with our food. I wasn't even sure where to start. The smell was unbelievable. My brain didn't know what to think, but my mouth watered. I decided to start with something familiar, reaching for the mashed potatoes as Mom poked at her salad, which was more pieces of chicken and ranch than it was lettuce and other veggies. Right before I went to take a bite, I glanced over at the kitchen and saw Laverne poking her head over the top of the saloon style door, waiting to see me take my first bite. Her bushy head disappeared as soon as we made eye contact, like she had been caught snooping, and I smiled.

The second the potatoes hit my tongue, I decided I was never going back to California unless I could take Momma Laverne with me. They were rich and buttery, with little chunks of potato and even some potato skins in them. I had never had them as anything but a pureed, snow-white mass. I reached eagerly for the corn on the cob and took a bite, enjoying the way it squirted in the most unladylike fashion over my chin. I glanced up at my mom, who was frowning at me, and rolled my eyes when she pushed the napkins towards me. Not now, Mother. Busy getting lost in food heaven here. My exploration into the collards and yams was more tentative but if this is what Southern cooking had to offer, we should've moved years ago. There goes my waistline.

About twenty minutes later, I was leaning back in the booth. My mom had long since pushed her half-eaten salad to the side and had watched me eat like I was seconds away from starvation. I was so dang full they were going to have to roll me out of here. I was not entirely sure I could even fit in my mom's little sports car either. Through my sated bliss, I caught sight of Maria slipping into the bathroom. Full or not, I still desperately wanted to find out about that bruise. Which felt more than a little hypocritical, as I had secrets of my own that I was in no hurry to share. Pushing that pesky thought to the side, I got up to follow her.

The tiny bathroom had two stalls that looked like they should've been one, and the fluorescent light overhead was flickering like it was barely hanging onto life. Unlike the restaurant, it reeked of cleaning products and a cheap lemony spray that made me feel like I was suffocating. I wanted to leave immediately but instead made a show of checking my makeup in the mirror, waiting for Maria to come out of the last stall. She must not have heard me come in, because she had taken her jacket off and hadn't pulled it back on quite yet. I turned to her as she looked up at me, and we both froze. It wasn't just *two* bruises, it was several. In her cut-off tank top, I could see them scattered everywhere. Her arms, her chest, her abdomen. I literally felt sick.

"I thought I locked the door."

"You didn't."

"You don't know anything."

"Not saying I do." We stared at each other for a minute, and then she looked down. Now that I was here, I had no idea what to say. She was clearly uncomfortable. But I knew that look in her eyes cause I had seen it countless times in my own. The fear, the shame, the wondering why. So, I just said something that countless people had told me. A little tidbit of truth I was still fighting to believe. "You're not alone, you know. And it's not your fault."

She looked up at me, "You think you know me—"

"I think I'm a girl in a really, really gross bathroom who saw something I couldn't just ignore."

She glanced at the floor again and then muttered, "I have to get back to work. Some of us have bills to pay."

I didn't take offense. Not only was it true, but I saw it for what it was, a defensive barb meant to keep people away. I looked at her for a minute, taking in her beat-up sneakers, torn skinny jeans, and makeup-less face. We were so different, we came from different worlds, but somehow, I had a feeling we were very much the same. Except she was softer than I was. And I had already started outrunning my demons and, though I had a long way to go, she was still running with them at her side. I had been there once. "I'll go back to my table. Sorry for sneaking up on you."

At the table, Mom was fending off Laverne, who was trying to give her an entire pie. Mom gave in and thanked her for her hospitality. Momma Laverne winked at me as Mom headed for the door, and I smiled at her before grabbing the pen sitting on top of the check and writing my number on a spare napkin. If Maria wanted, I was here. I refused to let another girl dance with her demons alone. Not if I could help it.

Chapter Two

Jackson

After leaving Little Miss High and Mighty behind, the four of us made our way over to the clubhouse. Mac's dad had just opened the place a few weeks ago, somewhere for people to go, hang out, and ride if they wanted. A few of the local community had raised hell when he had proposed what was essentially a motorcycle club, but not many people had the balls to stand up to August Mills and stay standing. He was the kind of guy everyone liked, and also one who took shit from no one. People stood up straighter whenever he walked in the room.

A huge sign hung across the shiny new bay doors. "Steel Saints MC BBQ and Fundraiser." After parking our bikes out front, Mac wandered off to find his dad. The second I walked through the front door of the clubhouse, the smell hit me—barbecue, baked beans, something buttery and sweet that made my stomach grumble like it hadn't been fed in a week. And over all of it, the unmistakable scent of a lavender-scented cleaner. Which meant one thing: Hannah Mills was in full-blown event mode. We made our way down the hallway, past a series of rooms that Mr. Mills hadn't figured out a use for yet.

"You boys better not be tracking mud in my kitchen!" All three of us stopped just outside the kitchen door, frozen like we'd just gotten our hands caught in the cookie jar.

Dalton peeled off his boots mid-step like his life depended on it, fumbling as he hopped on one foot. "We wouldn't dare, Mom."

Diego followed suit but he was smirking at me as he tossed his boots into a room. I did the same, and Dalton closed the door. If we were lucky, we would remember to grab them before she found them. I frowned at Diego. "What?"

"Oh, nothing. Just thinking how you just got your ass chewed by a five-foot, blonde missile."I rolled my eyes. "Dude, whatever. She should've been paying attention."

Dalton snorted. "You *barely* missed flattening her. I just wish I'd had popcorn."

"Yeah," Diego added, nudging my shoulder. "That 'princess' crack really sealed your fate. Nice opener, Romeo."

I groaned. "Can we *not* rehash this again?" A pair of hazel eyes flashed in my mind, bright, angry, guarded.

Mac pushed the door open behind us, arms full of folding chairs. He raised an eyebrow but kept his mouth shut, not adding to the conversation he just walked into. Classic Mac—stoic until someone really earned his two cents.

"Hey Ma," he said, brushing past us into the kitchen. "Dad said you wanted some more chairs in here?"

"By the table" she answered, not even turning. She was elbow-deep in potato salad, moving like a tornado in an apron. "And *Jackson*—I better not hear one more word about you driving like your skull's full of marbles. My husband didn't start this so you could ride through town like your own private demolition derby."

"Yes ma'am," I muttered, casting a side eye at Diego and Dalton who were grinning like a pair of fools.

She paused long enough to give me the patented Mom Glare—the one that somehow combined deep affection with the promise of violence. "That license of yours didn't come with a death wish, I should hope. And if you think for one second I won't make you spend the entire event picking gum off picnic tables, you'd better think again."

I nodded my assent and beat a hasty retreat towards the garage, "Won't happen again, ma'am." Not like I would ever see that girl again. Thank fuck for that.

Dalton cackled. "That's what you get for almost running over the new girl."

"Would've served him right if she kicked his ass," Diego added, grabbing a deviled egg off a tray as he went through the kitchen and instantly getting smacked with a wooden spoon.

"You've got ten fingers, Diego," Hannah said, cool as anything. "I can take a few if you don't keep them to yourself. And that bottle of dish soap over there? Don't think that just cause I ain't your momma, I won't wash your mouth out."

He followed me, grinning like an idiot. "Sorry, ma'am."

"Hands off until I say so," she added, then looked back at me just as I opened the door. "And if you ever *do* manage to speak to that girl again, maybe try leading with something that doesn't sound like it came from an overweight trucker in the back of a Love's Truck Stop."

"I wasn't flirting," I grumbled.

Dalton laughed, "You called her *princess*, man."

"It's a *word*."

"It's a *death wish*," Diego said. "She looked at you like you were a bug she was debating squashing."

"She did squash him. She had a hell of a look in her eye," Dalton agreed. "I liked her."

"Of course you did," I snapped. "She hated *me*."

"You gotta admit, though," Dalton said, "she was kind of hot." He dodged the apple Hannah lobbed at his head and hastily shut the door behind us. Clint, a friend of his dad and the owner of a seriously badass Indian Scout, eyed the rolling apple before giving us an admonishing look.

"Don't go pissing off Mrs. Mills, you three. You oughta know better than that." I was about to say something to him when it dawned on me what Dalton had just said.

"Hot?! Dude, she almost bit my head off!"

Dalton slung an arm around my shoulder, all grinning sympathy. "Welcome to Georgia, buddy. Where the girls don't play and you *really* shouldn't try to impress them by almost turning them into roadkill."

I shoved him off, half-laughing despite myself. "Remind me why I hang out with you losers?"

"Because we're pretty, and we make you look better by comparison," Diego shot back.

Just then, the side door creaked open and in walked August Mills, sweat glistening on his brow, clipboard in hand. The whole room shifted like it always did when he stepped in. Not from fear. Just respect. He glanced at us. "Mac in the kitchen?"

I nodded. "Yes sir. He was bringing in those chairs last I saw."

He bent, grabbed the apple off the floor and tossed it to us. Diego caught it easily, gave it a wipe on his shirt, and took a bite. "Mrs. Mills kicked us out."

"That's my girl. You boys stay out of her way unless she asks for you, ok? Why don't you go outside? Make yourselves useful. See if Silas needs help." He gave Dalton a squeeze on the shoulder as he passed. The kitchen door closed behind him and the sound of Hannah's delighted squeal echoed around the room. I couldn't help but smile. Those two were always messing with each other.

Outside, I could hear the deep rumble of bikes pulling in, kids laughing, someone blasting Lynyrd Skynyrd a little too loud. The fundraiser was in full swing, and this—this kitchen, this chaos, this family—was the heart of it.

And for all the teasing, all the yelling, all the clatter and sass and barking orders…I couldn't help but feel like I was exactly where I was supposed to be. Even if one blonde girl with a razor tongue had wrecked my pride in a parking lot. Whatever. Not like she'd crossed my mind again or anything. I mean, seriously. What was her problem? If she hadn't went freaking mental, I would've just apologized and went on my way. Probably. But "man child with small dick syndrome"? Like hell was I just going to sit down and take that shit.

Diego interrupted my thoughts, bumping his shoulder against mine. "Thinking of her again, lover boy?"

"Shut up, man."

Mac came up behind us. "Come on, leave the guy alone. Not his fault some strange chick destroyed his fragile ego."

"Fragile?!"

Dalton laughed. "We better go find something to do before Dad comes back out here. But it's a good thing that was a one-off thing. Not sure you could take another hit."

I gaped at him, then threw myself at him. We wrestled for a bit, Clint and a few others hollering at us for being idiots, before Mac pulled us apart. "All right, all right. Dalton was right. We gotta go help."

Fragile. Fucking fragile. Those damned hazel eyes flashed in my mind again. There had been an odd look to them. And it suddenly dawned on me what it was.

Fragility.

She had been crying.

Chapter Three

⸸ **Holly** ⸸

Summer passed in a blur of heat, sweat, and the kind of silence that sticks to your skin. I made a point of stopping in at Laverne's as often as I could. Partly for the pie. Mostly for Maria. Unfortunately, Maria made a point of avoiding me. And she never did text. I understood, even if it was maddening. Sometimes when you're so lost in the dark, you forget to look around for a light switch.

My mom slowly turned our new place into a home. She didn't say she missed the ocean, but she left the blue wingbacks untouched and bought throw pillows the exact shade of sea glass. Dad filled the shelves with lighthouse figurines, one after another, until the house looked like it was waiting for a shore that would never come. Dad developed an obsession with lighthouse figurines. You can take the family out of Cali, but you can't take the Cali out of the family.

Every now and then, I would wake up in a cold sweat, my parents rushing into my room, my screams having shattered the peaceful Southern night. When I was awake, I could avoid the past for the most part—I had become really good at shoving everything down. But nothing, literally nothing, could erase what had happened. Sometimes, I could still smell his fucking cologne. Little things like that. Dad had to stop wearing any cologne at all. I hated that he had to do that all 'cause I couldn't get a grip on myself.

As school loomed closer, I let Mom drag me shopping. And I surprised even myself when I ended up with bags full of color. Enough was enough, I told myself. Besides, that black hoodie I had lived in was entirely too warm for this climate.

One night, about two months before school was set to start, we were all sat at the ridiculously large dining room table. Why we needed a table for ten, I had no idea. I had just taken a bite of chicken when I looked up to find my mom watching me expectantly.

"What?"

"It's almost time for school!"

"Yeah?"

She glanced at my dad, who was intent on his green beans. "A new school, in a new place! Isn't that exciting?"

I blinked at her. I was completely starting over as a freaking senior, where friendships were already formed, plans already made. And I was about to be thrown in the middle like a blonde wrench. "Sure, Mom. Super exciting." Her smile dropped briefly at my lack of enthusiasm, but she plastered it back in place with practiced ease. She reached into a bag she had at her feet that I hadn't noticed. I froze when she laid out three shiny brochures. Private schools.

No fucking way.

"I've picked out three! You would do so well at Brendwylle. It's all girls, and I've already talked to the dean. Did you know-"

"You cannot actually be serious." She stared at me, frozen mid-sentence. I glanced at my dad. "Tell me she's not freaking serious?"

"Bug, just let your mom tell you about them. It may surprise you!"

I stood, my chair making an ugly sound on the wooden floor. "A freaking private school? Yeah, that sounds great. Let's just pretend like nothing has changed. I'm just some girl. Some bubble head whose biggest problem is whether I have the latest tech or designer handbag."

The sheer thought of being surrounded by all that...all that *fake* made me sick. I ran my hands through my hair. I couldn't do it. No way. Private school? I had been to private school. Grew up in private school. Met *him* in private school. I had been the girl with the crown. The popular girl. And no one had seen me falling apart—because no one gave a damn beyond how I looked. What my grades were. What competition I had just won.

My dad stood too, making his way over to me. When he reached for me, I jerked away. I didn't want to be touched right now. My mom still sat at the table, those damn brochures spread out before her like a trap. Dad glanced at her, then back at me. "What would you have us do, bug?"

I forced myself to pause, to anchor myself. *In the now. Live in the now.* With effort, I looked up at him. Striving to keep my voice steady, I met his eyes. "Public school. I just want to finish this last year in public school."

"Public school?!" My mother's voice was a screech of disbelief. "Holly, honey. I know you've been through a lot, but public school? You've never been in public school." Every time she said "public school", she might as well have been saying something like "mass murder." Her eye even started twitching, and she pressed a carefully manicured nail to the muscle jumping there.

"Yes, Mother. Public school."

"Are you sure, bug?"

I looked back at my dad. He had always been fair, and he loved me fiercely. Even I could acknowledge that the man spoiled me rotten. I was his only child, after all. But he was also a doctor, and he had a clinical approach. I knew he would listen to my side, without letting emotion play a part, unlike my mother, who appeared to be having a midlife crisis. "Yes, Daddy. I can't be surrounded by a bunch of girls who are just like the me… the me before. Before everything. I just can't."

He seemed to consider this, sitting back down at the table. For a minute, the room was quiet. My mom reached for his hand, and he intertwined his fingers with hers before squeezing them gently. "David?"

"Hush, Ruth, honey. It's just one year. If she wants to go to public school, I don't see why not." He smiled gently at me. "If that's what you want, I will see about getting you enrolled. Now, would you please sit? I would like to finish dinner."

My heart was starting to slow back down, my hands not shaking as much. Mom was tucking those stupid brochures back in the bag. I took my seat, reaching for my water and taking a sip. Guess that was that. Holly McCarthy, straight-A student and Miss Jr High School USA Pageant winner, was going to public school. Go Raiders.

Chapter Four

❧ **Jackson** ❧

By end of August, the heat had settled over our trailer like a wet wool blanket and refused to leave.

The box fan in my bedroom window rattled like it was two weeks from death. It shoved around air that was only a degree cooler than my sweat. The thin curtains fluttered, doing absolutely nothing to block the sunlight or the view of the neighbor's busted Chevy up on cinder blocks.

Welcome to paradise.

"Jax?" Mom's voice floated down the narrow hallway, thin and scratchy. "Baby, you up?"

I scrubbed a hand over my face. My phone said 10:17 a.m. I'd gotten in around three after helping Mac's dad clean up from another late-night hangout at the clubhouse. I'd have slept 'til noon if I'd had the choice.

"Yeah," I called back, swinging my legs off the mattress. The springs squealed loud enough to make me wince. "I'm up."

I stepped down onto the warped floor, carefully avoiding the soft spot near the dresser where the wood had started to give. One day, my foot was going straight through it and they'd have to bury me under the damn trailer. Maybe that would finally boost the property value. The hallway smelled like stale smoke, cheap vanilla body spray, and the faint sour edge of old beer. The AC unit in the living room window growled like it wanted to quit life. Couldn't blame it.

Mom lay half-curled on the couch, one arm flung over her eyes. An empty bottle of boxed wine sat on the coffee table, next to an ashtray overflowing with half-smoked cigarettes. The TV was still on some home shopping channel, the volume low. A woman with perfect hair who was very excited about knives.

"Morning," I said softly. No reaction. Sometimes she responded. Sometimes she didn't. Mom had become…background noise. Like the AC struggling in the window, or the dented coffee table, or the peeling laminate. I didn't try again. Talking to her when she was like this only made the silence feel louder.

The kitchen was a galley barely big enough for one person. Lino curled at the edges. The fridge hummed like a dying animal and had a dent in the side from when Mom's last boyfriend had kicked it during an argument. I'd put my fist through his truck window later that night. Funny how he hadn't come back after that.

I filled the ancient coffee maker, scooped in the cheap grounds, and hit brew. The smell was bitter but familiar. I grabbed the mail off the counter while it worked. A shut-off notice for the electric, a credit card bill we'd never pay, a glossy postcard about "BUY A HOME WITH 0 DOWN!" that I wanted to set on fire.

The disability check had hit two days ago. Rent was paid. The rest of it…we'd limp through the month, same as always. As long as nothing big broke, we'd be fine. "Fine" being the Stretch Armstrong of words. The coffee machine gurgled. I poured a mug and carried it to Mom, set it on the table, then went back to the kitchen and dialed the number on the voicemail slip for her disability. Ten minutes of automated hell and one bored-sounding woman later, Mom's case was "updated" and we were clear for another month.

I hung up and leaned on the counter, letting my forehead thunk softly against the cabinet door. For a second, I let myself imagine what it would be like to live in one of the big houses I rode past on the way to the clubhouse. Fresh paint. Real brick. Driveway not held together by weeds. A mom who woke up early on purpose, not because of a hangover. A dad who, I don't know, existed.

I thought of the girl from the parking lot. The blonde with the hazel eyes and the voice like broken glass. The way her clothes had fit. The car her parents had been driving. Out-of-state plates. Money practically screaming off them.

Princess.

She'd looked at me like I was something she'd scrape off her boot. And yeah, that pissed me off. But some ugly part of me also figured she probably went home to granite countertops and stainless-steel appliances and a mom who cooked dinner that didn't come out of a box.

I groaned, pushing off the counter and checking in on Mom before escaping down the hallway. Five minutes later, I was standing under the world's most anemic shower stream, letting lukewarm water run over my head. The plastic curtain stuck to my back. The shampoo was the cheap brand that burned your eyes if you even thought about opening them. The pipes clanged every time someone flushed in the neighboring trailer. I braced my hands on the wall and let myself say it out loud in the steam, where no one could hear.

"I'm getting out of here."

A promise. A prayer. A threat. I wasn't going to end up face-down on a couch that smelled like cigarettes and Merlot. I wasn't going to disappear into a bottle because life got hard.

I'd seen what that did.

I'd seen what it turned people into.

I was going to become *that*.

College, if I somehow scraped together the grades and money. Maybe a football scholarship. Maybe something else. I didn't know exactly what my way out would look like, but I knew it wasn't going to be a lifetime of disability checks and hangovers and hoping the landlord didn't raise rent. I shut off the water, towel-dried, pulled on my shirt and jeans, and laced my boots.

My bike was waiting out front under the slanted carport—my one beautiful thing in this world. Black as night. Gold pinstripes. Chrome polished within an inch of its life. Helmet hanging from the handlebar, visor scratched slightly at the corner from a drop two summers ago. A gift from August and Hannah when I turned sixteen. I ran my thumb over the paint like I always did. *Keep me alive today, baby. I'll keep you clean.* She fired up on the second try. Smooth. Confident. I eased onto the road, gravel spitting behind me.

The heat hit like opening an oven door. The helmet trapped my sweat. The air tasted like exhaust and dust. And still, with the engine vibrating beneath me and the wind clawing at my shirt, it felt like freedom. The closer I got to the clubhouse, the more the scenery shifted. Trailers gave way to small, tired houses. Those turned into newer builds, manicured lawns, actual trees that someone watered on purpose. By the time I turned onto the road that led out to the Mills' property, it was like I'd ridden into a different world.

The Steel Saints sign loomed ahead. The bay doors were rolled up, fans blasting inside. Rows of bikes gleamed in the sun. The smell of grease, gasoline, and last night's barbecue drifted out to meet me. Home. The real one. I parked near the other bikes and peeled off my helmet, running a hand through my damp hair. Before I could take three steps, Dalton came barreling out the side door like a golden retriever with ADHD.

"There he is!" he crowed. "Sleeping Beauty. Finally come to pull his weight."

"Morning to you too, jackass." I nudged his shoulder. "You're just pissed because August made you get up at eight."

"Seven," he corrected with a shudder. "There was sunlight and everything. It was disgusting. Child abuse, frankly."

"Pretty sure you're eighteen," I said. "Not a child."

He clapped a hand to his chest. "Don't strip my identity from me. I'm emotionally fragile."

"You're something," Diego said, appearing behind him with a box of school supplies balanced on his hip. Sweat darkened his collar. "Jax, you're late. Hannah's on the warpath. I barely escaped with my life."

"She throw a spoon at you again?" I asked.

"A spatula this time," he said solemnly. "Upgraded model. More surface area for pain."

"Would y'all shut up," Mac said as he stepped out behind them, a clipboard in hand. He looked annoyingly put-together for this time of day. Hair neat, T-shirt clean, expression somewhere between exasperated and fond. "We've got tables to set up, banners to hang, and my dad's already chewing gravel because somebody"—he looked at Dalton—"forgot to order enough hot dog buns."

Dalton threw his hands up. "We live in the South; who the hell buys out Walmart's hot dog buns in one night?"

"Literally everyone with a grill," I said. "You gonna stand here debating bread economics or hand me something to do?"

Mac snorted. "Garage needs sweeping. Kids will be in and out all afternoon. Can't have them tripping over your mess."

"My mess?" I repeated, offended. "Pretty sure the oil spill over there has your bike's name all over it."

"Argue later," Diego cut in. "Hannah hears y'all slacking, she's gonna put us to work peeling potatoes with our teeth."

We got moving. Banners went up. Tables unfolded, legs squeaking on the concrete. We hauled cases of notebooks, boxes of crayons, backpacks lined with cartoon characters and sports logos. Sweat dripped down my back. Somebody turned up the radio in the corner, classic rock bleeding into the summer heat.

Inside the garage, boxes of crayons, glue sticks, and folders were stacked in uneven towers. August wanted this year's school supply drive bigger than ever. Said the kids in Redwood needed it. He wasn't wrong. Redwood was…Redwood. A lot of us lived in places like mine. Too many. Most parents did their best. Some didn't. I grabbed a box of backpacks and hauled it to the main table. Mac worked next to me, organizing things like he was alphabetizing his soul.

"You good?" he asked quietly.

"Yeah," I lied.

He didn't push. Just nodded once, the way he did when he saw a play building on the field before anyone else. Then the side door cracked open again and Dalton headed for the table. "We need more zip ties," he announced. "Mom said if we don't have the banners hung straight, she'll personally rearrange our spines."

"Sounds right," I said.

Diego leaned over. "Hey, Jackson, you hear Redwood might get a new girl this year?"

My stomach dropped before I could stop it.

Dalton smirked. "Hazel eyes. Blonde hair. Voice sharp enough to slice deli meat?"

"Don't start," I warned.

"Princess," Diego sang under his breath.

"Oh my God," I snapped. "It was one parking lot argument. Months ago."

"And yet," Dalton said, "the legend remains."

I threw a crayon box at him. He dodged. Barely.

"She's probably going to Brendwylle or Saint Catherine's or whatever school the rich kids get custom uniforms from," I added.

Dalton shrugged. "Dad has been talking to her dad. He's some big shot over at the hospital, and Mom wants his wallet for the charities and shit. You never know, she may show up at Redwood. Then you can continue your star-crossed lovers arc. Like Romeo and Juliet, if Romeo had a busted trailer and Juliet had one of those twelve-step skincare routines you see on TV."

"I hate you," I said.

He slung an arm around my shoulder. "Yeah, but I make your life interesting."

"Interesting is overrated."

"Tell that to your quarterback stats," Diego said. "Coach still won't shut up about your arm."

I rolled my eyes, but something warm flickered in my chest. Football was the one thing I had that felt easy. Natural. Right. Ball in my hand. Crowd screaming. Dalton trash-talking on my left. Diego blocking on my right.

Mac first on the field with us, then in the stands after he graduated. Yeah. That part of my life, I could deal with.

What I couldn't deal with was the image that flashed in the back of my mind every time someone mentioned a blonde girl. Too pretty for her own good. Hazel eyes. Sharp tongue. A crack in her armor I hadn't seen until later. Broken recognizes broken. Even if you hate the person standing in front of you.

"Hey!" Hannah's voice shrieked from inside the kitchen. "If those banners aren't hung in the next five minutes, I'm tying you boys up with them myself!"

We scrambled because in the hierarchy of menacing forces in this world, it went: Hannah Mills, God, whatever was living under Dalton's bed, and the IRS. In that order. I snatched a bundle of zip ties on my way out the door, dodging around Clint and a couple other guys. Mac climbed up a ladder and Diego handed him the banner we were supposed to be hanging.

Dalton yelled, "A little to the left!" Mac and Diego flipped him off.

For a while, it was easy to forget the electric bill notice on the counter at home. The soft patch in my floor. The way Mom's hands sometimes shook when she thought I wasn't looking. Here, I was just Jackson. One of the guys. A kid with a bike and a purpose. This was the stuff that made everything bearable. Quarterback. Living two separate lives and praying the one I loved most never got swallowed by the one I was born into.

↓ **Holly** ↓

I tugged at the lacy edges of the tank top and eyed myself in the mirror. Behind me, my closet appeared to have exploded. I had no idea what to wear. It wasn't my first "first day of school," but I was a bundle of nerves. My hair? Carefully styled in gentle beach waves. Makeup? A touch of mascara, wickedly sharp eyeliner, and some color in my cheeks. I had on a cute pair of sandals and had donned my favorite cut-off jeans. But I couldn't get the damn shirt right. I groaned, ripping it off and tossing it onto the bed. My gentle beach waves had somehow survived the chaos, but if I kept going, they were gonna turn into a fuzzy tsunami.

I turned when a knock on my door dragged me from my rampage. If I wanted to be on time, I had to leave soon. I had approximately a million shirts. And I didn't like any of them. Sigh. My mom poked her head in, eyes widening at the carnage. When I didn't say anything, she pushed her way into the room and shut the door behind me. In her hands, she had a small brown bag, and she held it out to me with a soft smile. "You look gorgeous, honey. But maybe this is what you're looking for?" I looked between her and the bag with more than a little skepticism before accepting the gift.

I opened it up and pulled out a shirt so unlike anything my mother had ever gotten for me before. It was a dark green, with gold stitching and some swirly gold sequins. It was partially off shoulder, and, based on the hemline, it would show just a sliver of belly. I slid it on and froze.

The green pulled the gold from my eyes like it had been waiting there all along. I stepped closer to the mirror, tilting my head. For the first time in months, I didn't look washed out. I looked…awake. The vivid greens and browns, the gold rings around my irises. I tugged at the hem where it hovered just above my belly button and eyed my mother questioningly. She shrugged and offered a small smile.

"It's public school. I'm sure they've seen worse. What's that thing you kids say? Go big or go home?"

I couldn't knock that she was trying, really trying to connect with me. It was something she didn't do very often, but when she did, it was in a quiet way that showed just how much she loved me. Part of me was still angry with her for missing the signs, and I was in no hurry to go on a mother-daughter date or something. But I could at least appreciate the cute shirt. "Thank you, mom. I love it." Her face blossomed with a smile of relief that went from ear to ear. I tried to not be bitter. If she hadn't wanted us to be close, maybe she should've paid attention.

Glancing at the clock, I realized I was officially running late. Mom followed me out of my bedroom door and downstairs as I grabbed the last of my things. Pressing a kiss to her cheek and shouting a goodbye to my father, I ran out the door. Public school. What a trip. At least I wasn't taking a bus. No, my '76 teal Mustang was my pride and joy. Custom black leather seating. Matte black rims. She was a thing of beauty. Dad had the original engine pulled and replaced with a rebuilt 302. The thing growled like it had something to prove. She was the one good thing to come out of that year. My mother nearly had a heart attack the first time I spun tires.

As I rounded the corner of Opal Ave, Redwood High loomed in the distance. Looking at its massive, worn brick exterior, I briefly pondered the logic of taking such an expensive car to a building whose definition of expensive was probably upgrading to toilets that didn't use a pull handle to flush. I was going to stick out like a sore thumb. But then I brushed the thought to the side. I was the new girl. In senior year. I was already going to stick out. Might as well look good while doing it. I pulled into the lot, and heads turned. Where the shit was student parking?

Did they have student parking? I rolled the window down and made eye contact with a skinny, red-haired guy.

Flashing him a megawatt smile, I said, "Hi, you might've picked up on this already, but I'm new. Is there student parking?"

He blinked at me, clutching a heavy-looking AP Chemistry book to his chest. The engine grumbled as it idled, turning even more heads, and I fought to keep the friendly smile on my face. *Come on, numb skull. Simple question here.* Finally, he visibly shook himself and pointed towards a small driveway area that wrapped around the back of the building. Nodding my thanks, I followed it to a small parking lot that was tucked into a back corner and labeled with a faded sign. "Student Parking Only. Pass required."

I was so busy wondering what a pass was and how I was to go about getting one that I almost missed the line of bikes parked in front. A familiar black Harley with gold pinstripes seemed to mock me. It was flashy and obnoxious, just like its owner. Great, that freaking idiot must go here. Yay, me.

I found a spot for Sally, the name I had given my Mustang for obvious reasons, and took a minute to steel myself before going inside.

Was I late? Yup.

Did I care? Not particularly.

I eyed the throng of students around me, divided into obvious cliques.

Public or private school, they had at least one thing in common. How did this many people fit in one building? . I grabbed my bag and checked my makeup in the mirror one last time. Ready. Set. Action. One year. I could do one more year. At least there were no fucking pageants. There appeared to be two entrances, and I opted for the main one, assuming it would be closest to the office. I had to get my schedule and find out about a parking pass. If someone tried towing Sally, they were losing fingers.

I ignored the whispers and stares as I made my way up the steps. Hi, yes. New girl. Not a unicorn. Fuck off. Not to sound shallow, but sometimes being pretty really sucked. A group of jocks wolf-whistled at me and I flipped them the bird without sparing them a glance. Their cackling laughter followed me inside.

Holy fluorescents. At the far end of the hallway was a set of stairs. Between here and there, art lined the wall opposite a massive display of trophies. The linoleum looked like it had been around since I started grade school. I almost missed the door to my left. A small, nondescript wooden thing that had an easily missed label, "Office." I read the flyers stapled and taped haphazardly to the walls. Anything to buy myself a bit of time. Eventually, I realized I was in the way of everyone coming through the doors so I stepped forward and pushed the surprisingly heavy door open.

Faded blue carpets. A receptionist barely visible behind a mountain of a desk. Three other doors labeled nurse, counselor, and principal. She must not have heard me come in because she didn't even look up. I waited for a minute, for her to notice. But, realizing she would've just kept typing away forever, I spoke up.

"Excuse me? Hello?"

She yelped and looked up at me. "Heck, young lady. Where did you come from?"

Her accent was so thick I could barely understand her.

I pointed at the door behind me. "I'm the new senior? Holly McCarthy? From California?"

She stood, clapping her hands. "Oh, honey! You're our California girl! Welcome to Redwood High! I'm Miss Morrison. You're going to be wanting your schedule, I suppose?"

She had bouncy brown hair done up in an elaborate, poofy, wavy mess. A checkered blue headband clung to the top of her head, and she had nails that looked to be about ten inches long. She looked at me expectantly, bangs fluttering in the breeze coming from a desk fan.

"Uhm, yeah. Yes. That would be me. And I wanted to ask about a parking pass too?"

"All right, honey. We can definitely do that for you! Now, your parents and your old school sent over all your records, filled out most forms, right? But there are just a few that I need you to do. And, for that parking pass, it's $50. You'll need your make, model, and license plate number, too." She continued with a flurry of information that made my head hurt. I took the papers she held out to me on a clipboard covered in stickers and pen markings. I flipped through them as she talked, telling me about the school,my schedule, and my lunch hour. I looked up at her when she paused, to find her staring at me expectantly again.

"Huh?"

"I was asking if you wanted a tour? Or I could get a student ambassador to come show you to your classes?"

"Oh, no. Thanks. I'll figure it out."

She nodded, "Ok, then. Go ahead and fill out those papers for me. You'll be a bit late for first period, but I'll write you a pass."

I filled out the forms as quickly as I could before digging $50 out of my bag and handing everything over to her. The bell had rung at some point, and I found myself standing in an empty hallway, glaring at a glossy map of the building. A freaking map. I hate maps. I had failed geography. Twice. The first hour was English, and I decided to just start up the stairs. Worst comes to worst, if I couldn't find the room, I could go hide on the roof. The stairs were worn from countless feet, chipped in places, and gum permanently adhering to the surface in spots. I glanced at my schedule again.

The class was in 202, which had to be on the second floor, right? My locker number was 238. So, maybe I would get lucky and they would be near each other. I huffed as I continued up the stairs. Evidently, public schools couldn't afford elevators. Sigh. When I got to the second floor, I shoved the door open and was met with a woosh of cool air accompanied by the smell of bleach. Delightful. Each side of the long hallways was lined with doors, and glancing at the numbers next to them, I opted to go right. Sure enough, at the very end of the hall, I found 202. No hideaway roof time for me. The door was open and I could hear a man droning on about Shakespeare.

When I knocked on the door, the teacher stopped midsentence and turned to me. He was small and pudgy, a hideous tweed suit and a bulging belly pushing the buttons of his white collared shirt to the max. Every head in the room swiveled in my direction. I was quite used to being the center of attention, having lived half my life on a stage, so I looked over the curious faces to the man staring at me. He blinked owlishly at me over a pair of glasses, "Yes?"

I held my hall pass aloft like a weapon or a shield. "I'm your new student." He eyed the pass in my hand like it might bite, then made his way to me. As he took it from me, the room was quiet except for a few errant whispers until he looked up at me again.

"Holly McCarthy?" I nodded. 'Welcome to Redwood. I'm Mr. Brown. I believe there are a few extra seats in the back."

In the back. Through the throng of teenagers. I nodded again, and he watched me as I picked my way through the mess of bags tossed haphazardly on the floor. A few girls looked me up and down with a sneer. Some smiled at me. The guys either completely ignored me, stared at me, or, in the case of one brave yet foolish soul, winked suggestively. I found an empty chair in the middle of the back row and plopped down in it.

Let the games begin.

Once I had my seat, Mr. Brown continued his speech on the fine qualities of Shakespearean writing. I took out a notebook and pencil, to pretend at doing something, and stared resolutely at the whiteboard. No one spoke to me. And I was just fine with that.

First and second period passed by in a blur. I made my way to my locker, navigating the cramped hallways and evidently giving enough of a fuck-off vibe that no one stopped me. My locker looked like it had been through World War I and had the battle scars to prove it. Of course, the stupid thing wouldn't open. I cursed at it. Kicked it. Yanked on the little handle like it owed me money. I was standing there scowling at it when an overly bright "Hello" startled me out of my staring contest with the worn red metal.

A group of girls stood behind me. Tiny skirts, tight tops. Perfectly done hair. Great. Cheerleaders. I offered them a tight-lipped smile. They were exactly the kind of girls I had been hoping to avoid. "You must be Holly!"

Another tight-lipped smile, my eyes darting around for an exit strategy. "Yup, that's me."

"Welcome to Redwood!"

God help me if one more person said that I was going to hurl. "Thanks."

The girl was oblivious to my discomfort. "I'm Miranda. This is Jazzie, or Jasmine. And Taylor and Megan." The three girls gathered behind their leader waved at me in unison, and I eyed them warily.

"Can I just say you are *so* pretty. Like, for real." Miranda's friends all nodded and I was blinded by too-white smiles. "You have *got* to try out for the cheer squad. I know it's senior year, but you're an athlete. I can tell. I can totally make room for you. It'll be like my little welcome gift. I'm the cheer captain."

Yeah, no shit, Barbie. I picked that up the second you cornered me. I glanced at my watch. "Um, thank you. That's sweet. But I'm really not a cheer type of person."

Miranda's fake smile faltered, and her friends stared at me like they were shocked I'd dared to turn down their queen. But she recovered quickly and reached for my hand. I jerked it back like I'd been burned. I hated being touched. After everything, it made my skin crawl. I rubbed at my hands like I could erase the feeling. *Deep breaths*, I told myself. *You're here. He's there. In and out.*

She nodded like she understood. Something I highly doubted. "Yeah, of course. I am so sorry. It being your first day, I'm probably just overwhelming you! Silly me. You think on it, and just let me know, ok?"

She turned to her friends expectantly and held her hand out. I watched them scramble before one of them—Taylor, I think—put a pen and paper in Miranda's hand. Miranda scribbled something on it before handing the paper to me. I took it. Reluctantly. A quick glance showed a series of digits in an elegant script. Her number.

"Thanks. I appreciate it." The lie was smooth off my lips. *Now, please go away.* Thankfully, they did, and I breathed a sigh of relief. I had neither the time nor the energy to hunt down the cafeteria and face that fiasco, so instead I made my way to Sally. Hunkering down in the back seat, I pulled a granola bar and a bottle of water out of my bag. Not exactly a five-course meal, but it would work. I scrolled through my phone, ignoring the friend requests that my inbox was full of. People from back home, and even a few from today. Since when did passing someone in a hallway warrant friendship? Maybe I was too cynical.

I lay there for a bit. The back seat was tiny, but if I curled my knees to my chest, I could steal a moment of quiet. The sun beat through the windows, warming the black leather and filling the air with that rich, comforting scent. Mixed with the soft sweetness of my coconut air freshener, it was oddly soothing. Familiar. Safe. Just for a second, it felt like home. And it soothed my fraying nerves. My alarm went off on my phone, signaling fifteen minutes before third period. I was halfway through my day. I sighed, crawling out of the seat which stuck to my thighs.

As I dug my schedule out of the bag, my eyes found that group of now-familiar bikes. I glared at them, but was grateful that I had yet to run across their riders. Returning my attention to the crumpled paper, I scanned it for where I was to be next. Room 117, some elective I needed to graduate. I was halfway to the stairs when movement under the front alcove caught my eye.

Miranda. And her entourage.

They had some poor girl cornered, her back to the wall like a trapped animal. My stomach twisted. I fucking hated bullies. But it was my first day. I needed to keep my head down. Blend in.

One foot on the first step. One second from walking away.

"Jesus, look at you. Where the fuck did you even get that shirt? I mean, you could've at least gotten it in your size. Which is what? An XXL?"

I balled my fists as the cackle of mean girls filled my ears. I wasn't the only one in the hallway. I hated this. How could people just walk on by like this was ok? No one ever stepped in. I should know but, still, I was on the fence. Did this poor chick really need the new girl to step in?

But the second I heard her voice, my mind was made up.

"Miranda, come on. It's the first day of school. We're freaking seniors. Please just leave me alone."

Maria.

Oh, hell no. I spun so fast that the walls around me blurred and marched right up to the little group cornering the girl I had been trying to befriend all summer. They parted for me, giving me a clear shot to Miranda, who turned to me, surprised.

"Hey, Miranda, right?"

She gave me a sickly-sweet smile, "Hi, Holly! Change your mind about cheerleading?"

"No. I hate cheerleading almost as much as I hate pick-me bitches who think it's ok to bully other people just to make themselves feel better."

Someone behind me gasped. I looked over Miranda's shoulder at Maria, who was shaking her head like she was trying to tell me to stop. Miranda's jaw dropped, and then her face turned a very unattractive red color. Like a beet. "What did you just say to me?"

"You heard me. Now, fuck off."

"Do you know who I am?"

I rolled my eyes at the cliche line. "Did you know I don't give a damn? Get a better hobby. Don't you have some shitty routine to practice? A shitty boyfriend you need to text?"

I heard a male voice behind me. We must have drawn a crowd. Typical. They wouldn't stop to help someone but for a show? The chance to watch a cat fight? They were all over that. Miranda took a step towards me, shoving her face in mine. I didn't budge, wrinkling my nose at her floral perfume and raising a single eyebrow at her. *Come on. Do something. I dare you. I've got anger issues and a busload of trauma. I'll lay into your ass until you feel two inches tall.*

"Ok, new girl. I see you. Think you're hot shit? Well, let me tell you something. I own this place. I was doing you a favor. Now? I'm going to make your life a living hell. You're gonna wish you had never crossed that line for some chick you don't even know."

"Get out of my face, Miranda. Ten years from now you'll be dressing in designer to hide how much you hate your life. That girl behind you? She'll be somebody. She's already twice the person you'll ever be. So: fuck off."

Miranda's mouth moved, but no words came out. The whispering behind me grew louder. Just when I thought she was going to burst from the indignation, she stomped her foot and marched off, shouting that I would be sorry over her shoulder as her little posse followed behind her. I glared at her retreating back, then I turned my attention to Maria as the bell rang and the crowd began to disperse.

"Hi."

She stared at me, beat-up backpack clutched to her chest, and that same jean jacket hiding the bruises I knew were underneath. "Do you have a death wish?"

I shrugged. "Honestly? Yeah, a little."

"That was social suicide."

"I know. I just don't care. It's senior year, and I'm a stranger in a small town. I've already accepted my fate as an outsider."

She squinted at me, pretty brown eyes taking me in. The bell rang again, and she shrugged her backpack over her shoulder. "Well, new girl. We're gonna be late. What's your next class?"

"Ummm, I have no idea. Some elective. Room 117?"

"Oh, like half the senior class is in that class. Stupid freaking graduation requirements, am I right?"

"Are you?"

"Am I what?"

"In the class?"

"Yup." She popped the P. "Wanna follow me? Seal your fate as a social outcast?"

"I thought I already did that when I called Miranda a pick me bitch."

She grinned, "Yeah, you totally did. That made my day. But hanging out with me is like the nail in the coffin."

"Why?"

"I moved here a couple years ago. I'm not pretty enough to be a cheerleader, not smart enough to be in any academic club. My hand-eye coordination is shit, so sports is out of the question. And Miranda has made it her life's mission to torment me."

"Hmm, a California loner and the school's head outcast. Seems like a perfect match." My attempt at humor was lousy, but at least I was trying.

Maria laughed and headed up the stairs, "By the way, I'm sorry I never texted you."

"It's ok."

"It's not. It was kinda rude. But, well, you know."

"What I saw in the bathroom."

"What you *think* you saw." I cast a skeptical side eye at her and she scoffed, "Listen, let's just agree to never talk about it. And we can brave Hurricane Miranda together. Bet you're more used to those than I am."

"What, to hurricanes? Yeah, I've been through a few." Figuratively and literally. "Fine, friends with secrets. Like friends with benefits but more fun and less complicated."

Maria laughed again, "Yeah sure, blondie. Whatever you say."

⚡ Jackson ⚡

I sat on the crumbling brick wall that lined the parking lot, the late summer sun warming the brick as I watched the teal Mustang pull in like it owned the place. It was old school—sleek, loud, and unapologetically pretty. I had never seen that car before. Not in town, definitely not at school. It stopped, the engine purring, before continuing across the blacktop and turning for the student lot. Dalton was going on about something his mom had caught him doing, and Diego was calling him a dumbass. Neither of them was aware that something else had caught my attention.

When she stepped out like she was exiting a movie scene, I stood up and swore. Blonde hair, long tan legs, shorts that skirted the dress code by about a millimeter. A green top hung off her shoulder and she straightened as she looked around the place. She didn't look nervous. She didn't look lost. She looked like she'd been *waiting* for this entrance. I saw her pause when she noticed our bikes but she shook her head and continued inside. I watched her go, watched every head turn as she made her way up the steps.

"You've gotta be kidding me," I muttered.

Dalton followed my gaze and gave a low whistle. "That the new girl? I was right! Romeo and Juliet here we come!"

"You mean Malibu Barbie," I said, not bothering to hide the disdain.

"Pretty sure she's more Cheerleader Assassin than Barbie," Diego chimed in, squinting toward the car. "Remember what she called you?"

"I remember. That tongue could cut glass," Dalton replied.

I glared at them. "What does that have to do with her showing up here of all places?" They both shrugged.

"Well, ya know…even if she hates you, maybe she would give your best bud a chance," Dalton smirked. "I would be happy to give her a personal tour."

I rolled my eyes. "Jesus, Dalton. Grow up. You've got fucking issues."

"Hey, I'm just saying. Some of us have magnetic personalities."

"You're a walking code of conduct violation," Rodney muttered from where he leaned against the school's brick wall, arms folded across his chest. He also played on the football team with us and kind of just lurked around. Dalton grinned like it was a compliment.

"Bet Coach puts you on the bench if he hears that shit," Diego said.

"I'm not worried. He loves me."

"You've been benched three times for skipping weights," I pointed out.

"Technicalities." The warning bell rang, pulling us from our conversation. I glanced at the door again, but she had already disappeared inside.

"Let's go before Coach decides we need a pre-practice lap around the entire goddamn school," Rodney said, pushing off the wall. He was trying so hard to fill Mac's shoes, as the new LB1. The whole team was meeting at the field. As we made our way toward the locker rooms to stash our stuff, the conversation turned toward the weekend.

"We still good for Friday?" I asked.

"Yeah," Dalton replied. "I heard Lindsay's throwing something at her place. Her parents are out of town."

"Doesn't she have a boyfriend?"

Dalton shrugged. "She certainly didn't seem to when she was all over me the other day."

Diego made a sound of disgust. "Man, seriously?"

"Relax, Saint Diego," Dalton teased. "We can't all be pious little virgins."

"I'm not—Jesus. I'm just not a jackass."

"That's because he's got eyes for one girl," I grinned, elbowing him. "What was her name again? Maria? That one chick Miranda's always being a bitch to?"

Diego flushed, immediately defensive. "I do not—look, I barely know her."

"But you want to."

"Bet she does," Rodney said with a smirk.

Diego groaned and shoved open the locker room door. "I hate you all."

"Hey, didn't your dad say he needed help at the clubhouse this weekend?" I directed the question over my shoulder as I opened my locker.

"Yeah. Saturday morning. Didn't say for what, though."

"Cool. I'll be there. Got nothing better to do."

"Same. If I survive this week," Diego grumbled.

The rest of the day passed in a blur of classes and Coach barking about footwork. I didn't see the blonde again, though Dalton and Diego proudly informed me they had discovered her name from one of the cheerleaders always hanging around us. Holly McCarthy. From California, of all places. Fitting. At the end of the lunch hour, we made our way back inside. There was some sort of commotion over by the stairs.

"Miranda's on the warpath again," Dalton muttered. Diego's face darkened, his brow furrowed. We all knew Miranda's preference for victim. And whether he admitted it or not, it bothered the hell out of the guy.

Sure enough, Maria was cowered back against the wall. But, much to my surprise, she wasn't the one Miranda had her attention on.

Malibu. Again.

Standing tall. Standing *loud*. Miranda's nose was about an inch from Malibu's. And the chick didn't seem the least bit fazed. The crowd parted a bit, allowing us close enough to see her raise one eyebrow in a quiet challenge. Oh, cat fight.

"Did she just call Miranda a pick-me bitch?" Diego asked, leaning a bit closer to the two girls who looked about a second away from tearing each other's faces off.

"I think she did," Dalton cocked his head, watching the drama unfold.

I crossed my arms and watched as Malibu, aka Holly McCarthy, verbally dismantled the most feared girl in the school without blinking. That same sharp tongue that had laid into me, ripping Miranda to bits. The crowd was eating it up. Miranda looked like she might explode. Holly? She didn't flinch.

I shook my head as Miranda stormed off, Holly watching her go with a gleam in her eye. "Still don't like her," I muttered. "But damn. She's got balls." My friends all nodded in agreement, and with that, we headed to third period.

Chapter Five

↓ Holly ↓

A few months later, Maria and I were sitting in my room. Next week was finals, and, after that, the blessed relief of Christmas break. The first time I brought Maria home, my mother nearly hit the floor. I could see the emotions at war on her face. On one hand, I had made a friend. On the other, said friend dressed in faded thrift store T-shirts and beat-up sneakers. Maria won her over pretty quickly, though, showing up at our front door with a plate of hojarascas. Since then, much to my dismay, Mom has treated her like a charity case. Maria hasn't seemed to mind though, and has become very good at fending off my mother.

She was droning off about science and reading from one of the many textbooks scattered around us.

I was barely listening, opting instead to munch on the chips I had snagged from the kitchen and glaring at the handprint bruise on her arm. How could I possibly focus on what happened when you combined this chemical with that? I couldn't. Not when that bruise was staring back at me. It was like every bruise on her made me feel *his* hands on me again. I barely repressed a shudder. To make myself feel better, I imagined what sulfuric acid and hydrogen peroxide would do to a pervert's skin. See? That's science. I *was* studying.

About two weeks ago, Maria had finally opened up to me about Jesse,

"

her boyfriend, but it was the barest of details. She had stopped hiding her bruises when it was just the two of us. I knew feeling that pressure, that need, to hide the truth was an awful thing. I knew how badly it sucked. But those marks pissed me off. I frowned at the offending blue on her tawny skin. Either she was ignoring my heavy gaze or she was oblivious. It was hard to tell with her. A knock on the door distracted me momentarily, and Maria quickly pulled the blanket over her bare arms. My dad poked his head in and smiled at us.

"How goes it, girls?"

"Great! I think we're just about done," Maria chirped.

"Science is the root of all evil, closely followed by math," I stated bluntly.

My dad laughed. "Careful, science and math are how I pay our bills. It's pretty important. I was thinking of ordering a pizza for dinner. Would you like to stay, Maria?"

"Oh, Mr. McCarthy, I really appreciate the offer but I actually have to get going pretty soon. I'm expected home."

Home. I gripped the bowl of chips in my lap so tightly I think I heard the plastic protest. Maria's grandma was super old, and super sick. And freaking Jesse, the boyfriend from Hell, lived with them. So, the only way food got on their table was if Maria cooked it. I wondered briefly if I could sneak into Maria's Uber and finally meet the son of a bitch.

Expected home. Are you kidding me? Like a maid out past her curfew. Like it would kill him to warm up a damn hotdog or something. Cup of noodles. Frozen lasagna. Hell, even I know how to work an oven and I am dangerous in the kitchen. And not in a good way.

"Holly, honey?" My dad's slightly concerned voice pulled me from my thinking; he appeared to be waiting for an answer. I blinked owlishly at him, and he repeated himself, "What kind of pizza?"

"Oh, um…BBQ chicken? With pineapple." He gave me a thumbs up and shut the door behind him as he left. Maria teased me about my weird taste in pizza and then started again on the science study guide. My pizza was weird, but it was delicious. You know what's weird and not delicious? A man putting his hands on you. Fuck him. Fuck this. I had been quiet long enough. With that, I slammed my bowl of chips down so hard on the textbook that some of them fell out of the bowl.

"Why?"

"Why what?"

I pulled the blankets off her and gestured to the bruise there. Maria blushed furiously and I said, "I know we haven't known each other for long, but this is stupid. Am I supposed to just pretend you're super accident prone? Or maybe you gave yourself that mark? You told me about Jesse and I appreciate that. But be for real."

"Holly, come on…"

"No, Maria. I want answers. Starting with why you put up with it."

"I don't put up with anything."

"Oh, for Christ's sake." I glared at her and she glared back, until her brown eyes started watering and she looked away.

"You don't get it."

I get more than you think. An old memory tried pushing its way to the front of my mind. Mahogany body spray. Soft large hands. The sound of my tights ripping. I shook my head, shoving that shit back down into the box I kept it in. A small box with a tight lid, shoved into the darkest corners of my mind. Maria wiped at a tear, and I said "Try me."

She sighed, folding her hands in her lap and picking at the skin around her fingernails. "He doesn't mean it, ok? He just…he is super passionate. And we've only been together for a year. So, I'm still learning his cues, you know? It's not all bad, Holly. He's so funny and he is really nice to my abuela…"

I had been in the same place she was in now. Well, maybe not the exact same. It had been a modeling coach that had been handsy with me, not my boyfriend. And I had been a lot younger. But, still. I had spent years blaming myself. Maybe if I hadn't looked at him so much. Maybe if I had made sure I was never alone with him. Maybe this, maybe that. But eventually, I realized that even if I had danced naked in front of the motherfucker, I was twelve and he was in his damn thirties, and he had no right to put his hands on me. Absolutely none.

I swallowed, thinking back to the trial.

To my trophy case back home.

How they found him not guilty.

After all he had done. All those memories neatly tucked away so I could manage day by day. I had felt so alone. Sometimes still do. Like hell was my newfound bestie gonna put up with the same shit I had to.

"No."

"What?"

"You don't hurt the people you love."

"But—"

"No buts. It's not ok. You love someone, their pain is your pain. And you do everything you can to keep them safe. So, no. It's abuse. And he's an asshole. It's that simple. There shouldn't be any cues, any triggers. You are not his punching bag, even when he's having a shit day."

"You don't understand."

I looked at her. At the bruises. The bags under her eyes. And I realized that if I wanted to get through to her, there was only one way. Stupid fucking boxes. I closed my eyes, mentally preparing myself to open up everything I had carefully sealed away with duct tape and bright yellow caution ribbon. Swallowing thickly, I looked at the far wall and then back to her. "Yeah, I do. More than you think.

"Growing up in Cali, my mom put me in a ton of these competitions. Beauty pageants, contests, challenges…you name it. And I was really, really good. When I was eleven, I had already won a bunch of stuff. And, one day, after a show, a guy named Scott Lauren came up to my mom.

"He seemed so nice. He was a modeling agent, and a judge. He was practically famous in our world, you know? My mom was so excited. This was like my ticket to the big leagues. And everything was fine for a few months. Then, on my twelfth birthday, he called me to his office and said he had a special surprise for me. For the birthday girl."

I saw the moment the lightbulb went off in her head. Her brown eyes widened and her mouth dropped open in horror. It suddenly dawned on me that my cheeks were wet. I hadn't talked about this in so long, but the pain was still there.

"Four years, Maria. Four fucking years. And I wasn't the only one. When my mom finally caught on, she raised hell. But I never competed again. Being on stage makes me sick. Still does. That's why we moved. Why I have these scars on my hands, from breaking my trophies. Why I don't like being touched. So, yeah. I do understand. Some guys just suck. They are scum of the Earth. And Jesse is one of those guys."

Maria launched herself across the bed, wrapping her arms around me. At first, I stiffened. Girl, I literally just said I didn't like being touched. But this felt different. This was Maria, my friend. And it felt so good to finally be seen. So I leaned into her, and, for a few minutes, we both cried, soaking each other's shoulders and turning into a couple of snot-nosed goblins. Eventually, I pulled back from her and wiped my eyes with the back of my hand. "Please don't go back to him, Maria."

Her brown eyes were soulful, older than her seventeen years, and she shook her head. "I love him. What that man did to you was awful. But Jesse isn't like that. He isn't perfect, but he's not Scott Lauren."

I wanted to scream and throw the textbook. "I know he's not. But Maria, Jesse is awful. He's an asshole."

"But he's mine. My asshole. For better or worse. He loves me."

I stared at her, and she looked away, "Does he, though? Or is he just using you? Abusing you? In the name of love. He. Doesn't. Love. You." I grabbed her arm, holding her bruise up to the light. "This isn't love."

She stood abruptly and yanked her arm back. "Ok, I get you're concerned or whatever, but you don't get to judge me. You don't get to act like you know better. So, just stop. Stop making this about you."

"About me? You can't be serious. I am just telling you what everyone else is thinking. This isn't about me."

"Whatever. I gotta go make dinner."

I scoffed. "Fine. Go back to him. But if you ever get tired of being his fucking punching bag, you'll know where I'll be."

She whipped towards me, her defensiveness morphing into anger. "Yeah, kind of hard to miss your mansion."

I knew I wasn't imagining the undercurrent of bitterness in her voice. "What's that supposed to mean?"

She headed for the door but tossed venomous words over her shoulder, "Congrats, Holly. You escaped the bad guy. Was it really so hard? Is it still? In your big, white house and your designer clothes? You guys could afford to move across the freaking country to avoid him. That's not an option for me. I love him. And I am staying. And I am choosing to fight for what we have. It is so different from what happened to you. I appreciate you telling me. It means a lot, really it does. And what happened to you is awful. But it's not the same. I wouldn't expect you to understand."

I rocked back on my heels like she had hit me. My shirt was still damp from her tears, and I could see the spot of wetness on hers. I thought it had helped, to tell her the truth. I thought she understood. Clearly fucking not. I blinked back a new wave of tears, the warmth of anger spreading in my chest. "Fine. Don't let my privilege hit your ass on the way out."

I watched her go, trying to force myself to breathe. *Please turn around. Just one glance up at my window.* But she didn't. I could see the set in her shoulders even from here. After her Uber disappeared from view, I turned and stood for a minute staring at my bed and the books still scattered there. I wanted to scream, but the last thing I needed right now was my mom or dad all up in my business. Grinding my teeth, I picked the books up one by one and chucked them as hard as I could across the room. The thud of them hitting the walls did nothing to dull my anger. Or the dull ache. I had fucking trusted her, and she had turned it against me. Who did that?

Throwing myself back onto my bed, I buried my face into my pillow. Only then did I allow myself to scream until my throat ached. The raw, thorn-like tenderness that had become so familiar to me. My mom's voice came through the door, asking if I was alright. Guess I hadn't been as quiet as I meant to be. When I yelled that I was fine, I wasn't the least bit surprised when she took it at face value and left me to my misery. Just like old times. Me and my ghosts and a mom who was too caught up in being perfect to care.

That night, I took my pizza to my room. Amidst the textbooks and papers

I had yet to clean up, I nibbled on my dinner and stared into a corner. Part of me was livid. I had opened up to her., and she had thrown it in my face. I had cried. I hated crying. What did she think I wanted? A pity party? No. I just wanted her to know she wasn't alone and she was worth more.

Like it had been easy to leave everything I knew behind. The way my mom had looked at me in the months before, during, and after the trial. That sorrowful look, the one full of regret. I couldn't stand it. So, I had stopped looking back at her. And when he walked down the courthouse stairs a free man? Well, I just stopped talking about it all, 'cause it hadn't ever done me a lick of good. That's when I just shoved it all to the back of my mind. Out of sight and all that.

My mom came in at some point, taking my plate and pressing a kiss to my head. She eyed the textbooks and my disheveled appearance. I knew that, in her own way, she cared, just as much as I knew that Maria hadn't meant it. Not really. That didn't mean her words didn't sting. I just wanted so badly to help her. And maybe to run him over with a really big truck. Multiple times. Thud, thump, you son of a bitch. I chortled at the image, then wondered if this classified me as mentally unstable. Whatever. I would give her the weekend. And on Monday, she was going to realize I didn't give up so easily. She was stuck with me, whether she liked it or not. She turned eighteen in a few months, and we were almost half-way done with our last year of school. Sky's the limit.

I spent the weekend alternating between staring at my phone, praying it would ring, and running through my textbooks one more time. The air had gotten decidedly cooler, winter firmly having Georgia in her grasp after a brief struggle. At one point, I yeeted my geography book from the balcony and then regretted that decision when I had to go outside in the biting cold to get it back. Maria hadn't reached out. Not once. My mom was hovering, like she always did. And dad had some major surgery and a sick kid to save. So, it was just me and my study guides and my circling thoughts. And those stupid memories that hadn't wanted to go back in their box.

The nightmares had come back worse than before.

Suddenly, the rumble of motorcycles ripped me from my concentration.

Oh, and there was that. Much to my *sheer* delight, there was evidently a motorcycle club not even ten minutes down the street. I think mom's soul departed this mortal plane when she found out. I could live with it, for the most part, but there was a certain group of by now very familiar bikes that seemed to take a sick pleasure in revving their engines as they drove by.

Micropenis-possessing man children.

I flipped off the bikes as they went by. I had only caught sight of their owners once or twice in school. They were jocks. Big shock there. And players. Especially that blonde one. I only paid them any attention because one of them had a habit of staring at Maria like she had been put on this Earth to save him. And Jackson? That douche couldn't be further from my mind, thank you very much. He was lucky I remembered his name.

I huffed and grabbed my geography textbook off the ground. With it in hand, I headed back inside to find my mom. I couldn't get my mind to shut up, and there was only one other person loud enough to drown them out. She who didn't know *how* to shut up. I found her sitting in the primary living room. She looked up at me as I walked in, muting her show and smiling hesitantly at me. I held up my flashcards like a weapon. "Quiz me?" I was almost blinded by the sheer joy in her ear-to-ear smile.

"Oh my goodness, yes!"

"Geez, Mom. It's geography. Not the cure for cancer."

"Right, right. Ok. What can I do?" TV off, she crossed her legs and patted the seat next to her. I sat, turning to face her, and handed her the cards.

"Answers on the front, questions on the back."

She nodded eagerly, that little line in her brow furrowed in concentration. For the next several hours, she quizzed me until I considered burning the first globe I found. When I finally went to bed that night, I stared at the ceiling. When the same damn engines pulled me from almost sleep, I got up and grabbed the heaviest textbook I could find. Hurrying so I wouldn't miss them, I went down the stairs and out the front door. It was a beautiful, if not a little chilly, night and I tried to enjoy it a little as I walked down the driveway. Right as they went past my home, I threw that book with everything I had. It didn't hit them, but it did scare the shit out of them, judging by the shouts and the squealing of tires in the dark.

Take that.

Come Monday, I'd had my fill of studying and was ready to find Maria. I pulled into the parking lot a little too quickly, Sally protesting as I accidentally hit the curb. Sorry, girl. But there was one thing I wanted to do before I went inside. I was tired. Finals had me stressed. My bestie was going through hell. And someone was going to get their ass kicked. I found "someone" pretty quickly. Four jocks were leaning up against the worn brick, laughing at some joke I hadn't been privy to. The quiet guy—Rodney I think—nudged his buddies when he saw me heading over. Dalton gave me a wide, friendly grin before winking at me and saying, "Hey, gorgeous."

I scoffed at him. "Oh, fucking save it for one of the cheerleaders constantly hanging off you." He held up his hands in an "I surrender" gesture as I fixed each one of them with a hard stare. "Which one of you miscreants thinks it so damn funny to hold your throttle down every time you drive past my house?"

They looked at each other and then Jackson, King Asshole himself, stepped towards me. "What's wrong, princess? Don't like us disturbing your peace?"

"I'm going to show you peace disturbance if you keep messing with me."

He rolled his eyes, "Oh, you mean like throwing a textbook at us? Right. Very scary."

I moved closer to him. "I don't know what I've done to make you act like a damn fool, or maybe that just comes naturally to you. Newsflash? Being a dick doesn't look good on anyone. Keep pushing." I didn't give him a chance to answer before stomping away. My sour mood didn't improve when Maria didn't show up for school.

Not that day. Not that week. She missed finals. And she missed every call.

I was so damn worried about her I was sick. I questioned the teachers, even cornered the principal. I threw a tantrum when they told me it was confidential but there were "extenuating circumstances" and to "not worry." After about two weeks, I begged my father to look into it. An address, a name, a freaking welfare check. He promised he would. I was going mad feeling so useless. He and Mom had some sort of holiday gala at the hospital with the Board of Directors and a bunch of important people. I managed to convince them to let me stay home. One of those sudden, winter storms came rolling in and my windows damn near rattled. I was sitting at my desk, trying to stalk Maria on social media for some hint of her whereabouts, when my doorbell rang. I about jumped ten feet in the air as the sweet, tinkling chime echoed throughout the otherwise empty house.

I had a whole rant ready for whoever was behind that door but my misplaced ire dissipated as quickly as smoke on the air.

Maria.

She was soaked from head to toe. She must have walked here.

Worse? Her busted lip. Her black eye. The swollen jaw. How she cradled her arm. Her bottom lip trembled and she looked up at me, "I didn't know where else to go."

"Ohmigawd, get inside before you freeze to death." I was almost too afraid to touch her but, as gently as I could, I pulled her inside. "Maria, where have you been? What happened? Where is he? I will fucking kill him with my bare hands. My bare hands, you hear me? Why haven't you answered any of my calls?" She shivered violently so I steered her into the kitchen where I quickly made a cup of hot cocoa and shoved it into her hands.

Still, she said nothing.

I ran upstairs, grabbing a change of clothes. She was bigger than I was, but it would have to work. I snagged a blanket from the back of the couch before rejoining her in the kitchen.

After she was changed, and not shaking like a maraca, I looked at her expectantly. She wouldn't meet my eyes. "Maria?"

She finally looked up. "I'm sorry I've been gone. I'm sorry for what I said. I didn't mean it. I'm so sorry."

I shook my head. "It's ok. I'm not mad. Talk to me. According to the many therapists I've seen, saying awful shit is something called a defense mechanism. I know I've done it."

She started sobbing, a heartbroken, desolate sound. I still wasn't a huge fan of touch, but my friend needed me. Oh God, she looked awful. I was almost afraid to put my arms around her, worried she would shatter at the slightest pressure. She was warming up but still shaking. She buried her face in my shoulder, and I just held her like I had wish someone had held me. Her next words were so quiet, I almost missed them. But then the three shocking words seemed to echo around the room.

"I'm pregnant, Holly."

Chapter Six

⸸ Holly ⸸

Most people would ask their parents before setting up their pregnant seventeen-year-old friend in the guest bedroom.

I am not most people.

I offered to take Maria back to her house to grab her things and she promptly had a panic attack. The thought of seeing him again sent her over the edge. So, fuck that. I just ordered her a bunch of new clothes, new sheets, new everything. With my dad's credit card. A charge he may or may not question later. Whatever. A problem for later me. At first, Maria protested, but later I walked past her room and found her hugging a hideous fuzzy neon purple sweater to her chest like it was a lifeline. I promptly ordered a bunch more purple shit.

The first morning Maria joined us for breakfast, my parents were surprised but didn't question it. The second, my dad simply grabbed another plate. By the third, my mom was gripping her coffee mug so hard I was afraid it would break, and my dad was watching us two with a knowing look in his eye. Ever the surgeon putting the pieces together. On the fifth night, when Maria was in the shower and Amazon had dropped off even more boxes, my dad asked what was up. I explained everything best I could, trying to walk the line between "not my story to tell" and "yeah, I may have used your credit card without permission but there's a good reason." I then fixed him with a look that dared him to challenge the new arrangements. He had simply nodded and walked out.

The next morning, I overheard him on the phone. I may or may not have eavesdropped long enough to realize he was getting Maria's grandma in home care. That's when I knew he was on our side. I told Maria, and she sobbed. Again. So much crying. I blame the hormones. She cried at dinner too, thanking him. My mom watched everything with a thin-lipped smile.

By this point, winter break was in full swing. I had hoped the cold would deter the bikes but I was not so lucky. Jackson and his merry band of idiots had stopped destroying my peace of mind but still drove by daily, albeit quietly. Not that it mattered much. Maria and I both were barely clinging to sanity. What a pair we made.

One day, I was in the kitchen with Maria while she made herself a cup of peppermint tea. It had taken a hot minute before she would do anything in the kitchen, like she was afraid the cabinets wouldn't open for her, or the dishwasher might attack her. But either she was finally comfortable or the need for peppermint tea was strong enough that she overcame her fear of cutlery. Evidently it helped the morning sickness. She still doesn't talk a lot which was why I was a bit shocked to hear her voice.

"You ever see snow before, hermana?"

"Snow?" I shook my head, and joined her at the window. Sure enough, thick white flurries are falling from the sky, layering over the world like it could cover up anything ugly if it tried hard enough. It never snowed back home. "Snow! Ohmigawd Maria, it's snowing! Look! I thought it never snowed in Georgia?"

She smiled, her first in a long time, "Yeah, Christmas miracle, I guess. You got a snow jacket in that big closet of yours?"

As a matter of fact, I did. I had been dying to play in the snow since I was a kid. I needed to know what it felt like, and even though I knew Georgia had, quite literally, a snowball's chance in hell of a white Christmas…I had hoped we would get lucky. I grabbed Maria's free hand and pulled her towards the stairs. After changing quickly, I found her in the hallway in a knee-length purple and silver parka. Mine was red and gold and flashy.

Completely ridiculous. I loved it. Back downstairs, I found our front yard almost completely covered already. I turned to Maria, who hovered behind me. "This seems like a lot."

She shrugged. "It is. I can't really remember a storm like this."

"This is awesome!"

She shrugged again, but was fighting a smile. "Sure. But it's cold too."

I cast her a sideways glance, "Can you even feel the cold through that jacket? Is it safe for the baby?"

Maria's hand hovered over her belly, which was still flat. "I am fairly confident the baby will be fine. You know, I have an appointment in a couple of weeks."

"What? Really?"

"Yeah, but…I don't want to go alone. I was wondering, would you want to go with me? You don't have to."

Tears pricked the backs of my eyes, and I blinked them away before nodding furiously. "Yes, absolutely. Yes."

She smiled at me, and then walked out into the curtain of white. I watched as she stood, face tilted towards the sky. She kicked a little at the snow by her feet, which easily covered her boots. Looking back at me, she winked before allowing herself to fall backwards. She landed with a soft whoop sound, and just lay there. I was beginning to worry until a sound filled the air. It was soft, hesitant, but hopeful. Beautiful. She was laughing. With a smile, I ran out to her and threw myself belly-down onto the ground beside her.

Maria introduced me to the ancient art of a snowball fight. Turns out, I was quite good at it. Which was how we both found ourselves panting and wet and happy an hour later. My dad pulled up in his beloved Buick, but another guy got out of the passenger side. I didn't recognize him, though something about his hulking form and dark eyes was familiar. Maria definitely did and immediately froze. "Oh, boy," she muttered as she stood up next to me. Almost unconsciously, she reached for my hand. I let her. And frowned at the newcomer that was making my friend nervous as they approached.

"Hi, Mr. Mills." Maria offered up a soft, hesitant smile at the big man who immediately engulfed her in hug. She all but disappeared but managed to send me a wide-eyed look from under his arms.

My dad stopped between us and reached for me. I dodged his reach but stepped closer as he made the introductions. "Bug, honey. This is August Mills. He runs the motorcycle club down the road. And he sits on the hospital board. You might know his sons? Dalton and Maverick? Dalton is in your grade; Maverick graduated a couple years ahead of you."

August Mills released Maria, who stepped closer to me, looking a bit frazzled. "You must be Holly. Your father has told me a lot about you." His Southern accent was thick, but somehow warm? I frowned at him again, trying to decide if he was trustworthy or not.

Dad was staring at me expectantly so I forced up a thin lipped smile. He didn't seem like a bad dude, I guess. But I am not kidding when I say the guy was huge. He made my dad look like a toddler. His bright blue eyes, which were a replica of his son's, were open and friendly. But still. Trust issues and all that. I didn't say a word until I looked over at my dad again and found him with a vein pulsing in his neck. Sighing, I bared my teeth in what I was hoping was a friendly smile and said, "Hi."

Mr. Mills didn't seem the least bit fazed by me and turned to Maria who had been watching the whole exchange. "I hear you've been staying with the McCarthys?" Maria looked between me, my dad, and back to Mr. Mills. She suddenly became very interested in the roughed-up snow at her feet and nodded mutely. "Well, you know if you need anything to let me and Hannah know. Anything at all, darling. That good-for-nothing boyfriend of yours…" His blue eyes darkened in a way that made him look about hundred times scarier. "I never did like him."

Well. If I was Jesse, I would be moving to the next county. Or country. New planet? The leader of the Steel Saints was definitely not the kind of guy you wanted to piss off. There was a bit of an awkward silence as we all stared at him. Then my dad cleared his throat and said, "Are you sure I can't get you to stay for dinner, August?"

The big man shook his head. "Thanks but Hannah is making fried chicken and I'll be damned if I miss that. But"—he turned his attention back to Maria and I—"the Saints are hosting a sort of winter gathering in a couple weeks, right before school starts. Snowball fights if the weather cooperates, hot cocoa, bonfire. Y'all should come!"

My dad nodded eagerly, his head bobbing so hard I was afraid it would fall off. Mr. Mills must be a big deal. "Absolutely, we will be there! Are you sure I can't give you a ride to the clubhouse?"

We will?! Aw, fuck me. I knew exactly who else would be there. I wondered if Mr. Mills knew just how much of a pain in the ass his son and his friends were. Mr. Mills was reassuring my dad that it was just a short walk, and he would be fine. Maria excused herself, then grabbed me by the hand again, all but yanking me back towards the house. Once inside, she stripped out of her winter gear quickly and turned to me with a huff.

"Ohmigawd. I've never been to the club house. Like, never. But the Mills? They are like everything to this town. Everything. Jesse never let me go over there. Ever. And now? I'm freaking rotund and pregnant and I look like a lumpy pillow! Hi, everyone. I'm Maria, the town hoe. The pregnant teen. The oddity. Nice to meet ya!"

She was speaking rapidly, growing flushed. I put my hands on her shoulders, "Girl, breathe. It's not that deep. And rotund? You're pregnant. Not a donut. Fuck what everyone else thinks. You're beautiful." She gave me a skeptical look, and I shook her playfully, "You're fine. Plus, I know of at least one person who will be happy to see you." Her skepticism turned to confusion and she frowned at me. "Oh come on, I don't even like the idiots. I literally just moved here. But Diego drools over you."

"Diego?"

"Yes. His friends are all assholes, so he probably is too. But whatever. Curly brown hair? Dimples? Running back on the football team?"

"He doesn't like me! He doesn't even talk to me!"

I scoffed, "Yes, 'cause teenage boys are known for being eloquent and in tune with their emotions."

She rolled her eyes. "Fine. But good thing it'll be snowing. Otherwise there might be a fire, outside of the one Mr. Mills is planning."

Now it was my turn to be confused, "Huh?"

My dad came in, gave us an odd look, and headed towards the kitchen where my mom was making dinner. Maria stepped back to let him pass and then leaned towards me. Her stage whisper was conspiratorial. "You and Jackson."

I spluttered with indignation. "Are you insane? Are the hormones getting to you? Is this some kind of pregnancy mania?"

She smiled sweetly. "You guys pass each other in the hallway, glaring like you are on opposite teams at the Super Bowl or something. And didn't you like, 'My Little Pony' his bike the other week?"

About a week ago, she and I were out maternity shopping. We had come across the boys, and Jackson had made some dumbass comment about her being my pet project. Sure, Diego ripped him a new one. But when they got back to their bikes? I might have bought a super glittery, foul-smelling perfume from a nearby boutique. And up-ended it over his bike and in his helmet. I smiled at the memory before shaking my head. "We hate each other. He's an entitled, pompous man child."

Maria headed towards the kitchen, and said over her shoulder, "Exactly, gasoline meet match." I rolled my eyes and followed her. My mom was putting the finishing touches on a honey dijon chicken dish. It was her specialty, and she didn't cook often, so I was pleasantly surprised when the familiar aroma greeted us. She had her back to us, graying strawberry blonde curls tied back with a piece of ribbon. Her over-the-top sundress and heels made her look like she had stepped off the pages of a Martha Stewart catalogue. As we took a seat at the kitchen island, she turned to us.

Her smile was forced as she glanced at Maria and then at me before saying with a saccharine sweetness, "Holly, please go ahead and set the table. Maria, be a dear and get the salad out of the fridge."

Maria eagerly hopped from her seat, happy to help. My mother watched her as she walked to the fridge. I knew that look. The carefully placed, fake smile. Great. Mom was up to something. Tonight was going to be a shit storm. When dinner was finally ready, we all sat at the table in a tense silence. Maria was either oblivious or somehow managing to ignore it. Then again, she was used to dinners with Jesse, which I was sure were about a hundred times worse. My dad shook his head at my mother, who clenched her wine glass like a weapon and ignored him with pursed lips. I'd had enough. I slammed my fork on my plate, hard enough for the glassware to rattle. My dad's eyes shot over to mine; my mom simply raised her chin and avoided my glare.

"What? What's up?"

My mom cleared her throat, set her wine glass down after taking a dainty sip, and looked over at Maria. My friend was hunched, but she met my mother's gaze with a soft smile. "Maria, dear. How long will you be staying with us?"

Before Maria could answer, I said, "Is there a problem?"

My mother finally looked over at me. "Of course not. I understand the need for a temporary solution. But this isn't sustainable."

"Temporary? Sustainable?" My dad and Maria were silent, watching us.

"Holly, your father and I have been very tolerant—"

I cut her off with a snarl, "You cannot be serious, mother. Are you actually trying to kick her out?"

"Holly, you never exactly asked-"

Again, I didn't let her finish. "What's the issue, Mother? We have plenty of room. Plenty of food. Plenty of fucking money. So what's wrong with Maria staying with us?"

My dad cleared his throat, "Holly, language. Just hear your mother out. Maria, maybe you should go upstairs?"

Maria started to get up, but I stopped her. "First of all, no. You don't get to banish her to her room. Second of all, language?" Maria slowly sank back into her chair.

"Holly, there are plenty of programs that are designed to help single mothers. As a matter of fact, I know of one about two hours from here. She can get the support she needs. They will help her find a home for the child so she can finish her education. And this way, you too can focus on schooling. We just moved here, dear. We're not in any place to take care of...your friend."

Maria gasped, her eyes shining with unshed tears and her hand going protectively to her stomach. I stood, shaking and fought consciously keep my voice steady. "No."

"Excuse me, we are the adults here."

I looked over at my father. "You agree with her?"

My father pinched his nose between his forefingers before looking back at me, "Holly, I want to help your friend. But your mother and I are a team. In order to keep this family functioning, we must be on the same page."

"The same page? Even if it's the wrong one? She literally just assumed Maria wasn't keeping *her* baby." Dad had done this before. Agreed with mom just to keep the peace. As a matter of fact, us moving here was one of the few times he had ever laid his foot down. I'm over it. I can see in his eyes that he didn't think this is right. And I was fucking fed up with my mother's shit. I turned back to her.

"No. You don't get to do to Maria what you did to me. You don't get to sweep the shit under the rug. You don't get to act like everything is ok. This isn't about your precious image, Mother. And how dare you suggest Maria give up her baby? Try thinking of literally anyone other than yourself for once."

My mother stood too. "What are you saying?!"

Maria looked like she wanted to crawl under the table. Maybe she should've gone to her room. But I had left this unsaid long enough. "You saw all the signs. Or maybe you were so caught up in the spotlight, you were blinded by it. All the times he *touched* me? Longer than he should? More than he should? You either saw that, or you were too focused on being perfect to notice. I'm not sure which is worse. It's always been about you, about your image, about your reputation. Well, news flash, Mother, life isn't some fucking fairytale."

"Holly Elizabeth McCarthy, watch your mouth!"

My dad stood too, his eyes haunted. "Holly, honey."

I turned to him. "For once in your life, stand up to your wife, Dad. She was supposed to be my mother. She was supposed to protect me. And when she couldn't do that, she barely knew how to support me in the aftermath, so she didn't even try. I am over it, Dad. I am tired of being your perfect baby girl. I am not her anymore. And Maria needs someone in the same way I needed someone. So, she stays. End of story."

I turned to leave and gestured for Maria to come with me. Neither of my parents made a move to stop us. I didn't know what was next. But I would keep Maria here, where she was safe, or die trying. Silently, Maria followed me to my room where I threw myself onto my bed. She sat next to me and after a few minutes, she whispered quietly, "You didn't have to do that."

I didn't reply, just reached for her hand and squeezed tight as the sound of my parents arguing echoed throughout the house.

Chapter Seven

I was supposed to be helping the guys set up for Mrs. Mills' party. She was ecstatic. Snow was falling heavy outside when I came in, which would make for one hell of a snowball fight later.

I was not ecstatic.

Two weeks ago, a Malibu Menace upended cupcake hell on my bike and helmet. And I still hadn't managed to get all the glitter out. I was going to have to get a new helmet. I loved this helmet; it was custom, a gift from Mr. Mills.

I scrubbed harder.

Fucking Malibu.

A low laugh dragged my attention to the door, and I found Dalton smirking at me, and wearing a pair of elf ears, which made his almost 6six-foot-tall self look ridiculous. "You still trying to clean that shit?"

I glowered at him in response. "Clearly."

He squatted next to me, leaned forward to sniff the air, and screwed his nose when he caught a whiff of the evil, sickly sweet vanilla cupcake smell. "Damn, bro. She got you good. Maybe next time, try not to say stupid shit?"

"It was a joke." A stupid joke, sure. But still.

"Yeah, try telling her that. Or Diego. Shit pissed him off."

I shook my head and rubbed a microfiber cloth across the top of my helmet. "And he still wants to say he doesn't have feelings for that chick."

Dalton shrugged, standing and saying, "Mom wanted me to tell you, and I quote, to quit feeling sorry for yourself and come help. I'm not sure your helmet is salvageable, man. At least you got most of the glitter off the bike."

For the record, if my Harley had become permanently sparkly, I would've lost my shit. I hang my helmet from the handlebars and go to follow him. "What all still needs done?"

"Diego's working on setting the bonfire up. He's got a mountain of wood, and I'm mildly concerned he's going to burn the county down. Mac and Dad are making sure tables and shit are set up. Silas and Cliff are trying to get the garage cleared. Mom is scaring everyone out of the kitchen. Can't even steal a damn meatball without her seeing. I was gonna see if you wanted to help me hang up the last of the streamers and stuff."

I gestured for him to lead the way. As we made our way from the garage and outside, I was blinded by the light on the snow. It must have stopped a while ago, but there was easily a foot. It came over my boots and I frowned at it, shaking the cold wet off before it could seep inside and soak my socks. Blue and silver foil, polar bear blow-ups, and the giant oak in the front yard was bare except for about a million twinkle lights. I could hear Mrs. Mills shouting something inside, and over yonder Diego was stacking lumber. The teepee shaped pile was taller than him, and I briefly wondered if Dalton was right. I figured if it was a true danger, Mr. Mills would have stepped in, so we just left him to it.

About two hours later, I was sitting in the kitchen with Dalton and Mac and sipping on a cup of hot chocolate when Diego came in. He immediately glared at me, and I rolled my eyes. "Dude, how long you gonna stay mad at me?"

"Long as I damn well want."

"Come on, man."

Dalton slid Diego a cup of cocoa. "He didn't mean it. Sometimes he just has more balls than brain."

I frowned at him before looking back at Diego, who was still glaring at me, "You called her a pet, Jackson. Like, who the fuck does that? After all the shit she's been through?"

"I was just trying to piss off Malibu."

"Yeah well, it was fucking stupid."

"I'm not knocking that." Malibu kind of has a way of making me irrational. That damn tongue of hers. The fucking glitter. And they say I have anger issues.

Mac was watching us in that careful way of his. "How about we just agree sometimes we can all be dumbasses and move on?"

"Maverick Edward, you watch your mouth." Mrs. Mills came breezing into the kitchen and fixed her son with a firm look. He smiled at her and her face softened. Literally the only time the guy smiles. We're a messed-up bunch.

"Hey, now that she's ditched the ex—"

Diego groaned and sank into a chair. "Don't even go there."

Dalton looked between us and I saw the moment the same thought I had crossed his mind. "Shit, man. He's right. Goal is open!" He held his arms up in a touch down gesture. Diego flipped him the middle finger, but before he could respond further, Mrs. Mills swooped in and grabbed our half-finished mugs.

"Maybe y'all should've spent more time sipping and less time gabbing. Guests are starting to arrive. Go out and greet them. Smile. Be friendly."

She shooed us out the door, and the four of us headed to the parking lot. We could hear car doors and scattered chatter now that we're out of the kitchen. She must have super hearing or an eerie form of intuition. Wouldn't surprise me.

"Jackson! Guys! Can you believe this snow?"

I looked over at Rodney. Several of our teammates were following him. Dalton raised his hand in greeting, calling several of them by name. Mac made his way over, giving Rodney shit about filling his shoes. I sucked at names but joined the throng with ease. Diego was joking around with another wide receiver, and I was laughing at some joke I barely heard when I turned and saw *her*.

Malibu.

Stepping out of her daddy's Buick like she owned the place. She was wearing some red sweater dress with a black belt that accented her waist. Black boots that were probably going to get her knocked out in the snowball fight. And a little red Santa hat perched on her mess of blonde curls. Hazel eyes scanned the area like she was looking for a threat. They narrowed when they landed on me. Threat. Found.

"Dude, you're drooling."

"Fuck off." I shoved Dalton into the nearest snowbank.

"He's not the only one," Mac muttered. I turned to him, confused, until I saw Diego staring hard enough at Maria that I was surprised the girl wasn't smoldering. Maria had on a fuzzy purple sweater and leggings, neither of which made much of an effort to hide her slight baby bump. Some people whispered as they passed, the McCarthys making their way over to Mr. and Mrs. Mills. Every whisper was met with a glare from Holly so sharp, I half expected to see spots of blood red in the snow. She shielded Maria with her body, probably unconsciously. But I was starting to realize how much I had probably fucked up with my "pet project" comment.

Later, after dinner, Mac's dad got a little over serious with teams for the snowball fight. In an attempt to make it a fair fight, he split up the football team randomly. Mac and I were on one team, along with Rodney and a couple other guys, plus a few people from the neighborhood, and Holly's dad. Dalton was riling his team up, Diego jumping on the balls of his feet like this was legit. Maria and several of the wives sat on the sidelines. I expected Malibu to join them, but she made her way over to Dalton, who watched her in the way one might watch a lioness. She said something to him, and I was too far away to hear. But he looked over at me and mouthed, "Oh shit."

I just grinned.

When Mac's dad blew the whistle, it was almost immediate chaos. I mean, zero planning. Just one side aggressively hurling bundles of snow at the other. No method, no strategy. It was fucking awesome. About ten minutes in, the noise finally dipped while everyone scrambled to reload. I bent to tighten my laces—then took a snowball the size of a damn melon square in the face. Knocked me flat on my ass. I spat out ice, blinked through the snow in my lashes, and looked up, ready to raise hell.

Dalton? Diego? Nope. Malibu.

She was *grinning.* Not that sharp, defensive smirk I'd gotten used to—this was real. Unfiltered. Her cheeks were pink, her hair full of snow, and for the first time since I met her, she actually looked like a kid having fun. Damn near stopped my heart.

Then one of my own teammates nailed her from the side—hard. She stumbled, smile faltering. I retraced the ball to who had thrown it, and reacted before I could stop myself.

"Hey!" I barked. "Watch where you're throwing!"

The guy blinked at me. "You do realize she's on *Dalton's* team, right?"

Yeah, I realized. Didn't make me feel any less pissed.

Across the field, Dalton caught my eye. He was grinning like a bastard. "Gonna need you to stop flirting with my MVP, Morgan!" he called

."Tell your MVP to stop hitting me in the face!" I shot back, but my heart wasn't in it. She laughed, loud, bright, unguarded, and any thought of payback went right out the window. The rest of the match, my aim went to hell. I missed more than I hit, too busy keeping an eye on *her.* Making sure nobody threw too hard. I told myself it was just good sportsmanship.

Even I didn't believe that shit.

Chapter Eight

⸸ **Holly** ⸸

The beginning of the end.

Spring semester, senior year.

I could get through this. I glanced at Maria, who sat hunched in the passenger seat of Sally. We could get through this. Her baby bump was almost invisible under her baggy shirt. I'd told her approximately a million times that hiding her growing belly was just silly. I think it's adorable. She loves her baby. And fuck what everyone else thinks. Little bit in there is a girl. Found that out just last week. At least, the doctor said she's mostly sure it's a girl. I'm running with it. I've already started buying baby clothes, much to Maria's chagrin. She doesn't know it yet, but we're going to be besties.

"We're gonna get through this, you know?"

She glanced at me. "Uh-huh."

"Ah, how bad can it be? The emotionally scarred California girl and the pregnant loner?"

This time, she groaned and slid lower in her seat. "I'm not sure I can do this. People already talk."

"Let 'em. Who gives a shit what they think? If it helps, let everything they say bounce off of me. I'm tougher than I look. I can handle it."

"You shouldn't have to handle it."

"I shouldn't have to handle half the shit I've been through yet here I am. Now, come on, I've got to stop by the office before class starts."

I cut the engine on Sally, sliding out of my seat and into the weak sunlight peppering the parking lot. Maria came around the side of the car, surprising me when she looped her arm through mine. I let her cling to me, knowing she probably needed the support. Sure enough, as we climbed the steps into the brick and linoleum halls, whispers followed us. Maria held her head high, but the hand she had on my bicep trembled. One girl in some God-awful ripped jeans wouldn't stop staring, so I stared back, glaring a hole into her soul until she looked away. I swung by the office to "follow up" on the schedule and locker change my dad had requested, funny how quickly things move when a surgeon makes a call, and then we headed for our lockers.

As Maria put her things away, keeping only what she needed for first period, I watched a gaggle of theater kids plaster prom posters all over the walls. "Already?" I muttered, half to myself. "And what kind of theme is Fae Festivities? We are not wearing wings." I directed that last bit to Maria who turned as they hung up the last of the posters.

"I'm not going to prom."

I scoffed. "Yes, you are."

She shook her head vehemently. "Um, no?"

"Maria—"

"Holly, how many pregnant fairies do you know?"

"Well, seeing as how I know exactly zero fairies, I would say none."

She rolled her eyes. "You know what I mean. Come May, I won't even be able to fit in a dress."

"Oh, I'll find you a dress. I don't know if you noticed this, but I'm kind of rich. I can afford a tailor."

"Gonna need one."

My head whipped towards the girl who said that shit so fast, I felt my neck pop. Jasmine. One of Miranda's friends. "Holly, ignore it." I barely heard Maria as I marched over to that bubble bitch. I *know* she had meant for us to hear.

"Hey, Jazzie right?"

"So?"

"That girl over there? She could wear a fucking burlap sack and would still outshine you. Your hair? That is the *cheapest* perm I have ever seen in my life. And I hope you know a good oral surgeon. You're gonna need more than braces to fix that overbite. But please. Go on. Keep talking."

Jasmine stared at me, jaw slightly ajar, face red. Her eyes shone with tears and her friends shrank back from me like I might bite. Fucking try me. I just might. Miranda wasn't around, but I was sure my words would get back to her. Good. Maria had been through enough. I turned on my heel when the bell rang, making my way back to my friend. Looping my arm through hers once again, I all but marched her to first period.

"Girl, you have lost your marbles."

"Yeah. A long time ago."

A couple weeks later, things had mostly died down. Maria was disappearing to a bathroom twice a day to hurl, minimum. Morning sickness was more like an all-day sickness, and random smells just sent her spiraling. The cafeteria was always rocky territory. One Friday, I watched her carefully as we approached the double doors, propped open for the flood of students.

It was 50/50. Either she would eat everything in sight, or we would be spending lunch period in the handicap stall. But she visibly brightened when the smell of chicken hit us. I had packed a bagged lunch, safe foods for her. But evidently the baby was feeling chicken, and she bee-lined for it like a hound on a scent. I followed dutifully, smiling a little. I eyed the chicken sandwich, warm under the foil, as it was handed to me. I had never been a big fan of cafeteria food. Fuck it; if I didn't like it, Maria would probably eat it.

Snagging some fresh fruit and a cookie, I found an empty table and sat down. Maria joined me a few minutes later with a bag of apple slices and a piece of cheese. I wasn't entirely sure where she had gotten the cheese, but I watched as she put the cheese, apples, and an unhealthy amount of honey mustard on her chicken sandwich. What in the actual fuck? Maria caught me watching her and grinned around a mouthful of chicken. Great, now I was going to hurl. Just as I was about to comment on her weird pregnancy taste buds, she looked over my shoulder and her eyes widened.

Turning, I saw Miranda and her boyfriend making their way over to us. Oh, come the fuck on. I thought we were past this. I eyed her as she got closer, and Maria quietly continued devouring her sandwich. Sure enough, Queen Bimbo stopped at our otherwise empty table and sneered at us. The cafeteria slowly grew quiet. Evidently there was a show about to go down. I had neither the tickets nor the script, yet here we were. Rustling sounds made me glance over my shoulder, and I caught Maria unabashedly snatching my sandwich. I watched her for a second, both of us completely ignoring Miranda until her annoyingly twinkle-shine voice shattered my peace of mind.

"Excuse me."

I turned back to her, "You're excused."

She rolled her eyes. "Hilarious. So, Maria, tell me. We've all been dying to know—how does it feel being the only knocked-up chick in school?" Her boyfriend snickered, ever the dutiful fan boy.

Maria set her sandwich down, staring at her plate. "Miranda, shut the fuck up," I snarled.

"No, I mean seriously. Does a guy beating the shit out of you just turn you on that much? I mean, I hate to kink shame, but, honestly. Hey, whose last name is the baby getting?"

I stood and would've found myself nose to nose with the bitch, but some guy got between us.

No. Not some guy.

Diego.

"Get your fucking girl, Austin, or I am going to lay you out on this floor." I hadn't quite noticed how tall Diego was, but he seemed even bigger when pissed. The dude towered over Miranda's boyfriend, who seemed a bit stupefied at first, but evidently he wasn't the brightest bulb.

"Who the fuck you talking to, Gonzalez?"

Diego stepped forward, the two boys chest to chest. Out of the corner of my eye, I could see Maria slowly pick her sandwich back up. Just when I thought they were about to start a fist fight in the middle of the cafeteria, another voice entered the fray.

"You really need to sit down, dude." I glanced to my left and found Dalton there, his words were a-not-so carefully-veiled threat. His usually bright blue eyes were dark, like a sky that had been clear only moments before. Rodney, another guy on the football team, was there too, and right behind them? Jackson. It was Jackson who stepped forward, wedging himself between Diego and Austin.

"Take your girl and fuck off. Or I swear to God, I will get you kicked you off the damn team."

"Austin!" Miranda pulled on her boyfriend, who jerked his arm from her grip.

"Shut up, Miranda. Let's go."

I made a shoo gesture, and Miranda's lip curled in a snarl. But she followed Austin out of the cafeteria and the tension seemed to leave the room with them. I turned back to Maria, who was finishing her sandwich. Diego glared at the door, and, after a minute, he took a seat next to her. She blinked at him and then looked up at me. I shrugged. And then watched, mystified, as Jackson and the rest of them sat down too. Um, ok?

"So, what? You're Pregnancy Secret Service now?" Jackson ignored me, stealing the orange from my tray. I frowned at him and looked around the table. "Hello? Anyone? I had that handled."

Diego was whispering to Maria who was still watching him carefully, and Jackson tossed the peel to the side before looking up at me.

"Sure you did, Malibu."

"Malibu?!"

"Yeah, it's better than princess, don't ya think?"

I glared at him and Dalton snickered, so I glared at him too. Maria giggled. Great. Just great. Was this my life now? I glanced again at Diego and the look on his face as he watched my bestie? Yeah. That right there told me he wasn't going anywhere anytime soon. I glanced over at Jackson and found him watching me. I raised an eyebrow at him and he shook his head before dragging a hand through his hair. When he looked back at me and then away again, I swear I felt my eye start to twitch. Out of the corner of my eye, I noticed Maria glancing back and forth between the two of us. Yeah, this wasn't weird at all.

Our table sat in a tense silence until the bell rang. The boys walked with us to the door where we gathered in a group, totally blocking the flow of traffic. Diego was still watching Maria carefully, and she casually edged behind me until she was almost shielded from his view. I frowned at Diego in warning—one he may not have noticed but his friends did. Jackson frowned back, and Rodney nudged Diego who seemed to visibly shake himself. Dalton grinned like this entire thing was just a soap opera he was lucky enough to be privy to.

"Well, this has been an absolute blast. Really. But I am pretty sure if I keep missing class, Coach is going to hang me from the goalpost. And then let Jackson here use me for target practice."

Diego snorted. "Oh, well, you would be fine then. Jackson can't punt for shit."

Jackson glared at the two of them, "Bullshit. My punt is just fine. Waldo here couldn't hit the broadside of a barn." He jerked his thumb at Dalton who feigned insult. Maria poked her head out from behind me, and I glanced down at her.

The guys seemed completely content to continue arguing about who could hit what but Maria cleared her throat, surprising them into silence. "We should really get going. I would very much like to not be a high school dropout and a teen mom. That would just be the cherry on top."

I smiled at her. "You would be the cutest teen mom ever, dominating the shit out of that show."

She blinked at me, "What show?"

"Teen Mom?"

She glanced at the guys who all looked equally confused. "Yeah, I think you're the only one who knows what that is." She waddled off before I could reply, waving goodbye over her shoulder to our unlikely companions. I hurried to follow her, not having the least bit of desire to be in the middle of their shit. I caught up to her as we headed to our next class. We were definitely late but neither of us seemed to be in any hurry. I wasn't quite sure how our schedules ended up being the exact same but I would bet money my dad and Mr. Mills had something to do with it.

"Hey, that was weird right?"

I tilted my head. "I mean, kind of. I wasn't expecting the others to jump in, but Diego makes sense."

"It does?"

"Girl, you are so deep in denial…you could be living in Denali and not know it."

She side-eyed me. "Ok, first, that made no sense. Good try though. And secondly, I am not in denial."

"He really likes you, Maria."

"No accounting for taste."

"Oh hush, you and Lil Bit are a catch."

"And you'll fight anyone who says otherwise?"

"Damn straight."

When we got to class, we slid to the back of the classroom under the disapproving stare of the teacher who hadn't appreciated us interrupting her lecture. Maria offered her an apologetic smile before carefully sliding into her seat. The desks were those old-fashioned kind, where the chair and the table were connected. Before long, she wouldn't be able to fit in them. Guess we would just cross that bridge when we got there. The teacher droned on about psychology, Maria taking careful notes. I doodled in my notebook, occasionally glancing around the room. When Maria looked over at me, I proudly held up my crude drawing of me and Lil Bit in Sally. Lil Bit was driving, pacifier in her mouth. Maria shook her head at me, and I smiled proudly.

For the next couple of weeks, life was normal. Ish. Every day, the guys sat with us at lunch. Diego doted on Maria. At first, she resisted. I could see that fearful look in her eyes, that uncertainty. I prayed she got over that hesitance to trust, to love. I still hadn't. But doesn't mean she wouldn't. Dalton was growing on me, as much as I hated to admit it. He was like a puppy. A labrador puppy. Or maybe a golden retriever. His infallible cheer, twisted humor. After he finally stopped hitting on me, he was actually quite fun to be around.

Now, Jackson. He was a different story. I did not like that fucker. That arrogant, rude, boy band wannabe. Pain in my ass. And I swear to God, if he didn't stop calling me Malibu…I was going to prison for murder.

Prom was slowly creeping up. I could tell it made Maria incredibly nervous. Which was how we found ourselves sitting on the hood of Sally, debating dress shopping. Well, I was debating. She was just nodding and picking at her nails, blatantly refusing to help me choose a shop. I was stuck between Formally Yours or Bridals by Lori. Maybe both? Maria was still convinced we wouldn't be able to find anything that would fit her now very visible baby bump. When the guys came out of the school and made their way to us, I hopped off the hood and spun towards Dalton.

"Bridals by Lori or Formally Yours?"

"The hell did you just say?" Dalton's blue eyes were puzzled, comically so.

Jackson blinked. "Are we supposed to know what that means?"

Diego helped Maria off the hood. "They're dress shops, dumbasses. Hannah shops there for gala events and shit."

Dalton gave him a weird look, "And you know that how?"

I groaned. "Maria, come on. These dolts are useless. Bridals by Lori or Formally Yours?"

"Jesus, Malibu. Is it really such a big deal? Just freaking pick one. It's just a dance. How you look is not that important."

I fixed Jackson with a withering look. "Right, says the guy who spends more time on his hair than I do." I gestured to his boot cut jeans, old rock T-shirt, and carefully styled hair. Hair that looked like the wind had just been caressing it, and jeans that hugged a really nice ass. Not that I noticed.

"Aw chucks, didn't think you noticed me that much."

I flipped him off and then gave Maria a pleading look. "Maria, please?"

She looked over at me. "I don't know, Holly. Which one do you think has a maternity section?"

I groaned. "Any store has a maternity section if you have a good enough tailor."

"Something only a spoiled, rich chick would say."

I spun towards Jackson. "The fuck did you just call me?"

"Oh, lay off. My house could fit in your living room."

Diego piped up. "You don't live in a house. You live in a trailer."

"Dude, shut up. Not important."

"Just saying."

Jackson glared at him before turning back to me. "Like I said, just pick one, Malibu. And get Maria home before she falls asleep in the parking lot."

I glanced over at my friend, who was looking a bit pale and swaying gently. She was always tired lately. I was so focused on her that I almost missed Jackson's parting remark.

"You'll look beautiful in whatever you wear, anyways."

Beautiful.

He actually thought I was beautiful? My chest gave a stupid little flutter I crushed fast. Nope. Not going there. Not with him. Or anyone, for that matter.

That night, after dinner and a shower, I checked on Maria before heading to bed. She slept soundly in her room. My parents had long since given up the fight, and she was here to stay until she was able to get on her feet. I was ready to get the room next to hers set up for the nursery but she had asked me to wait. She was still working at that diner in what little spare time she had, insisting she needed the money to save up for her own place. I worried about her but had stopped trying to convince her to stay home when I realized that Diego kept a careful watch over here while she worked. Whatever made her happy.

I was grateful we had made some friends, unlikely as they were. She needed the support. And to be honest? It was nice for me too. These guys? Maria? They weren't fake. Sometimes rude, often annoying. But real.

And Jackson? Well...he thought I was beautiful. Which made me just a little giddy.

Chapter Nine

✒ Jackson ✒

Lying on my bed, hands intertwined behind my head and facing the ceiling, I thought about the future. Which, to be honest, wasn't something I did often. Another day, same routine—me and the guys trailing after long tan legs and Maria's new waddle. Holly's sway? Damn near lethal. I groaned. *Focus, dumbass.* I couldn't stay in this shit hole forever. I tried to envision what my future might look like, but in between the mess of my thoughts was a distinctive pair of hazel eyes that danced in and out of view.

I rolled out of bed and walked as quietly as I could to the kitchen. If I was lucky, there just might be something edible in the fridge. I didn't pay much mind to my mother, who was passed out on the couch drunk. Again. Dodging the soft spots on the floor of our beat-up trailer, I managed to make it to the fridge. Grimacing at the contents, sour milk and moldy mystery meat, I glanced over my shoulder at Mom before heading out the door and down the rickety stairs.

The blessing and the curse of living in a trailer park, I could walk right over to my best friend's house. The faded green siding was still a shit ton nicer than ours, and the flowers lining the sides said someone actually gave a damn. I had met Diego ages ago, when we were both barely big enough to walk up the steps on our own. Now, I just walked through his door without knocking.

His mom worked nights at the nursing home, which was where I assumed she was now. Diego was chilling in front of the TV, playing some video game. He glanced over his shoulder when he heard someone come in but went back to his game when he saw it was just me. "There's pizza in the fridge, and Mom left some arroz con pollo on the stove. Have at it."

He knew why I had come, fully aware of what was going on at home. I had stopped being embarrassed a long time ago. Grabbing a chipped plate out of the cabinet, I took a massive scoop of the rice dish and a soda out of the fridge before sitting by Diego. I watched him play for a minute, until he died and hollered obscenities in Spanish at the TV. Then he put his controller down and turned to me. "Mom sleeping?"

"Yuppers."

"What the fuck, man."

I shrugged. "She was breathing when I left." He shook his head, disappearing into the kitchen and reappearing a minute later with a plate and drink of his own. "Your mom is a damn good cook."

He nodded around a mouthful of food and we sat there in comfortable silence until we had both finished eating.

"So, what's up?"

I glanced at him. "What do you mean?"

"Come on, man. We've known each other since forever. I can tell something is on your mind."

I rolled my neck, relishing the pop, before picking up the remote and scrolling through the channels. "I dunno. It's almost time for prom."

"Thinking of asking her out?"

I gave him a droll look, not bothering to ask who he was referring to. "You gonna ask Maria?"

"God, I want to. But Holly scares me a little."

"Meh, she's harmless."

He blinked at me. "Harmless? Are we talking about the same girl?" I laughed and he smirked before getting serious again. "Ok, but seriously. What's on your mind?"

I settled on a channel playing *Hacksaw Ridge* before putting the remote down and saying, "I was just thinking. After prom, that's it. We're pretty much done. So, what's next?"

He scratched at the stubble on his cheek. "Shit, man. I ain't got a clue. I mean, Dalton is going to UGA. He's got that scholarship. Pretty sure Mac is staying here, helping his old man. Me? To be honest…"

"Maria."

"Yeah. It may be corny as fuck but that's all I want. She's all I want. What about you?"

I frowned at the TV and watched Desmond go back for yet another soldier, the wheels spinning in my head. "That's the thing, man. I haven't a damn clue." On the screen, Desmond lowered himself on that fraying rope. I nodded towards the screen. "Maybe that?"

Diego looked between me and the TV in confusion. "Acting?"

I rolled my eyes. "No, dumbass. Enlisting."

He raised his eyebrows, "Enlisting? In what? The military?"

"Dude, you are not that slow."

"Yeah, yeah, I know. It's just…I wasn't expecting that."

"Could be good for me."

"I guess?"

"Making a difference and shit."

"If you say so."

"Plus, I would get all the girls."

"Right, that's a great reason to risk your life."

I threw a throw pillow at him. "It's just a thought."

"What branch?"

I shrugged. "No idea."

He studied me. "Trying to imagine you with a buzz cut. Hate to tell you, but you would look weird as fuck." I flipped him off and he smirked but then he tilted his head to the side before squinting at me. "What about Holly?"

"What 'bout her?"

"I mean, I'm no Cupid. And we all know Dalton's the resident player. But even I can see there's something there."

I frowned at him, "There's nothing between me and Malibu."

"Uh-huh."

"She hates me."

"Riñen a menudo los amantes, por el gusto de hacer las paces."

"The hell does that mean?"

"Something Mom says. Google it." Silence filled the room yet again, before he stood and made his way to the kitchen. "Mom made tres leches. Want a piece?" I nodded and when he came back with two pieces, we finished the movie and watched the next one that came on.

Eventually, I went home. My Mom was still passed the fuck out on the couch. I frowned at her, watching the steady rise and fall of her chest. She had been like this since my dad left when I was like eleven. The bottle on the table caught the light from the TV. Half empty. Or half full. Depends how you look at it.

I stared at it longer than I meant to. Not seeing the amber glass but the future everyone swore I'd end up in. Especially the damn school counselor who looked at me like I was already a lost cause.

But, once upon a time, my Mom had been the kind to make cake. Like Diego's mom. The house had smelled like sugar and vanilla instead of sour wine and regret. Then she lost herself in the bottle. I swore I'd never be the guy staring at the bottom of one, looking for answers that weren't there. Sighing, I pulled a faded afghan over her shoulder before going to my room. Right before I fell asleep, I googled what Diego had said to me before shutting my phone off.

Malibu and I just weren't happening. That wasn't how these kinds of stories went.

Chapter Ten

⸸ **Holly** ⸸

I lounged in an old-fashioned, high-backed chair facing the dressing rooms. Scrolling through my phone, I waited for Maria to come out in yet another dress. The jingle of a curtain sliding back called my attention, and I looked up to see my bestie looking gloomy and sad in a behemoth of a silver gown.

I raised a single eyebrow. "You look like cotton candy. Boring, sad cotton candy."

"Holly!"

"What? I love you. But this is even worse than the last one. And don't try telling me you like it, 'cause you look like you left your Xanax at home."

She threw her hands up, visibly hiding tears. "I don't even know why I'm trying!"

"You're not trying!"

"What's that mean?" She crossed her arms, now pouting.

"Girl, you walked in here and basically grabbed the ugliest damn dresses off the rack like you had a point to prove. No offense." I directed that last bit to the sales girl, Arlene, who hovered nearby. She shrugged and smiled.

"That's easy for you to say! You looked amazing in everything you put on."

"Well, duh. That's 'cause I am trying. I've known what I wanted my prom dress to look like since I started high school. Sure, it's changed a bit but the fundamentals are still the same." I looked over at Arlene who nodded eagerly. Neither of them needed to know that I really couldn't give a rat's ass about prom. What was the point? I had my fill of dressing up and looking pretty for other people long ago. But I'd be damned if I was going to ruin Maria's time.

"It's not that easy."

Ha, you're telling me. "Why not?"

Maria huffed, stomping her foot and then gestured to her belly. While it was currently hidden under a mountain of tulle, she was indeed sporting a prominent baby bump. She was now almost six months pregnant. "Come on, Holly. You've got a body most girls would kill for. I have a bit of a hiccup in my grand, senior year plan."

Part of me shrank at the mention of my body, of the insinuation that I would be found desirable. Never fucking again. I forced down the revulsion and stood, tossing my phone on the chair. "Is that what she is?"

"Huh?"

"Is she an inconvenience? A hiccup?"

"Of course not!"

"Then stop treating her like one! Swing that belly! Don't be shy! I mean, the whole fucking town already knows you're pregnant. Not like it's a big secret."

Maria started chewing on her bottom lip and rubbing small circles on her belly. I glanced over at Arlene who stepped forward and said, "If you will allow me, let's try this. What was your dream dress? What did it look like?"

Maria glanced at me, then back at Arlene who waited patiently before sighing. "Sweetheart neckline, trumpet silhouette. Lots of sequins." Arlene smiled before turning to dart off.

"And purple if you've got it!" I hollered at her retreating figure. I turned back to Maria, who shook her head at me, and I winked at her before ushering her back into the dressing room. "Go ahead and get the Stay Puft Marshmallow Man off so we can give him a proper burial. With fire."

Arlene came back a few minutes later, pulling a rack with four dresses on it. "Now, I have a few dresses here. You can try them all on, of course. But I think I have the perfect one, if you want to start with that?"

Maria poked her head out from behind the curtain and reached her hand out, "Sure, why not." Arlene handed her a black garment bag before standing back by me. A couple seconds later, Maria called for help and Arlene ducked inside to get her zipped up. Then, much to my surprise, the sound of Maria crying filled the room. And my girl waddled out looking like a radiant sunset. Blushing pink melting into a royal, rich plum that flowed around her feet. The multitude of sequins caught the light and I could see that Arlene had gone to town with her pins and things, making it fit just right.

"Oh, Maria. You're gonna break hearts. I almost feel bad for Diego. He may not survive the night."

"He hasn't even asked me yet."

"He will."

She ran her hands down the sides of the dress, over her now very visible bump. "What do you think?"

"What do *you* think?"

Her smile was soft, hesitant but hopeful. "I love it so much."

Arlene clapped her hands. "It'll take alterations, of course. But that is no problem! We can get it back to you in time for your big night!"

Maria made her way over to me and reached for my hand. "Holly, *mi hermana*, are you sure? This dress..."

I waved her off. "I am positive. And so is Dad. Whatever we want, he said. Right? And, if this is what you want, it's what you'll get."

She gave me a watery smile before wrapping her arms around me. "I love you."

Here, in this brightly lit store, a little piece of my heart felt like it had slipped back into place. The cracks still visible, sure. But I felt a bit more whole. Being there for Maria, in the way I wish someone had been there for me...it was healing in ways I couldn't have even begun to fathom. Squeezing her gently I whispered, "I love you too."

After a minute, I stepped back and said, "Go ahead and get that off so we can go eat. I am starving." While Arlene helped Maria out of the dress, and marked where tailoring would be needed, I made my way up to the register. My dress hung behind the counter, needing a bit taken off the hem and a couple nips and tucks. It was a stunner. Black lace overlay clinging to satin gold like sin and silk. The lace was an intricate pattern and the neckline plunged far enough that I was probably going to have my mother gasping dramatically. But my favorite part was the sheer gold cape that hung off either shoulder, trailing behind me like smoke whenever I moved. If I had to wear a damn dress again, it was going to be one that would've made the old bags at the pageants clutch their pearls.

By the time Maria had made it up to the front, I had already paid and was waiting for her by the door. Arlene gave us details on how long the tailoring would take, and an estimate on when it would be done but promised to call if they were finished sooner. Maria looped her arm through mine as we made our way out into the weak, spring sunshine. Winter had finally loosened its grip and warmth was desperately trying to creep its way into the soil and air around us. She pulled out her phone as we walked along the row of shops, on the hunt for something to eat. I was down for pretty much anything, content to just follow the pregnant lady's nose. Which led us both to our favorite spot.

"I swear, if Momma Laverne has her lemon pie today, I might cry," Maria groaned, sniffing dramatically.

I laughed. "You've cried like six times already."

"Pregnancy. I contain multitudes."

The bell above Momma Laverne's door jingled as I pulled it open, warmth and the smell of grease and sugar wrapping around us like a hug.

Let me just tell Diego where we are."

I raised an eyebrow and she blushed furiously, mumbling something about seeing if he wanted to join us. "He needs to hurry the heck up," I teased.

"What do you mean?"

"Asking you to prom!"

Her eyes brightened when I held the door open for her, and she sniffed the air like a hound dog. "I'm not worried about it. What about you and Jackson?"

I tripped over the entry rug. "What about it?"

I almost said us. There is no us. There could never be an us. Sure, the guy was handsome. I could admire those gray eyes. That jawline. Wonder what his hair would feel like if I ran my hands threw it. Dreaming was harmless. But a relationship? With Jackson Morgan? So far from harmless it was in a different fucking galaxy. I focused again on Maria who was oblivious to my inner monologue.

"I mean, in between ripping each other's heads off, you guys have been making moon eyes at each other the last few weeks."

Stepping up to the counter, I opted to order for us instead of answering, but found Maria watching me expectantly. Before I could speak, a warm, familiar voice cut in.

"Well hey now," Momma Laverne called from behind the register, sliding her glasses down her nose to get a better look at us. "How's my girls doin' today?"

Maria's whole face lit up. "Hi, Mama Laverne."

I leaned against the counter. "We're starving."

She clicked her tongue. "Mm-hmm. Starving, huh? Or just dramatic?"

"Both," I said.

She laughed, deep and rich, like Sunday morning gospel. "What we celebrating? Y'all look like you done spent somebody's money."

Maria's hand drifted instinctively to her belly. "We found our prom dresses."

"Well now," she said, eyes softening as she looked Maria up and down like she could see the gown through denim and cotton. "Ain't nothing wrong with a girl feeling beautiful. Baby or no baby." Her gaze slid to me. "And you? You finally pick something that don't look like you fixing to start a revolution?"

I raised an eyebrow. "No promises."

She smirked. "That's what I was afraid of."

I rattled off our order and she scribbled it down. Grabbing our drinks and a little #8 sign, we made our way to the table and I said, "I dunno, I just..." I looked at my friend, her open and kind eyes. I knew she wouldn't judge me but still I hesitated, "Big truth?" It was something we had gotten into the habit of asking before laying down something ugly, like our way of saying "brace for impact".

She nodded. "Hit me."

"I want to feel normal. Act normal. I see the way you and Diego are, and a part of me wants that. But there's also a part of me that remembers what it feels like to be touched without my permission. My brain hasn't quite gotten the memo that it's safe. And anytime a guy looks at me or brushes up against me, I just can't breathe. Everything in me yanks on the emergency brake. Being used like that...it made everything real, feel unsafe."

Maria's lower lip wobbled. "It'll get better."

I offered her a thin smile. "I sure hope so." I wasn't really quite ready to believe that.

A waitress walked over with our food and about two seconds later, Diego and Jackson walked over. Maria wiped at her eyes, banishing any tears that might have been there and gave Diego a huge smile. His neck turned crimson as he pulled up a chair beside her. He stole a fry, then whispered something in her ear that had her blushing too.

Jackson wouldn't meet either of our eyes as he sat at the end of the table. I glanced between him and my chicken wrap. Had he heard any of that? God, I hope not. Finally, he looked up and his eyes met mine. A shudder ran through me at the steely gaze. The rage in his gray eyes. What the fuck? I frowned at him but he just shook his head and suddenly pushed back from the table and made his way over to the counter. I watched him go but my attention was pulled from him by a hand clasping on my shoulder and I jerked from the sudden grip, frowning at the intrusion.

"Well if it isn't Mamacita and Malibu, the prettiest and deadliest duo this side of the Mason-Dixon." Dalton's smile was broad and unwavering, even under the weight of the three frowns that were now aimed in his direction.

"Dude, shut up before you get stabbed with a fork." Mac rolled his eyes at his brother's antics before heading to join Jackson at the counter. I hadn't hung out with Mac too much. He had already graduated by the time I got to Redwood, but the times I had met him, I had been struck by just how similar he and his father were.

Unfazed, Dalton pulled up a chair beside me and asked, "So, how was shopping? Find what you wanted?"

Maria nodded eagerly, "Oh yeah, it only took me ten years but we found the perfect dresses."

"Whatever you wear will be perfect." Diego winked at Maria. She blushed again and Dalton feigned gagging while I hid a smile behind my drink. Jackson and Mac rejoined us a minute later with little numbers of their own.

The table dissolved into easy banter. When Momma Laverne came over with a basket of fries and an extra side of ranch no one had ordered, Dalton fixed her with a charming grin and I swear she rolled her eyes so hard they almost clattered on the tile.

"Boy, if you grin at me like that again, I'm telling your mama," she said, setting the basket down with a thump.

Dalton pressed a hand to his chest. "Momma Laverne, I would never."

"Mm-hmm. You're a damn playah." She turned to Mac. "And you. Quit letting him talk before he thinks. You the older one."

Mac smirked. "Yes, ma'am."

She shifted her gaze to Jackson, who was still pretending I didn't exist. Her eyes narrowed just slightly. "And you," she said, tapping the table near him. "If you keep scowling like that, you gonna scare my paying customers."

Jackson blinked. "Sorry, ma'am."

"Don't apologize. Fix it."

Dalton snorted. Diego excused himself, and Mama Laverne's eyes tracked him like she already knew something was about to go down.

She leaned in just slightly toward Maria. "You eating enough, baby?"

Maria nodded. "Yes, ma'am."

"Good. That little one need strength. And don't you let none of these knuckleheads stress you out." Her voice softened on that last part, protective without making a show of it.

She straightened, hands on hips, surveying the table like a general reviewing troops.

"Y'all act right. I ain't breaking up no wrestling match in my dining room again."

"That was one time," Dalton muttered.

"Three," she corrected.

Then she walked off, but not before giving me a look. Not questioning. Not prying. Just… knowing. Mac threw a fry at his brother, who caught it and promptly ate it. Diego rejoined, sliding a cupcake towards Maria who was teasing Mac and trying to drag Jackson into the conversation. She hadn't yet noticed the cupcake, which had a flower on top and tiny square piece of paper.

I gently kicked her under the table and her eyes swung to mine, brow furrowed. I looked pointedly at the table, where the cupcake sat, and she looked down. Diego was trying to desperately appear casual, arms crossed on the table, but he was fidgeting like mad. Mac elbowed his brother, who finally shut up and Jackson picked now as the perfect time to stare at me. I ignored him, of course. I focused all my attention on Maria who was staring at the cupcake like it might bite her and blinking furiously. She glanced at me again and I gave her a reassuring smile.

With a trembling hand, she reached for the note and just barely loud enough for the rest of us to here read it aloud: "Please let me take my two favorite girls to the dance." She was crying in earnest now, which appeared to freak Diego out.

"Maria, honey, I think he was hoping for a yes or no…"

"Ye-eee-ss," it was a broken reply, but a reply none the less. She turned and threw herself into Diego who was more than happy to wrap his arms around her.

I squirmed in my seat, not really loving the feel of being in a rom-com. I gave in, glancing over at Jackson, who had stopped staring at me at some point and was fiddling with his phone. Dalton whooped, and Mac clapped his friend on the back. A few patrons smiled and shook their heads. My phone buzzed.

Jackson: "We need to talk."

I glanced up at him and found him frowning at me.

Me: No.

His frown morphed into a glare and, maintaining eye contact, I put my phone back down on the table and ignored it when it buzzed again. And again. And again. Until I turned it off. He looked like he was going to implode. I abhorred pity and had vowed long ago to never attend another party.

Brushing it off, I asked Maria and Diego, "So, is it official? You two are a thing now?" Their answering smiles told me all I needed to know. I nodded, reaching for a fry. I looked Diego in the eye and smiled. "You know what'll happen to you if you hurt her, right?" I bit the fry in half, aggressively. Suggestively. The look on his face told me he got the hint. And that I wasn't kidding.

Dalton began laughing. "Shit, it's about time. You've been ogling her since fucking sophomore year."

Diego glared at him and Maria looked between the two, "Sophomore year? I didn't move here until sophomore year."

Jackson was intent on boring holes into my soul, the rest of the table apparently oblivious as Mac said, "Yeah, basically the second he saw you."

"It was kinda sad, like a puppy."

"And then he found out you weren't single."

"And he was a very sad, kicked puppy. Ain't that right Jackson?"

Jackson looked over at Dalton when his name was said. "Yeah."

I honestly wasn't sure he knew what he was agreeing to—a sentiment the rest of the table apparently shared as Mac glanced between Jackson and I. His blue eyes were astute, narrowed, as he got a read on the tension between the two of us. Maria nudged me under the table, and I raised an eyebrow at her. She was still in Diego's arms but mouthed to me, "You good?"

I nodded before refocusing on my plate. I didn't need a white knight. I sure as hell didn't want one. If Jackson had heard something, he just needed to drop it. And that was that.

Maria hadn't been in a hurry to leave and, by the time I had managed to wrest her from Diego's hold, it was getting late. We shouted goodbyes to Mama as we hustled out the door. For once, I was glad to be home. Away from the weight of sharp as steel, gray eyes. My mom greeted us as we made our way through the main living room. Some medical drama was playing on the TV which meant my dad must be on call. Mom didn't dare watch it with him around lest he yell at the TV any time they got something wrong. She smiled at us, pausing a dramatic scene. "Hey girls! Have fun?"

Maria smiled back at her, a decided glow on her tawny skin. "Yes! We found the most beautiful dresses. And guess what?"

Mom cocked her head, raising a carefully shaped eyebrow at her.

"Diego asked me to prom!"

Mom squealed, getting up from the couch and wrapping Maria in a hug. Over the past few weeks, she had warmed up to my friend and had even begun treating Maria the way she deserved. Like family. "Oh my goodness, sweetheart! That is just wonderful. The two of you will make such a lovely pair. I bet he cleans up well." She winked at Maria, who giggled, before turning her attention to me. "What about you?"

"What about me?"

"Do you have a date?"

I scoffed. "In the words of the great Daya, this queen don't need a king." For a split second, I pictured Jackson in a tuxedo. He sure as hell would clean up nice too. Then I all but beat that picture out of my mind. *No, ma'am. No way, no how.*

Mom frowned at me and then sighed. The look of disappointment in her eyes pissed me off. *Sorry, Mommy Dearest. The perfect daughter you have is gone. Get over it.* For a second, I was sure she would say something. But, like always, she simply changed the conversation to a less touchy topic. "Maria, dear. You got mail today. I put it on your bed."

I all but dragged Maria up the stairs, eager to get away from my mother and into the quiet of my bedroom. Maria headed to her room and I continued down the hall towards my sanctuary. I froze when Maria's small scream shattered the air, spinning on my heels and running towards her.

She stood at the foot of the bed, a box of preserved roses scattered around her feet. In her trembling hand, she held a small note and her tear-filled eyes met mine as I made my way towards her. I took the note when she held it up to me and ground my teeth together so hard, I was surprised none of them broke.

Little dove, little dove. What am I to do with you? Are you really going to keep a baby from her father? I can't let that slide. See you soon.

I tossed it to the floor with the roses and pulled Maria into my side. She was shaking. Terrified. I wasn't going to lie—it scared me a little too. I wasn't surprised he knew where she was. But to reach out like this? That mother-fucker. I held her tighter as her cries quieted.

"It's going to be ok, Maria. I promise. I got you."

Once I had gotten her calmed down, I cleaned up the roses and the note and took it all to the nearest fireplace. Setting that shit on fire made me feel marginally better. Seeing Maria like this…it sucked. For so many reasons. I wanted to fix it, make it all better. I was scared and angry for my friend. But, even if I would never admit it out loud, watching her go through this brought up painful memories. Memories I had worked hard to bury deep inside. I checked on her one last time and was surprised to find her asleep in bed. It was a fitful rest, I'm sure. But a deep one brought on by the stress of pregnancy and shitty men. Quietly, I closed the door to my room. My mom hadn't even come upstairs, apparently not even the least bit alarmed by the commotion.

I laid in bed and, for a several minutes, just stared at my phone.

To do it, or not to do it?

Send the text?

Order some DoorDash, take a nap, and forget about it all?

Fuck it. I was sending the text.

Me: "Hey."

He replied immediately.

Jackson: "Oh, so now you want to talk?"

I itched to say something smart.

Me: "Maria's ex is still around. He left her a note here. Scared the shit of her."

The three dots letting me know he was typing appeared and disappeared. After a couple minutes, his reply finally came through.

Jackson: "You guys ok?"

Me: "We're fine. Just thought Diego would want to know. I don't have his number."

Jackson: "Yeah, he's weird about giving it out."

Me: "Oh."

Yes, Holly. Very eloquent of you.

Jackson: "About what I heard..."

Me: "Don't worry about it."

Jackson: "Are you kidding?'

Me: "I'm serious, Jackson. Leave it."

Jackson: "Fuck that, Malibu. Talk to me."

Me: "Pass."

Jackson: "Holly, let me help. I'm going insane here."

Me: "I can't Jackson. Ok? If you heard me, then you know. I just can't. Please."

Jackson: "I know what it's like. Not trusting people. Not being able to open up. But even someone like you can't do it alone."

Me: "Someone like me?"

Jackson: "You've got a tongue like a knife. But I've met my share of monsters. You aren't one. And you didn't deserve that, Malibu. I want... idk. I want to make it better. Somehow."

I wanted so badly to reply to him, but a little piece of my heart warned me it would end badly. Even if the rest of my heart was screaming to let him in. I shut my phone off and put it in the drawer of my nightstand. Out of sight, out of mind. For now. I was better off alone. Whether he liked it or not, alone was safe. Alone was easy. So alone I would stay.

✒ Jackson ✒

I stared at her name on my screen for a long time, my fingers curling into a fist. *Someone hurt her.* That's why she'd moved? Someone had taken this…this gorgeous firestorm of a girl, and had turned her cold. Fury burned through every vein and I wanted to do something. I couldn't sit still. But then I froze as the thought occurred to me.

If it was public record, that wasn't wrong…right? Just information anyone could see. My jaw ached from clenching as I pulled up my search engine and typed in her name. It didn't take long. Articles. So many goddamn articles. My throat closed as I scrolled, bile rising higher with every headline. My Malibu wasn't the only one. That bastard had hurt *others.* And they'd let him walk.

I saw his name over and over again. *Scott Lauren.*

My vision tunneled, rage settling into something cold and certain.

Count your days, I thought, memorizing every detail of his face on the screen. *Because if the law won't finish it, I damn sure will. One day.*

Chapter Eleven

⊹ **Holly** ⊹

"You really need to think of your future, dear."

I blinked at the guidance counselor, biting my tongue instead of telling her any dreams of the future I'd once had had vanished the second my childhood burned down around me. When you get wrenched from the innocence of being young and dumb, when the ugliness of life throws curveballs you never saw coming…You don't think about *after*. You just think about the *now*. How to survive. How to stop the bleeding. But she was staring at me expectantly still so I took the packet she held out to me. I thumbed through it. My transcripts, a How-To guide on writing a good admission essay, the best schools for the most popular majors.

"You are very bright, Ms. McCarthy. I understand you've been through quite a lot." She hesitated and then reached over and grabbed my hand that was resting on her desk. "Don't let the bad guys win." I smiled thinly, thanking her for her time and all but running from the office.

Maria waited for me outside, having just completed her own guidance nightmare. She had decided after the 3D ultrasound to put a hold on college until she could get herself on her feet. Find a good place, a steady job, and be the best mom she could be. My mom was flabbergasted, insisting Maria needed to go to college, but I understood where she was coming from. And I wasn't going to push my bestie to do something she didn't want. It's not like college was going anywhere. Right this second, or ten years from now. If she wanted to get a degree, great. If not, that was fine too. And I figured the same went for me. I had no idea what I wanted to do. Once upon a time, I had dreamed of coaching other girls to dominate the stage like I once had. But the thought nearly had me vomiting now.

"Hey, have fun?"

I waved my packet at Maria, "Loads. Wanna skip last period and go grab some food?"

"Oh heck yes. Momma Laverne's?"

"I could go for that."

Last period was basically just a filler course—something to keep seniors occupied until prom, which was this weekend. After that, graduation. And then? Sky's the limit. Or so the giant poster outside the counselor's office said. Maria linked her arm through mine, leaning on me heavily. She was so pregnant I was genuinely concerned that if I poked her belly too hard, a baby would fall out. We made our way outside and I helped her slide into Sally. I tossed the useless "Preparing For Your Future" file in the back seat and headed towards our favorite spot.

Momma Laverne greeted us warmly, yelling from the kitchen in that boisterous way I had come to learn was uniquely her's. Maria shoved herself into a booth, the only one with spacing big enough for her now. I slid across from her right as Momma came up to us with two waters.

"How are my favorite girls?"

"Hungry," I gave her a half smile and she winked at me.

Maria rubbed her belly and said, "In between getting the shit kicked out of me, my stomach is rumbling. I could eat a horse."

Momma Laverne leaned down, placing a gentle hand on Maria's belly. She didn't ask permission; she didn't need to. She might as well be blood, as much time as we've spent in this diner. "There's my favorite little nugget. You be nice to your momma now, you hear?" She straightened and said, "The usual I assume?" Maria and I didn't even need menus. We almost always got the same thing. Pork steak for her, fried chicken for me. Yes freaking please! I watched Momma bustle away, ample bosom bumping into tables as she went. Like the sweetest bull in the China shop.

I glanced over at Maria and found her rubbing her belly and chewing on her lip—a habit when she was nervous or worried about something. "What's on your mind?"

She shrugged. "The future. Worrying like I always do."

"About what?"

"I dunno…will I be a good mom? Is choosing to not go to college a bad decision? How long will I have put up with her dang sperm donor?"

I grabbed a warm biscuit from the plate Momma had dropped off and drizzled honey on it before replying, "Ok, one. Yes. Absolutely yes. You will be a wonderful mom. Second, I can't answer that one. Tragically, I do not have the powers to see into the future. But if it's what you feel is best, and you're just worrying about what everyone else will think? Fuck 'em. And lastly, my offer to kill him still stands. Diego would probably help. They would never find the body."

She cracked a smile. "Murder is illegal, Holly."

I licked honey from my fingers. "Only if you get caught."

She laughed. "I'm pretty sure that's not how it works."

I smiled back at her. She might be my only friend in the world. But she was a good one. And I would be damned if I was going to let anyone dim that glow. I envied her a little, if I was being honest. After all she had been through, she still had a light. A kindness in her eyes. She was beautiful inside and out. Maybe one day she would rub off on me. I watched as she attacked the tray of biscuits in a way benefiting a pregnant queen. Shortly after, Momma interrupted my racing thoughts with our food.

In between bites of collards, Maria peppered me with questions.

"You're not going to college?"

"Negative, ghostrider."

"But you're so smart!"

I would shrug, and she would change subject at the speed of light.

"Are you sure you don't want a bite?"

"Pass."

"Are you excited for prom?"

"Eh."

"And it doesn't bother you that Diego and I are going together?"

"Why would it?"

Every now and then, Momma would appear, refilling our drinks and showering us with tidbits of wisdom. Eventually, after an obnoxiously large piece of pie, Maria and I sat back in our seats. As happy and fat as two ticks on a one-eyed dog, as Momma would say. When I realized Maria was slowly falling asleep in the booth, I paid our ticket and helped her up. I was fixing to follow her out the door when Momma stopped me.

"Holly, honey, can I talk to you?

"Uhm…"

Maria glanced between her and I, "Go ahead, I'll just wait in the car."

I tossed her the keys and turned to Momma Laverne, "What's up?"

"I just want to say you are a damn good girl, taking care of your friend like that."

"Oh, well…"

She raised a hand, "No, don't downplay what you do, sweetie. I just wanted you to hear it from someone. You are a good kid. You didn't deserve what happened to you, and I'm sorry it did. If I ever get my hands on that sombitch, I'm feeding him a pie *Help* style. That all being said, I am real glad you're here. And whatever you decide to do with your future, I know it'll be amazing."

A feeling I had almost forgotten crept its way into my chest. A feeling that came from being loved and accepted. Something my own mother had made me feel when I was young. Before it all. But now, standing in this dank diner with a woman who had become family, I felt a little piece of my heart slip back into place. Fighting to keep the tears back, I did my best to wrap my arms around her. She engulfed me in a hug and squeezed gently. Sniffling, I stepped back. "Thanks Momma. I better go. Maria's waiting." She smiled softly at me and shooed me out the door.

I was still floating on something awful close to Cloud Nine when I made my way around the corner and into the parking lot. Much to my surprise, Maria wasn't in the car. She was just standing there, clutching a note in shaking hands. Fucking deja vu. I hurried to her, and she handed it to me without a word.

Little dove, can't wait to see how pretty you look in your dress. See you soon.

I glared at it, before pulling my phone out and taking a picture. Crumpling it, I threw it to the ground as I sent the picture to Diego. After last time, I had gotten Diego's number the very next day. The slightest hint that Maria might be in danger and I was pretty sure he would've sold me his bike. This time, his response was instant.

Diego: "She ok?"

Me: "She will be, I'm taking her home now. Leaving Laverne's."

Diego: "Let me know when y'all get home."

I ushered Maria into the passenger seat, looking around us and second-guessing every shadow. It was a feeling I did not miss.

When we got home, my mom and dad could immediately tell something was off. Maria bolted upstairs, leaving me to explain what had happened. I did so, briefly. My mom's whole face pinched like she had swallowed a lemon, the way it did when she was really mad but trying to maintain face. Eyes narrowed, lips nothing more than thin lines. My dad's face grew stormy, and he marched out of the room muttering something about calling August and the sheriff. Mom looked like she wanted to ask me something but I hurried off before she could start a conversation I wasn't ready to have.

Upstairs, I knocked on Maria's closed door and told her that Dad was calling Mr. Mills. I also reminded her to check in with Diego, who was probably champing at the bit to run Jesse over with his bike. When she didn't respond, I went to my room and took a shower—letting the hot water wash away the sins of the past and the shadows that plagued me. Dad came in when I was sitting at my vanity, braiding my wet hair.

"You ok, bug?"

I nodded, looking at him in the mirror's reflection. "Yeah, just wish he would leave us alone."

"August and I are taking care of it. You know your mom and I won't let anything happen to our girls."

I sighed, folding my hands in my lap. Our girls. I was elated that they considered Maria one of their own. I already loved her like a sister. But the truth is…they already *had* let something happen to their first girl. Something really fucking awful. Something that made my skin crawl every time a guy brushed up against me. Something that made me shrink back from the way Jackson would sometimes look at me. Memories that made me hate who I had been. And who I was. Dreading who I would become. "I am just so tired of seeing the bad guys win, Daddy."

The admission surprised him as much as it did me. Even more surprising were the tears in his eyes when he stepped closer, bending down and hugging me from behind. I stiffened but slowly let myself lean into his touch. The same touch that had once made me feel safe and secure and loved. God, part of me wanted that so bad. Maybe one day. But right now? I was still a hot mess. In this moment though, I could just be a girl getting a hug from her dad and that would have to be enough.

That night, as I was lying in bed, I woke up to my door creaking open. In the light spilling from the hall into my dark room, I could see Maria's silhouette and scooted over as she crawled into bed next to me without a word. She must have been having nightmares again. I didn't mind the company. I even welcomed it. Cause those nightmares that came and went for her? They were every damn night for me. Her breathing eventually evened out and I rolled over, letting sleep come over me. It had been a long damn day. I made a mental note to figure out what pie Momma had referred to. Something about help? I snuggled deeper under my covers and filed it away for another day.

The next couple of days were spent convincing Maria to still go to prom. She was scared, I could see that, but I didn't want that douche ruining her night and told her as much. I even brought Diego over and eavesdropped as he told her over and over again that he would never let someone hurt her. My mom even gave it her best shot, telling Maria all about the makeup artist she had hired, and fawning over the dresses when they were delivered to the house. True to form, she adored Maria's dress. Mine? Well, it left her speechless. Pretty sure she almost fainted.

Which just made me love it all the more. At first, prom was just something I was doing for Maria but as it got closer, I found myself growing excited.

The morning of, I still wasn't sure I had convinced Maria to go. But as I was going through my mother's jewelry case, Maria barged in. Panting. Out of breath like she had run a mile.

"Ok, here's the deal."

I raised an eyebrow at her, putting Mom's pearl and diamond earrings back into the case. Too flashy.

"I will try on the dress. With the alterations. If it fits, I go. If it doesn't fit, I stay. It's like a coin toss."

"…that dress was custom tailored for you, by some of the best seamstresses in Georgia. If my mother is to be believed."

"Exactly. So if it doesn't fit, it's a sign."

"Uh-huh." She frowned at me, so I picked up a necklace and held it out to her. I knew my jewels and this was a gorgeous opal and pink tourmaline pendant that my dad had gifted Mom for one of their anniversaries. "This would go so pretty with your dress."

She walked over and took it from me. "It's beautiful. But why do I get the feeling I could buy a house with this?"

"Try a small apartment," I quipped.

She shook her head at me, "I dunno, Holly. Y'all already paid for my dress. My shoes. And the way your mom talks RuPaul himself is coming to do our makeup."

"Who the hell is RuPaul?"

She blinked at me. "Wow. That's just sad." She edged closer to me, eyeing the jewelry box. Pointing at a black diamond choker that I had literally never seen my mother wear she said, "That would look great on you."

"My poor mom is going to have a heart attack."

"Why? You look amazing in your dress!"

I shrugged, taking the choker and making sure she still had the opal pendant. "I dunno. I guess Mom is just used to me being in pageant type dresses. Which are a bit more like yours. My dress is just a bit too—" I hesitated, trying to find the right word.

"Edgy?"

I nodded. "Yeah."

We headed downstairs and Maria reached over, squeezing my hand. "I'm not a mom yet but just thinking about my little girl growing up, graduating high school, getting a date to prom. It doesn't seem real to me. Like I can't even imagine. So…I guess for your mom, it's probably the same. She still sees you as the little girl you used to be."

I stopped at the bottom of the stairs, eyeing my mom who was chatting animatedly with my dad. She hadn't noticed us yet, and his back was to us. I squeezed Maria's hand back. "I'm not that little girl. And I don't ever want to be. I used to blame her. I kinda still do, but I don't hate her."

"Does she know that?"

I opened my mouth but stopped. I didn't have an answer to that, to be honest. Mom finally turned to us, squealing. "Ok, girls. It's show time!"

I forced back a cringe. She used to say that same thing every time, right before I took the stage. But if Maria could hold her head high despite everything she was going through, so could I. So, I smiled at Mom, even though the movement felt foreign. Mom faltered, before hesitatingly smiling back at me. "Um, so…the makeup artist will be here in a few hours. I figure we eat. Your dad and I need to refine our threats to the boys. You girls can shower. I'll do your hair. And by then it'll be makeup time!"

Maria surprised us all by bouncing on her toes. Well, it was more like a wobble. But it was still cute, watching her teeter around in excitement. We spent the morning exactly as Mom suggested. Maria ate her weight in waffles and took a shower so long I was quite surprised it didn't use up all our water. She came out smelling like cherries and sandalwood. It was a scent uniquely hers. A scent that enveloped me as she stomped her way into my room and brandished her razor at me. I eyed it with suspicion. "What?"

"I can't reach. Like anything. Not my legs. Not my armpits. Not that annoying tiny sprig of hair on my big toe. I barely managed to shave off the obscene line of hair that has appeared without invitation on my belly."

"Please tell me you're not asking me what I think you're asking."

She stomped her foot. "Please, Holly!"

I waved my hands at her toweled form, "He won't even *see* your legs in that dress!"

"Holly!"

"Oh for Christ's sake. Can't you ask Mom?"

"Ohmigawd I cannot ask your mom to shave my legs!"

"Why the hell not? And why am I the first pick?"

Maria pointed her razor at my door, shaking it like a baton. "Well, who else do I have? The cat?"

I dragged a hand across my face. "Are you like 100% sure that Diego isn't like…into that? Maybe he likes a little extra hair!"

She made a general face of disgust and brandished the razor at me again. When I fixed her with a look, she pouted, brown eyes begging me to give in. In the depths of them, I could see a glimmer of her pain. The need for this night to be perfect if nothing else was.

Which was how I found myself shaving my best friend's legs as she laid on my bathroom floor. 'Cause she couldn't stand for long and I didn't trust myself to work on a vertical canvas that wasn't me. When I was done, she preened in the mirror before flouncing out of my room with an ear-to-ear grin. The things you do for the people you love. I hopped in the shower and hurried over to my mom's room after blow-drying my hair. I had highlights put in a couple days ago, and the mixture of honey blonde and caramel was eye-catching. Throwing on my silk robe, I made my way towards Mom's room where she was already working on Maria's hair.

I perched on a nearby settee, watching the two of them. They were chatting animatedly, completely enthralled with just how many curls they could pile on Maria's head. If I hadn't been watching so closely, I would've missed it. For a second, one split second, Maria stopped smiling. Her eyes dimmed. Her brow furrowed. Then my mom said something and immediately, her jovial attitude was back in place. I frowned at her, but she didn't see. A little piece of my heart broke as I recognized what she was doing. Something I had done a million times. Putting on a mask, wearing a front so others didn't see that you were crying inside.

Maria's phone buzzed, and her hand trembled just so slightly as she slid it under her leg without checking it. This night was supposed to be about glitter and gowns. But I couldn't shake the feeling that something ugly was coming for us.

CHAPTER 11 * HOLLY

Mom and Dad had wanted to hire a limo, but I knew the threats Jesse had made were not to be taken lightly. I insisted that we would be safer if we had a getaway car in case he did show up. Instead of waiting for a driver, we could just dip if things got dicey. Mom was still hesitant, but I could see that Dad understood. When Maria chimed in, agreeing with me, that was that. It was for Maria that I agreed to let Diego drive. I made several dark promises about what would happen to him if he was not gentle with Sally, but I knew it would make Maria happy, riding up front with her date by her side.

'Which is how I found myself crammed into the backseat with Jackson next to me. They had ridden their bikes to my place and, when Maria and I had walked out, I deliberately focused on watching Diego light up and twirling her around. Even then, I didn't miss the way Jackson looked at me. The way his eyes looked me up and down, his gaze feeling like a caress that made me shudder. But not my usual shudder. Oh, no. This was my traitorous body being surprisingly appreciative of the way this ridiculously good-looking eighteen-year-old biker was staring at me like I was the last drop of clean water on a polluted Earth.

I thought he would say something, but he didn't. He was leaning up against Sally, and I walked over, leaving Maria and Diego to whisper to each other like conspirators. Maybe I should've said something at least moderately friendly, but the heat in his gaze as he watched me left me feeling unsteady. So instead, I said, "Let's maybe not lean up against my car and scratch the paint?"

His eyes morphed from a molten gray to an icy steel. "You sit on the hood of your car all the damn time."

"So? That's different."

He shook his head, jaw tense, and looked away from me, "Yeah, ok, Malibu. Whatever you say."

I opened my mouth to snark back but was distracted by Maria coming up behind me. She hugged me as best she could and said, "Y'all ready to get this show on the road? Or are you just gonna stay here and make moon eyes at each other?

I sputtered. Jackson rolled his eyes. Diego chuckled. I threw the door open and climbed in, shaking Jackson off when he reached for my elbow. My next step made me wish I'd taken the help—my heel caught, and I stumbled forward, arms flailing like a drunk chicken. Then heat. A big hand on my hip. Another at the small of my back. Steady. Firm. Unmistakably *him.* The contact froze me in place. The world went quiet. I could've sworn the whole damn car tilted with us. I turned, breath catching when his eyes met mine—dark, unreadable, *dangerous.* For a moment, neither of us moved. Not until his thumb brushed a sliver of exposed skin, feather-light. I shivered, tore myself away, and practically dove into the back seat.

Diego eased Sally out of the drive as Mom stood crying in the driveway, waving us goodbye, and Dad was taking a million pictures. I waved awkwardly to them and Maria blew kisses. She and Diego eased into a natural banter and I remained turned to the window, back to the man beside me. Neither one of us spoke a word until we got to the downtown hotel. When he climbed out first, he turned to help me out. Blatantly aware I was being a petulant child, I shooed his hands away and he threw his arms up, completely exasperated with me, then watched in cool amusement as I nearly fell on my face.

I made my way over to Maria who held her phone out to me. "Take a picture of me and Diego in front of Sally?"

I snapped the picture, but when I went to hand her phone back, she passed it to Diego and pulled me to her side. I stood a full head over her, but she tucked herself under my arm and said, "Us, next. You're not getting away that easy." I couldn't help but smile as Diego took several photos of the two of us. Maria, resplendent in her gradient gown. And me. I didn't look like a naive beauty queen anymore. Tonight, I was something new. Not the girl I used to be. Not the girl who got hurt. But something that bloomed from the ashes of both. Someone who was content to be her friend's backup dancer, instead of center stage. I was more than happy to trail behind her as she eagerly pulled Diego towards the conference center turned ballroom.

The room was beautifully decorated, I had to admit—even for a public school whose halls were clad in peeling, faded linoleum. A banner hung above the entrance, fairy lights draped along the top. I craned my neck to read it: *"A Night Between Worlds—Welcome All Fae."* Inside, more fairy lights cascaded from the ceiling, like iridescent droplets of rain. A refreshment table, styled to resemble clustered tree stumps, held bowls of punch, bottles of water, and glittering trays of snacks. Silk flowers littered the floor and the whole room was cast in a soft glow.

Music was already thrumming through the speakers that lined the room. Couples danced, and others mingled in corners. Maria pressed a kiss to my cheek and all but dragged Diego to the dance floor. I smiled softly, watching the way he was incredibly gentle with her. Ever mindful of her comfort, and the baby's. Out of the corner of my eye, I saw Jackson head over to where Rodney and Dalton were hanging with a few other football players. I grabbed a bottle of water and made myself comfortable on the green, velvet-clad chairs. Glaring at any would be dance partners who found the balls to come up to me until they slunk off with their tails between their legs.

After a few songs, Maria disentangled herself from Diego. He went towards his friends, and she headed towards me. She reached for me, pulling me to my feet, and said, "You can't think I'm going to just let you sit here all night? As beautiful as we both look, let's rock this dance floor."

I smiled, playfully bowing and gesturing towards the open space as the DJ put on some catchy pop tune. "You are damn right. Lead the way, Your Majesty!" She laughed, and I let her lead me into an empty spot on the crowded floor. We twirled around the dance floor, laughing so hard our sides hurt. It felt good—*free,* even—to just be girls for a night instead of broken things pretending to be fine.

Just as my feet began to ache something fierce, Maria stopped and pulled me close so she didn't have to shout over the music. Her face was pink, and there was a faint shine to her forehead. "I gotta go get some water before I pass out."

"Um, yeah, that would definitely not be a good idea. Diego would lose his shit. I'll meet you over there. I gotta pee!" She waddled off to the refreshment table, and I headed out the room. Bathrooms were just down the hall. I was touching up my makeup when a shrill scream split the air in two. My hair immediately stood up on end, and abandoning the small clutch I had brought with me, I ran as quickly as I could back to the ballroom. Having spent most of my life in heels of various sizes, I could still move fairly fast in the fuckers. As I got closer, I could make out the sounds of a fight. Pushing through the crowd, I dodged two guys who went down in a tangle of fists. I squinted in the dim light, realizing it was one of the football players and a guy I had never seen before.

Finally at the center of the mess, I looked around erratically for Maria, hoping I was wrong. But when I caught sight of her tear-streaked face, I knew I wasn't. We ran to each other, and I enveloped her in my arms. Fucking Jesse. And he had brought friends. I glanced one more time at the fight, realizing that not only had Diego stepped in, but so had Jackson, Rodney, Dalton, and half the football team. Jesse and his buddies were vastly outnumbered. The guys had it handled, so, keeping Maria tight against my side, I began to usher her out of the room. Diego had left the keys in the car, and I was beyond grateful that I had trusted my gut.

We had barely made it halfway towards the door, when Jesse blocked our path. I had never met him before, but I recognized him from pictures and there was no mistaking the way Maria cowered against me. I pulled her even closer before practically spitting my words at him. "Move. We're leaving."

His laugh was cold and cruel, and I recognized this as a different kind of evil I had never faced before. My heart thudded in my throat, fear clawing its way from where I kept it shoved deep down. He took a step closer, grabbing my arm so tight I knew it would leave a mark, and trying to wrench me away from Maria. "Little dove thinks she can keep my kid from me. *My* fucking kid."

I refused to let go, even as his grip on me became painful. And then suddenly, Jesse wasn't in front of me anymore. Jackson was. Jesse hit the floor, groaning, and Jackson stood over him with that lethal glare. I backed away as Jackson shielded us with his body and snarled, "Touch her again and I'll make sure you don't get back up." He glanced at me, and I just stared at him until he jerked his head towards the door.

It felt like it took years to get across that parking lot, but once I had Maria settled, I ran over to the driver's side and jumped in. Sally's tires shrieked a protest as I peeled out of the parking lot. Maria was still crying, and I kept one hand on the wheel as I used the other to reach for her. I pretended not to notice just how badly I was shaking. "It's ok, we are going to go home. Daddy will take care of it. Jesse won't dare come near the house. It's ok." I wasn't sure who I was trying to convince, me or her. I drove even faster, eager to be in the safety of home. Several police vehicles flew past us, sirens blaring. I noticed Maria flinch at the onslaught of sound and squeezed her hand again. I couldn't stop fucking shaking.

I pulled into the driveway and Maria remained frozen in the passenger seat even after I parked. As I helped her towards the house, I realized she was also shaking like a maraca. My mom called from the living room, "You girls are home super early!"

As she turned to face us, her face fell. She rushed towards us, and I was surprised when she got on Maria's other side, helping me support my friend as we all but carried her to the couch. "David! You better get down here!" My mom's shout was almost immediately followed by the thundering of footsteps. I was still standing, hovering over Maria who huddled on the couch, her pale complexion a violent contrast to the bright colors of her gown, like a cruel taunt.

I turned to my dad as he entered, and something in my face had him crossing the room in three quick strides to embrace me. I began to shake in earnest, the subtle tremors evolving into a full-blown earthquake as adrenaline ravaged my body. He held me tight, running soothing hands down my back, and said, "Tell me what happened."

Maria looked up at him and spoke for the first time since we left the dance, "Jesse. He showed up, like he said he would. Had a bunch of his friends with him." Her lower lip trembled and she buried her face in her hands as she sobbed, "He ruined everything." My mom sat on the couch beside her, pulling Maria into her arms.

"I never should've left you. I'm sorry. I'm so sorry. I wasn't thinking."

Maria looked at me, eyes red and makeup smeared. "It's not your fault. What were you supposed to do? Wear a diaper so you stayed glued by my side? If anyone should be apologizing, it should be me. I ruined the night for everyone."

"That's enough girls. No more apologies from either of you. The only fault lies with that son of a bitch."

I expected my mom to correct dad's language, but she simply frowned and said, "Your father is absolutely right. This is not on you. And that boy is going to be in a cell by night's end, you mark my words. I will drag him there myself." Her pretty face was flushed pink in anger and, distantly, I remembered that my mom had responded similarly when I had confessed what Scott Lauren had been doing. I had forgotten her anger, her fire, when she had decided to start a clean slate in Georgia. She had swept it all under the rug the second we started packing, deciding for us all that it was done and over. But she hadn't stopped to ask if the rest of us were ready to move on. As the shaking subsided, I saw my mother in a whole new light. It wasn't that she didn't care; it was that she just didn't know how to be real.

My dad left the room to make calls, and not even thirty minutes later a deputy and August Mills showed up in the living room. Maria and I gave our statements and then promptly ran upstairs to hide in our rooms. She kept trying to apologize to me, and I kept shutting her down. I wasn't mad. I didn't blame her. How could I? She was just someone who was trying to stay standing in the face of a hurricane. I knew how that felt. I helped her out of her dress, and she helped me out of mine. We both cried, lamenting the loss of what should've been a perfect night. At some point, it grew late and Maria eventually fell into a fitful sleep in her bed, so I snuck out quietly to mine.

I lay in bed staring at the ceiling, but sleep just wouldn't come. Not after all that shouting, not after Jesse's hand on me; not after Jackson stepping in like that. My arm still ached, and my brain wouldn't shut up. Every time I closed my eyes, I saw that room. Still shining like it hadn't caught onto the ruination of the evening. And the way Jackson had looked at me, like I mattered. I hated that it made my chest hurt in some confusing, impossible way. I tossed and turned, trying to decipher the millions of thoughts racing through my head. But nothing was working.

Before I could fully process what I was doing, I slid my feet into a pair of slippers and grabbed my keys from the dresser. As I headed downstairs towards the front door, I froze at my dad's voice.

"Just where do you think you are going, bug?"

I turned slowly to find my dad standing with his arms crossed and frowning at me, Mom at his elbow and watching me with a look I didn't quite understand. "I just…I dunno. I gotta make sure they're ok."

They. Who is they? There was only one person on my mind, no matter how hard I tried to shove him out.

My dad opened his mouth but before he could say something, my mom put a small hand on his forearm. "Let her go, David." I glanced between them, hesitating. But at a small nod from my dad, I slipped outside into the cool of the night. A few minutes later, I sat behind the wheel of Sally, idling in his front yard. I only knew where he lived cause I had dropped Maria off with Diego a few times. Now, I eyed the shoddy trailer and tried convincing myself this wasn't the dumbest thing I'd ever done. There was no going back without looking like a complete idiot.

I tapped an unsteady rhythm on the steering wheel. I didn't care if he was hurt. I didn't. Scout's honor and all that. I just…couldn't sleep. Couldn't stop picturing that fight, fists flying, Jackson taking a hit that knocked him flat, and getting right back up. I mean, he had helped me get Maria out of there. So it was only right I thanked him. A little voice in the back of my head whispered I could've just sent him a text and I promptly told that voice to shut the fuck up. I got out of the car, still considering bolting no matter how stupid it made me look.

The door swung open, and there he was—messy hair, bruised cheek, still breathing but looking like he'd been dragged through hell and back. I froze at the bottom of the stairs, looking up at him like a robber in the night getting caught red handed.

"Well," Jackson drawled, shutting the door and leaning against the rickety railing, "if it isn't Malibu. What are you doing here?"

I crossed my arms, a shield against the way my chest twisted at the sight of him. "Couldn't sleep."

"I'm touched that you would lose sleep over me."

"Don't flatter yourself. Just making sure you're not dead."

He smirked, but it didn't reach his eyes. "Sweet of you. Didn't think you cared." He made his way down the steps, closer and closer until he was right there. My eyes darted to his busted knuckles and he shoved his hands in his pockets.

God, he could make me want to scream and…something else. Something I refused to name. He was so close to me. Why was he so damn close? He smelled like soap and faint motor oil, and something woodsy. Everything about being here felt like a mistake I couldn't stop making. Like a freight train on a broken track. "I didn't say I don't care," I blurted, words too sharp, too brittle. "I just—"

Jackson looked skyward, like he might find remnants of his patience there. "Just what? We're at each other's throats all the time. And even when I do try to be nice, you bite my damn head off. You think I don't notice?"

My temper flared to life, a safe place to hide and I couldn't swallow my next words quick enough. "You think I wanted to sneak out and come here? You think I wanted to worry about you? I tried not to, but I couldn't stop thinking—" I finally managed to bite down on the words before I confessed what scared me most.

"So, you do care," he said quietly, like it cost him something to admit.

"I just wanted to say thank you. For protecting Maria. That's all."

He blinked at me, and let out a dry, humorless laugh. "Jesse grabbed you, Holly," Jackson bit out. The muscle in his jaw ticked, and those gray eyes flashed.

My heart stumbled in my chest. "I…what?" I blinked at him, confusion tangling with a rising tide of something else—fear, maybe. Memory. I didn't want to think about his hands on me, didn't want to feel that old panic clawing up my throat.

Jackson stepped closer, eyes blazing, his voice rough and shaking like he barely had control of it. "I wasn't protecting Maria," he spat, every word sharp enough to cut. "I was protecting *you.*"

The silence that followed pressed on my chest like a weight. I shouldn't be standing this close to him, shouldn't notice the way his breath brushed my face, the way his lips were just…there. Easy distance to close. Too easy. My heart lurched, panic bubbling beneath the pull in my stomach. Because this was the first time in years I'd felt something like this—a spark, a want—and it terrified me. After everything that happened before, the thought of wanting someone again felt wrong, broken, like crossing a line I wasn't ready to step over.

But God help me, I wanted to.

My eyes flicked to his mouth before I could stop myself. He saw it, of course he saw it, and for one endless heartbeat, it felt like he might lean in. I swore the air changed between us, heavy and electric, every nerve in my body begging him to move closer. Close the distance. What would he taste like? Would I regret it?

"Don't," he murmured, voice low and rough, like he was holding himself back, too.

My breath caught. "Don't what?" I whispered, hating how shaky it sounded.

"Look at me like that." His jaw tightened, eyes dark. "Like you're thinking about something neither of us is ready for."

And he was right. I wasn't ready. But maybe I wanted to be.

The moment shattered when he stepped back, dragging a hand down his face like this whole thing was exhausting to him. "Doesn't matter," he said, voice flat now. "I'm leaving."

The ground tilted beneath me. "What?"

"Georgia. The Saints. All of it. I enlisted. Basic training starts in a couple weeks."

My throat burned. I didn't know why it hurt so much, why those words sliced deeper than they had any right to. It wasn't like I *liked* him. Not like that. Not enough for this to feel like a loss. Except…maybe I did. And that truth scared me more than anything. I swallowed it all down. The fear, the hurt, the confusing ache. "Oh."

Jackson gave another humorless laugh. "Yeah. So, good news, you can stop worrying about me."

I didn't say a word. Couldn't. Not when every thought screamed too loud and not a single one made sense. I turned to leave, and as I walked back to my car, I almost looked back over my shoulder. Almost said something, almost begged him not to go.

But burying it was easier. Safer.

"Night, Malibu," he said softly.

"Night," I whispered back, getting in my car and driving away before my heart could betray me any more than it already had.

Chapter Twelve

⚜ **Holly** ⚜

The morning after prom should've come with a warning label.

May cause nausea, emotional instability, and a sudden desire to fake your own death.

I groaned into my pillow, which smelled faintly like expensive lavender detergent and the tears I absolutely did not cry last night. My head pounded. My eyes burned. And every time I blinked, I saw *him*—a bruised cheekbone, a shattered expression, the way he'd said he was leaving like it didn't rip something open in me.

Stupid.

Stupid, stupid, stupid.

I rolled onto my back, staring at the ceiling like it had personally wronged me. Honestly, it might have. The fan wobbled overhead in a way that suggested imminent decapitation. Maybe that wouldn't be so bad. Quick. Clean. No emotions. Prom really said, "Let's traumatize the entire friend group and ruin your sleep schedule." I was mid-wallow when someone knocked once—no hesitation, no politeness—then shoved the door open.

Maria.

She looked like she'd run a marathon on zero sleep: messy bun, hoodie stretched over her growing bump, determination radiating off her in waves. "We're going to the lake," she announced.

I stared. "What?"

She marched straight to my closet like she owned the place (she did not) and pulled out a duffel bag. "Pack."

"Maria, what the hell are you talking about?"

She didn't even look at me. "Hannah's orders."

That gave me pause. I had met Hannah Mills only briefly at the Saints' winter get-to-together. Dalton spoke of her like she was a deity. Mac spoke of her like she was a drill sergeant. Maria spoke of her like she was a terrifying mix of both.

"Hannah?" I repeated. "Mac and Dalton's mom?"

"Yes." Stuff, stuff, stuff. Clothes flying everywhere. "She saw everybody this morning and said—and I quote—'These children need Jesus, sunlight, and forty-eight hours away from drama before I lose my religion.' Then she threw Mac the keys to the cabin and shoved us out the door."

I blinked. "She...threw him keys?"

Maria paused only long enough to give me a wide-eyed, meaningful look. "Holly. She hit him in the face with them."

Holy shit. I wasn't prepared to meet a Southern hurricane disguised as a woman.

"So this is...a family trip?" I asked warily.

"More like court-ordered emotional rehab," Maria muttered. "We're going."

"We?" I repeated. "Who's 'we'?"

"Me, you, Mac, Diego—" She hesitated. "—and Jackson."

My soul left my body. "Aw, that's sweet. Pass."

"Holly, it's happening."

"I'm not spending an entire weekend in a confined wooden structure with that *boy*."

Maria dropped a stack of shorts into the bag, unimpressed. "He's going."

"I'll stay home."

"You can't."

"Watch me."

She planted both hands on her hips. "Listen to me very carefully. You met the woman. This isn't a suggestion. This is Hannah Mills. Mac looked her in the eye and said 'Yes ma'am' like she was the president."

I choked. "What does that have to do with me?"

"She said you're going too."

"By name?"

Maria leveled me with a look. "Holly," she said slowly. "She said—and again, I quote—'Bring the blonde one too. The sharp-tongued one. That child needs rest.'"

My mouth fell open. "My tongue is not—"

Maria slowly raised her eyebrows.

"Ok," I muttered. "Maybe a little sharp."

"Like a machete," she said.

I threw a sock at her. Missed. Then groaned and flopped back onto the bed.

This was a nightmare. A sun-soaked, mosquito-infested, Jackson-filled nightmare. And the worst part? A tiny, traitorous piece of me wanted to go. Wanted to see him. Wanted to figure out why last night felt like the ground shifting under my feet. I looked up to find Maria stuffing my bright red bikini into my bag and groaned again. She glanced at me, offered a cheery wink, before zipping it shut and heading for the door.

"You've got like, fifteen minutes. Hurry up and get ready."

"This is a cruel and unusual punishment."

She didn't answer, just hummed as she shut the door behind her.

In my bathroom a few minutes later, I reapplied my mascara for the third time, then immediately scrubbed it off because I looked like someone trying too hard, then reapplied it again because I looked dead, then wiped half of it away because it clumped, then dropped the tube and said several unladylike words that would've made my mother faint. Every few seconds I told myself, "You don't care if Jackson's there."

Which was hilarious, because the second I said his name—even internally—my pulse jumped like it was training for a marathon.

By the time I grabbed my duffel bag and stomped downstairs, I'd made peace with the fact that I looked...fine. I was aiming for fine. Fine was safe.

Fine didn't feel anything. Outside, the Mills' massive truck took up most of our driveway. It was one of those vehicles you could probably tow a barn with. Or an entire town.

Dalton sat in the truck bed eating Doritos and waving them around like he was conducting an orchestra. He shoved them into a cooler that was strapped down before hopping off the tailgate when he saw me. Mac leaned against the hood with the air of a man who had been ready to leave ten years ago. Diego was talking to Maria in low, sweet tones. And Jackson—

He was leaning against the passenger door, arms crossed, jaw shadowed with last night's bruises. He looked like someone who wished he was anywhere else. But he also smiled a little when he glanced over at Maria and Diego. His eyes flicked over my way when he heard me. They swept over me so quickly I almost convinced myself I'd imagined it.

"About time," he said, pushing off the door.

"Could say the same," I shot back. "You look like you slept in a ditch."

Dalton hooted from the truck bed. "He basically did! Their AC broke again last night."

Jackson flipped him off without breaking eye contact with me. Typical.

Maria tugged on my sleeve. "You ready?"

"As I'll ever be," I muttered.

Mac jerked a thumb toward the truck. "Let's go. Mom said if we weren't out of the driveway by nine, she'd 'light a fire under all our asses.' I don't want to find out what that means."

We piled in. Or tried to. The truck was not meant for four football players, a pregnant girl, and me with my stress aura taking up half the available oxygen. Dalton slid into the back seat behind Mac, who was driving. Diego shoved himself into the middle of the front seat, that tiny little part every truck seemed to have that they definitely shouldn't. Maria climbed in next and sat half on Diego, half on thin air.

That left me smashed against the right door in the back, Jackson trapped between me and Dalton, his forearm brushing my arm every time we hit a bump. Perfect. Amazing. Love that for me.

"Move," Jackson muttered.

"I can't," I hissed. "I have no leg room."

"Maybe try having smaller thighs."

I glared at him. "Maybe try having less of an ego."

Dalton cackled so loudly, Mac turned the radio up to drown him out. Maria reached back and squeezed my hand like she was telling me to behave. As if that ever worked. The drive took forever. Trees blurred past in a green smear, the early summer sunlight slanting through the windshield. Diego kept up a steady stream of chatter with Maria, trying not to stare at her too obviously. Dalton was halfway out the window yelling at cows. Mac was muttering under his breath about "damn kids" like he was forty-seven and not twenty. And Jackson just stared out the window, jaw tight, tapping his thumb against his knee like he was trying not to feel the way our arms kept brushing. Every time it happened, the air between us tensed—sharp, bright, almost painful. Like a spark without a flame. Yet.

I hated it. I hated him. I hated how I didn't hate any of it.

We turned down the long gravel road that led to the Mills' cabin. I didn't know what to expect, but it definitely wasn't the stunning two-story lake house tucked under towering pines, the water shimmering like glass behind it.

I stopped when I got out the truck, staring. "Holy shit," I breathed.

Dalton walked past me. "Right? Told you it was awesome."

"I didn't know you had…this," I said.

"Correction," he said. "Mom has this. And by extension, we have this. Which means now you have this too, temporarily. As in, don't get too attached."

I rolled my eyes and dragged my bag inside.

Maria froze halfway through the doorway, blinking rapidly. "It's so… clean."

Mac snorted. "It's a cabin, not a hospital. Relax."

"Cabins can be dirty," Maria whispered like she was confessing a felony.

"Everything's dirty to you, you germ goblin," Dalton said.

Maria ignored him and walked straight toward the glass doors overlooking the lake. I could practically see the thought form in her head before she said it. "We should go swimming."

Diego perked up immediately. "Now?"

"Yes," she said with complete conviction.

"But we just got here," Mac said.

Maria didn't blink. "And?"

I pinched the bridge of my nose. "Maria, honey, you're pregnant. Maybe just let's get settled first—"

She turned, hands on her hips, looking absolutely ready to fight me. "I am pregnant, not made of porcelain. It's a lake. I want to swim before the boys turn it into testosterone soup."

Dalton threw his shirt at her. "You wound me."

"You deserve it," she fired back.

Jackson had wandered out onto the deck, leaning on the railing, staring at the water with a look I couldn't place. Something soft. Something tired. My stomach tightened.

Maria nudged me. "Let's go get changed."

"I don't want to—" I trailed off because even I didn't know how to finish that sentence. Also, because I was still staring at Jackson and multi-tasking had never been a skill of mine.

She looked at me like she was reading the words I wasn't saying. "You don't have to be afraid to want things, *hermana*."

I swallowed hard, unable to answer.

Maria lifted her chin and said brightly, "Thirty minutes. Everyone changed. At the dock."

Then she marched off to find her swimsuit like she was leading a military mission. None of us moved, waiting for her to realize, and a second later she was back. "I have no idea where I'm going."

Diego picked up her bag, I grabbed mine, and Mac led our little entourage up the stairs to the bedrooms. She and I were going to be sharing a cute little room with a massive king-size bed and Diego set her bag down before she shooed him out the door so we could change. Maria immediately started rummaging through her bag like a woman on a mission.

"You're sure you're ok to swim?" I asked.

She shot me a flat look. "Holly, I'm fine. I can float."

"People who 'float' don't go around saying they're rotund."

"You said I wasn't rotund."

"That was me being nice."

She reached into her bag and pulled out a purple maternity swimsuit that looked *shockingly* cute, then paused to squint at me. "Where's yours?"

I held up the one-piece I had added to my bag after she left. Black. Simple. Conservative. Safe. The emotional equivalent of a brick wall. Maria stared at it like it offended her ancestors.

"No."

"Yes."

"No."

"Maria—"

She marched over, plucked it from my hands, tossed it onto the bed, then went back to my duffel like a general conducting a search-and-seizure raid. She let out a triumphant little sound when she found it. The red one. The one that made me look like I had a waistline sculpted by the gods. The one I had privately planned to wear in my room and then never again.

Maria shoved it at me. "Put. It. On."

I wanted to argue. I did. But she was looking at me with those big brown mom-friend eyes, and I caved like a wet cardboard box. Ten minutes later, I was standing in front of the mirror wearing something that should have come with caution tape. Maria let out a low appreciative whistle.

"Damn, *hermana*. Jackson's gonna die."

"Maria."

"He deserves it."

"Maria."

"He does! Mr. Macho Man, no feelings. Take that."

"Maria."

She winked at me, grabbed her towel, and waddled—yes, waddled, I said what I said—toward the stairs. I stood alone for a second, staring at the girl in the mirror. Legs too long. Stomach too tight. Skin that still didn't always feel like mine. And beneath it, the quietest sliver of something that hadn't existed in years. Want. I swallowed hard, grabbed my towel which I wrapped around me like armor, and followed.

Outside, Maria was hustling toward the shoreline with a determination I couldn't help but admire. I stood there watching her, knowing just how badly she needed this after the disaster that was prom. Then Mac cleared his throat and I looked over at him. He looked pointedly from me to the purple menace who was kicking off her flip-flops.

I groaned. "Oh my God. I'm responsible for her, aren't I?"

"Yes," all four boys said in unison.

I frowned at Diego, who was watching Maria closely. "Why aren't you chasing after her?"

Jackson folded his arms. "Because she listens to you."

I blinked. "No she doesn't."

"Yes she does," Diego said.

"Maria," I yelled, "Sunscreen! Sunscreen!"

Nothing. No reaction. I gave the four of them a pointed look and then we all trudged after the pregnant woman about to yeet herself into a lake.

She went to step off the dock and it wobbled precariously, which meant she did too. Diego was there in an instant. "Easy," he said softly, offering both hands like she was made of clouds.

She smiled at him, the kind that could melt a glacier. "*Gracias*, Diego."

He turned bright red. "Yeah. Yeah, of course."

I had to look away because it felt like intruding on something private. Something soft and new.

Dalton, on the other hand, was across the dock announcing at top volume, "Mac hit me with a noodle and I'm pressing charges!"

Mac smacked him with the neon pool noodle again. "It was an accident the first time. This time was because you're annoying."

Jackson was shirtless—of course he was—sitting at the edge of the dock with his feet in the water, pretending not to listen but smiling that crooked grin that was so him. His hair was brushed back. His shoulders were broad. His jaw was bruised. My chest tightened so fast I almost tripped on the last step. I caught myself, but not before my towel fell leaving in my bare skinned glory. Jackson's head snapped around, probably ready with some asshole remark, but the second his eyes landed on me—he froze. Actually froze. Like someone had unplugged his entire brain. His mouth opened slightly. Then shut. Then opened again like a fish desperately trying to survive on land. His eyes dragged over me once, then jerked away like the sun had slapped him.

Good. Suffer.

I tried to walk normally, like a girl who wasn't painfully aware of every square inch of exposed skin. The wood was warm against my feet. The lake smelled like pine and sunscreen and summer.

Maria eased into the water with Diego, who kept one hand hovering near her back like he was ready to catch her if gravity betrayed her.

Dalton cannonballed off the end of the dock and came up screaming, "Fuck! That's cold."

Mac dunked him under the water with one hand. "Hush."

Chaos. Pure chaos.

And Jackson. He stared at the water like it had personally wronged him, shoulders tight, jaw ticking. Every few seconds his gaze flicked toward me, then snapped away like touching a hot stove. I stopped beside him, arms crossed, voice low. "You planning to jump, or just brood dramatically?"

"I don't brood."

"You literally *are* brooding. Right now. In front of me."

He cracked his neck, eyes still on the water. "Maybe I'm thinking."

"You thinking usually looks like brooding."

"Malibu."

"Jackson."

That earned me a sideways glance. Slow. Careful. Like he was afraid if he looked directly at me, something inside him would break. I sat down next to him, close enough to feel the heat from his skin. He sucked in a breath like the proximity hurt.

"Relax," I muttered. "I'm not here to bite."

"You don't have to bite," he said quietly. "You do plenty of damage with just your mouth."

My heart stuttered. I tried very hard not to imagine any alternative meanings to that sentence.

"Are you trying to flirt with me or piss me off?" I asked.

"Yes."

I hated how good he was at this. How my pulse jumped every time his knee brushed mine.

"Malibu," he murmured, almost under his breath.

"Hmm?"

"Go swim."

"You go swim."

Before either of us could say a word, we were shoved off the dock. Dalton at some point had climbed back onto it and used the distraction to creep up behind us.

Jackson surfaced with a curse then huffed something that might have been a laugh, then immediately looked horrified with himself for doing it.

God. He was stupidly cute. This time when he glanced at me, I wasn't able to hold back my smile. Dalton stood in the dock triumphantly. We ignored him.

I swam backward farther into the lake, holding Jackson's gaze.

"Come on, Morgan," I teased. "Or are you scared of a little cold water?"

He splashed me, and I shrieked as freezing water exploded over me.

Dalton cheered. Mac yelled at him for almost knocking the dock loose. Maria cackled like a gremlin.

I glared at Jackson. Then I dove. Straight at him. When I surfaced inches away, he went perfectly still. We were almost nose to nose.

I pushed my wet hair back. "I grew up on the water. I got moves you don't even know."

He swallowed.

Then—voice low, almost strangled—said: "Is that so?"

And just like that, I felt my cheeks go as red as my swimsuit.

The lake water was cold enough to make my bones file complaints with HR, but after the first shock, it felt good—clean, alive, like something I hadn't felt since California. Maria eventually perched on the lower dock steps, letting the water lap at her legs. Dalton dragged Diego away from her and the two of them got into a wrestling match in the water. Mac joined in, and Dalton did his best to drown his brother. Jackson did his usual routine—act like he wasn't watching me, fail spectacularly, then pretend he had been looking at a tree the whole time.

The chaos eventually tapered off, and by late afternoon, the six of us drifted into the lazy warmth of the day like sleepy lizards. Maria and I sprawled out on towels near the waterline while the boys took turns roughhousing and occasionally "checking the firewood situation," which I suspected was code for "let's stand somewhere and secretly watch the girls."

Maria nudged me with her elbow, eyes closed behind her sunglasses. "You know he keeps staring."

"Please," I said, pretending to be unbothered. "They stare because we're the only women here and one of them is literally pregnant."

She hummed, unimpressed. "Uh-huh. And the other one is wearing red."

I smacked her with my towel.

A soft breeze combed through the trees. I glanced over my shoulder, watching Mac carry one of the coolers to the deck where Jackson was pulling off the cover of a massive silver grill. Everything felt warm and loud and alive. For the first time in a long time, Maria's face didn't look pinched. She was sun-drowsy and glowing, one hand idly resting on her stomach.

"You happy?" I asked quietly.

She didn't open her eyes. "I forgot I could be."

My throat tightened. "Good. You deserve this."

She smiled, soft and vulnerable in a way that made me want to throw a rock at Jesse's skull. By sunset, the grill had been conquered by Mac and Jackson—who turned out to cook like two dads hosting a Super Bowl party. The picnic table was a chaotic spread of burgers, chips, grilled corn, Dalton's "secret sauce" (which Mac repeatedly warned everyone *not* to eat), and a pitcher of sweet tea so sugary I felt my teeth vibrate.

Maria ate like she hadn't seen food in four days, and Diego hovered so hard I thought he might cut her hot dog for her. Dalton told some horrific story about accidentally eating a bug in practice last season.

Maria gagged, laughing. "Dalton, stop!"

"No, keep going," I said. "This is the most entertaining part of my week."

Jackson snorted into his sweet tea. I pretended not to notice.

But every so often, his eyes flicked to me. Every so often, mine flicked back. A magnet I kept pretending wasn't there. The sky drained from gold to navy. Crickets started their nightly concert. The lake shimmered in the last bit of light. I wandered down toward the dock for a moment to breathe. The air tasted like pine sap and charcoal. Mac yelled at Dalton for throwing Doritos into the fire pit. I stood at the edge of the water, toes curling over the wood, and tried not to think about the way Jackson had looked at me today. Tried and failed.

"You good Malibu?" a low voice said behind me.

I turned as he walked toward me, hands in his pockets, shoulders tense like he wasn't sure if he was allowed to stand this close. "You following me?" I asked lightly.

"If I say yes, you'll hit me."

"Probably."

A ghost of a smile. "Then no. Pure coincidence."

We stood in silence for a moment, both of us watching the water like it had answers.

He nudged my shoulder with his. "Hey."

"Hey what?"

"You were good today," he said, voice low. "With Maria. With… everything."

I rolled my eyes because anything else would've been too much. "Yeah, well. I got dragged here against my will. But it's against my upbringing to be a party pooper."

His jaw clenched. "You don't give yourself enough credit."

"And you give yourself too much."

"That's fair," he admitted, making me snort.

He took a breath like he had more to say, then didn't say it. His fingers brushed mine—accidental or not, I couldn't tell. And I was stupidly aware of it. Of him. The warmth. The gravity. It scared me. But it didn't make me step back.

"Malibu," he murmured.

I swallowed. "Yeah?"

He didn't get to say whatever he was thinking before Dalton yelled from the fire pit, "Hey! Stop making eyes at her and come help with the firewood!"

"Not making eyes," Jackson muttered, ears going pink.

"Definitely making eyes," I whispered.

He glared at me. "You're impossible."

"And you're slow."

We walked back together—close enough to touch, far enough not to. The fire crackled as night settled fully around us, sparks drifting up into the trees like tiny fireflies. Dalton was trying to toast marshmallows three at a time. Mac confiscated them before he lit the entire county on fire. Maria curled up with her tea while Diego sat on the log beside her, picking at a guitar like the thing was part of him. I didn't even know he played. He definitely didn't tell anyone he could *sing*. But when he opened his mouth—just softly, gently—it was…beautiful. Deep and warm and a little unsteady, like someone testing courage. Maria stared at him like he'd hung the moon. When the song tapered off, there was a tiny, reverent silence.

Then Dalton ruined it by whisper-yelling, "Bro, you could've been pulling girls this whole time."

Mac threw a leftover hotdog at him. I laughed. Hard. Diego played another song, something low and sweet and in Spanish that had Maria swaying with her eyes closed.

Then Jackson stood and held out a hand toward me. Not forceful. Not cocky. Just…an offering. The entire group went dead silent except for Diego's singing, like I was a deer about to bolt. My heart hammered because this was too public, too vulnerable, too much. Dancing meant touching. Touching meant remembering. Remembering meant spiraling. But Jackson's eyes were steady. Not demanding. Not teasing. Just asking.

"Holly," he said quietly, "dance with me?"

Everyone waited. I hesitated, part of me still fearing things that weren't him. But this wasn't…that. There was no need to run from this. Right?

Only one way to find out. So I swallowed. Lifted my chin. And put my hand in his. Jackson led me just outside the firelight—close enough for warmth, far enough for privacy. One hand settled at my waist, slow and cautious, like he was touching something fragile. I rested my hand on his shoulder because anything else would've set my nerves on fire. We swayed. Just that. Just swaying.

"You're shaking," he murmured.

"I'm cold."

"You're lying."

"Yeah," I whispered. "I am."

He didn't push. He didn't ask. He just held me steady.

The fire popped behind us. The guitar thrummed quietly. And for somewhere between one breath and the next—I forgot to be afraid.

Jackson dipped his head slightly, voice rough. "Holly?"

"Yeah?"

His forehead touched mine.

"Leaving for basic doesn't mean leaving you. You know that, right?"

"Yeah." I wasn't sure if I believed that. But maybe I was starting to. Under the firelight, with his heartbeat tapping against my palm, something in me finally, quietly clicked into place.

Chapter Thirteen

✏ **Jackson** ✏

I woke up Sunday morning with Diego's elbow jammed into my spine. Technically, we had a bed. A queen. Large enough for two grown men. Technically. In reality, Diego slept like he was reenacting a homicide, and I ended up half off the mattress, clinging to the edge like the hero in an action movie refusing to fall from the skyscraper. I shoved him. He groaned, rolled, and took the blanket with him. Figures. We'd crashed in the spare room—one of the few spaces August and Hannah never fully finished decorating. Bed, dresser, nightstand. Functional. No nonsense. It smelled like cedar and laundry detergent. Mac had his room. Dalton had the room across the hall. And the girls got August and Hannah's room because it was the only one with a bathroom attached—plus, Hannah would've murdered us if we'd stuck a pregnant girl anywhere else.

I stretched, bones popping, and made my way to the kitchen. The cabin was quiet. Warm. Early sun slanted through the windows and painted the whole place gold. The coffee pot was full. Mac had set it on a timer before we all went to bed. I grabbed a mug and filled it to the brim. Black. Hot enough to maim. Exactly how I needed it. I'd only gotten a couple hours of sleep. Every time I drifted off, I jolted awake thinking about Holly's waist in my hand. The way she smelled like coconut sunscreen and lake water. The way she'd looked at me like I wasn't just some jock from a busted trailer.

Like maybe I was something more. Footsteps padded behind me, and I didn't even have to turn around.

"Morning," Holly mumbled, voice soft and scratchy with sleep.

I turned. And almost aspirated my own soul. Matching silk pajamas. Shorts that were basically a suggestion. Tank top that clung like she'd been poured into it. Blonde hair in a messy knot. Eyes heavy from sleep. She looked…soft. Feminine. Disarmed. A version of Holly I'd never seen before. The kind of girl I'd burn in hell for. Without thinking, I handed her the steaming mug. She took it like she trusted me not to poison her.

She sniffed the coffee, recoiled, and marched to the fridge. "Absolutely not. I am not raw-dogging caffeine like a psychopath." She grabbed the creamer. Not just "a splash." Half the mug. Maybe more.

"You want some coffee with your sugar?" I asked.

She sipped it with a blissful sigh. "Yes. It's perfect."

I stared at her. "That's not coffee."

"It has coffee *in* it."

"Barely."

"Maybe that's why it's good."

I wanted to roll my eyes so hard they detached. Instead, I found myself watching her. The way she curled her fingers around the mug. The way her bare legs brushed against each other as she shifted her weight. The way the morning light traced her shoulders, her collarbone. I didn't know where to put my hands. Or my sanity.

"So," she said, staring into her mug like it held state secrets, "about last night." She finally raised her eyes, expression unreadable. "What was it?"

God, I hated not having the answers sometimes. I could tell she needed them. Clarity meant safety to her. So, I kept my voice low. Gentle. Controlled. Gave her the only answer I had. "It was real."

Her breath hitched.

But then she shook her head, shutters slamming back down. "Doesn't matter."

"It does to me."

She gave a bitter, crooked almost-smile. "You're leaving, Jackson."

Yeah. That was the anvil over both our heads. I stepped closer. Just a fraction. Enough that her shoulder almost brushed my chest. "Holly," I said, slow and raw. "I'm leaving. I'm not disappearing."

She looked away like the words hurt. "It's not that simple."

"I know."

I forced a laugh, rough around the edges. "I'm not simple. You're not simple. Nothing about us is simple."

She scoffed into her coffee. "Tell me something I don't know."

We stood in the stillness, steam rising between us. And God, I wanted to reach for her. Wanted to tuck that messy hair behind her ear. Wanted to pull her close and pretend basic training didn't exist. Instead, I poured myself another cup of coffee and said, "Let's go outside. Air's good this early."

She hesitated. Then nodded once. We stepped out onto the porch, lake fog curling around our ankles. For a moment, we just stood there, side by side, watching the world wake up.

She whispered, "I'm scared."

I turned to look at her, heart thudding. "Of me?"

"No." Her voice cracked. "Of…wanting something. He hurt me, Jackson. Badly."

My throat tightened, I gripped my cup so hard I was surprised it didn't crack. "I know. But Holly…I would never hurt you. Never."

She looked out over the lake and her next words were so quiet I wasn't sure I heard them. "I think I am starting to get that."

Our shoulders touched. Light. Barely. Like a promise neither of us was brave enough to say out loud yet. Then the cabin door behind us banged open.

"Good morning, children!" Dalton hollered. "Who wants eggs?!"

Holly sighed dramatically. "And the moment is dead."

I couldn't stop the grin. "Yeah. He's good for that."

She hid her smile behind her mug. But she smiled. And that felt like winning something I didn't even know I'd been competing for.

Breakfast with the guys was always a feral experience, but this morning it felt like it was happening in slow motion. Mac stood at the stove flipping pancakes with the precision of a neurosurgeon. Dalton was aggressively stealing them off the cooling rack like a raccoon in human form. Diego sat at the table, rubbing sleep out of his eyes while Maria loudly proclaimed that coffee was, in fact, not bad for pregnant women in moderation and then poured herself a cup that nearly overflowed. And Holly padded around the kitchen in those damn silk pajamas, sipping her dessert-in-a-mug coffee, avoiding eye contact with me like looking at me too long might melt something she didn't want melted.

The whole place smelled like syrup and butter and safety. I should have felt peaceful. Instead, something ugly and electric twisted tight beneath my ribs. Five days. I had five days before I left. Before I wasn't *here* anymore. Before early mornings meant drill instructors screaming, and not Holly with bedhead and creamer breath. Before the only people I saw were strangers in uniforms—not Mac, not Dalton, not Diego, not Maria. Not her. My fork hovered halfway to my mouth before I noticed I hadn't taken a bite in five minutes.

"Jackson," Dalton said around a mouthful of stolen pancake, "you good?"

It was such a stupid question. Such a Dalton question. The easy answer—the lie—stuck in my throat. "—yeah," I managed.

Diego looked up, sharper than the rest. "He's thinking again. Dangerous."

"Shut up," I muttered, but it came out tired.

Mac slid into the seat across from me, tapping his fingers against the table. "Five days."

I didn't ask how he knew what was in my head. Mac always knew.

"Big change," he said softly. "It's ok to freak out about it."

Dalton snorted. "I freaked out when I lost my favorite hoodie. This is, like, ten times worse."

Diego deadpanned, "Dalton, you nearly cried because you thought a squirrel stole it."

"The squirrel *was suspicious*," Dalton argued.

Holly laughed—quiet but real—and something warm pushed through the fear coiled inside me.

I chewed one bite, two, forcing my stomach to accept food. "I'm not freaking out."

Maria raised a brow. "Your hand is literally shaking."

I looked down. Damn it. It was.

Holly set her mug down. "It'd be weird if you *weren't* scared," she said, voice way gentler than I was prepared for. "Basic is…huge. And brave. And…" Her eyes flicked up to mine. "You're allowed to feel whatever you feel."

I swallowed hard. We all stared at her. Because hearing *her* say that? Yeah. That hit somewhere I wasn't armored. "Thanks," I said quietly. She nodded, cheeks pink like maybe she hadn't meant to say all that out loud.

Mac clapped me on the back. "We're proud of you."

Dalton slapped the other shoulder. Hard. On purpose. "Yeah, but like… don't die."

"Dalton," Maria hissed.

"What?! Someone had to say it!"

I groaned. Underneath the table, Holly's leg brushed mine.

By noon we were stripping beds, loading bags, folding towels, and pretending this wasn't the last carefree morning I'd have in a long time. Mac carried the trash to the truck. Maria marched around threatening to disembowel us all because none of us were willing to let her lift anything heavier than a bag of chips. Diego lugged a box of leftover snacks across the deck, grumbling. Dalton sprayed himself with bug repellant like he was painting a fence. Holly was stuffing her bag into the truck, face slightly pinched like she didn't love the idea of going home either. The air felt thick. Heavy. Like a balloon stretched too tight.

We piled into August's massive truck. Holly climbed into the back beside me. The first thirty minutes of the drive were quiet—radio humming, Dalton telling some story none of us were listening to, Maria half-asleep on Diego's shoulder. But every bump, every turn, every shift of the truck had Holly's leg sliding against mine. By the fourth time, something in me snapped. Fuck it. I reached over and let my fingers brush the back of her hand.

She froze.

I almost pulled away. Almost told myself I'd misread everything. Almost reminded myself she was soft and clean and lake-water sweet and I was…me. Then her fingers curled around mine. She didn't look at me. Didn't speak. Just…held on. Tight. Like she needed the contact just as badly as I did. My chest squeezed. Hard. Painful. Perfect. I laced our fingers fully, palm to palm, and her shoulders sagged like she'd been holding her breath all day.

Outside the window, the lake disappeared behind the pine trees. The cabin faded from view. And time kept moving—pulling me toward the thing I'd chosen, and away from the girl I was terrified to leave. But she didn't let go. Not once. Not even when we turned onto the road that led home. The ride back into town felt shorter than the drive out, which was bullshit because the miles were the same. It was everything else that had changed.

By the time we rolled into Holly's neighborhood, the sun was low, throwing long shadows from all the perfect, expensive houses with their perfect, expensive lawns. The truck looked wrong here. Too loud. Too rough around the edges. Kind of like me. Mac pulled into the McCarthy driveway. Dalton leaned forward between the seats. "All right, princess. You and Maria get out before your HOA fines us just for existing."

"Shut up," Holly muttered, but there wasn't much heat in it. Maria unbuckled slowly, one hand cradling her stomach. She hesitated, then twisted to look at us.

"Thank you," she said softly. "For…all of it."

Dalton pressed his palm to his chest. "I am always available for water fights and emotional support."

Diego smiled, eyes warm. "Anytime, Maria."

Holly's fingers tightened around mine once more, shielded by her duffel and the angle of our bodies. No one had said anything, but I knew Mac had noticed. He noticed everything. She finally pulled her hand free, slow like the separation cost her something, then reached for the door handle.

"Bye," she said, almost too quickly. "Thanks for not letting Dalton drown anyone."

"No promises next time," I said.

She rolled her eyes, but her lips twitched. Then she and Maria climbed out. Her parents' porch light clicked on automatically, casting them in a warm halo as they walked up the steps. Holly turned just before they went inside. Her gaze found mine through the windshield. For a second, everything else went quiet. She lifted her hand in a small wave. I dipped my chin. That was it. Mac pulled away. Diego and I were dropped off next, two sagging trailers at the edge of the park.

"Diego hopped out, banging the door shut behind him. "Later, man."

"Yeah," I said. "Later."

Mac met my eyes in the side mirror. "You call if you need anything this week. You hear me?"

"Yes, Dad," I deadpanned.

His gaze sharpened. "Smart-ass."

Then they were gone. The truck roared off, leaving me standing in the gravel, dust settling around my boots. The quiet hit hard. Our trailer looked the same as always—siding a little warped, porch steps a little crooked. The box fan in my bedroom window still rattled. The plastic flamingo Mrs. Hargrove had stuck in her patch of dirt two lots down leered at me like it knew all my secrets. I climbed the stairs and pushed the door open.

Mom was exactly where I expected: curled on her side on the couch, the empty wine box shoved under the coffee table. The TV played an infomercial about a mop that could allegedly change your life. I tugged a blanket over her shoulders. She barely stirred.

"Hi, Mom," I murmured.

Then I went to my room, dropped my bag on the floor, and flopped onto the mattress. The springs screamed in protest. The ceiling stared back at me. Silence pressed in. I lasted maybe thirty seconds before I grabbed my phone. My thumb hovered over her name. Holly. I had no idea what the rules were here. No idea what I was allowed to say without blowing this up or making it heavier than she could carry right now. Fuck the rules.

Me: Get home ok?

I stared at the message for a second, then hit send before I could overthink it—which, for me, meant I only overthought it for six full seconds instead of thirty. The bubbles showed up almost immediately.

Holly: You were literally in my driveway when I got home, genius.

I huffed out something that wasn't quite a laugh. Already felt better.

Me: Yeah, but you know. Gotta make sure you didn't trip on your way to the door. That bikini looked hazardous.

The dots appeared, then vanished. Appeared again.

Holly: Wow. Misogyny AND concern. A two-for-one deal. Also, I wasn't wearing that bikini when you guys dropped me off. Day dreaming much?

I smirked at the screen.

Me: You didn't seem very concerned about male objectification when you were staring at my chest.

Message sent. Immediate regret. Two agonizingly long seconds. Then:

Holly: LMAO. Please. You WISH I was staring.

A pause.

Ok...maybe I was a little.

My heart slammed against my ribs.

She was still there. Still doing this. Still meeting me in the middle where the joking rubbed shoulders with something realer, sharper, scarier. I rolled onto my back, thumb flying, but before I could respond, she sent another message.

Holly: This weekend was good. The cabin. The lake. The dancing. Don't get used to me being nice though.

Me: Too late. Already adjusted my expectations.

Holly: Bold of you.

Me: That's what they're sending me to basic for. My boldness.

Holly: Pretty sure it's for your inability to shut up and listen.

Me: Aw, I didn't know you paid attention to me like that.

Three blinking dots. Longer this time.

Holly: I'm still figuring out what I feel. But "don't like you" isn't really accurate anymore.

The breath left my lungs in a rush.

Me: Same. For the record, the lake was the second most beautiful thing I saw this weekend.

Holly: Oh yeah?

Me: Yeah.

The seconds stretched. My chest hurt. In a good way. In a terrifying way.

Holly: You're still leaving.

Me: I am.

Holly: I'm scared. I know I said that already. Just gonna be honest. This... whatever it is? It's a lot.

Me: We can be scared together.

Holly: You're not allowed to be scared. You're the strong one.

I tapped my fingers against my knee, then typed.

Me: That's not how it works, Malibu. I can be scared AND strong. So can you.

No reply for a long moment. After a minute she sent back:

Holly: You're annoyingly good at saying the right thing, Dr. Phil.

Me: Don't tell anyone. It'll ruin my rep.

Holly: Too late. I already know you're a softie.

Me: Lies.

Holly: Sure. Keep telling yourself that.

I swallowed, a smile tugging at my mouth even as my eyes burned.

Me: I should let you sleep. Gonna be a long week.

Holly: Yeah. Probably.

Me: Thanks for... everything.

Holly: You don't have to thank me, Jackson.

Me: I want to.

Holly: Goodnight Jackson.

Me: Goodnight, Malibu.

I set the phone on my chest and closed my eyes. The fear was still there. So was the tight, anxious buzz that came with the thought of leaving, of screaming sergeants and endless drills and being stripped down to nothing so they could build me back up. But under it, braided into it now, was something else. She'd held my hand in the truck. She'd danced with me by the fire. She'd admitted she didn't not like me. I fell asleep with her name on my screen and the echo of her hand in mine. And for the first time since signing those enlistment papers, the idea of leaving hurt for a reason that wasn't just getting out—it hurt because of what I'd just started to find.

<h1 align="center">Chapter Fourteen</h1>

⸸ Holly ⸸

It had been eight weeks since Jackson left. Not that I was counting. Or noticed. But at some point yesterday, a desperate and rampant rage to do something burned through me. Thus, I'd been up all night.

Twelve hours. Zero sleep. A pattern I had been doomed to repeat ever since he left.

Just me, my laptop, a legal pad, and a brain running laps on a track that went nowhere. Well…nowhere except Bumfuck, Egypt.

Mac? Playing right-hand man to his dad with the Saints. They had been making updates to the inner and outer workings of the club, literally and figuratively.

Dalton? Had considered Georgia Tech but ended up running off to University of Georgia with a fancy full-ride football scholarship, and was apparently loving it.

Maria and Diego? Baby-proofing her new apartment. Momma Laverne and my dad had pulled some strings to secure a decent, little place just ten minutes away. Maria had been reluctant at first, hesitant to accept such a large favor but I there was joy in her eyes when she first saw the place.

And Jackson? Yeah. *Fucking Jackson.* He left me. Us.

Fuck.

Somewhere between my third cup of coffee and contemplating whether

140

to set my guidance counselor's office on fire, I realized I couldn't just…stay here. Rotting in my parents' house. Waiting for life to happen. Once, I'd wanted to be a beauty coach. Maybe an influencer. That was a lifetime ago. Now? Just the thought made me want to gag.

So what did I want? I was flipping through that stupid career packet when it hit me. Hard. More than anything, I wanted to make a difference. To be there for the people who needed it most. Short of becoming Batman, I had an even better idea. And that's when the doomscrolling and googling began.

Did you know 20.4% of businesses failed in the first year? And almost 70% were dead by year ten?

How fucking depressing is that?

But not mine. I didn't have the name yet—Phoenix, Ashes Rising, Victor's Haven—whatever. I *did* know what it would be: a shelter for women. Women like Maria. Women like me. Women who'd been used as doormats by small-dick men and were done with it. Somewhere they could get a boost. A step up. A safe place to rebuild without becoming another statistic.

For it to succeed, I needed a business degree. And the best business school in Georgia was the Terry College of Business at UGA. So, that was where I was going. Come hell or high water.

Thus the giant stack of papers I was brandishing at my confused mother who was just trying to eat her avocado toast. She blinked at me, sleep still heavily present in her own eyes. When she made no move to grab the papers, I shook them insistently at my dad who paused mid-sip of his expensive Brazilian coffee. He hesitated before taking it from me, giving me one of those long-suffering looks, and began to leaf through it.

"Bug, while I do so enjoy these games, could I get a hint?"

"I'm going to school."

Mom's eyes widened. "I thought you didn't want to go to college."

"I didn't. But I changed my mind."

Dad handed the papers to Mom, who took another dainty bite of her toast before scanning them. He eyed me. "Business school?"

"I'm going to start a business."

"Yes, bug. I figured that much out."

Mom put the papers on the table and gestured for me to sit down. "Whatever for?"

"A women's shelter for survivors of domestic and sexual violence."

Dad choked on his coffee, and Mom's eyes practically pop out of her head as I took a seat and reached for the carafe. I didn't say anything as I poured yet another cup of coffee. My dad watched me make it just the way I liked it, and I think Mom's eye started twitching from the silence. Just as I took a sip, he said, "A shelter?"

"Yup."

"Holly, honey, are you sure?"

"Yes, Mother."

Mom and dad shared a look, a million things passing between the two of them. Dad reached for her hand, and she intertwined her fingers with his. I eyed their joined hands for a minute. Her dainty fingers so different from his equally delicate ones. Her's being small and slim from years of being a house-wife. His being quick and steady, but small enough to fit under a child's ribcage. Finally, Dad broke the silence and brought my attention back to him. "Ok."

I glanced between the two of them. "Ok?"

Mom nodded. "If that's what you want."

I hesitated, waiting for the shoe to drop. This had come completely out of left field, yet they caught the fly ball like it was a game of toss. They both went back to their breakfast and I frowned. Maybe they hadn't heard me? "I want to open a shelter for women, so I am going to business school." I enunciated each word carefully, slowly.

"Have you applied?" Dad smoothed a newspaper out on the table and didn't bother looking up.

"I heard the University of Georgia is amazing." Mom dropped a sugar cube in her tea and glanced at me with a soft smile.

I had expected a fight. Or at least some discontent. Their easy acceptance was mildly off-putting. Maybe they were just glad their daughter wasn't languishing in the house? Or were tired of seeing a zombified, overly-caffeinated heathen wandering around aimlessly in fuzzy pajama pants? Whatever. I wasn't about to look a gift horse in the mouth. I had a ramshackle business plan, and a college admission essay to write. I headed back to my room, grabbing a piece of toast on my way and firing off a text to Maria with my free hand.

Me: Lunch?
Maria: She lives!
Me: I was thinking Mama's.
Maria: It's been 84 years....
Me: Maria.
Maria: I thought she was all but lost...
Me: OMFG
Maria: LOL love you...give me a few and I will meet you there. Diego will probably tag along, if that's all right? He is overbearing to say the least now that the baby is gonna be here soon.
Me: You say that as if he hasn't always been overbearing.
Maria: Meh, I think it's sweet.
Me: If you say so. Meet in an hour?
Maria: Yup!

I tossed my phone down on the bed and headed for the shower. God knows I needed one. Now that I had an actual plan in place, my brain seemed to have calmed down a bit. Leaving the house didn't seem like such an impossible task. I let the hot water run over me, hoping it would wash the last of my worries down the drain. I dressed carefully, even applying a bit of makeup before heading back downstairs. My dad had already left for the hospital but I found Mom mid soon-to-be-forgotten crafting project in the sun room.

"Hey, I'm going to grab lunch with Maria."

Mom angrily shook the tangled ball of yarn, frowning at it like she was appalled by its audacity to not cooperate. She barely glanced up at me. "Ok, sweetie. Have fun, tell her I said hi."

Outside, I cringed when I was buffeted by the summer heat and hurried towards the carport where poor Sally had languished these last few weeks.

She roared to life like she was eager to get back on the road and I left tread marks as I spun tires out of the driveway, something I was sure Mom would get on to me for later. I passed the Saints' clubhouse on the way, admiring the work they had done in the last few weeks. I spotted Mr. Greyson in the parking lot and he waved as I drove by. I hadn't really gotten to know him, but I knew he was like an uncle to Dalton and Mac, so I honked in reply.

Not too long after, I pulled into the parking lot of Momma Laverne's. I spotted Diego's beat-up Nissan he had borrowed from his mom to help Maria get around. Sure enough, they were at a booth close to the kitchen and Maria smiled at me when I walked through the door. I went to slide in across from them but stopped right before I nearly landed in Dalton's lap. He gave me a cheeky grin and winked. "Hey, it's all good if you want to have a seat."

I frowned at him and went to grab a chair from a nearby table but was stopped by Mac on Dalton's other side. He shoved his brother from the booth and gave me a friendly half smile before nodding at the seat next to him. Dalton took the chair from me and flipped it around, resting his arms on the back of it. Maria was seated almost sideways on the opposite side of the booth, her back against Diego's chest and incredibly prominent belly straining the cloth of her shirt. "Ignore the party-crashing oaf, *hermana*. Diego texted Mac, figured we could have a nice little get-together, but someone is evidently home for the weekend."

Dalton raised his hands in surrender. "Hey, I can leave. Just thought y'all would be missing me."

Mac shook his head and Diego threw an empty straw wrapper at him. Maria pushed my tea towards me, half sweet and half unsweet, just how I liked it. I accepted it eagerly before reaching for a biscuit off the plate in front of us. Before coming to Georgia, biscuits weren't a snack or even an appetizer. They were flavorless, often dry, and all together just sad. But Momma's biscuits were fluffy, buttery pillows and I could've happily eaten ten of them. Drizzling honey on one, I took a bite before raising an eyebrow inquisitively at Maria, who was staring at me.

She shrugged, shifting in a hopeless attempt to find a more comfortable position. "I'm just glad to see you out of the house. Thought maybe you were gonna die in there."

"Yeah, it's like a certain guy who just happens to be a friend of ours left and took your extroverted-ness with him." Dalton popped nearly a whole biscuit in his mouth before waggling his brows at me.

"Ok, one, extroverted-ness isn't a word and, two, he has nothing to do with it. I was trying to figure out what I wanted to do with my life. Like all responsible soon-to-be adults."

"Sure, sure."

I glared at him but before I could come up with a retort, Maria said, "So, did you?"

"Did I what?"

"Figure out your next steps." She shifted again, and Diego wrapped a comforting arm around her shoulders and kissed the top of her head. Offering her a biscuit, he turned his attention to me, and suddenly I was stage shy as I realized they were all staring at me.

"Actually, yeah. I'm going to apply to UGA."

Dalton threw his hands in the air. "Oh yeah! Roomies! Go Dawgs! Uga, Uga!"

We all stared at him, and he gave an abashed grin. Mac shook his head before asking, "What major?"

"Business. I want to open one when I graduate." I wasn't ready to tell them my plans yet. Maybe Maria. Maybe later.

Maria squealed and clapped her hands together. "That's so cool. Will you be able to start with Dalton?"

Dalton had already been to Athens and back a few times, knee deep in football and team bonding shit. I looked over at him and he mouthed, "Uga, Uga!"

I rolled my eyes and reached for another biscuit. "I doubt it. Spring, if I get in."

"Oh, you'll get in." Diego gave me a friendly grin, and I surprised myself when I returned it. Just then, Momma made her way over with a tray laden with food. She laid out the feast, Dalton eyeing it like a man half starved, and winked at me.

"Hey, honey. Haven't seen you in a hot minute. I've missed that pretty face. How's my girl?"

"What about my pretty face?" Dalton said around a mouthful of fries, earning a grimace from the table and a stern look from Momma. He resumed attacking his burger like it owed him lunch money.

"Hey Momma, looking good!"

"Don't I know it." She winked at me and sashayed her more than ample hips. "Now before we were interrupted, you were fixing to tell me what was on that big, beautiful brain."

"Actually, I was just telling them that I'm going to apply to UGA. Business school."

"Go Dawgs! Sic 'Em! Woof! Woof! Woof!" This time, Mac threw a piece of fried okra at Dalton's head and frowned at him.

"Oh, that's right. Get it, girl!" She beamed at me. "You are going to go far, sweetie." She turned her attention to Maria. "Hey there little mama, how are we feeling?"

"I need a good lawyer so I can serve up an eviction notice." Diego handed her a glass of water, and she took a sip before saying, "I love her, but I need her out."

"You have a name yet?"

"No ma'am, just waiting till I hold her. See what feels right."

"That's a good plan, baby. Good plan. It'll be here before ya know it. Yall enjoy your food, if you haven't already inhaled it." She ruffled Dalton's hair before heading back to the kitchen.

I eyed my chicken fried steak eagerly and tucked into the deliciousness that was Momma Laverne's cooking. A comfortable silence settled over the table. My mind was still racing, going over a list of things I needed to do to get in to UGA. But this kind of racing was more peaceful, less hectic.

"It's nice having the gang back together. Look at us. Adults and shit." Dalton stretched in his chair, having demolished his cheeseburger.

Mac rolled his eyes. "Y'all are not nearly old enough to be called adults."

Dalton frowned at him. "Oh, but you are old man?"

Mac flipped him off, and Maria laughed. An easy banter started up, and I half listened as I ate. Until a certain name was brought up. My traitorous ears perked up and I looked up, reaching for my tea.

"Yeah, I haven't heard from him but that's typical, I think?"

"I got a letter, like once. Letting me know he wasn't dead but kinda wished he was."

"He should be back towards the end of September, right? October, at the latest?"

"Pretty sure."

"Gawd, I miss his ornery ass. Nobody tell him I said that shit, though." Dalton fixed the table with a glare and Diego chortled.

"Jackson's coming back?" Everyone looked at me as I tried to force the words to be completely nonchalant. I glanced at Maria and the slight smile I saw on her face told me she wasn't fooled.

Mac nodded, "Basic is thirteen weeks. Then MOS. Then he'll be back for a bit before he goes to more training. From what I understand. Mom's throwing him a welcome home party."

"Yeah, she's crazy excited. Still like, over two months away and she's already planning a menu. BBQ, by the way. If anyone is interested. Mom is sending Dad to get a brisket from that butcher she likes. Two hour drive. For a piece of meat."

Diego opened his mouth to say something, but just then, Maria groaned and made a slight whimpering sound as she closed her eyes. The entire table froze, and she startled a little when she opened them back up and found us all staring at her.

"*Mi corazon?*" Diego's eyes were a mask of worry, but she shooshed him.

"I'm fine, everyone. Promise. Braxton Hicks. They're a bitch." Diego bent closer to her ear, whispering Spanish and she reached behind her head, placing a hand on his neck. Dalton cleared his throat and started clearing plates from the table. I stood, and walked to kneel by Maria. She was seated facing the end of the booth, her back resting against Diego's side. I could see the pain and exhaustion in her eyes. "I'm fine, *hermana*. I promise."

I reached for her, placing a hand on her belly and smiling when I felt a gentle kick in response. "Hey Lil Bit, you causing your momma some grief? That's not very nice." Maria put her hand over mine and squeezed gently. Mac and Dalton had cleared the table, taking plates to the kitchen, but returned with several pieces of pie in to-go containers. "You, and me, pizza night before Lil Bit gets here?" She nodded eagerly and held both hands out to me. I pulled her to her feet, steadying her as she wobbled a bit.

She wrapped me in an awkward hug and said, "Yes, absolutely. My place? It's not much but...I wanna show it off."

"Hell yeah, I'm down with that. You can help me edit my admissions essay. You were always better at writing than me." She smiled at me and I bid everyone goodbye before grabbing a piece of pie and heading for the door. Momma hollered a farewell from the kitchen, telling me to behave myself, and I winced as I stepped from the cool interior of the restaurant into the smothering heat of a Georgia summer. As I slid behind the wheel of Sally, I put the AC on full blast and, despite my best efforts, thought of Jackson. I don't know why I was so shocked he would be coming home. It made sense. I guess I had just wrapped myself in a little cocoon or something.

Whatever. Not like it was a big deal. Whether he was here or there, he had made it clear that he wanted nothing to do with me, so, my confused heart could just take a chill pill. I had bigger things to focus on.

When I got back home, I shouted a hello to Mom as I headed up the stairs. Before I got too far, she stopped me. "Hey! How was lunch?"

I turned to her, frowning when I realized she had something behind her back. "Good. Everyone says hi."

She nodded and then whipped out a little red bag that was overflowing with glittery gold tissue paper. I turned, heading back down the stairs and grabbed it from her. "Turns out Georgia is really big on school pride. It was surprisingly easy to rustle up some goodies while you were out!"

"I was only gone for a bit..." I trailed off as I pulled a black hoodie from the bag. "Georgia" was emblazoned across the front in bold red lettering. I dug further, pulling out a fat stuffed bulldog and a rather hideous hat with a big red pompom on top. "Mom, I haven't even gotten in yet."

"Oh, pish-posh. Technicalities. You're gonna do great things. I always knew it."

I eyed her for a minute, not missing the irony that Momma Laverne had literally just said the same thing. She waited for me to say something, but I couldn't help but wonder if she had really let me down or…if I had just been a hurt kid looking for someone to blame. I don't know. Call it my era of healing. But I was happy. I had friends, a future, and, whether I liked it or not, parents who loved me and were stubbornly a part of my life. I held up the stuffed dog, "Uga, Uga."

Mom tilted her head, "Huh?"

"Something Dalton wouldn't shut up about. Their mascot, Uga."

"Oh."

"Thank you, Mom. I appreciate it. And…I'm sorry. That it's taken me so long. To, you know, see it."

She blinked furiously, and clasped her hands in front of her to hide the tremble, "See what?"

"That you love me."

Her bottom lip trembled, but she didn't make a move to embrace me. "Always. And I'm sorry too."

I hesitated before taking the last few steps and embracing her. I genuinely couldn't remember the last time I had willing initiated a hug with my mom. But, maybe, this was how healing happened. Not loud, not sudden. Just small, little moments that fixed what was broken behind the scenes. "I'm going to go work on my essay, get started on the application."

She rubbed my back and a singular tear slipped down her cheek as I headed to my room. I had my pie in one hand, my mom's gift bag in the other. Time to focus on the future. Make something of it. Of myself. I tossed the bag down on my bed and sent another text to Maria.

Me: Pizza, Friday?

Her response was immediate, as always.

Maria: If I last that long. Be prepared to take me to the hospital. Might want to put some plastic covers on Sally's seat.

Me: Hey, I love Lil Bit but we are going to have beef if she messes up my car.

Maria: LOL I'll be sure to let her know Auntie Holly's car is off limits.

My thumb hovered over the screen before I sent my next message.

Me: I think my mom and I are getting better.

Maria: Oh yeah?

Me: Yeah, whole ooey gooey moment.

Maria: That's great. Healing is good. I should know. Still working on my end though.

Me: Yeah.

Maria: Imma take a nap. Diego went back to his mom's for a bit, so it's quiet here for once.

Me: Ok, love you. Get some sleep.

Maria: Don't have to tell me twice. Love you.

I grabbed my laptop from my desk, settling crisscrossed applesauce on my bed. Scrolling through UGA's website, I gnawed on my lip as I summoned the courage to open my email. I was surprised to find a response from Undergraduate Admissions already. Like I suspected, it was too late for fall enrollment but I could start in spring. I went through the to-do list they shared with me and decided to start with the shorter of the two required essays. After a few hours, I was eating the pecan pie when my dad knocked on the door. I looked up at him as he let himself in.

"Hey, bug. Whatcha up to?"

I gestured to my laptop with my pie. "Admission essays."

"Fun, fun. Heard you and your mom talked."

"Yeah, sort of."

"That's great, bug. Keep it up."

I smiled at him as he turned to leave. "Let me know if there is anything you need."

A few minutes later, I heard my mother's laughter peal throughout the house as I worked on the paragraph that was giving me the most trouble. For the first time in a very long time, I was excited for the future. And when I finally came down from my room to join them for dinner, there was a lightness to my parents that hadn't been there before.

Chapter Fifteen

⚜

⸸ **Holly** ⸸

Friday evening I found myself juggling two large pizzas, a little gift bag, and a file folder that contained my admissions essays as I nudged my way into Maria's house. The place was tiny—one bedroom, one bath, a kitchen you could sneeze in and hit three walls at once—but she'd made it cozy in that Maria way. The thin carpet was spotless, the walls freshly painted in a soft gray, and there were purple daisies in a vase on the island, holding court like royalty over the clutter of mail and prenatal vitamins. A massive white Dutch oven sat on the stove like she was preparing to feed a battalion instead of just herself.

Maria was sprawled on the couch, her belly rising like a small planet under her T-shirt. She made a valiant effort to roll upright when she saw me, but I shook my head.

"Girl, stop before you hurt yourself. Where are the plates?"

She flopped back down with a groan. "Paper plates. Cabinet next to the stove."

I flipped the lid of the pizza box open, plates in hand. "One or two pieces?"

"Heartburn says one. Stomach says two."

I handed her a plate, balancing it on her belly like a makeshift TV tray, and settled into the armchair. For a few blessed minutes, we just ate. The only sound was Maria's occasional burp and the muffled groan that followed.

She broke first. "I am so ready to not be pregnant. Whoever said pregnancy is beautiful is a liar."

I smirked around my slice. "It'll be beautiful when you're holding Lil Bit in your arms. Right now, yeah…not so much."

She made a face but didn't argue. Then she perked up. "Hey—did you bring your packet thing?"

"It's right there." I jerked my chin at the folder. "Rewrote that damn essay about thirty times. If they don't let me in after this, I'm suing for emotional distress."

"I'm sure it's fantastic."

"Or it's garbage and I'm about to waste the last three months of my life." I tossed my crust back into the box. "Submitting this is the last step, and then…waiting game."

Maria reached for the coffee table to drop her plate but missed completely. It flopped onto the floor. She sighed like the world had just ended.

I rolled my eyes, scooped it up, and tossed it. On my way back, I grabbed my essay and the gift bag. Shoving both into her lap, I squeezed onto the couch beside her.

Her brows arched. "What's this?"

"Just some essentials. You know—for when you're officially someone's mom and have zero time to shower."

She dug into the tissue paper like a kid at Christmas. Out came fuzzy socks, a giant chocolate bar, a self-care kit, and a mug that read "Good Moms Say Bad Words." She laughed so hard her belly wobbled like a water balloon. "You are ridiculous. And I love it."

"Good. Now balance that out by tearing me to shreds." I handed her the essay.

Maria put on an exaggeratedly serious face, pushing up invisible glasses like she was about to deliver a presidential address. She cleared her throat loudly. "'Education is the doorway to a brighter future,'" she declaimed, voice booming. "Really, *hermana*? A *doorway*? What are you, a motivational poster from 1997?"

I groaned and face-planted into a pillow. "It sounded better in my head!"

"Mm-hmm." She flipped the page with a dramatic flourish. "'With dedication, I can achieve anything I set my mind to.' Classic. Very Miss America. Do you also dream of world peace?"

I hurled a pizza crust at her. "Keep reading. It gets better. I swear."

She grinned but continued, her voice softening as she reached the middle. "'As a survivor of sexual assault, I understand that resilience isn't just a word—it's a fight. College is my chance to reclaim the future that was almost stolen from me.'"

Her hand dropped, eyes shining with unshed tears. "Oh, Holly…"

I jabbed a finger at her. "Don't you *dare* cry. You're basically a human water balloon right now. If you cry, I cry, and then it's Niagara Falls in here."

She sniffled, laughing wetly. "It's just pregnancy hormones."

"Uh-huh." My cheeks burned, but I forced a smirk. "Finish it before I regret letting you touch it."

She shook her head fondly, eyes darting back to the page. "You don't give yourself enough credit, you know? You sound strong. Like someone who knows who she is."

"Fake it till you make it." I picked at a piece of pepperoni. "Now, are you gonna keep roasting me, or—"

A sharp intake of breath cut me off and I looked over at her. Maria's eyes had widened to the size of saucer plates, and she was staring at her belly.

"Uh… Holly?"

"What?" My stomach dropped at her tone.

"Either I just peed myself…or your essay broke my water."

The slice slid out of my hand, landing face-down on the carpet. "Oh my God. Oh my God!"

Her deadpan stare did nothing to calm me. "Don't panic."

"I'm not panicking," I lied, already tripping over myself to grab the hospital bag.

"Ok. Hospital bag—where is it?"

"Hall closet." She winced, shifting on the couch. "And for the love of God, hurry."

I bolted, grabbed the duffel, and came back to find her struggling to stand. "How do you plan on fitting me into your Barbie car?"

"Sally is not a Barbie car." I hooked an arm under her. "She is a *classic*. And she's about to be the classiest ambulance in town."

The car in question sat in the driveway gleaming in the light, all curves and chrome, smug as hell. My pride and joy. She smelled faintly of old leather and motor oil, with a dash of vanilla from the air freshener I hung off the mirror last month. She was built for long drives with the windows down and a killer playlist, not chauffeuring a woman who looked like she was smuggling a watermelon under her ribs. I pursed my lips, Maria leaning heavily against my side as we both contemplated the beautiful car we were about to soak in baby juice.

Maria squinted at Sally like she was the enemy. "Your car is—"

I held up my hands defensively. "Don't drag Sally into this. She didn't ask to be born that way."

"She wasn't designed to haul a pregnant woman in active labor. Holly, there's barely enough space for *you* in there."

"Relax. She's got plenty of room." I hurried to pop the passenger door, the hinges groaning like they knew we were about to attempt the impossible. "Ok, here's the plan: you slide in sideways, butt-first, then pivot your legs—"

Maria gave me a flat look. "Do I look like I can *pivot*?"

"Fine. Less pivot, more…shove."

Her laugh came out strangled, half a groan. "If you start quoting Ross Geller at me, I swear to God—"

But we tried it anyway. She braced her hands on the roof, angled herself sideways, and we both realized instantly this was going to be a full-contact sport. Her belly bumped the dash, her hip caught on the seat frame, and the seatbelt buckle jabbed her thigh.

"This car," Maria grunted, breath coming in sharp bursts, "was built for cigarettes and bad decisions, not a nine-pound baby trying to escape."

"Don't insult her when she's doing her best!" I huffed, putting my shoulder into it. The sight of me shoving my pregnant best friend into my vintage Mustang probably belonged on some kind of "what not to do" PSA, but damn it, we were committed now.

"Ow, Holly!"

"Sorry! Almost there! Just—pivot, for the love of God!"

With a final grunt, she popped into the seat like a cork into a bottle. Both of us sat there panting like we'd just wrestled a bear.

Maria let her head fall back dramatically. "Comfortable," she deadpanned. "Like a turkey in a toaster oven."

"Perfect fit," I said, trying to catch my breath.

She cracked one eye open at me. "If I give birth in this seat…you are never getting that out. You know that right?"

I attempted to click her seatbelt into place, gave up the fight, and patted Sally's dash. "Don't listen to her, baby girl. You've got this. Just get us there and I'll give you a wax and polish after."

Maria groaned. "If you talk to your car one more time, I'm walking."

"Good luck with that." I started the engine, and Sally purred like she was eager to see her mission through.

And then, of course, the second I pulled out of the driveway, brake lights flared ahead of me. I slammed the brakes, Maria screeched, and the Mustang fishtailed just enough to make my heart leap into my throat.

"Barbie car," Maria hissed, clutching the dash as another contraction hit.

"We're alive, aren't we?" I shot her a grin, though my hands white-knuckled. "Totally fine."

I peeled out of the driveway with one hand on the wheel and the other dialing Diego. He picked up instantly.

"The eagle is landing!" I shouted. Next to me, Maria propped her knees on the dash and cradled her belly.

"Huh?"

"The chicken is flying the coop!"

Maria groaned, clutching the dash. "My baby is not a bird!"

There was another beat of silence. Then Diego's voice cracked: "…wait. Oh fuck."

"Now he gets it," I muttered.

A clattering sound followed, and his voice went faint as if he'd dropped the phone. "I'm going to be a father! I'm a dad! A dad!"

I rolled my eyes, but Maria's soft laugh seemed to ease her pain, even if just for a moment.

A second later, Dalton's voice cut in. "Idiot dropped his phone. And left it. I'll drop it by the hospital later. Good luck? Does this make me an uncle?"

I looked down at my phone on my lap and started to respond.

"Focus on the road, Holly!" Maria hissed, another contraction apparently hitting as her pretty face screwed like a twist of pain.

"I *am* focusing!" I shot back, though my hands were shaking on the wheel. "Mostly."

By the time I screeched up to the hospital, my nerves were sparking like live wires. I half dragged, half guided Maria through the automatic doors. We got her into a room, and suddenly everything blurred—nurses wheeling monitors, snapping on gloves, checking charts. I stuck to Maria's side like Velcro, clutching the little cup of ice chips like it was sacred.

Normally, this was Maria's role. She was the calm one, the sunshine. She could make a thunderstorm feel like a spring shower with just a smile. But labor had twisted that sunshine into lightning, sharp and relentless. Every time a contraction hit, she clenched her jaw and let out a noise somewhere between a growl and a scream, and I realized she wasn't going to be able to talk me through this one.

Which meant the job fell to me. God help us all.

"Ok, ok, remember what that slightly mildewy doula said," I said, shoving an ice chip at her. "In and out, steady breaths, channel your inner zen goddess—"

Her eyes flicked open long enough to pin me, and through gritted teeth she whispered, "*Hermana*... you're babbling."

That one word stopped me cold. Babbling. Me. Holly McCarthy, professional smartass and world-class sulker, not known for running my mouth unless it was dripping with sarcasm. And here I was, rattling on like a bad infomercial because the silence felt like it might kill us both.

"Right," I muttered quickly, pressing the cool cloth to her forehead instead. "Deluxe comfort package it is. Handholding, forehead dabbing, and questionable pep talks. All included, free of charge."

Another contraction slammed through her, and she reached out like a drowning woman, grabbing my hand. Bones cracked. I hissed.

"Ok, ow, bones are supposed to stay inside skin—but you're doing amazing!"

Her face twisted, then softened for half a second. "You're… something, you know that?"

"Exactly. That's my gift." I leaned down and brushed damp strands of hair off her forehead, feeling her sweat stick to my fingers. "You're welcome."

She let out a shaky laugh that broke into a groan, and my chest squeezed. This wasn't the Maria I knew—the one who could cook for twenty bikers without breaking a sweat, who could talk Diego down from a temper faster than anyone else. This was raw Maria. Human Maria. And it scared the hell out of me, but it also made me fiercely determined.

"I got you," I whispered, so low only she could hear it under the beeping monitors and shuffling nurses. "You're not alone. Not for one second. Even if you break every bone in my hand, I'm right here."

Her lips trembled into something like a smile. "Auntie Holly in training."

"Damn right." My voice cracked on the words, but I grinned anyway.

Another contraction ripped through her, and she practically tried to climb off the bed, dragging me with her. I scrambled, pressed the cloth to her forehead, and started babbling again before she could sink into the pain.

"Ok, ok, let's think of something else. Pizza. Imagine pizza. No, wait, not pizza, you'd puke. Puppies. Imagine a thousand tiny golden retriever puppies running around in sweaters. Or, no, wait, better—Diego trying to change a diaper. He's gagging. He's crying. He's screaming for backup—"

Maria's laugh broke free, wet and shaky, but real. "Stop—you're going to make me lose focus—"

"Good," I said, relief flooding me. "Focus on laughing, not on crushing my knuckles into dust."

She groaned but held tighter. Another wave came, and I swear my hand was going to be mangled forever, but I didn't care. I kept talking, kept joking, because it was the only thing I could give her. My words. My stubborn refusal to let her do this alone.

Her face twisted, eyes bright with tears, but through it all, she still managed to squeeze out, "You're a good friend."

I swallowed the lump in my throat and forced a grin. "Takes one to know one, sunshine." And for a split second, even in the chaos, her smile made the whole room feel brighter.

Then Diego burst in, wide-eyed and frantic.

"Diego!" I pointed to Maria's free hand. "You get that side!"

He rushed to Maria's side, nearly tripping over the cords on the floor. She grabbed both our hands, eyes blazing. "Neither of you are allowed to pass out before I do this."

Labor was chaos. Maria shouted, Diego paled, and I tried desperately not to look *down there*.

Don't look.

Don't look.

Ohmigawd, I looked.

And now I'm going to be sick. I may need to go to therapy. *Again.*

"Ok, push!" a nurse encouraged.

What even *was* that—holy shit, was that a head? That was a head. That was a whole human head trying to crawl out of my best friend.

Nope. Nope nope nope.

I snapped my gaze back to Maria's face, but it was too late, the image was seared into my brain forever. I leaned in. "You've got this, Maria. One more big—"

She roared, crushing our hands. I nearly blacked out from the pressure. Diego's eyes widened as the joints in his head popped but still he murmured words of comfort in Spanish.

And then, suddenly, there it was. A wriggling, crying, absolutely horrifying little miracle.

"Ohmigawd this is so cool," I whispered.

"I'm going to vomit," Diego groaned.

"Don't you dare," Maria snapped, sweaty and glowing, clutching her baby to her chest. Diego suddenly seemed to forget all about his nausea as he leaned towards the tiny human loudly announcing its presence to the world. A perfect little girl. My throat tightened as I watched Maria cry and laugh all at once.

The room finally quieted after the storm. Machines beeped softly, nurses shuffled out with tired smiles, and Maria lay in the bed, cradling a tiny bundle swaddled so tight it looked like a burrito. Diego hovered close, eyes shining like he'd just been handed the entire galaxy.

And me? I stood off to the side, trying to wrap my head around the fact that the thing squirming in Maria's arms had been inside her half an hour ago.

It was…incredible. Terrifying. Beautiful. All at once.

The sight of Maria's face, sweaty, tear-streaked, glowing with relief, made my throat tighten. She looked like herself again. Sunshine Maria, but brighter. Stronger. The storm had passed and left something holy in its wake.

A nurse motioned to me, and before I could argue, I had a baby in my arms. A whole human. Tiny, warm, smelling faintly like milk and hospital sheets. She blinked up at me, her eyes dark and cloudy, little fingers curling instinctively around mine. She looked so much like her mama.

My chest clenched so hard I thought I might actually keel over.

"Hi," I whispered, because what the hell else do you say to a brand-new person? "I'm Auntie Holly. I make bad decisions and worse jokes, but you'll love me, I promise."

She made a sound that was somewhere between a squeak and a sigh, and my heart turned inside out.

Nope. Not happening. I could *not* be getting emotional over a baby burrito named Jewel. That was too on the nose. Too perfect.

I shoved her gently back into Diegos's waiting arms, my hands trembling. I could hear Maria in the shower, and headed out to the hall.

My brain betrayed me with a flash of an image I hadn't asked for: broad shoulders in a pressed uniform, strong hands holding a baby like it was made of glass. A soft smile tugging at lips that weren't meant for softness.

My stomach flipped.

Absolutely not.

I shook my head hard, like I could rattle the thought loose. "Oh hell no," I muttered. "Brain, you can keep your little fantasy family slideshow to yourself. I've got plans. College. A business."

Still, the ghost of that image lingered, tucked somewhere deep and traitorous. The fluorescent lights of the hallway hummed overhead, the linoleum gleamed sterile and too bright, and the adrenaline still buzzed in my veins like I'd swallowed a beehive. I leaned against the wall and pressed my palms to my eyes.

Nineteen. That's all I was. Soon to be twenty. Kids weren't in my game plan. Not now. Maybe not ever. I wanted independence. A degree. A business with my name on the sign. A life that was mine alone before I even thought about sharing it with anyone else.

But the sight of Maria with her baby, Diego crying quietly at her side—it carved a soft ache into me I didn't know what to do with. Like I was peeking through a window into a life that wasn't mine, and part of me wasn't sure if I wanted to look away.

I snorted at myself, trying to shake it off. "Get it together, McCarthy. You've got essays to submit and pizza to eat, not diapers to change." Straightening, I squared my shoulders and forced my feet back toward Maria's room. Because the truth was, I wasn't ready for that life.

But I was ready to stand beside Maria as she stepped into hers.

And maybe, just maybe, someday I'd figure out the rest.

Chapter Sixteen

‡ **Holly** ‡

September blurred into spit-up, sleepless nights, and the kind of diaper blowouts that deserved their own crime scene tape. I'd submitted my college application at the end of August, hit "send," and nearly threw up in the process. Now all I could do was wait. And stalk my mailbox. And maybe threaten it once or twice under my breath in between stress-eating Oreos.

Every afternoon, I trudged down the driveway, checking for the fat envelope that would change my life. Instead, I got bills, junk ads, and once, a glossy pamphlet about tractor parts. Nothing screams "bright academic future" like spark plugs and hay balers.

With my application sent off, all I could do was wait, and waiting was torture. I didn't have the patience for it, so I threw myself into the one distraction available: Maria and Jewel. Which meant spending a lot more time at the clubhouse than I ever expected. And it wasn't just Jewel who got welcomed like royalty. Yeah, the guys all lined up to take turns holding her like she was the crown jewel of the Steel Saints (pun intended), but what threw me off was how they treated me. These were gruff, scarred, leather cut wearing bikers, and yet every time I walked in, someone shoved a soda in my hand, someone else pulled up a chair, and before I knew it, I was smack in the middle of the chaos. Like...family. The kind of family I didn't exactly ask for, but maybe needed.

Dalton, of course, decided to push this whole newfound bond thing further. Which was how I found myself lounging in an overstuffed armchair as he unveiled a rather hair-brained idea. "You're around us enough," he said, smirking. "You should learn to ride."

"That's a terrible idea," Mac muttered from across the room.

"Best idea," Dalton insisted.

"Worst," Mac fired back.

Maria and Diego exchanged a look, equal parts amused and horrified. Maria bounced Jewel on her hip, eyes dancing.

Dalton shoved a helmet at me. "C'mon, Holly."

Against all logic, I put it on. Dalton ran me through a rushed tutorial—clutch, throttle, brake—while Mac muttered about life insurance policies. As Dalton talked, word spread around the place about what was about to go down. A California princess about to ride a motorcycle for the first time? Not a show you wanted to miss, apparently. Even Hannah had meandered out onto the porch, wiping her hands on a tea towel.

After a bit, Dalton asked if I'd got it.

"I think so?" He stepped back, and gestured for me to go. Then I twisted the throttle.

The bike rocketed forward, straight toward the warehouse wall. Bikers scattered; I heard Diego roared with laughter. Maria squealed, and Jewel decided to join in the noise and squealed too. Dalton yelled, "Clutch! Clutch!"

I screamed. Dalton lunged, grabbed the handlebars, and yanked them sideways at the last second. We skidded to a stop inches from destruction. For a beat, silence. Then the room erupted with laughter.

Dalton patted my helmet, wheezing with laughter. "Not bad—for a first try."

"First and last try! I almost Road Runnered through your wall!" I shouted, yanking the helmet off.

Mac rubbed his temples. "Told you this was a horrible fucking idea."

Diego grinned. "Best entertainment we've had in weeks."

I wanted to be mad, but instead I found myself laughing too—louder than I'd laughed in months.

One quiet afternoon at Maria's place, Maria had finally crashed hard on the couch, mouth open, snoring soft little whistles. I crept over to Jewel's bassinet. She was wide awake, gurgling, fists waving at nothing.

"Hey, Lil Bit," I whispered, scooping her up. She was warm and heavy in my arms, and I couldn't help myself—I lifted her like Rafiki presenting Simba to the Pride Lands. "Behold! The new queen of the Steel Saints!"

Jewel blinked, then let out a bubbling giggle that hit me square in the chest. Spit bubbles clung to her chin, her tiny fists batting the air triumphantly.

I lowered her close, my voice fierce. "Listen here, tiny human. I don't do diapers. I don't do lullabies. But I swear on Sally, if anyone ever hurts you, I will murder them and hide the body where even the FBI can't find it."

Jewel squealed, delighted, as if she approved of my murder vows.

"Good," I muttered, bouncing her gently. "Glad we understand each other."

I sat with her, rocking gently, my thoughts drifting. If I felt this protective over one baby, what would it mean to protect women and kids who had no one else? Survivors like me, like the ones I'd read about, who needed a safe place to land? Jewel wasn't just a baby—she was proof. Proof that new beginnings were possible. And that was what I wanted my future to be about. Not diapers or midnight feedings, but giving people their second chance.

A knock came at the front door, and I startled so hard I almost dropped Jewel. Maria woke up with a very lady-like grunt and stretched before heading for the door. In swept a tall, lithe woman with red hair and blue eyes, balancing a casserole dish, a canvas tote, and a basket of baby supplies, as if she were single-handedly provisioning a small country.

Maria lit up. "Hannah!"

I freeze. Oh. Shit.

Because this wasn't just any grandma barging in with casseroles and Pampers. This was *Hannah Mills*. Mac and Dalton's mother. The woman people mentioned in the clubhouse with reverence and a little fear. The one I tended to avoid, though I would never admit it.

Hannah leaned down to kiss Maria's cheek, eyes sharp and kind all at once. She set her haul on the counter, and I swear half the kitchen rattled under the weight.

"New mom care package," Hannah announced briskly. "Soup, burp cloths, lanolin cream—don't ask, just use it. And a little something for you too."

Maria's eyes glistened as she rooted through the bags, laughing softly. "You didn't have to—"

"Of course I did," Hannah cut her off. "You're family. We take care of family."

Her gaze shifted then, landing on me. Jewel squirmed in my arms, drooling happily down my shoulder. Hannah's eyebrow arched. "Hi, Holly. Seems you can't outrun me forever. I've heard a lot about you."

Shit. I had been caught.

"Hi," I manage. "All lies you've heard. Unless they were flattering, then absolutely true."

Her mouth twitched, like I'd passed a test. She held out her arms. I hesitated, then surrendered Jewel carefully. Hannah settled the baby with practiced ease, kissed her forehead, then looked back at me.

"Maria told me a little about your plan."

Maria looked up at her name, pausing her hunt for a vase to put the pretty flowers Hannah had brought in. "I hope that's ok."

My mouth went dry. "Uh…yeah. It's fine. Just college, you know. Hopefully. If the mailbox ever decides to cooperate."

Hannah smirked, but not unkindly. "And after that?"

I swallowed, glancing at Maria, who was watching me with an encouraging smile. "Well, actually. I…I've got this idea. A shelter. For women. And kids. Survivors. A place where people don't have to feel like they're broken."

The words tumbled out before I could stop them, and my cheeks burned. I hadn't really told a lot of people about this, outside of Maria and my parents. But something about Hannah just dragged it out of me. I waited for her to laugh, or pat me on the head, or tell me I was too young.

Instead, her expression sharpened. "Good. We need more women thinking that way. You've got passion, and Maria says you're smart." She leaned in slightly. "Don't wait until you're thirty. Start building now. Start small. Think big. You're not alone in this. Remember that."

Heat prickled behind my eyes. Someone was taking me seriously. Someone who wasn't Maria.

I nodded. "Ok. Yeah. I can do that."

Hannah's smile was fierce. "I know you can."

One night not long after, Hannah invited me out for dinner. Just the two of us. I thought it was going to be awkward—me sitting across from this fierce, no-nonsense woman who somehow ran circles around bikers twice her size—but it wasn't. We talked for hours. About school. About my essay. About the shelter I wanted to build one day. And instead of treating me like some kid with a pipe dream, Hannah leaned in like every word mattered.

She told me about grant programs, local nonprofits, and even women she knew who'd been through hell and back and could use a place like the one I was imagining. She sketched ideas on the back of a napkin, asked questions that made my brain spin in the best way, and by the time the waitress shooed us out for closing, I realized something: Hannah Mills was a force to be reckoned with and one hell of a lady to have on my side.

Weeks rolled on in a blur of baby duty, late-night bottles, and mailbox stalking. Every day when I got home from hanging out at the clubhouse or Maria's apartment, I'd check our box at the end of the driveway like it owed me money. Nothing. Bills. Flyers. Once, a pizza coupon that wasn't even valid anymore.

Then one Tuesday afternoon, there it was. A fat envelope, stamped "University of Georgia."

I froze on the gravel drive, heart slamming against my ribs. For a second, I just stared. Then I snatched it out, tore it open with shaking hands, and scanned the first line.

Congratulations. We are pleased to offer you admission to the University of Georgia...

My knees buckled. I reread it twice, three times, the words blurring until they finally stuck.

"I got in," I whispered. Then louder: "I got in!" I screeched for joy and danced a weird little jig. The neighbor's hound exploded into frantic barking across the road, and I laughed so hard I almost fell in the ditch. I tore up the porch steps, flung open the door, and nearly collided with my mom, who had come halfway down the hall at the noise.

"I got in!" I shout, waving the letter. "Mom, I got into UGA!"

Her face crumpled and she dropped the towel she was holding, pulling me into her arms, and for the first time in years, I let her. "Oh, baby. I'm so proud of you."

I swallowed hard. I hadn't heard that the day I told her what he did. But maybe we were both learning. Because after everything…her distance when I needed her most, the silence after the assault, all the ways she didn't show up, I needed to hear that more than anything. Getting into UGA wasn't the bravest thing I'd ever done. But maybe she was trying. Maybe we both were.

It wasn't a long moment. Her phone rang in the kitchen and she hurried off towards it. But it was enough. A stitch in a seam that had been frayed for years.

I tucked the letter to my chest, my whole body vibrating. I couldn't sit still. I needed to tell someone else—someone who would *get it*.

I fired off a text to Maria who confirmed she was still at the clubhouse, and so was Hannah.

Hannah Mills had shown up with casseroles and baby ointment and, somehow, with steel-backed belief in *me*. She'd taken me seriously when I said "shelter," when everyone else just smiled politely. She'd told me to start now. And now—I had a brick. A foundation.

The clubhouse was five minutes away. My legs felt like springs as I grabbed Sally's keys and ran out the door. She roared to life, and I flew down the back road, heart hammering in time with the engine. For once, I wasn't the screw-up. I wasn't the broken girl with sharp edges. I was a young woman with a future.

I don't think my feet even touched the ground as I sprinted up the clubhouse steps. The letter crinkled in my fist, and Sally still ticked hot in the lot, but I didn't care—I had news. The kind of news that made my chest feel too small for my ribs.

I shoved the door open and practically shouted it at the room. "I got in!" Heads turned. Conversations stopped. For one awful second, I wondered if maybe I'd overdone it. Then Maria shrieked, nearly toppling off her chair with Jewel in her arms, and Hannah beamed like she'd known all along.

"You did it!" Maria clapped and Jewel blew a spit bubble.

I waved the fat envelope over my head like it was a trophy. "Spring semester, baby! Athens is gonna have no idea what hit it."

Hannah crossed the room with that purposeful stride of hers and pulled me into a hug so fierce I thought she might crack my spine. "I knew you could. Didn't I say? Didn't I tell you?"

"Yes, ma'am, you did," I wheezed into her shoulder.

Dalton's voice rang out from behind the bar, dripping with mischief. "Well, look at us—college buddies."

I turned, narrowing my eyes. "College buddies?"

"Sure," he said, grinning, arms spread like it was obvious. "I'm on a football scholarship, psychology major. Same campus. Same stomping grounds. I'll even show you the best coffee spots so you don't flunk out first semester."

I snorted. "Oh please. If anything, I'll be tutoring you."

Dalton held a hand to his chest in mock offense. "Bold words from a late-start freshman. Guess we'll see who's carrying whose GPA."

The room bubbled with laughter and congratulations. Someone shoved a soda into my hand. Someone else slapped me on the back hard enough to make me stumble. Even Mac gave me a rare, approving nod from his corner.

Maria's eyes shone as she reached for me. "See? You were so worried, and look at you now."

"I was two seconds away from bribing the mailman," I admitted, flopping into the chair beside her. Jewel gurgled at me, fist jammed in her mouth.

"Your niece approves," Maria added, tilting the baby toward me.

"I'll forgive her for drooling on my shirt, then," I said, tickling Jewel's foot.

My whole body hummed with adrenaline, joy fizzing through me like soda bubbles. For once, the future didn't feel like a fog—it felt real. Concrete. Like something I could reach out and grab.

Hannah settled beside me, her expression softer than I'd ever seen it. "You've taken the first step, Holly. And now we start building. We'll make that shelter happen, one way or another."

My throat tightened, and I nodded quickly before I embarrassed myself by crying in front of a room full of bikers.

I was mid-ramble about course catalogs and dorm options when the door opened and somehow the loud room got even louder. I peered over the shoulders of the people closest to me...and froze. Then slowly stood.

Because Jackson Morgan was home.

The quarterback. The Marine. The boy who grew up in this clubhouse, the kid Hannah practically raised. He was back from basic, taller, sharper, his smile sparking the room like a flare.

The Saints roared his name. Men clapped him on the back, dragging him into hugs. Hannah's eyes shone, August beamed, and even Mac was smiling.

Thirteen weeks gone, and Jackson Morgan wasn't the boy who'd left. The buzzed haircut made his jaw look sharper, his shoulders broader. The uniform clung in all the right places— dress blues and muscle, a clean edge to everything about him. He filled the doorway like he owned it, sunlight haloing him from behind.

My brain short-circuited.

Holy hell.

He looked good. Too good. Unfair-to-humanity good. My stomach flipped in a way that made zero sense.

I couldn't move. Couldn't breathe. My acceptance letter crinkled in my fist as the whole room swirled around me, voices rising, laughter spilling. He was swallowed in embraces and slaps on the back, and still my feet stayed glued to the floor.

He laughed—deep, rougher than I remembered. Like the boy I'd sparred with had been sanded down into something steadier. A man.

And then his eyes found mine.

The sound around me dropped out. I was back on that porch thirteen weeks ago, his breath warm against my lips, his voice low and rough: *Don't. Don't start something you're not ready to finish.*

And then all the insanely confusing bullshit at the lake house.

He cut through the crowd, boots heavy on the clubhouse floor, shoulders filling every inch of that damn uniform. Everyone surged toward him like a tide—slaps on the back, shouts of "Semper fi!"—but his eyes stayed on me.

Great. Fantastic. Exactly what I needed: the human embodiment of unfinished business striding toward me like he owned the oxygen in the room.

I straightened, forcing my chin up. Defensive mode: *on.* "Well, well," I said loudly, before my throat could betray me. "Look who survived boot camp."

A ripple of laughter moved through the guys nearby. Jackson's mouth twitched, like he was trying not to grin. "Good to see you too, Malibu."

Malibu. Damn him. The nickname hit its mark, same as always, a lazy little reminder of every fight and almost-kiss we'd ever had.

I folded my arms, letting the acceptance letter crinkle loudly in my fist. "You missed a lot while you were off getting screamed at by men in funny hats. Jewel was born. Dalton nearly killed me teaching me to ride. Oh, and I got into college."

That landed—his smirk flickered, pride breaking through. "Yeah? Congratulations."

"Thanks," I said, tilting my chin. "Guess I'll be a Bulldog now too. You gonna be able to keep up with me?"

He cocked his head, watching me the way a cat watches a bird that thinks it's safe on a branch. "You always did run a little ahead, Malibu."

I glanced behind me, gauging the distance between the chair I had just vacated and where I now stood in case my legs were to give out. Because beneath the banter, beneath the armor, there was a heat in his voice that said he hadn't forgotten either—that night on the porch, that almost-kiss, that cut-short moment that had lived rent-free in my brain ever since.

So I did what I do best. My smile was sharp enough to draw blood. "Careful, Marine. Don't start something you're not ready to finish."

The words hit him like a slap and a dare at once. His eyes darkened, his jaw ticked, and for one suspended beat I thought maybe he'd close the distance and prove me wrong.

But then Hannah's voice cut in, proud and calm as ever, breaking the spell. "Boys, girls, simmer down. We celebrate Holly's acceptance *and* Jackson's return tonight. They've both earned it."

The crowd cheered, the moment broke, and I tried to remember how my lungs worked. Dalton immediately climbed onto a chair like some kind of overgrown toddler, waving his soda can overhead. "Ladies and gentlemen, may I present—our resident genius and our shiny new Marine!"

The room whooped, Maria laughing so hard Jewel startled in her arms. Even Mac cracked a grin, which around here was basically the equivalent of a standing ovation. Dalton pointed his can at me, then at Jackson. "Now, I'm not saying there's a competition brewing, but…one of you is gonna trip over your own ego first semester."

"Semester?" Diego drawled, smirking. "Pretty sure the Marines don't hand out midterms. He's got a few more months of getting yelled at ahead."

Laughter rolled, and Jackson ducked his head with a grin, not denying it. He'd be gone again in days, off to Camp Geiger and infantry school, but tonight? Tonight he was here.

Dalton scowled like he'd been personally attacked. "Fine! Then Holly's gonna have to carry the team GPA on her own, and Jackson's just gonna flex in a uniform until people love him."

Jackson ducked his head with a grin, and the Saints ate it up—clapping, ribbing, the kind of rowdy love that made your ribs ache.

Hannah didn't even need to raise her voice. She just fixed Dalton with *the look*, and he hopped off the chair so fast it was like gravity tripled just for him. "Yes ma'am," he muttered, and I leaned into Maria's side, tickling Jewel's bare toes. The atmosphere was triumphant, and maybe I was basking in it. Just a little. I laughed until my cheeks hurt, until Jewel's spit bubbles felt like a crown on my shoulder, until for a second I let myself believe life could stay this loud and simple.

By the time the night wound down, the clubhouse had gone soft around the edges—guys drifting to cards in the back, Hannah herding stragglers toward the door, Maria rocking Jewel half-asleep against her chest. I tucked my acceptance letter back into my pocket, ready to head home before I crashed face-first on the couch.

That's when Jackson found me by the door. Not with some grand gesture, not with that cocky swagger he'd perfected years ago—just standing there, uniform jacket unbuttoned, eyes steady like he'd been waiting.

"Congrats again," he said quietly. "On Georgia."

"Thanks." My voice came out softer than I meant it to. "Congrats on… surviving boot camp without getting your head shaved all the way bald."

His smile twitched. "Close call."

For a second, neither of us moved. The noise of the clubhouse faded, and it was just the two of us, thirteen weeks stretched tight between us.

"You look…" He stopped, cleared his throat, tried again. "Different. In a good way."

My stupid heart tripped. "So do you. Guess getting screamed at by grown adults every day for three months works wonders."

That earned me a laugh—low, warmer than I wanted it to be. His eyes flicked down, then back. I hitched my bag higher on my shoulder, needing armor. "Don't get used to me saying this, but…it's good you're back, Jackson."

His jaw tightened like he was holding something back. I tried—and failed—not to notice the way his eyes dipped to my mouth. My pulse tripped. Then his hand came up, rough palm grazing my cheek.

"Yeah," he said quietly. "It's good to see you too, Malibu."

It wasn't a confession, but it landed heavy in my chest all the same. I didn't mean to lean into his touch, but I did. Didn't mean to hold my breath when his thumb dragged lightly across my bottom lip, either.

A crash from inside shattered the spell. The look in Jackson's eyes as he glanced towards the noise made me want to find the guy who had made the sound and suggest he find a place to hide. I took the opportunity to slink off into the night, hurrying home before we crossed a line.

Back in my room, I slid the acceptance letter under my pillow like a secret and lay flat, staring at the ceiling fan cutting lazy circles in the dark. I should've been high on adrenaline—college, a future, Hannah's belief tucked in my pocket. But all I could hear was his voice again, that last night before he left.

Don't start something you're not ready to finish.

He'd meant it as caution. Maybe even care. But it had felt like rejection, and I'd spent thirteen weeks pretending it didn't matter. Pretending I didn't want him anyway. Tonight blew all that to pieces. The way he looked at me, like he'd been holding his breath just as long. The way neither of us could quite say it, but both of us knew.

I rolled onto my side, pressing my fist against my mouth to keep from groaning at myself. I had UGA. I had a plan. I had a future. So why did one stupid almost-kiss and one stupid Marine still have the power to undo me?

Chapter Seventeen

✒ Jackson ✒

The first thing that hit me when I rolled back into town on boot leave wasn't the smell of motor oil or the sight of bikes lined up outside the clubhouse—it was her.

Holly.

She wasn't the sharp-tongued girl I remembered spitting fire at me in the school parking lot. She was standing there, evening sun coming through the window and catching in her hair, laughing at something Maria said. I barely registered the baby Maria was holding. She damn near knocked the wind out of me. Like she always did. But this wasn't like last time. Not just because she was beautiful—though God help me, she was—but because she was *different*. Stronger. Softer around the edges but also…unshakable.

I'd left her three months ago on the edge of something—anger, pain, maybe even hope. I came back to find her carrying herself like someone who knew her own worth, even if she didn't believe it all the way yet. A lot had changed in three months. And I didn't know what the hell to do with the feeling in my chest when I saw that change. Pride. Fear. Want.

Basic had beaten a lot into me—discipline, grit, the ability to hold my tongue when some guy twice my size screamed in my face. I thought I'd come out of it sharper, better, and maybe I had. But standing here, all I could think was how unprepared I still felt. Not for the Corps. For *her*. For this.

After the party, I had watched her drive away then I went inside and found Dalton sitting on the couch. "Do me a favor," I said, dropping on the couch next to him, trying to sound casual. "Keep an eye on Holly when she's at UGA."

Dalton raised an eyebrow. "Keep an eye on her, huh? You mean like bodyguard duty, or more like babysitting Malibu before she verbally eviscerates some poor bastard who looks at her wrong?"

I clenched my jaw. "She doesn't need babysitting. I just…I don't go there. You do. So just…watch her back."

Dalton smirked, taking a pull from his beer. "Sure. But I expect hazard pay. That girl's got a mouth like a buzzsaw. One wrong move and I'm gonna need worker's comp."

I glared at him but couldn't stop the corner of my mouth from twitching. "You'll survive."

"Yeah," Dalton said, grin widening. "But I ain't makin' any promises about my sanity."

I only had a few days before Camp Geiger and infantry school, but it mattered knowing someone would have her back while I was gone again. Clapping him on the shoulder, I gave Hannah a kiss on the cheek and headed outside where Diego was waiting to give me a ride home. In front of the familiar trailer, I paused before going inside, and headed for the ramshackle shed to check on the other girl I had missed. My Harley sat under the dust cover, and I ran my hands over it before covering it back up. Resigned to my fate, I headed inside.

I wanted to be surprised when I found my mother sitting half-drunk on the couch, TV glow flickering against her face. I wasn't. She barely stirred when I came in. Had she even noticed my absence?

I'd left Atlanta thinking I was tough. I came back realizing I'd only been half-built before. Now I could run until my lungs gave out, push through pain until it blurred into background noise, fire a rifle until the stock bruised me raw and still hold it steady. But there are some things they don't teach you how to fight. Like the silence of a house where your mother lives but never really *is.*

"Jackson," she slurred, eyes glassy, trying to push herself upright before giving up and slumping back.

"Yeah, Ma. It's me."

"You look.…Different." Her brow furrowed in confusion as she took in my uniform and she tried to stand before falling back.

"I graduated Basic, Ma. I did it. I'm a Marine now." She didn't respond. Her blanket had slid to the floor, and I picked it up, tucking it back around her shoulders. I hated myself for the tenderness—hated how I still craved something she couldn't give. She smelled like whiskey and the cheap perfume she never stopped wearing. I pressed my lips tight and sat with her for a minute, staring at the ceiling fan turning lazy circles above us.

I'd faced drill instructors who made it their mission to grind me down to nothing. I'd pushed through twenty-mile humps with blisters bleeding through my boots. But none of it scared me the way leaving again in a few days did. Back to Camp Geiger. Away from my mother. Away from the Saints. The thought of some far-off battlefield didn't gut me half as much as the idea of saying goodbye again—especially to *her.*

Her flame. Her heat. The pull I couldn't shake.

And maybe that was the real problem. I didn't want distance. I wanted more of it. More of her.

I hadn't planned on stopping by. Hell, I told myself I wouldn't. But Sally was parked in her driveway like a taunt. I almost kept driving. Almost. Then I noticed her sitting on her porch, head tilted towards the sky and bathed in moonlight. Next thing I know, I was parking next to her car. She didn't look at me, seemingly intent on the stars above her.

She sat there, hood up on some oversized sweatshirt, hair spilling over her shoulders. Bare feet, blue nail polish, that soft hum in her throat she probably didn't realize she was making. She looked…peaceful. Which somehow made my chest hurt worse.

"You stalking me, Marine?"

"No. Just making sure you're real."

She looked over then, a half-smile ghosting her lips. "Careful. Reality's overrated."

Her eyes were that impossible kind of hazel—sunlight trapped in green glass. They never just looked at you; they *searched.* And when they landed on me, I swear the air changed temperature. I stopped in front of her. "Mind if I sit?"

She shrugged. "Free country."

For a minute we just sat there, legs dangling, the night humming around us. It was stupidly perfect—summer air, crickets, that faint smell of motor oil and lilacs.

"You leave tomorrow?" she asked finally.

"Yeah."

She nodded, eyes fixed ahead. "You just got back."

"Didn't want to go without saying goodbye."

"You could've texted."

"Would've," I said. "But maybe I wanted to see you smile."

She turned then, lips parted like she might say something smart, but no words came. I reached for her hand before I could think better of it. "Holly—"

"Don't," she said softly. "If you say something real, I might believe it."

"Maybe I want you to."

The air between us snapped tight. She didn't move when I leaned in, just breathed, slow, shallow, like she was trying to decide if this was a bad idea. Our noses brushed first. A tiny static crack in the dark. Then her lips grazed mine—quick, uncertain. Just enough for me to get a taste of coffee and something sweet. She started to pull back, but I followed, deepening it just enough to make the world tilt.

It wasn't practiced. It wasn't smooth. It was the kind of kiss that happened when both people were terrified and too far gone to stop. Her fingers found the front of my jacket; mine slid up the back of her neck, holding her there like something sacred. A quiet sound escaped her, half sigh, half surprise, and I swear I felt it down to my bones. I knew right then and there I was hooked. I threaded her soft hair between my fingers, determined to memorize everything about her.

When we finally broke apart, neither of us spoke. Just stared, breathing hard, hearts doing their own drum solo.

"Well," she whispered, voice shaky but laced with humor. "Guess you're bad at following your own advice."

"Yeah," I managed. "Guess I am."

She smiled and kissed me again.

This one was slower, surer. The kind that says, *we'll deal with the consequences later.*

Then she pulled back, thumb brushing the edge of my jaw. "Don't make me regret that."

"Wouldn't dare."

She got up, and I let her pull me with her. I wrapped my hands around her waist, pulling her body into mine. Trying to memorize every curve. Then the porch light started flickering frantically. It stopped, and then when neither of us moved, it began to disco the porch. She groaned and stepped away from me. I hated to let her go. She looked back once before opening her door and stepping inside. "Maybe while you're away, you can read a book on communication. These mixed signals really make a girl's head spin."

I grinned at her. "What was mixed about that kiss?"

She rolled her eyes, and when she shut the door behind her, I had to practically drag myself off that porch. I got home, checked on Mom—still asleep, still curled on her side like she was waiting for someone to wake her who never would—and finally stumbled to my room. I dropped onto the mattress, staring at the ceiling, replaying every second of that kiss like my brain was stuck on a loop. Her lips. Her hands in my jacket. I must've drifted halfway to sleep, because the knock on the door nearly sent me into cardiac arrest. Three taps. Soft. Hesitant.

I ran a hand over my face, stood, and padded down the hall. The TV flickered on the couch where Mom slept, dust motes drifting through the blue glow. When I cracked the door open Holly stood there. Barefaced. Hair down. Hands shoved into the sleeves of a massive sweatshirt like she was holding herself together by the threads. My heart did something stupid.

"Can I—?" she started, swallowing hard. "Can I come in?"

I stepped aside so fast I nearly tripped. She slipped past me, eyes adjusting to the dim, taking in the mismatched furniture, the sagging couch, my mom asleep two feet away. Embarrassment crawled up my neck. "It's not—" I started.

But she whispered, "Jackson." Just my name. Soft. Reassuring. And the shame deflated out of me like a punctured tire. She walked toward the hallway. Slowly. Like she was memorizing everything. The photos. The chipped paint. The scuffed floorboards. And not one hint of judgment touched her face. I followed her, heartbeat doing its best impression of a machine gun. When she reached my doorway, she stopped. Looked inside. My room wasn't much—cheap sheets, cracked dresser, boots lined up neat along the wall—but her breath caught like it meant something anyway.

We stepped inside and she turned to face me. For a second I forgot how to inhale.

Holly lifted her hands, barely brushing the hem of my T-shirt. "Is this ok?" she whispered.

My voice didn't work. I nodded. Her fingers slid up, skimming my ribs, my chest, my shoulders. Slow. Deliberate. Testing. Her hand shook once—barely—but I felt it like a lightning strike. God, it killed me. Every instinct in me screamed to reach for her, to pull her in, to deepen this. But I stayed still. Perfectly still. If she wanted distance, she'd get it. If she wanted closeness, she'd take it. If she wanted control, it was hers. She smoothed her palm over my collarbone, tracing muscle like she was learning a new language. "Ok," she whispered to herself. "Ok. I can do this."

She wasn't talking to me. Not really. She was talking to the old ghosts. I felt her touch everywhere. "I'm… not used to wanting to," she said quietly, eyes fixed on the fabric beneath her hand. "Usually, I want to run. Or freeze. Or…disappear."

I swallowed hard. "You're here. That's what matters."

Her laugh was shaky, more of a surrender than anything. Still, I didn't move. Not an inch. Just breathed slow so she could feel the rise and fall under her palm. Her hand slid up my chest, trembling but determined.

"This feels...weird," she murmured. Her voice tightened on the last word. "But good weird. Not bad weird."

"Good weird is allowed," I said softly.

She nodded once, eyes darting up, then back to her own hand like she couldn't trust herself to look at me too long.

"I keep expecting my brain to freak out," she whispered. "Tell me to stop. Tell me I'm doing something wrong. But it's...quiet."

Her thumb traced my collarbone.

"And that scares me," she admitted. "Because I want to keep touching you. And wanting is...complicated."

My throat felt too tight for words, but I forced them out. "You're allowed to want things, Holly."

"I know," she said automatically—then paused. "Actually...I don't. Not really. But I'm trying." Her fingers drifted to my shoulder, following the seam of my shirt, slow and searching.

"I need you to know something," she said, voice low but steadier now. "I'm not doing this because of the kiss. Or because you're leaving again. I'm doing it because I chose to come here. I chose you. This moment."

I swear I almost broke right there. Her palm flattened over my sternum. "Is this ok?" she asked.

"Whatever you want," I said, "Whatever you need. It's fine by me."

Her breath hitched—but she didn't pull away. Instead she rested her forehead against my chest, her voice muffled. "Good. Because I want to know what it feels like to touch someone without bracing for pain."

My hands clenched at my sides. I couldn't touch her yet. Not unless she asked. Not unless she showed me she was steady enough. She slid her hand down my ribs, over my stomach, then back up again—mapping me with trembling fingers. My pulse punched against her palm, and she froze before finally looked up at me—eyes glassy but bright, cheeks flushed, courage battling fear. "I want something good tonight," she said. "Something that's mine. Not something taken from me."

I let out a breath I hadn't realized I was holding. "Tell me what you want me to do, Malibu."

She swallowed, pressing her hand firmly against my chest.

"Just...stay still," she murmured. "And let me learn you. At my pace."

"Whatever you want," I said again. And meant every word.

Her fingers drifted up my throat, along my jaw, the side of my face. Slow. Deliberate.

Claiming ground inch by inch. She was breathing harder now—soft little pulls of air she was trying (and failing) to hide. Her hands were warm on my stomach, tracing slow, unsure lines like she was learning a language she hadn't spoken in years. Then she pulled back just enough to look up at me, hair falling across her cheek, eyes wide and scared and wanting all at once.

"Jackson?" she whispered.

"Yeah, Malibu?"

Her throat bobbed. "Can...can I ask you something?"

"Anything."

She closed her eyes for half a second like she needed to steady herself, then whispered, "I just want to feel you. Skin on skin. Just before you go."

The words hit like a fist to my chest. Not lust. Not shock. Just... *trust.* The kind that made your knees go weak.

"You sure?" I asked, voice rough.

"Yes." A breath. "Please."

I exhaled slowly, carefully—like if I moved wrong the whole moment might shatter. "Ok," I said softly. "Come here."

She stepped closer, fingers curling into the hem of her sweatshirt. And then, slowly—giving her time to stop, to rethink, to run if she needed—I lifted it up and over her head.

A simple bra. Bare shoulders. Bare stomach. Nothing sexual in her eyes. Just honesty. She was letting me see her—really see her—without armor.

My breath left me in one long exhale. "Holly..."

"Don't look at me like that," she said quickly, but her voice wavered. "Like I'm breakable."

"You're not breakable," I said. "You're brave. That's what I'm looking at."

Her cheeks flushed, lips parting, and she whispered, "Your turn."

I swallowed once, then tugged my shirt over my head and tossed it onto the foot of the bed. And the second I did, she froze. Not with fear. With… something else entirely. Her eyes swept over my chest, the tattoo over my ribs, the faint scars from all the dumb shit I'd done over the years. She reached out—slow, intentional—and pressed both palms to my chest.

My damn heartbeat stuttered under her hands.

She stepped closer, until her forehead rested against my collarbone. The press of her stomach to mine, bare skin to bare skin, made every muscle in my body go rigid—but not for the reason I expected.

Her arms slid around my waist, tentative at first, then firmer when she realized I wasn't going anywhere. I wrapped my arms around her carefully— slow, visible, giving her every second to stop me if she needed.

She didn't. Instead, she buried her face in my throat and whispered, "I didn't think I'd ever want to be this close to anyone again."

My arms tightened fractionally—not pulling her closer, just holding her there like she was something precious and breakable, even if she insisted she wasn't.

"You don't have to rush anything," I murmured into her hair. "We can do this however you need."

"I know." Her fingertips traced the line of my spine. "And that's why I want this. You."

We stood there like that—slow breaths syncing, skin-to-skin, her heartbeat rabbiting against my chest—until her muscles softened and her shaking eased.

After a minute, she said, "Can we…lie down? Not for anything more. Just…to be close."

"You never have to explain wanting something," I said. "Come here."

I guided her to the bed—letting her climb in first, letting her choose the position—and when she settled on her side, I slid in behind her. Not touching. Not yet. Letting her decide how far she wanted this to go. Then she reached back, took my hand, and pulled my arm around her waist. Her back pressed to my chest, bare skin warm against mine, her breath stuttering before finally settling.

After a long, trembling moment, she said it—quiet, fragile, but real: "Jackson…don't forget this. Don't forget me."

I rested my chin on the top of her head. "Impossible."

Her fingers tangled with mine. And for the first time in my life, I fell asleep holding something I was terrified to lose.

Chapter Eighteen

⌒ↂ⌒

⳽ **Holly** ⳽

I woke to warmth that didn't belong to me. For one calm, impossible second, my brain didn't question it. Didn't brace. Didn't run. It just… existed. Wrapped in heat and steady breath and quiet safety. Then the world clicked back into place. Jackson's arm was draped across my waist, his chest solid against my back, our bare skin pressed together like it was normal.

My heart forgot how to beat correctly. I tried easing out from under his arm—slow, careful, the kind of stealth move you make when you're sneaking back into the house at two a.m. and praying the floorboards don't rat you out. But his fingers twitched, then curled against my hip.

"Holly?" His voice was gravel-soft, heavy with sleep.

I froze, halfway upright and looking like a raccoon caught stealing chips.

"Hi," I croaked. Smooth.

He blinked himself awake enough to register me hovering like a guilty ghost. "You ok?"

Two words. That was all. No panic, no suspicion, no pressure—just checking in. It made everything inside me twist. "I didn't want to wake you," I muttered, which wasn't even close to the truth.

"You didn't. But you also don't have to sneak out like you're escaping a hostage negotiation."

Heat burned up my neck. God, kill me now. "I wasn't sneaking. I was… relocating."

His mouth twitched. "Real stealthy."

I groaned into my hands. "This is so embarrassing."

"Why?" he asked, gently tugging one hand away from my face. "You didn't do anything wrong."

Something in my chest pulled tight—like a knot that had been there for years suddenly got tired of being knotted. I pulled my knees up, leaning against the ancient headboard. "Last night was…a lot."

"Yeah," he agreed quietly. "For me too."

That startled me enough to look at him. Really look. The nervous edges around his eyes, the careful space he kept between us, like he didn't want to spook me.

"For you?" I asked.

He nodded once. "I've never been trusted with anything like that."

My throat tightened. "I feel stupid. Like my brain thinks I deserve an award for…lying here. Not freaking out. Like—'congrats, Holly, you touched someone without imploding.'"

His expression softened, a small, genuine thing. "Seems like a big deal to me."

I stared at my hands, cheeks hot. "It doesn't make sense."

"Sometimes the stuff that works doesn't make sense," he said. "Doesn't mean it's wrong."

Something inside me shifted. A tiny click. A quiet easing I didn't know I'd been waiting for.

"Do you regret it?" he asked.

"No." The answer came without hesitation. "I just don't know what to do with it now."

"Me either."

I got up and pulled my sweatshirt over my head. "I should go. Before your mom wakes up and thinks I broke in to steal your innocence or something."

He huffed a laugh. "She wouldn't notice if a marching band set up in the living room."

Fair. I hesitated in the doorway. "Last night…mattered. Even if it feels stupid to admit that."

"It wasn't stupid," he said firmly. "It was brave."

That word hit in a place I didn't let people touch. I swallowed, nodded once, and slipped out. "See you around, Jackson," I said softly.

His answering smile was small, real. "Yeah, Malibu. You will."

Next thing I knew, he had left for training. And I'd barely wrapped my head around the idea of starting college before my father was pulling strings, making phone calls, greasing palms—whatever it took to make sure I didn't have to set foot in a dorm. "It's not negotiable, bug," he'd said in that surgeon's tone of his, clipped and precise. "You're not ready for that environment."

For once, I didn't argue. He was right. Throw me into a building crammed with strangers, and I'd either lock myself in my room until spring or pick a fight with the first girl who breathed too loudly. Probably both.

So instead, I stood in the middle of a two-bedroom apartment on the edge of Athens with the keys digging into my palm and the overwhelming sense that I didn't deserve any of it. Polished hardwood floors. Granite counters. A balcony big enough to throw parties I'd never host. School was still a couple of months out, but my hammering heart hadn't gotten the memo. There was nothing to freak out about…yet.

Maria whistled low when she walked in, Jewel bouncing on her hip. "Girl, this place is bigger than my whole house."

I was sitting cross legged on the floor and guilt immediately churned in my gut. "I know. I feel—"

"Stop." She turned so fast she almost tripped. Her eyes snapped, sharp as knives. "Don't you dare apologize. You hear me? Don't. You didn't steal this. You didn't cheat for it. You use it."

I blinked, caught between shame and gratitude. "But—"

"Shut the heck up," Maria cut in, smirking now. "Seriously. You're not allowed to feel bad for something that makes your life easier. You've had enough hard already."

Jewel gurgled as if seconding the point, reaching sticky fingers toward my face. I laughed, the sound rusty but real, and let Maria boss me into hanging curtains and rearranging furniture until the apartment felt less like a showroom and more like a home. We made a game out of it. Maria held up two sets of curtains and crouched down in front of Jewel like it was a royal decree. "All right, *princesa*, left or right? Which one's worthy of our girl here?"

Jewel squealed, grabbed a fistful of the left panel, and promptly stuffed it into her mouth.

Maria cackled. "Done. Decision made. You can't argue with baby logic."

I shook my head, smiling in spite of myself. "So my décor is going to be determined by whatever tastes good to an infant?"

"Exactly," Maria said, already climbing onto a chair to hang the chosen set. "Kid's got better instincts than either of us."

For the first time since I'd walked into the apartment, the knot of guilt in my stomach loosened. It wasn't about how much I had compared to her. It was about filling the space with people who made it feel alive. And with Maria and Jewel in it, my apartment finally felt like it belonged to me.

Still, when Maria left that night, the silence pressed down like a weight. I curled up on the couch, staring at the neat rows of books I hadn't read yet and the perfectly folded blankets I didn't want to use. Everything felt too clean, too empty, too much.

The days blurred after that. I bounced between the clubhouse, my apartment, quick visits with my parents, and afternoons at Maria's—Jewel babbling on the floor while we folded laundry or cooked together. And then there were the damn mixers. Every week another glossy flyer or email telling me I *had* to show up to some "welcome event" if I wanted the "real college experience." If the real college experience meant warm soda, sticky floors, and people shouting in my ear, then I'd take a hard pass. I went to two out of obligation before swearing off them entirely.

And always in the background, Jackson. Gone for training, unreachable except for the rare text that hit my phone like a lightning strike. Our moment on the porch had changed everything. Our moment in his room had changed *me*.

I'd never admit it out loud, as that involved witnesses and feeling, but I missed him. Missed the calm in his voice, the way his gray eyes saw right through me, the way he made silence feel safe.

I ached for another kiss. Not the fairytale kind. The real one. The inconvenient, ruin-your-dignity kind. Which was entirely his fault. At night, when things got too quiet and my brain tried to drag me back into old patterns. Clenched hands. Tight breaths. That rush of heat behind the eyes that I refused to let fall. And then something new happened— something I pretended wasn't happening. My brain went looking for the memory of Jackson's arm around me. Not the kiss. Not the heat. The *weight*. That slow, steady rise and fall of his chest under my cheek. The grounding of his heartbeat. The way he didn't rush or expect anything. Just…existed.

It was ridiculous. Silly. EMDR-without-the-beeping levels of nonsense. But the tightness eased. My hands steadied, my lungs didn't fight the air I filled them with. Damn. Should've sent myself a copay.

By the time classes started in earnest, life was chaos in the usual way. Lecture halls crammed with bodies, professors droning about syllabi, endless lines at the coffee shop. I sat in the back with my notebook open, hood pulled low, trying to disappear into the noise. Some days I managed. Others, I couldn't stop my hands from trembling, couldn't block the memories when a stranger's laugh hit too sharp, too close. But I kept showing up. One day at a time, one class at a time.

There were moments that surprised me. Like the day my history professor fired off a question about the Reconstruction Amendments. The room went dead silent, two hundred students ducking their heads. Against my better judgment, my hand went up. My voice shook, but the answer came out clean, and the professor gave me a quick nod of approval before moving on. I sat there grinning like an idiot, heat crawling up my neck, and fully aware I was acting like a toddler given a dollar in a candy store. It was the tiniest thing, but for once, I didn't feel invisible.

Other days, doubt hit harder. I'd leave class with a headache, staring at the flood of students around me, wondering if I belonged here at all. If

I was only fooling myself into thinking I could be normal. If I'd made a mistake choosing this path.

At two in the morning, the questions got worse. I'd sit hunched over my desk, notes scattered everywhere, some math problem staring back at me like Satan and a bored Greek philosopher had personally designed it. I was convinced the teacher had beef with me specifically. Or maybe it was just my sanity he wanted to see ruined. My chest would tighten until I caved and grabbed my phone.

Hannah answered once, her voice thick with sleep but gentle. "Breathe, Holly. Walk me through the problem."

I contemplated faking a bad connection. I eyed the discarded chocolate bar wrapper that would make a very convincing static sound. Then I closed my eyes and forced myself to breathe like a semi-functioning, self-respecting adult.

Another time it was Maria, who didn't even bother pretending to know what a unilateral equation was. "Hell if I know, *chica*. But I'll stay on the line while you figure it out. Maybe Jewel will wake up and give us both the answer." We laughed until my shoulders finally unclenched. And then I finished the damn equation.

They were small things, maybe insignificant to anyone else. But to me, they were proof I wasn't drowning. Proof I could keep going.

And then life threw in Dalton.

It was a Thursday morning, already too hot for March, the Georgia sun pretending it was July as I hustled toward the science building. My backpack strap cut into my shoulder, my sneakers slapped against the pavement, and my heart was pounding—not because of exercise but because I was late. Again.

And then the sun vanished. I nearly smacked into him.

Dalton Mills. Six foot of smug jock, leather jacket slung over his shoulder like we weren't all sweating through our clothes. He stood square in my path, grinning like he'd been waiting for this exact moment just to derail me.

"Morning, Malibu."

I blinked. "What—"

Before I could finish, he shoved a cup into my hands. Not coffee. No. This thing was a monstrosity, the Starbucks version of a sugar-loaded middle finger. Whipped cream piled a mile high, caramel dripping down the sides, condensation already soaking the cardboard sleeve.

"What's this?"

"Your breakfast." He looked far too pleased with himself. "Courtesy of yours truly."

Suspicion flared so fast I almost dropped the cup. "Did Jackson put you up to this?"

Dalton cocked his head, feigning confusion so badly I wanted to slap him. "Who?"

I narrowed my eyes. "Don't start."

"Never heard of him." His grin sharpened. "Tall guy, buzzcut, likes to boss people around? Nope. Doesn't ring a bell."

My stomach did an irritating little flip I refused to acknowledge. I clutched the cup tighter. "How did you even know what I drink?"

Dalton leaned in just close enough for me to smell leather and aftershave, his voice dropping into a conspiratorial drawl. "Maria."

"She wouldn't," I frowned, though deep down I knew she absolutely would.

"Oh, she would. Turns out your girl's easy. Promised her I'd babysit Jewel this weekend, and suddenly she's singing like a canary." He smirked. "You should be thanking me, really. Now you get your coffee, *and* Maria gets a night off. Everybody wins."

I stared at him, speechless, and briefly contemplated dumping it over his head and slapping the shit out of him. But that was probably the exhaustion talking.

He nodded at the cup. "Go on. Don't waste it. You look like you need it."

I hated that he was right. Against my better judgment, I took a sip. Cold, sweet coffee hit my tongue, caffeine sparking through my veins. My eyelids fluttered, and a sound escaped—half sigh, half groan.

Dalton's grin went feral. "Knew it. Got the Malibu stamp of approval."

I scowled up at him. "Not yet."

"Yet, she says." He started walking backward into the crowd, still smirking like he'd just won something. "You're welcome. And don't forget to tell Maria she owes me the title of world's best babysitter."

And then he was gone, swallowed by the flood of students, leaving me clutching a cup big enough to drown in and wondering what the hell just happened. Shaking my head but not stupid enough to refuse free caffeinated goodness, I resumed the trudge to class. Just as I stepped inside, met with the blessed rush of cold air, my phone buzzed with an incoming text. I checked it, expecting Maria. It was not.

Jackson: Morning Malibu. Enjoy the coffee?

Me: Stalker. I am perfectly capable of taking care of myself.

Jackson: Don't I know it.

What was that supposed to mean?

Me: Aren't you supposed to be running laps or something?

Jackson: I can take a second to say good morning.

I tried desperately to ignore the butterflies in my belly and frowned at my phone. I typed a response. Deleted it. Typed another. Deleted that too.

Jackson: Don't over think it, Malibu. I can see you typing. And I don't have to imagine it too hard to see that cute, little line you get between your eyebrows when you're thinking. Have a good day.

My thumb hovered over the screen for a stupidly long time after his dot went gray. I had half a dozen replies drafted—sharp, sarcastic, defensive— and I deleted every single one. Telling him off would be easier. Telling myself off for caring would be easier still. But I couldn't get the image of him waiting somewhere, rough and impatient and earnest, out of my head. The butterfly thing in my stomach did not care for my dignity.

I shoved the phone into my pocket and stumbled into class, late again. The professor said something about primary sources, and I pretended to take notes while my brain replayed the text like a bad song on loop. I kept checking my phone and eventually realized I was acting utterly pathetic which resulted in me turning it off and shoving it into the bottom of my bag.

The week fell into a rhythm. Jackson's messages were short but steady. I had come to expect a good morning, and the occasional good night. When I showed Maria the string of simple messages, she had a total fangirl moment and squealed loud enough it woke up Jewel.

Dalton kept appearing like an inconvenient traffic cone—there when you needed to swerve around, impossible to ignore. Hannah called a couple of nights to make sure I wasn't dissolving alone, that old-fashioned voice soft around the edges that kept me grounded and focused on the mission. Her words, not mine.

One night I stayed up until three trying to parse a chemistry problem that might as well have been a riddle written in a cipher. I texted Maria a picture of my scrawl. Her reply was a string of angry emojis and a single sentence.

Maria: Stop making my brain hurt, come over. I'll feed you until you stop yelling at molecules.

I went.

Maria's kitchen was chaos: a loud radio, two pans sizzling, a tiny person in the center of it all who thought splatting into a bowl was the highest form of art. Jewel handed me a soggy tamale and grinned like I was a god for existing. Sure, I visited my parents often. Was starting to look forward to seeing them, which was weird. Almost like I missed them. But this was my happy place. Then it was back to my too quiet apartment and hovering thoughts.

Eventually, I had to admit Dalton wasn't just a dumb jock. The guy was smart—like weirdly, *might actually solve world hunger if he stayed focused long enough* smart. Most weekends, we holed up in the clubhouse back room, folding chairs and busted tables buried under textbooks and highlighters like the detritus of an academic camping trip.

But the Friday before a big test, Maria pitched a different idea. Hannah volunteered to babysit Jewel, and Maria lit up like someone had handed her a week's vacation. She wasn't going to waste it in the clubhouse basement. So we ended up at my apartment.

Dalton stepped inside, whistling low. "You weren't kidding. This place is bigger than my mom's kitchen."

"Behave," Maria snapped, smacking his arm as she claimed the couch. "She already feels weird about it."

"I do not," I lied, dropping my backpack on the coffee table.

Diego came in with a box of snacks like reinforcements, and Mac slipped through the door last, muttering that his dad could handle things for one night. He didn't say much else, just claimed a chair in the corner—but somehow the whole room shifted quieter, more focused, like his presence set the tempo.

By the time Maria clapped her hands, snacks were spread across the table and half a forest's worth of flashcards stacked in front of us. "All right. No whining. No excuses. Holly, eyes up. Dalton, stop pretending you know the answer before I even flip the card."

Dalton smirked, leaning back in his chair. "I do know the answer. It's always C."

I groaned, dropping my head into my hands. "God, you're insufferable."

"Insufferable and passing."

A pen flew across the table. He caught it just in time, grinning wider. "What? You tolerate it from me sometimes."

"Key word: sometimes," I warned, aiming for the bowl of pretzels next.

Diego snorted from the couch. "Better watch it, *hermano*. She's got good aim."

"Please." Dalton tipped his chair back further, utterly smug. "She wouldn't kill the only guy keeping her awake with my quality jokes."

"Quality?" I muttered. "That word doesn't mean what you think it means."

Mac rolled his eyes but smiled a little, dragging the bowl of pretzels away from me and my quick hand. Maria slapped the next card down. "Focus, children. Save the flirting for after you pass this damn test."

Dalton's chair thunked back onto all fours. "Flirting? Absolutely not. I like my balls attached, thank you. And I don't even know who'd get to them first if I tried it—Holly, or Jackson."

I froze mid-chew, an Oreo hanging half way out of my mouth. "*Excuse me?*"

Dalton pointed the pretzel bowl at me like it was evidence. "I am not flirting with Malibu. I value my life too much."

The Oreo hit him square in the forehead.

"Do not call me that," I snapped.

Diego wheezed from the couch. Mac sipped his coffee, and reached for the Oreos like he was going to take those next. I snatched them before he could and glared at him. Maria groaned, scooping up the next flashcard like she was reconsidering all her life choices. "*Ay Dios mío…*you two are never going to survive this test."

We worked in fits and starts. Someone would shout an answer, someone else would argue the logic, and someone else would eat everything in sight while pretending they were only "refueling for academic excellence." That last someone may or may not have been me. Maria ran the whole thing like she was refereeing a prize fight, clapping her hands when we got too loud, passing snacks when we got too quiet.

At one point I got hung up on a stupid arithmetic problem, the kind of thing my hands could've done on autopilot if my brain wasn't busy tripping me up. Numbers blurred, my chest tightened, and frustration crawled under my skin. I was strongly considering dropping out entirely and finding a new career to invest in. Or, at the very least, setting the entire notebook on fire and calling it a day.

"Slide it over," Dalton said, voice even, not mocking. He pulled the napkin toward him, sketched out a quick diagram that actually made sense, and started explaining. Not in a teacher voice. Not in a condescending one. Just steady, clear, matter-of-fact—like he'd done this before. Which he probably had.

"You're making it harder than it is," he said, pen moving fast. "Look—split it like this. Simplify first, don't let the numbers bully you. One step at a time."

"You're not stupid, Holly," Mac said finally, voice flat but sure. "You just think too fast and trip yourself up. Slow down. That's all."

Somehow that landed harder than Dalton's whole napkin diagram. I snorted, trying to cover how much it calmed me. "You would both rather be elbows-deep in an engine."

Mac gave a one-shouldered shrug, eyes flicking up to mine. "Problem's a problem. Doesn't matter if it's fractions or carburetors—you figure it out piece by piece."

Dalton brandished his pen at his brother, "What he said. Now watch."

Between Dalton's diagrams and Mac's steady logic, the numbers finally lined up in my head, neat instead of snarled. When I blurted out the answer, triumphant and a little too loud, the room erupted like I'd just solved world peace.

Maria banged her hand on the table. "Yes! That's what I'm talking about!"

Dalton smirked, but there was pride under it, sharp and real. "Told you it wasn't that hard."

Mac's mouth twitched in the closest thing he ever gave to a grin. And Diego slid the Oreos closer to me, mouthing, "For victory."

And me? I laughed, shaky and breathless, but real. For once, the knot in my chest eased. It was ridiculous and small and perfect—the kind of night that made me feel like maybe I wasn't drowning. Or, if I were, that someone nearby gave a damn to throw me a buoy.

By the time the last flashcard had been conquered and the snack table raided down to crumbs, everyone was winding down. Diego started packing up the textbooks with military precision, Maria stretched on the couch like she was storing up one more hour of kid-free peace, and Mac disappeared into the kitchen, probably to see if he could wrangle one last cup of coffee from the pot before driving home.

I was ready to call it a night too, until my eyes landed on the library book poking out of my bag. My stomach dropped. "Shit. I gotta run to campus. This is due at midnight, and the librarian already hates me."

Dalton raised an eyebrow. "So, pay the late fee. Pretty sure you're not gonna starve over a couple bucks."

Heat rushed up my neck, fast and sharp but before I could say anything, Maria smacked Dalton on the shoulder with the kind of casual mom-whack that carried more sting than a punch. "Don't be an ass."

He blinked, rubbing his shoulder with a put-on wince. "What? I'm just saying—"

"Don't." Her glare shut him up faster than anything I could've said.

I ducked my head, grateful and mortified at the same time, shoving the book into my bag. "It'll take twenty minutes, tops. I'll be back."

Dalton sighed, already grabbing his jacket. "Yeah, well, no way you're walking across campus alone this late. Let's go."

"I don't need a babysitter," I shot back, but he ignored me, holding the door open like it was *his* apartment.

By the time I stepped past him, he was already humming —some loud, obnoxiously cheerful tune designed to crawl under my skin. It didn't work like it used to. We cut across campus under a sky that had started to lose its day-heat, students folding into the campus stream. The air had a crisp edge even in the sticky weeks, the way spring tried to bargain with why it existed in Georgia. My head was buzzing from equations and flashcards, but Dalton walked like the night belonged to him, hands shoved in his jacket, unbothered as ever.

"You kept up tonight," he said finally, voice even. Not smug, not mocking. Just fact.

I side-eyed him. "Kept up? Pretty sure you were two steps ahead of me the whole damn time."

His mouth twitched, the closest thing to a grin. "Only 'cause you psych yourself out. You're not slow, Blondie. You just fight the problem like it's out to get you. You're like that with most things."

My throat went tight, so I masked it with a shrug. "Wow. You do flashcards, and suddenly you're Freud. Thanks for the diagnosis, doc, but no thanks."

"Hilarious," he said, tone dry but steady. Then, after a beat, softer: "We'll keep at it. You'll get there. You're better than you used to be."

The words hit harder than I wanted them to, settling right in the spot I usually guarded with claws and sarcasm. I knew he wasn't talking about just math. I stared ahead, jaw tight, because if I looked at him, he'd see too much.

And of course, he didn't let me off that easy. His elbow nudged into mine, firm enough to jolt me a step sideways. "Don't get all misty on me, blondie. I'll revoke the compliment."

My head snapped his way as I glared at him. "You're insufferable."

"Yeah, but I'm right." The smirk was back, lazy and infuriating, like he'd planned the whole exchange just to watch me squirm.

We walked in silence for a few blocks. My phone vibrated, but I didn't look. My head was too full and too quiet in a different way. The silence stretched, comforting for the first time in a long while.

And then the laughing started out of nowhere, a group of guys from somewhere behind us, loud with too many beers and the kind of confidence that comes from never being told no. Someone whistled. A voice called, "Damn, Barbie is out past curfew!"

I didn't break stride. "Original," I called back over my shoulder. "Did you workshop that in the group chat or does it just come naturally?"

One of them laughed. The wrong kind of laugh. The kind that thinks it's winning.

"Wanna hang out?"

I stopped then—not because they told me to. Because I wanted to. I turned slowly, dragging my gaze over them like I was pricing clearance items at a thrift store. "Hang out?" I tilted my head. "With that haircut? Please. I have standards."

One of them puffed up, swaggering a step closer. "You got a mouth on you."

"Yeah," I said flatly. "It's attached to a brain. Try it sometime."

Dalton casually took one huge step between me and them, one shoulder forward like a shield, and smiled at the guys.

It wasn't his usual grin—the easy, "let's fuck with the world" grin. This was shorter, colder: a small curl at one corner of his mouth, the set of his jaw that said he could, if necessary, make you regret being alive. The way his smile cut through the crowd made them stop laughing mid-word like someone had turned off a radio.

"You boys lost?" he asked, voice calm as a lake. The tone didn't invite banter.

The closest one tried to swagger up to him, all bluster. He took one step, maybe two— then he faltered. He looked at Dalton like the math just went wrong and he wasn't sure why. They all glanced at each other before slinking back off into the night with their tails between their legs.

I didn't realize I'd started shaking until Dalton's hand found my waist, pressing, not tight but solid. I stiffened from the contact, but distantly my brain recognized it as safety and I didn't pull away. Slowly but surely, the night folded back into ordinary noise, and we found ourselves in front of the library.

We stood there for a beat, the sidewalk suddenly enormous and ordinary. My cheeks were hot with a shame I couldn't quite place—ashamed that I'd needed someone to stand up with me, ashamed that I felt the relief like a physical thing.

Dalton's shoulders relaxed. The grin returned, the old one, but softer, like he'd closed a book. "You good?"

I swallowed, feigning nonchalance as best I could. "I was about to eviscerate their egos before you interrupted."

He watched me for one second, then rolled his shoulders and muttered something about hazard pay. When he returned his attention to me, he bumped his shoulder into mine. "I think you already did that. Besides, you're not allowed to get picked on. Not on my watch."

The gratitude hit like a thing heavy and warm in my throat. I wanted to say something real, like thank you, but instead I said, "I'll add bodyguard to your job description."

"Perfect," he said, and his voice carried that ridiculous half-smirk that made me want to punch him for being infuriatingly kind.

I dropped off my book and wasn't the least bit surprised when Dalton walked me back to my apartment. This time, I didn't protest, and he joked about how thrilled his coach would be at the extra exercise. That night, when I crawled into my apartment and turned the key, my chest felt different, not lighter exactly, but like someone had tied a rope from me to the earth. I could breathe in a way I hadn't in years.

Jackson texted before I fell asleep.

Jackson: Good luck on Monday, Malibu.

I stared at the message, blinking at the glow. How the hell did he even know I had a test? Oh, right. His pet spy. Dalton. I typed a reply. Deleted it. Typed another.

Me: Copy that.

It wasn't much, but it felt like something. I hit send and dropped the phone on my nightstand. For the first time since the semester started, I believed I might actually be able to do this—not alone, not perfectly, but…enough.

Chapter Nineteen

❧❦❧

By Monday afternoon, my brain was fried, fingers ink-smudged from hours of notes, when a familiar shadow cut across the sidewalk. Dalton. Of course.

He matched my pace like he'd been waiting for me, hands shoved deep in his jacket pockets, grin tilted in that lazy, dangerous way that always made me want to smack him. "Well, look at that. McCarthy lives. Survived the test without combusting." He paused for effect. "Want some good news to go with your brain death?"

I narrowed my eyes. "Do I?"

He didn't wait. "Jackson's coming home. Mom's throwing a cookout Friday. Attendance is non-negotiable."

Heat rose before I could stop it. I forced my voice even. "Fine. I'll drive."

Dalton's brows flicked up, like he'd expected more of a fight. "Huh. That was easy." Then he peeled off toward his own class, smug as ever.

My phone was already in my hand before I even cleared the steps.

Me: You're coming home?

The reply was almost instant.

Jackson: Yeah, on leave. It was supposed to be a surprise. Remind me to pummel Dalton. Me: Noted.

A smile tried to break loose. I strangled it.

The week stretched and snapped at the same time. Tuesday tasted like cold coffee and graphite—my notes smudged, my brain a scraped-clean bowl. Jackson's messages were short, steady shots in the dark.

Jackson: Eat breakfast tomorrow. Non-negotiable.

Jackson: Got to the range today. Hands are wrecked. Worth it.

Jackson: You make it to class?

I started answering without overthinking.

Me: Fine. But only because Pop-Tarts count as breakfast.

Me: Don't shoot anyone. Or yourself.

Me: Yeah. Barely. But I was there.

Wednesday after lab, Maria kidnapped me under the guise of "errands" and dragged me through Target like we were preparing for an apocalypse, Jewel judging us from the cart seat like a tiny Roman empress.

Maria held two mascaras to the light. "Waterproof or extra black?"

"Waterproof. Always"

She tossed both in the basket. Jewel grabbed one, gnawed on the corner, and declared it superior by drool. We detoured through home goods because my apartment still looked like a rental catalogue threw up. Maria pointed at a plant. "You need something alive."

"I'm alive," I said.

"That's debatable," she said sweetly, and put the plant in the cart.

Thursday night, Hannah called just to ask what side I wanted to bring, like I wasn't the least reliable potluck participant on earth. "We'll take anything," she said, voice soft around the edges. "And don't fuss about it. Just come."

"I'll—" I stalled. "I'll bring a salad." Salads were safe, right? I hoped.

By the time I walked out of the bathroom on Friday evening, Dalton had already sprawled across my couch like he owned the place. Boots on my coffee table. Remote in one hand. My Pop-Tarts in the other.

"Jesus, Holly, what's taking so long?" he mumbled around a mouthful, crumbs scattering down his shirt.

I yanked the box out of his hands before he could finish the packet. "Stop eating all my food. And get your nasty boots off my table."

He only grinned wider, eyes flicking to the eyeliner I hadn't wiped off fast enough. "What's the holdup, anyway? You're not meeting the pope."

I walked over to the kitchen to grab my super boring, super safe Caesar salad and told myself this was normal. A cookout. People I loved. A boy I…refused to name. My phone buzzed.

Jackson: Leaving now. Save me a burger.

Me: Maybe.

I stared at the word for a stupidly long time, feeling twelve and thirty at once. I was so zoned in on my phone, I didn't hear Dalton walk up behind me, and when he tapped me on the shoulder, I nearly threw the salad at him.

"Whatcha doin'?" he drawled.

Heat crawled up my neck. "Mind your business."

"Mm-hmm." He stretched like a cat, perfectly at home. "Ready?"

"I have been ready," I snapped, grabbing my bag. "Now let's go before you eat all my food. We're late." We made it down to the lot, me storming ahead, Dalton sauntering behind. When I unlocked Sally, he stopped dead.

"You're kidding." His voice was flat. "We're taking this?"

"This," I said, patting the roof like a beloved pet, "is Sally. You will respect her. Or you can walk."

Dalton eyed the Mustang like it was a coffin. "Pretty sure I'm too tall to legally ride in that thing."

"Funny. Maria managed when she was literally giving birth. You'll survive."

He groaned but folded himself inside anyway, all six feet of him contorting into the passenger seat. His knees jammed the glovebox. His shoulders barely fit between the door and console.

"Christ," he muttered, fumbling with the seatbelt. "This is a clown coffin."

I slid into the driver's seat, revved the engine just to make him groan. "Quit whining, sardine. We've got a cookout to get to."

The ride was mercifully short, though Dalton filled it with complaints about his circulation and exaggerated groans every time I shifted gears. When we finally pulled into the clubhouse parking lot, the smell of hit me before the car even rolled to a stop.

The clubhouse buzzed with noise and smoke. Mr. Mills flipped burgers at the grill, the scent of charred meat curling through the air. Mac was holding court by the cooler, handing out beers like he owned stock in Bud Light, while Hannah shouted instructions from the porch, her wooden spoon tapping against her palm like a gavel.

I wove through the chaos until Maria flagged me down at a picnic table. "Eyeliner, huh?" Jewel was perched on her lap, already smearing applesauce into her curls.

"Hush you." I accepted the plate Maria handed me, ignoring her smirk.

"Eat," she ordered.

I was a sucker for a good burger, and my girl had loaded my plate. I'd just taken a bite when the air shifted. The kind of shift you felt in your spine before your brain caught up.

He was dressed casually. Jeans, a faded T-shirt. His old, familiar leather jacket straining to fit his shoulders which had all but doubled in width. What exactly did they feed Marines? Crayons and steroids? He was going to need a bigger size.

I realized I was staring, and everything inside me short-circuited. My lungs forgot how to work. My burger staged a mutiny, lodging halfway down my throat. I coughed, choked, saw spots. And because the universe hates me, Dalton had picked that exact moment to saunter over with a drink in hand. He set it down, clapped me on the back with way too much enthusiasm, and grinned like Christmas had come early.

"Easy there, blondie. Try breathing between bites."

I wanted the ground to swallow me whole. By the time I finally managed to wheeze in a full breath, my face was scarlet. Hannah, still perched like a queen on the porch, was smirking knowingly. Maria had both hands over her mouth, her shoulders shaking with laughter.

Perfect. Absolutely perfect. Jackson Morgan had been home all of thirty seconds, and the first thing he saw was me nearly dying on a burger. I chanced a glance at him and found him watching me with a half cocked smile. Lord, take me now.

The cookout slid into that easy rhythm the Mills clan always managed—kids darting between legs, somebody's speaker crooning classic rock, Maria perched on a bench fixing Jewel's hair while scolding Diego for sneaking her cookies. Dalton and Jackson had wrangled up a ramshackle football game, and I sat watching them play. Hannah eventually joined me, taking a seat at the table next to me. I caught her glancing from me to the field a few times. I don't think I wanted to know what that knowing gleam in her eyes meant.

The food was good, the chatter loud, and it was really just the perfect Friday after a very long week. God, I was ready for spring break. Every time Jackson tipped his head back to laugh, that low rasp rolling through the air, my chest did this stupid little twist. I found myself cataloguing things I shouldn't—the scar along his knuckle, the way his T-shirt clung at the shoulders, the new stillness about him. Like he'd learned to hold himself tighter. Like something in him had shifted.

I hated that I noticed. I hated that it mattered.

By the time the sun slid down and the plates sat empty, I was strung tight. So, when Hannah clapped her hands and announced, "Alright, kitchen duty! Holly, Jackson—you two can handle dishes."

My fork clattered against my plate.

"Wait," I spluttered but Jackson had already starting clearing plates and heading inside, leaving me with not much of a choice other than to follow. Hannah's eyes caught mine, bright with mischief, daring me to try and wriggle out. Which was how I ended up in the kitchen with Jackson Morgan at my side and no escape hatch in sight.

The sink steamed, bubbles frothing high, the whole kitchen hazy with grill smoke clinging to our clothes. I shoved my sleeves up and grabbed a plate like it was a weapon. He reached automatically for the towel, leaning one hip against the counter like he'd done it a thousand times. Like we weren't two people tiptoeing around a fault line.

For a while, it was just the quiet splash of water and the clink of ceramic. Too quiet. I could hear my own heartbeat over it.

Then his voice—low, rougher than I remembered. "You look good,

Malibu."

The plate nearly slipped from my hands. My throat went tight, but this time I didn't bother with the usual argument. He knew I hated the nickname. He also knew I wasn't going to stop him.

"Flattery, Marine?" I tried for sharp, but it came out thin, frayed at the edges.

His mouth twitched like he wanted to grin but thought better of it. "Not flattery. Just fact."

I focused hard on the soap bubbles, scrubbing like the plate had personally offended me. "You've been back five minutes and you're already insufferable."

That broke him—the grin came, softer than I'd seen in a long time. "Maybe. But it's good, seeing you. Better than I thought it'd be."

Something pulled in my chest, stupid and dangerous. I scrubbed harder, like I could drown it in suds. "You could've told me you were coming."

"Wanted to surprise you." His voice dropped lower, conspiratorial. "Didn't count on Dalton being a traitor."

That pulled a laugh out of me, sharp and unwilling. Our shoulders brushed when I handed him another plate. Neither of us moved away. The words slipped out before I could stop them. "Your texts…they help." My throat felt too tight, the admission small and raw.

His gray eyes caught mine, steady, unflinching. "Keeps me sane."

The air shifted. The room shrank until it was just soap bubbles and the heat rolling off him and my own pulse hammering in my ears. His fingers brushed mine. Not accidental. Not hurried. A test.

I didn't flinch.

Something dangerous and beautiful flickered in his expression. His jaw tightened like he was holding back a thousand things at once.

"Malibu…" His voice dropped into something low and rough. "You don't know what you do to me."

My breath stuttered. Heat licked up my neck. "Tell me," I whispered before I could talk myself out of it.

He blinked once, slow, like the request hit somewhere deep. "I don't know if I can," he admitted, voice gravel-soft. "But…" He swallowed. "I can show you."

Everything in me froze—then trembled. Fight or flight tugged at my ribs, my breath, the back of my throat. He waited. Didn't step in. Didn't push. Just stood there in the warm glow of the kitchen, bubbles clinging to his arms, looking at me like I was something worth waiting for.

I hesitated. One heartbeat. Two. "…ok."

Something in him loosened—a breath he'd been holding, maybe. Slowly, giving me every chance to stop him, he stepped behind me. His hand lifted, hovered, then gently brushed my hair aside. The touch alone sent a shiver up my spine. He leaned in.

The first kiss landed on that tender place between my neck and shoulder— soft, warm, devastating. My knees nearly buckled. A sound caught in my throat, half gasp, half plea.

His other hand found my waist, not gripping, just anchoring. Steady. Safe. He kissed the spot again, slower this time, like he wanted to memorize the way I reacted. Then he dragged his mouth up to my ear and gave the faintest nip to my earlobe. A whimper slipped out of me—small, helpless, completely involuntary. His breath trembled against my skin.

"That," he murmured, voice barely holding together. "That right there." His lips brushed my jaw, slow, reverent. "Feel your heartbeat?" he whispered. "How fast it is? How you swear if you looked down, you'd be floating off the floor?"

He pressed his forehead to my temple, breathing me in. "That's what you do to me, Holly. Every time I see you."

I opened my mouth to respond, to say something. Anything. But before I could, Maria's voice detonated from the next room. "Hey! Who let Jewel have a juice box?!"

We jerked apart like teenagers caught necking in the backseat. Jackson muttered a curse under his breath, and I nearly flung the plate at the sink. My hands wouldn't stop shaking as I shoved it at him. He caught it and then stopped me before I bolted from the room. "Breathe, Malibu."

"I *am* breathing."

He raised an eyebrow at me, then grinned. His way of saying, "I see you. You're safe. Are you ok? Are we ok?"

Who knew someone could say so much with just a look?

I couldn't help but smile back. *Yes. All is well.*

Somehow.

Later, sprawled in bed with the smell of smoke still clinging to my hair, I stared at the ceiling and replayed every damn second. My mom had been thrilled to have me back in the house, but I escaped her endless questions about college and found myself lying in bed. Eventually, I realized maybe I should've stayed in the kitchen, with *my* interrogator of a mother. At least Mom made my brain short-circuit instead of spiral. Unlike him.

His breath against my cheek. The way his whole body went rigid when I touched him. The sound of my name as I lured it from his lips. His mouth against my skin.

The second Maria's voice broke the spell, my courage evaporated faster than soap bubbles in hot water. But now I couldn't stop replaying it. The warmth of him, the taste of him, the look in his eyes when I pulled away. Groaning, I smacked a pillow over my face.

Sunday evening came too damn fast. The whole weekend blurred together—voices, smoke, laughter, Jewel toddling around with sticky fingers, Hannah orchestrating everything with her wooden spoon scepter. Jackson and I hadn't talked much, not really. A handful of words here, a brush of shoulders there. His hand finding mine under the table.

I found myself watching him when I thought no one else noticed—the way he leaned in to listen to August, how his mouth curved when Maria made some joke, the careful way he carried plates to Hannah without being asked.

Creepy. That's what it made me. A straight-up creep. And yet, I couldn't make myself stop. Even as I watched his headlights fade on his way back to Camp Geiger.

I made an excuse to stop by the clubhouse right as Jackson was getting ready to leave. He stood by his bike with Mac, nodding at something I couldn't hear. When he noticed me, he excused himself and crossed the yard in that calm, steady way that made my pulse act stupid.

He stopped an arm's length away. "Heading out soon."

I nodded like my skull was too heavy. "Camp Geiger."

"Yeah." The word was simple and full.

We didn't have the right words. I didn't even know what the right words would be. *Don't go* wasn't an option. *Wait for me* was a lie neither of us would tell.

"Text me when you get there," I said, aiming for practical and landing somewhere near pleading.

He studied my face like he was committing it to memory. "Eat breakfast," he countered. "Even when you don't feel like it."

My mouth twisted. "Bossy."

"Says you."

For a heartbeat, we stood there facing each other. Then he pulled me into him and I found myself wrapping my arms around him as he rested his chin on my shoulder. The kiss he pressed to the top of my head said more than any sentence could.

Then he swung his leg onto the bike, and the engine rolled through my ribs like thunder. He pulled away, not fast, not slow, just…inevitable. I watched until the road took him out of sight and then a little longer, because letting go took practice and I was still learning.

By the time Dalton and I were piled into Sally and heading back to Athens, the air had cooled, and the miles stretched out black and endless ahead of us.

We'd driven maybe ten minutes before Dalton spoke, drumming his fingers against the window. "Sooo…you and Jackson—"

I gripped the wheel tighter. "Finish that sentence and I'll toss you out right here."

Dalton angled a look at me, smirk curling slow. "Whatever, Holly. I can get a ride. I'm hot enough to hitch one, scary enough to not get robbed on the way."

I bit back a laugh and floored it a little harder than necessary. "You're insufferable."

"And yet," he said, settling deeper into the seat, "you keep letting me in your car. Makes me wonder who's really the crazy one here."

I turned up the radio until it rattled the windows, pretending the heat creeping up my neck was just from the weather.

Chapter Twenty

⸸ **Holly** ⸸

Finals week was hell.

The kind of hell where the devil wasn't fire and brimstone but highlighters that bled through thin paper, pencils were chewed down to nubs, and professors thought "comprehensive" meant "here's every miserable detail since the dawn of human history."

By Thursday, my apartment looked like the aftermath of a small academic tornado—coffee mugs, flashcards, and empty take out containers scattered like land mines.

"Why did I do this to myself?" I groaned at my ceiling sometime after midnight, surrounded by flashcards like confetti after a pity party. "I could've just…not. I could've burned this place to the ground instead."

Dalton, sprawled on my couch and half asleep, muttered something about not being equipped to put out fires. I frowned at his unhelpful ass and then got up to grab the stack of flashcards resting on his abdomen. That roused him a bit more, and he opened one bleary eye. "I really don't know why you're stressing so much."

"And I don't know why you're still here! Go home!"

"Um, I'm sorry. Have you seen my dorm room? Smelled it? It smells like vanilla and coconuts here. And the couch is comfy."

"Then help me study!"

"Holly, chill. You've got this. You're a lot smarter than you give yourself credit for. Don't make me tell Jackson on you."

Heat crept up my neck, and I glared at him before snatching the pillow he was resting on. His head fell back with a thump into the couch, and he watched as I went around gathering every pillow and throw blanket. I even took my Salt & Sea candle off the mantel before marching down the hallway and into my bedroom. He sat up, grinning, and laughed out loud when I slammed my door. I spread my notecards and books on my bedroom floor, gnawing on the eraser of my pencil. I kept sneaking glances at my phone, and finally gave in.

Me: Your pet spy is really annoying

When he didn't immediately reply, I sighed and took a picture of the chaos around me before sending it to Maria.

Me: I need pointers on pest control.

Her reply was almost instant.

Maria: What kind of pest?

Me: The 6 foot tall, blonde that has infested my couch kind.

She sent back a string of laughing emojis.

Maria: I thought he was helping you study.

Me: He was for a bit. Mostly he sleeps and eats my food.

Maria: Need me to come save you?

The thought was tempting. But I wasn't about to have her make the drive from Atlanta to Athens.

Me: I'll survive. He may not.

Heart emojis filled my screen and were followed by a picture of Jewel gnawing on a washcloth.

Maria: You got this.

I wasn't so sure. Finals had me questioning everything. Sure, my grades were good. Great, if I'm being honest. But this was different. Just one more week. One more God-awful, grueling week under fluorescent lights that made my head hurt. Then I was back home. And a sophomore. One step closer to my dream. Speaking of…I dragged my laptop closer to me and checked to see if Hannah had replied to my email. She was old-fashioned like that.

About a week ago, during Introduction to Entrepreneurship, the gears in my head had started spinning like a cracked-out gerbil on a wheel. So, I asked Hannah, *"Do I need a business plan now, or can I wait until I'm closer to launching? I know what I want it to look like in my head, but right now it's just...floating around. Not on paper."*

Hannah's response was blunt, something I could appreciate. *"If it's only in your head, it's still just a wish. Write it down. Plans don't have to be pretty; they just have to exist."*

I had just started to reply when my phone buzzed.

Jackson: What did he do now?

Me: Oh, so you don't deny him being your spy.

Jackson: Spy. Bodyguard. Whatever. What'd he do?

Me: Well, now I'm not telling.

Jackson: Malibu.

In a fit of playfulness not like me, I sent back a tongue out emoji.

Jackson: Careful. Some guys might think you're flirting.

My face went nuclear. If embarrassment were flammable, the whole damn room would've gone up in smoke. I tossed my phone down and went back to studying. Or pretended to. Suddenly focusing was impossible.

I buried myself in books, half-studying, half-replaying that stupid message comment in my head. Finals week turned into a blur of caffeine jitters, selective amnesia wishes, and enough Oreos to qualify as a food group. The exams ended, but the anxiety didn't. I refreshed the school portal so many times I was half-convinced I'd crash the server. And I kept eyeing my phone like it might bite me, but the day of my last final came and went. Dalton helpfully informed me that the teachers usually uploaded end-of-semester grades all at once. Which made me want to report college as a hate crime.

The grades hit my screen like fireworks. I blinked, reread, blinked again. Passed. Every class. And two of them? As. A choked laugh escaped before it turned into a shout, half-scream, half-triumph. I spun around my tiny apartment like an idiot, nearly tripping over a stack of books I'd been stress-sleeping on. Proof. I wasn't crazy for trying. I wasn't doomed to fail. *I had a shot.*

Maria was the first person I texted.

Me: School's out, babeeee. Your girl is officially free and smarter than she looks. Hot mess incoming.

My cheeks ached from smiling. I threw on a jacket, ran a brush through my hair, and headed for the door like a prisoner out on bail. The air outside was sharp with early summer, thick with honeysuckle, the kind of night that hummed with possibility.

And then I froze.

Because parked beside Sally was a motorcycle I knew too well.

Matte black, chrome catching the sunlight. My pulse skipped. And leaning against it, like he'd stepped straight out of one of my daydreams and into my parking lot, was a Marine with storm-gray eyes and a grin that dared me to breathe.

"On leave," Jackson said, casual like he hadn't just detonated my universe. He held up a second helmet, tilting it toward me. "Just for a bit before I get orders. Let's go for a ride."

I snorted, crossing my arms to hide the way my hands shook. "On that death trap? Not a chance. I like my bones inside of me, thanks."

His grin deepened, the kind that curled low in my stomach. "What's the matter, Malibu? Scared?"

I hesitated just long enough for Jackson's smirk to sharpen. He swung a leg over the bike, held the helmet out like a dare, and raised a brow.

"Last chance, Malibu. You in or out?"

"Ugh," I muttered, snatching it from him. "If I die, I'm blaming you in the afterlife."

He just grinned, like the thought of me haunting him was a perk.

The engine roared to life, loud enough to rattle my bones, and when he revved it, the sudden jolt slammed me against his back. Reflex had my arms clamping around his waist, and that's when it hit me—solid muscle under my palms, abs like carved stone flexing with the throttle. My face was buried against the broad line of his shoulders, and his scent—clean soap and something darker, something *him*—wrapped around me.

Fantastic. Just fantastic. At least the wind would whip away the drool.

"Hold on," he called over his shoulder, and if the cocky tilt of his head was anything to go by, he knew exactly what he was doing to me.

The bike surged forward, eating the road, and my heart forgot how to beat in any sort of normal rhythm. Fear bled into exhilaration, into something hotter, sharper, tangled up with the way every bump in the road pushed me closer to him. The night was alive with cicadas and possibility, and I clung tighter—not just to keep from falling off, but because for once, I didn't want to let go. As the engine's growl swallowed every second thought I had, Jackson leaned into the curve of the road, confident and reckless, and I held on like my life depended on it.

I told myself it was only adrenaline making my pulse misfire. Definitely not the fact that I could feel every line of his body through my fingertips. Definitely not the fact that when he tipped his head back and laughed into the wind, it sounded like freedom itself.

The highway slipped behind us, Athens giving way to backroads lined with pines that whispered in the dark. The wind tangled my hair, whipped it across my cheeks, but it couldn't cool the fire thrumming under my skin. He leaned into another curve, deliberately sharp, and I swore I felt him grin when I yelped and dug my fingers harder into his side.

"Relax," he shouted over the roar.

"Relax?" I yelled back. "You're trying to kill me!"

He just laughed again, low and rich, and revved the engine until the vibrations shuddered through both of us. My heart was a mess of panic and exhilaration, and underneath it all, the tiniest spark of something I didn't want to name.

When he finally slowed, we coasted into a clearing by the river just outside town. The rising moon spilled silver across the water, cicadas buzzing like static in the air. Jackson cut the engine, and the silence that followed felt louder than the ride itself.

I slid off the bike, legs shaky, lungs fighting to catch up. My helmet hit the seat with a thunk. "Well," I said, voice a little breathless. "That was…horrifying."

Jackson swung off too, tugging his helmet free, hair mussed from the wind. His grin softened, though, the edges curling into something gentler. He stepped closer, close enough that the warmth of him chased the night air away.

"You loved it," he murmured. "Didn't even scream that much."

I scoffed. "Only because I was too busy praying."

His chuckle was low, rolling through me like the rumble of the bike. "You're tougher than you think, Malibu. Always have been."

I blinked, trying to find a response. He turned away and started pulling things out of his saddlebag. First came a pack of Oreos. Then a family-sized bag of Doritos and a six-pack of Coke.

I blinked. "Wow. Real nutritious, Marine. You trying to give me a heart attack *and* a sugar crash in the same night?"

He shot me a look as he popped a soda tab. "Yeah, because your diet is the gold standard of health. You basically lived on junk food through finals week. And don't get me started on your caffeine addiction."

I narrowed my eyes. "Dalton is such a snitch."

He just shook his head, settled onto the grass like he had all the time in the world, and leaned back on his hands, watching the water. He didn't push, didn't fill the silence. Just sat there, steady as the moonlight.

I sat cross-legged in the grass beside him, staring at the soda in my hands as the condensation slid down the side. Jackson leaned back on his elbows, casual as ever, like the entire world wasn't tilting on its axis around him.

The question burned a hole in my chest until I couldn't keep it in. "What changed?"

His head turned, brow furrowing. "What do you mean?"

I laughed, sharp and shaky, eyes on the water. "Don't do that. Don't act like you don't know. It's been a year since that night after prom. You told me not to look at you like that." My voice cracked, the memory still a raw scrape in my chest. "I thought it was because you didn't want me. But all this—" I waved my hand in the air like I was trying to get rid of a fly, "This back and forth. All the little touches and the flirting. I want you, I don't. Oh, wait, maybe I do. It's driving me nuts."

He sat up, elbows on his knees, jaw tight. "Holly…" His voice was rough, careful, like he was picking his way through broken glass. "It wasn't that I didn't want you. Hell, that was the problem—I wanted you too much."

I froze.

He raked a hand through his hair, exhaling hard. "But you'd just gone through hell. You'd barely gotten out of California with your skin intact. I knew what had happened, what he'd done to you. And I was leaving for basic in a matter of weeks. I couldn't be the guy who lit a fuse in you and then disappeared. I couldn't put that weight on you—not when you were still fighting to breathe."

The words hit me like a punch, dredging up shadows I tried so hard to outrun.

"I didn't want you thinking you were just…another mess for me to walk away from," he said softly. "We were both too wrecked. And you deserved more than half of me before I left."

My throat burned. "So what changed? Was it the cabin? That night in your room? You're just going to leave again."

He looked at me then—really looked—like I was the one thing keeping him tied to this earth, steady and unflinching. "Because now I'm here. For however long I get, I'm here. And if all I've got is a few weeks and the chance to sit beside you, I'm not wasting it pretending I don't care. I just—I didn't know how to make you mine without hurting you. Or both of us. So, I just tried to push you away. I shouldn't have. And for me, everything since then has been to make up for that."

My heart wanted to believe him. God, it wanted to throw confetti and scream yes and sprint straight into whatever this was. But my brain? My brain was screaming bloody murder. *He'll leave. They always leave. He'll hurt you without even meaning to, and you'll be the idiot who let it happen.*

Healing wasn't linear. It was jagged, messy. One step forward, three steps back. Some days I could almost trick myself into thinking I was fine, normal even. Other days, the ghosts crawled under my skin and reminded me exactly how breakable I was. Sitting here beside him, the two halves of me—heart and head—were clawing at each other like alley cats. I hated that part of me still waited for people to prove me right. To prove that deep down, everyone leaves. Everyone takes. Everyone hurts.

So, while my heart wanted to leap at his words, I couldn't fully resist the urge to yank it back down where it belonged. Because wanting was dangerous. Wanting blurred the lines. What if I gave in, and it turned out I couldn't tell the difference between love and manipulation? What if I let him close enough, and he ended up just like the others—just another man who hurt me, even if he didn't mean to?

It was easier to believe in my scars than to believe in *him*—this storm-gray-eyed boy who didn't fawn, didn't flirt, didn't look at me like some broken doll or beauty queen on a shelf. He never tiptoed around me, never softened his edges to make me feel safe. He pushed back. He matched me jab for jab. And maybe that was why he scared me most of all—because he was real. Because he saw me, sharp tongue, jagged edges, mess and all, and didn't flinch.

I looked back over at him to find him still watching me. He didn't say anything. Didn't press me for answers or a response. But there was a look in his eyes I didn't yet fully understand. My heart thudded so hard it felt like it might bruise my ribs. Because for the first time, I realized he hadn't been rejecting me a year ago. He'd been protecting me. And everything since then…it might have actually been real. A little voice whispered that maybe this was ok, after all.

The world tilted again—only this time it felt less like falling and more like flying.

⚡ Jackson ⚡

She didn't even notice how stiff she'd gone, but I did. Shoulders locked, knuckles white around her Coke can, lips pressed tight. I'd just told her the truth, told her I'd wanted her a year ago, wanted her now, and it spooked her worse than the bike ride over here.

Couldn't blame her. She was all fire on the outside, sharp tongue and quick wit, but underneath she was stitched together with scars and nerves. I'd dropped a live grenade in her lap, and she didn't know whether to hold it or run.

I wasn't going to push. She'd had enough people in her life take without asking.

So I leaned back on my hands, let the silence stretch, and said casually, "The guys and I used to come here a lot. Back before life got complicated. Before football, before the Saints."

Her head tipped, curious despite herself.

"This riverbank we're sitting on?" I nodded at the slope. "Dalton and I rolled down it once, wrestling. He thought he could take me. Spoiler—he couldn't. I tossed his ass straight into the river. Clothes, shoes, everything. Hannah nearly skinned us when we came home dripping like swamp rats."

Her lips twitched. Not quite a smile. But close.

I was determined to see that tension in her shoulders ease so I kept going. "Couple years later, Diego bet Dalton he could climb the sycamore over there faster than him. Loser had to buy milkshakes for a week. Dalton made it halfway before the branch snapped. Landed flat on his back in the mud. Didn't just lose the bet—knocked the wind out of himself so bad we thought he was dying. Diego laughed so hard he fell out of the tree too."

A ghost of a smile curved her mouth. She tried to hide it by taking a sip of Coke.

Better. But not enough.

"You'd have liked seeing Mac back in the day," I said, smirking. "We thought he was untouchable. Cool, collected, always had the answers. Until one night we snuck back into the clubhouse around two in the morning."

That earned me a raised brow.

"We'd 'borrowed' some weed from a friend who didn't deserve it anyway. Came creeping in smelling like smoke, trying to act sober. Mac was the first through the door, thinking he could bluff his way past." I shook my head, laughing. "Hannah was sitting at the kitchen table waiting. Arms crossed. Didn't say a word at first. Just…stared. For such a little woman, she's scarier than any drill sergeant I've met."

Holly's lips twitched again.

"I swear, I thought she was gonna flay us alive. When she finally spoke, it was just: 'Do you three want to dig your own graves now or after breakfast?' Mac turned white as a sheet. Tried to stammer out some excuse about practicing 'field medicine,' which made no damn sense. Hannah just stared at him like she was shocked her firstborn could be so damn stupid."

That did it. Holly barked out a laugh, sharp and surprised, like she couldn't believe the sound came from her. Her hand flew to her mouth, eyes wide.

I grinned. "Yeah, you can laugh now. But you've never seen Hannah Mills coming at you in a dark kitchen with a wooden spatula in her hand."

She dropped her hand, shaking her head. And suddenly the laughter came easier, rolling out of her in waves.

"Field medicine," she gasped. "That's the best he could come up with? What was he treating, his ego?"

"Yep. And he stuck to it. Even when she grounded us from our bikes for a month. Dalton swore she had the hides she flayed off us hanging in her closet."

Now she was doubled over, Coke can rattling in her grip, tears pricking the corners of her eyes. And damn, if it wasn't the best thing I'd ever seen.

I wasn't done yet. I was like a starved man, and her laughter was my salvation. "Did I ever tell you about Dalton trying to impress a girl by jumping his dirt bike across a drainage ditch?"

Her eyes went wide. "Please tell me he didn't."

"Oh, he did. Swore he had it in the bag. We told him it was a bad idea, but you know Dalton. Stubborn as hell. Made it halfway, clipped the far edge, and bam." I clapped my hands together. "Straight into the ditch. Broke his wrist clean through."

She threw her head back, laughter echoing over the water. "Oh damn… Was she at least impressed?"

"Sure," I deadpanned. "Impressed with how fast the ambulance showed up."

She laughed so hard she nearly toppled over, catching herself on my arm. And my chest tightened, because I'd fight ten wars if it meant I could keep that sound alive.

I let her settle, then threw in the last round. "Diego once swore he'd wrestled a wild hog when we were all like ten."

She was already smiling. "Oh, this has to be good."

"Yeah. Claimed he pinned it down with his bare hands. Took us two days to figure out it wasn't a hog at all. It was Mrs. Calder's fat Labrador that had wandered out of her yard."

Her laugh cracked sharp, and she smacked my shoulder. "No way!"

"Swear on my life. Dog just rolled over for belly scratches, and Diego strutted home like he'd bagged a prize boar."

She was breathless now, cheeks pink, eyes shining in the moonlight.

"And me," I added, leaning in like I was sharing state secrets, "I was the picture of innocence. Scout's honor. If you don't count all the times I instigated shit or let my temper get the best of me."

Holly eyed me, gifting me with one of those rare smiles, before lying back in the grass and stretching with a sigh. She tucked her hands under her head and stared up at the night sky.

We sat there for a while. Eventually she rolled on her side, propped on one elbow, eyes still dancing. For once, she didn't look guarded. Didn't look like she was waiting for the next blow to land.

That was when it hit me: I'd bleed my throat raw, talk myself hoarse, spin every dumb story from our past twice over if it meant keeping her like this—unguarded, easy, alive. Her laugh was my new favorite sound. Not engines, not cheers at a game, not even the hum of conversation at the clubhouse.

If all I got before I left again was this night by the river, her laughter tangled in the cicadas, I'd guard it like treasure.

Chapter Twenty-One

⚔ **Holly** ⚔

Life didn't exactly change overnight—but something in me had. I wasn't ready to slap a label on whatever Jackson and I were dancing around. Not when the thought alone made my chest ache like I'd swallowed sunlight. But I kept finding myself near him. At the clubhouse after errands. On the back porch when he pretended to need a smoke break. Passing him a wrench in the garage even though I couldn't tell a socket from a screwdriver.

It wasn't that I'd planned it, more that some rhythm caught me and refused to let go. Hannah's sharp laugh from the kitchen, the rumble of bikes out front, Jackson's shoulder brushing mine when we leaned over the same pool table—it all knitted into a routine I hadn't realized I craved. Just when I thought I had the beat down, Maria threw a series of curveballs.

The first curveball was beige and box-shaped, parked crooked in front of the clubhouse like it already knew it didn't belong here.

"A minivan," I announced, arms crossed, surveying the battered Chrysler like it had personally offended me. "You're twenty-two, not fifty."

Maria slammed the trunk shut with more force than strictly necessary. "It's called practical, Holly. Look it up."

"Practical?" I tapped the faded sticker on the bumper. "'Baby on Board'? What's next, church bake sales and soccer practice?"

She adjusted her sunglasses, smirking. "You think I can't dominate a bake sale?"

"God help the PTA."

Behind us, Diego came down the steps with Jewel on his hip, shaking his head and looking too smug for a man carrying a diaper bag.

"Don't encourage her," I warned him. "She's already drunk on minivan power."

"I like it," Diego said, settling Jewel into the car seat with the efficiency of a man who'd practiced. "Plenty of room for snacks."

"Spoken like a true dad," I muttered.

"Spoken like a true man who doesn't want to stop every fifty miles."

I rolled my eyes and leaned down to Jewel. "Don't let them trick you, Jellybean. This thing is a coffin on wheels. Stick with me and we'll get you a convertible by sixteen."

Jewel giggled, jamming her unicorn in my face, and babbling something only she understood.

"Exactly my point," I said and kissed her cheek.

Hannah bustled out the door with a tote bag of Tupperware like she was sending them on a six-month voyage. "Breakfast burritos for tomorrow, casseroles for the day after, and pie for emergencies."

"Define emergency," Diego said, wrestling with the straps on Jewel's car seat.

"Any man pretending he doesn't need help," Hannah shot back. She shoved a thermos into Maria's hand. "Coffee. If you don't drink it, pour it on Diego."

Maria shot me a look as Hannah hurried back inside and tucked the thermos into the console. Then she hugged me tight, citrus lotion and warm cotton wrapping me in that maternal thing she carried without even trying.

"Listen to me, *chica*," she murmured into my hair. "Don't let fear steal your joy, you stubborn woman."

My throat clenched. "Rude," I muttered into her shoulder.

"True." She eased back, eyes dancing but serious underneath. "There's a kind of love that makes everything worse, and there's a kind that makes you brave. Learn which one you're holding."

My mouth went dry. "I'm not—" I started, then shut up. No sense lying to Maria. She read people like grocery lists.

Behind us, boots thudded on the steps—Mac and Dalton, their shoulders squared in that silent-brothers way. Jackson trailed after, hands shoved deep in his pockets, pretending he wasn't watching me. Which was adorable, because he absolutely was.

"Mom is at it again," Dalton muttered. "Keeps trying to shove half the kitchen into a cooler. Says you'll need it."

"She's not wrong," Mac said, deadpan. "Road food beats gas station jerky."

Diego smirked and clasped Dalton's hand, the unspoken kind of goodbye Saints men seemed fluent in.

Jackson crouched beside the car seat, his drawl honey over gravel. "You take care of those mountains, all right? They've been waiting on a boss."

Jewel squealed and jammed her unicorn against his face like she was crowning him. Jackson pretended to choke on it. "Oh, Sparkle, huh? Should've guessed."

Maria laughed, shaking her head. "You're fluent in baby now?"

Jackson grinned, eyes still on Jewel. "She's got a lot to say. Somebody's gotta translate."

Jewel clapped her hands, drool on her chin, like she agreed with every word.

The send-off turned into a whole procession. Somebody tossed in the last overnight bag. Somebody else double-checked the straps on the car seat. The Saints were like an ecosystem—everyone had a job.

Maria slid into the passenger seat, her eyes catching mine through the glass. "I'll be back before you miss me."

"Too late," I said, too soft for her to hear.

Diego started the engine, the minivan coughing to life like it hated its own existence. Jewel waved with both arms, enthusiasm trouncing fine motor skills. Maria blew us a kiss like a woman who believed in returns. I prayed that the death trap on wheels would get them to Montana, where Diego's extended family waited, and back again. Safely. In one piece. I was going to miss Maria like hell while she was gone. Jewel too. Maybe even Diego.

We watched until taillights were just a suggestion against the Georgia summer glare.

"Feels weird," Dalton muttered. "Quiet."

Mac nodded once. Jackson didn't say anything. Neither did I.

Hannah looped her arm through mine and tugged me toward the kitchen. "Come on. Help me hide the good pie from these locusts."

I let her drag me inside, the clubhouse swallowing me back into its clatter—the scrape of chairs, the thunk of pool balls breaking, the hum of voices rising to fill the new gap.

At the sink, I washed my hands and pretended my eyes weren't glassy. Out the window above the counter, the road stretched west, carrying Maria and her family toward the mountains.

Don't let fear steal your joy.

He took it all those years ago, I realized, glaring at the pies like they were responsible for my emotional growth. But I was going to steal it back. Come hell or high water.

The clubhouse always felt loudest after someone left.

Maria, Diego, and Jewel hadn't even been gone a week before the rhythm shifted. No more Maria humming in the kitchen, no more Diego leaning in doorways like a quiet guard dog, no more Jewel's squeals bouncing off the walls. The place was still full of people, but without them, the song was missing its harmony.

I told myself I was only hanging around more because my parents' house was five minutes away and because it was easier to blame Hannah for keeping me busy than admit I wanted to be there. That excuse lasted maybe two days before even I stopped believing it.

Truth was, I liked the noise. The scrape of chairs, the slam of screen doors, Hannah barking orders like a general in an apron. It kept me busy, gave me something to do with my hands—chopping onions, setting out plates, scribbling notes on the back of envelopes while Hannah grilled me about my plan.

Not a homework assignment. Not some neat little degree program goal. My plan. The shelter.

I'd floated the idea before—a place for women and kids who had nowhere else to go. My parents nodded politely, as though I'd just announced I wanted to major in philosophy. Maria hugged me like I'd already built it. But Hannah was different. She didn't just listen; she made me prove I meant it. She shoved a legal pad at me and said, *"Write it down before you lose your nerve."*

So I did. At the sticky clubhouse table, with the sound of poker chips clinking behind me, I scribbled half-baked budgets and bullet points while Hannah fired questions. *Where would the funding come from? How do you get people to trust you? Who's gonna keep the lights on?*

Half the time I didn't have answers, but she didn't let me quit. If I stumbled, she just raised a brow and said, *"So find out."*

It was terrifying. And addictive.

And then there was Jackson.

I never admitted it out loud, but he was everywhere. In the garage, bent over an engine, grease streaked across his cheek. At the pool table, leaning just close enough to make my pulse stumble. On the back steps, smoke curling around him while he stared at the night sky like it owed him secrets.

I told myself I wasn't orbiting him; I was orbiting the clubhouse. But it was a thin lie, and every time our shoulders brushed or our eyes caught across the room, it burned a little more.

The guys noticed. Dalton teased me constantly, like it was his new favorite sport. If I grabbed a beer from the fridge, he'd smirk and ask, "Gonna grab Jackson one too?" If I sat too close to the pool table, he'd lean over and whisper, "You keeping score or just staring at him?" He had a way of needling without ever quite crossing the line, and every time, Jackson's jaw tightened like he wanted to deck him.

Mac didn't tease. He just gave me those steady looks, the kind that made me wonder how much he saw without me saying a word. It was equal parts comforting and unnerving.

At night, I'd walk the short five minutes back to my parents' house, and my mom would glance up from her book to ask why I smelled like smoke and motor oil. I'd shrug and say Hannah was helping me with my business plan. Not a total lie. But it wasn't the whole truth either.

The whole truth was that I liked being there. I liked the rhythm, the noise, the way the clubhouse wrapped itself around me like a song I hadn't realized I'd been waiting to hear.

And, most of all, I liked the gravity of the man I kept pretending I wasn't falling into. One day, the sort of peaceful cadence I had found came to a screeching crescendo.

I was laughing at something Dalton said, and the oaf threw his arm around my shoulders, using his bulk to force me into a hug. Most people knew I wasn't great with touch, but Dalton had decided he was the exception at some point. Still, I pushed against him half-heartedly and gave him a kick in the shins for good measure.

Then Jackson's voice cut through the clubhouse like a knife. "You two need a room?"

The laughter died in my throat. The whole room shifted, conversations halting as eyes swung our way. I felt Dalton stiffen beside me. Out of the corner of my eye, I saw Mac start forward, only for Hannah to lift a hand and stop him.

"Excuse me?" My voice was ice.

Jackson's jaw clenched. "What? I'm just standing here while you two hang all over each other."

Heat flooded my face—not from shame, but from fury. He said that in front of *everyone.* "Hang all over him?" My words cracked sharp as a whip. "First of all, I wasn't hanging over anyone. And, even if I was, what the fuck does it matter to you? I can do what I want. I don't *belong* to you Jackson Morgan."

The silence that followed was suffocating. I could feel every pair of eyes on me, the weight of the room pressing down. Dalton lifted his hands, trying to defuse. "Hey, Holly was just laughing at my bad joke. That's it. No need to start a fight where there isn't one."

"Damn right there isn't." My glare stayed locked on Jackson for one last beat before I spun and stormed toward the door, my chest heaving.

Behind me, I heard Dalton's voice drop low, meant only for Jackson. "Dude, if you want her, biting her head off in front of everyone? That's the fastest way to lose her." Jackson muttered a slew of curses, and after a sharp word from Hannah, hurried after me.

I barged through the door leading into the garage with my head down, past a few of the members who were acting like they hadn't heard anything. I could still hear Jackson behind me as I rushed outside. I didn't make it three steps to my car before I slammed into a woman in heels and pearls.

Correction: not just any woman. My mother.

I stopped so fast, Jackson barreled into me from behind. His palm landed against the small of my back, steadying me before I went face-first into Ruth McCarthy's Dior.

Her eyes went wide, darting between us, me flushed and furious, Jackson hot on my heels, his hand on me like it belonged there. Right behind her was my father. The neurosurgeon who could remove a tumor the size of a grape from someone's brain but would rather swallow glass than referee his wife in public. He didn't say a word. He just looked.

At me.

At Jackson.

At the fact that Jackson's hand was still on my back.

Jackson felt it. The shift. His hand dropped like he'd been burned.

The lightbulb flicked on in my mother's eyes. Disapproval sharpened her features and she pursed her red lips.

"Mom—" I started.

She cut me off, her voice clipped. "What exactly is going on here?"

Before I could decide whether to lie or pick a fight, Hannah stepped out from the door behind us, wiping her hands on a towel. She must have followed at a discreet distance to make sure I didn't kill Jackson. Which, for the record, was still tempting. Even though the hand lingering on the small of my back was sending goosebumps up and down my spine. Hannah took in the scene with one sweeping glance—Mom in heels, me cornered, Jackson stiff at my side, Dad trying to become one with the wall—and arched one brow.

"Well," Hannah said, "if it isn't Ruth McCarthy."

My mother's chin lifted a fraction. "And you must be Hannah."

"Depends who's asking." Her small smile cut back the bite of her words but just barely.

Mom's eyes flicked around the clubhouse, lingering on the patched leather vests, the half-fixed ceiling fan, the scratches in the bar top. She looked like she'd stepped onto another planet. Her knuckles tightened around the poundcake she carried, edges blackened beneath the neat ribbon.

"I thought I'd…contribute something," she said at last, offering it out like proof she belonged.

Hannah didn't take it right away. She let the silence stretch just long enough to be uncomfortable, then plucked it from Ruth's hands. "Brave, bringing dessert into my kitchen."

"It's homemade," Ruth replied, defensive.

Hannah peeled back the wrap, sniffed. "Smells like it put up a good fight in the oven." She turned back towards the kitchen, and Mom followed dutifully behind her. "We'll figure out how to save it."

I glanced at my mom as a flush crept into her cheeks, not embarrassment, but irritation. She wasn't used to anyone, especially not another woman, cutting her down in public. For a long, tense moment, nobody moved. Dad studied the area around us like he might be expected to perform surgery later. Jackson shifted at my side, but Mac caught his eye and shook his head. The whole clubhouse was watching without watching, everyone pretending to mind their own business while the real show played out in front of them.

Finally, Mom exhaled through her nose, setting her jaw. "We'll see," she said, but the edge in her voice wasn't as sharp as before.

Hannah smirked, satisfied. "Oh, we will."

And just like that, the battle lines were drawn—not enemies, not allies, but two women who loved me in completely different ways, trying to figure out if they could stand each other long enough to fight on the same side. The air in the clubhouse went sharp, brittle. You could've heard a pin drop if not for the sound of my pulse pounding in my ears. Every man in the room suddenly remembered he had somewhere else to be. Chairs scraped. A cue ball clacked into a pocket. Boots scuffed the floor as the Saints made themselves scarce, one by one, until the place was nearly empty.

Dad stepped forward after the two women had disappeared back into the kitchen. "You're the Marine," he said.

It wasn't a question. I jerked my attention back to him as he scrutinized the man standing next to me.

Jackson straightened like someone had yanked an invisible string up his spine. "Yes, sir."

Dad's gaze did what it always did. Catalogued. Assessed. Measured. The way Jackson stood slightly in front of me but not possessively. The way he wasn't fidgeting.

"How long are you home?"

"A few weeks, sir."

"Mm."

Silence stretched. The kind that made most men squirm. Jackson didn't.

"My daughter," Dad said evenly, "has worked very hard to build something for herself."

"So have I, sir."

That made Dad's eyes lift properly. And I saw it. The smallest shift. Not approval. Recognition. A beat passed. Then another. Finally, Dad nodded once. "Good."

Behind us, Mom's voice floated out of the kitchen—tight and controlled. Hannah's answered, lower and sharper. Dad glanced toward the noise like a man spotting an incoming storm and deciding he did not, in fact, need to be outside for it.

"I'm going to…look around," he said mildly.

Translation: I refuse to be Switzerland in that kitchen.

He stepped past Jackson, paused just long enough to clap Mac lightly on the shoulder. And just like that, my father disappeared into the garage like he hadn't just silently evaluated the boy I'd nearly strangled five minutes ago. I watched him go.

"Coward," I muttered affectionately.

For a minute I just stood there. Unsure where to go. Eventually, I sighed, and, resigned to my fate, I turned and followed Denim and Dior towards the smell of food and burnt cake. I claimed a seat at the now-empty table. Jackson stood in the doorway, looking like he was already halfway gone. I caught him with a glare sharp enough to pin him in place. *Don't you dare,* my eyes said. He stayed, taking a seat next to me.

Mom's eyes snapped to me. "Holly, we need to talk. Privately."

"Actually," Hannah said, crossing her arms, "I think it's time we all talk. Together."

Mom turned her head, slow and deliberate. "Together?"

Hannah's smile sharpened. "You love your daughter, but I do too. This girl's got fire. Wants to build something that matters. I told her I'd help keep her pointed straight."

My mother blinked, surprise breaking through the disapproval for half a heartbeat. "She…told you about that? About her shelter?"

"Damn right she did," Hannah said. "She's not just daydreaming. She's putting in the work."

Mom studied her, pearls glinting, suspicion warring with something softer. "And you think you're the right person to guide her?"

Hannah leaned in, not an inch of ground ceded. "I think I'm someone who won't pat her on the head and tell her it's sweet but unrealistic. She doesn't need coddling. She needs pushing. And I can do that."

The air crackled between them. It was pearls against apron. Two women from different worlds circling, testing, daring the other to blink first. I glanced over at Jackson.

His jaw was clenched tight, the storm still written across his face, but when his gaze dropped to me, something shifted. The anger bled out of him, replaced by a flicker of something else, realization.

My hands were trembling. I hadn't even noticed until he did something about it.

Beneath the table, out of sight of the two women still sparring, Jackson reached for me. Big, rough palm closing around both my hands at once, steadying them. Steadying me.

I froze. But then the tightness in my shoulders gave way, the air rushing out of me in a shaky breath. Slowly, I let him wrap his hand around mine, grounding me the way no words could.

Hannah kept talking, Ruth kept bristling, but the tension in the room softened at the edges. Two women who had nothing in common except me found themselves circling toward some uneasy truce, while Jackson and I sat silent, tethered under the table like a secret.

Eventually, I couldn't take the air anymore. I slipped my hands from his, pushing up and heading for the porch. The screen door creaked behind me as the heavy summer dusk swallowed me up. I sucked in a lungful of air that didn't taste like motor oil and pride.

The boards creaked again a few minutes later. Jackson.

I didn't look at him. "If you came out here to defend what happened tonight, don't bother. I'm still pissed."

"I know." His voice was rough, ragged, the temper gone but the strain still in it. "I know, Holly. I just—fuck." He dragged both hands through his hair, pacing like a caged animal. "I don't want to be that guy. I don't. But you drive me out of my mind."

"Not my problem," I shot back, arms folded tight.

He turned, eyes fierce. "No, it is. It is, because I can't fucking breathe when I think about losing you, and I'm not even yours. You laugh with Dalton, and it's like I'm already—" He cut himself off, shaking his head hard. "Christ, I sound insane."

"You do," I said. But the way his voice cracked, the way he couldn't stop pacing, it knocked something loose in me.

He kept going, words tumbling. "I'm not making excuses. I'm just—fuck, Holly, I can't think straight around you. I've been in fights that should've killed me, and none of it scares me half as much as you do."

It threw me. The honesty. The rawness. Jackson Morgan, the one who swaggered and smirked like the world couldn't touch him, rambling like a fool over me.

So I kissed him.

Quick. Just a press of my mouth to his, stealing the words right out of him.

He went rigid. Frozen.

Panic snapped through me, and I spun, ready to bolt. Like I always did. But this time, his hand was faster, snapping around my waist and yanking me back like I was already his.

This kiss wasn't quick. It was searing. Hungry. His mouth claimed mine, his hands anchoring me like he was terrified I'd vanish. My fingers curled into his shirt, dragging him closer, closer, until the world blurred out. I forgot how to breathe. Forgot everything but him. Against my better judgement, my hand found its way to the back of his head. I ran my fingers through his hair, pulling on him like it was possible for us to get any closer. He groaned, his grip on my hips tightening as he deepened the kiss. When his tongue pressed against my lips, I didn't hesitate before opening to him and the moan that came from me was a foreign sound.

When we finally broke apart, I was gasping, forehead pressed against his chest. I closed my eyes, my brain working overtime to memorize the taste and smell of him. Heat and smoke, pine and musk. His heart slammed against my skin, wild and uneven, matching mine.

I glanced up, dizzy and dazed, and caught sight of movement in the window.

Two silhouettes ducked back like guilty teenagers caught peeping. Pearls and apron.

My jaw dropped. "Oh my God."

Jackson followed my gaze, and when he realized what I'd seen, his shoulders started to shake. A laugh broke out of him, low and unsteady.

"Unbelievable," I muttered, pressing my hands to my face. "My mother and Hannah Mills. Peeping Toms."

Jackson grinned, brushing his thumb across my cheek like he couldn't stop touching me. "Guess we put on a good show."

I groaned into my palms. But when he leaned down, lips brushing mine again, I didn't stop him. Instead I tucked my hands into the back pockets of his jeans and let the feel of him anchor me.

Chapter Twenty-Two

I didn't see it coming. One second she was fire and fury, telling me she didn't belong to me, and the next she was kissing me like I was the only man alive.

It wrecked me. Because Holly McCarthy wasn't mine—not really—but the taste of her said otherwise. And I knew if I screwed this up again, she'd walk, and I wouldn't get a second chance.

So, I stopped talking and started showing. No big announcements, no declarations in the middle of the clubhouse. Just…staying close. A palm at the small of her back when she squeezed past me at the bar. Fingers brushing hers when I passed the drink she wanted before she even reached for it. My knuckles grazing her thigh when I sat beside her, the room loud enough to hide the way her breath stuttered.

I quit pretending I wasn't looking. She'd catch me sometimes, eyes snapping up like she could feel it burning. I never looked away. Just held it, slow and lazy, like we were in on some joke no one else knew.

Couple of idiots tried their luck when my back was turned.

Probies, mostly. Too-wide grins, lines so bad even Hallmark would've told them to quit. They didn't get far. Holly didn't do "polite." She cut them down where they stood, her voice sharp enough to draw blood. One poor bastard tried to call her "sweetheart," and she filleted him so clean the whole room winced. I swear I saw the guy shrink two inches before he slunk off.

She didn't need my help. Hell, half the time I wanted to sit back with popcorn and watch the massacre.

Still, I saw red.

So when she walked away, I made sure to have a quiet word. No yelling, no theatrics. Just leaned in close enough for them to feel it in their bones. A look. A hum. My jaw flexing like I was two seconds from breaking theirs. Whatever I said—or didn't say—worked. Because later, when Holly came back in, that same probie damn near tripped over himself scrambling for the door.

She frowned after him. Looked at me.

I shrugged.

She narrowed her eyes.

I smirked. Wolfish. Unapologetic.

She shook her head, fighting a smile like she couldn't help herself. Then she walked away.

And yeah, I watched. Damn right I did.

Dalton, of course, had to make it worse. "Game night," he announced, hauling a goddamn fire extinguisher onto the table with a thunk. "Never know when these two might combust."

I couldn't help but grin. That slow, gloating kind of grin. Then I hooked an arm around Holly's waist and yanked her straight into my lap.

"Jackson!" she barked, squirming. "Put me down."

My arm just tightened around her, loving the sound of my name on her lips. "Then sit."

"You're an ass," she muttered, cheeks hot, fists batting at me and even elbowing me in the stomach. But she didn't get up. Didn't really want to. I could feel it in the way her body went from stiff to settled, like she hated herself for it.

Dalton rolled his eyes. "Christ, get a room. Some of us are here to win."

I forced myself not to wince. My own damn voice came back at me, sharp and ugly—*you two need a room?* I'd thrown it at them like a grenade, jealous and stupid, and all it bought me was Holly's fire.

I'd fucked up. No way around it.

And yet, if I hadn't? If she hadn't snapped back, if I hadn't chased her out to that porch, if she hadn't kissed me first—

I tightened my arm around her without thinking, like I was afraid she'd slip away if I let her breathe. Maybe I should be grateful my mouth had run off that night. Cost me some pride, sure. But it got me *this.*

Spades turned into war quick. Ten minutes in, Holly and I were snapping at each other about whether she should've thrown a Queen. Which is why neither of us noticed Dalton quietly stacking up tricks like he was running a casino.

She got up to grab a drink. Dalton slipped something out of his sleeve. I lunged, catching his wrist. Out slid an Ace.

"You son of a bitch!" I yelled, waving it like Exhibit A.

Dalton jerked free, scandalized and shouting protests.

Mac dragged a hand down his face. "We should've played Monopoly. At least then the cheating's honest."

I lunged across the table, grabbing Dalton in a headlock, both of us wrestling across the floor while the fire extinguisher rolled off the table like a referee calling time-out.

Holly leaned on the counter with her drink, smirking at us like we were a couple of idiots, which we were. But she was smiling. At me. And I'd take that any damn day.

Idiots, her eyes said.

Mine, my chest answered.

The days blurred into each other after that. Loud, messy, full of touches that probably looked casual to everyone else but weren't casual at all. Every morning shaved another sliver off the time we had, and every night I found some excuse to put my hands on her. A brush of my fingers. A hand at her hip. One more second burned into memory, like if I touched her enough, I could map her into me and never lose it.

Didn't matter. Time was still running out.

She didn't see it yet, or she pretended not to. The calendar bleeding down to nothing. But I felt it every damn night, lying awake and listening to the clubhouse go quiet around us. Every laugh, every spark in her eyes, every soft sound she made when she leaned against me…it was all getting carved into me.

Because when it ended, and it would end, I knew I wasn't walking away the same man. If anything was going to bring me home, it was the memory of her.

↓ **Holly** ↓

When I kissed Jackson, I hadn't realized I was signing up to be his. For him to be mine. Or maybe I had and just didn't want to admit it. He didn't say it out loud, but I felt it in the small things. The way his hand always seemed to find the small of my back, guiding without pushing. The way his eyes tracked a room, not just watching me, but watching for me.

Sometimes it was more than I could handle. His hand would land on my knee under the table, warm and steady, and before I even realized it my body jolted—reflex, fear wired into my bones.

He noticed. Every time. His hand would start to retreat, slow and careful, like he was giving me space. Like he'd rather cut off his own arm than scare me.

And every damn time, I caught him, my fingers wrapping around his wrist, dragging his hand right back where it was. My pulse screaming, my throat tight, but needing that contact anyway.

It scared me. Not because I didn't want it—I wanted it too much. But because the last time someone forced their way into my world, they hadn't protected anything. Least of all me.

So I kept my guard up, even as part of me leaned into the warmth of him. The voice in my head warned he could break me. The louder voice whispered he already was. Most days, it felt like I was walking a tightrope— balancing between fear and wanting, between the ghosts that still clawed at me and the man who made me feel almost safe. I didn't always trust myself to stay steady. Which was why I kept busy. Kept moving. If I let myself stop, let myself feel too much, I was afraid I'd fall.

I was constantly working with Hannah and my parents on the business.

We'd agreed not to wait until I graduated—people like Maria, people like me, didn't have time for that. They needed help now. When exams or life knocked me flat, Hannah picked up the slack. She wasn't about to let this dream stall out. And ever since Hannah begrudgingly served up that burnt pound cake, Mom had inserted herself into every step, insisting she'd have a say. And honestly? I didn't mind.

Some nights, when the clubhouse quieted down to the clink of bottles and the murmur of voices on the back porch, I'd pass by the window and see Hannah and my mother sitting together at the table with my legal pad between them. At first they circled each other like boxers—tap, tap, test the guard—but slowly the footwork changed. My mother started showing up with folders and tabs. Hannah started teasing her less and trusting her more. My dad just did his best to keep them from burning the whole county down. He and Mr. Mills were getting good at tag-teaming the dynamic duo that their wives made up.

One night I turned the corner and caught the tail end of a private conversation.

"—waiting for her to come to you won't fix what you broke," Hannah was saying, not unkindly. "Show up. Do the work. Don't talk about loving her; prove it."

"I am trying," my mother answered, and I heard the crack in her voice before she smoothed it away. "She's…stubborn."

"So are you." Hannah's mouth twitched. "She gets it honest."

They saw me a second later. The pad lay open on the table: cost projections, staffing notes, a messy list of grant targets my dad's office had spit out for her. For *us*.

"You're late honey," Mom said, brushing a crumb from her dress like she hadn't been caught caring. "Sit. We're arguing about names."

"We're not arguing," Hannah said. "We're just trying to figure out how to tell you your ideas are terrible."

"My names are not terrible," I said, instantly defensive. "They're heartfelt."

"'Haven House' is a bank," Hannah said. "Or a timeshare. Or a cult."

"'Second Dawn' sounds like a skincare line," my mom added, crisp.

"It's my business," I said, heat rising. "I'll name it what I want."

They shared a look—one of those quick, zipper-sealed expressions women had when they agreed on something without a word.

Hannah leaned back. "Good."

"Good?" I repeated, thrown.

Mom nodded once. "If you can't claim the name, you won't be able to claim the rest." I don't think she realized how much she just sounded like Hannah. She slid a pen toward me. "So claim it."

I stood there, suddenly aware that they weren't trying to take it from me; they were waiting for me to take it for myself. The heat in my cheeks shifted into something steadier.

"Fine," I said, snatching the pen. "How about...Willow's Harbor?" *Willow* was Hannah's idea—strong, rooted, bending without breaking. *Harbor* came from my mom.

The look they traded this time was pride, admiration, a truce drawn in ink and it settled something tight in my chest.

The nights got shorter. The air pressed hotter. The countdown got louder.

On the last week before he left, Jackson and I ended up alone in front of my parents' guesthouse, the one tucked back by the stand of trees where cicadas screamed like an orchestra. Mom hadn't exactly been thrilled about Jackson. Pretty sure her dream boyfriend for me wore loafers and carried a briefcase, not boots and camo that he swapped for leather on the weekends. But then she started catching the way he looked at me, like I was oxygen, and even she couldn't argue with that kind of devotion. Devotion that I had started to accept. The main house lights across the lawn flickered off and we lay across the hood of Sally underneath a hot summer sky full of stars.

I had laid my head on his chest, having given up the fight pretending I didn't care. As if I didn't feel the heat that came from the sparks between us. His arms were around me, my legs intertwined with his. Neither of us said a word; we didn't have to. His hand traced a lazy path up and down my back. I closed my eyes, trying to force away the voice in my head that reminded me that summer was almost over. And then, he would be gone. And I would be here. But I couldn't get it to shut up. I slid off the hood, pulling him with me.

He gave me a questioning look. "What's wrong, Malibu?"

I didn't know how to answer. There were simply too many things racing through my mind and not enough words. So, like I had on the porch all those months ago, I kissed him. The feel of his lips had become familiar to me. But the hundreds of kisses and stolen moments we had shared were not doing a thing to still the racing of my heart. So, with trembling hands, I pushed my hand under his shirt and ran my palm across his defined stomach. I felt his breath stutter, and as I started to trace the V of his abdomen before pulling at the waist of his jeans, he stopped me and stepped back.

I stood across from him and could feel every mile that was about to open between us. It had been a long time since I was so certain about something, even though it was making my whole body shake. I could see in his gray eyes that he had seen the line I had drawn in the sand, and how close I was to crossing it. How badly he wanted to cross it too. Then, not daring to break eye contact, I slipped my hand into my back pocket and pulled out the silver foil square like an offering. It had been burning a hole in my jeans all night. His eyes widened as he glanced from me to it and back again.

"We don't have to," he said first, hands flexing uselessly at his sides. "Holly, we don't."

"I know," I said. "But I want to. We've been dancing around it. I can't keep lying to myself. I…I want this. I want you. In a way I've never wanted someone before. Please."

He opened his mouth, closed it. Then he closed his large hand over mine. The foil crinkled and my breath caught. It nearly broke me, the way he was careful, the way he would rather go crazy than rush me. His thumb brushed my jaw, like a question mark. "Are you sure, Malibu?"

"Yes," I answered, shivering. "But slow."

His eyes sharped to a steel gray when I tugged his shirt over his head, but he never moved an inch. I knew he was waiting for permission to touch me. I closed my eyes, steeling myself, then guided his hand to my breast and encouraged him to explore the rest of me. My heart was trying desperately to escape my ribcage, and I gasped when he bent his head, burying his face in the crook of my neck. His lips traveled down my jaw, to the sweet spot where my neck met my shoulder, and then he kissed my collarbone. When he ran a calloused thumb over the skin of my breast, I didn't stop him. He tweaked my nipple through the fabric, taking the way I leaned into him as the green light that it was.

I slipped out of my top, letting it fall to the ground. The reverent way he looked at me as my bra followed just made me want this more. I kissed him again, surprising us both as I moaned when his tongue pressed against my lips and pulling him into me when I opened for him. He groaned, hands traveling over every inch of my skin. When he cupped my breast in his hand, I whimpered and he froze. But I smiled softly, and he didn't take his eyes off mine as he traced the curve of my body to my ass which he squeezed before lifting me up. I wrapped my legs around his waist as he laid us down in the grass. The moon was our only light, and I would be lying if I said I didn't love his infuriatingly patient touch, like he thought I might vanish if he pressed too hard.

I did vanish, a little. Everything blurred until there was only heat and him and the sound of my own pulse. When I flinched and closed my eyes as he touched my inner thigh, an echo of an unwelcome memory, I felt him go still above me.

"We can stop," he said into my hair, voice breaking. "Say it and I'll stop."

I swallowed, throat thick. "No," I whispered, and pulled him back to me. "I want to. Help me forget what his hands felt like on my skin."

His breath left him in a rough sound. He gathered me closer like we were the last two people in a world that had never once been kind. His hands weren't cages. They were doorways. Every place he touched rewrote something, and every place I touched said *mine* back to him in a language older than both of us. He slid my shorts off my legs, and settled himself between me. I bit my lip as I took the condom out of the wrapper, and we both trembled when I slid it on him. He gave me one last questioning look before lining up and sliding into me. I whimpered, but my grip on his thighs urged him to keep going. Slowly, we found a rhythm. And it felt *good*. I had been so afraid, for so long…but he made me feel whole.

Jackson was painfully gentle, the steady movement driving me insane. I wrapped my legs around his waist and pulled his face to mine. I kissed him, then trailed kisses down his jaw and over to his ear. I nipped at it, and he moaned, so I did it again. "Harder, handsome. Faster."

"Malibu…"

I dragged my nails down his back, lifting my hips to meet his and rolling my body under his, taking him even deeper. That was all it took.

A firestorm erupted.

He began to move, a slow, deep rhythm that quickly turned frantic. Each thrust dragged a gasp or a moan from my lips. The air filled with the sounds of our joining—skin slapping against skin, ragged breaths, the rustle of grass beneath us.

He drove into me, again and again, and we let ourselves drift, and somehow landed exactly where we were meant to. I let myself feel every hard ridge of his cock, and it was as if my body had been *made* for this, for him. The friction was exquisite, a building coil of pleasure so intense it bordered on pain.

Jackson groaned, "Fuck, Malibu. You feel so right." He picked up the pace, until he was slamming his body into mine. He muttered an oath, or maybe it was a prayer and buried in his face in my neck again, going faster still when I started moaning his name. "Malibu, baby. That might be my new favorite sound. Let me hear it again."

"Jackson…" I sobbed, my head thrashing side to side.

"Look at me," he ground out, his pace becoming desperate. "Holly, look at me."

My eyes flew open, fixed on his which were glazed with passion. In that moment, with his body pounding into mine, with the stars pricking the violet sky above us, the pain I had carried for so long drifted into the night.

"I've wanted you since senior year," Jackson gasped, his hips pistoning. "You have no idea. You've had my heart. You've had my *mind*. Every damn thought." He punctuated each confession with a deep, claiming thrust.

Chapter Twenty-Two

"You're all I see."

Something broke in me. A final wall, not shattered by force, but dissolved by the sheer, overwhelming truth of his words, by the physical proof of his desire rocking into my very core. A tear traced a path down the side of my face, cool against the flushed heat of my skin. He wiped it away with his thumb and then, never taking his eyes from mine, traced his way to my clit and began to rub circles there in time with each thrust.

My climax hit me suddenly, violently. My body arched off the ground, and I wrapped my arms around his neck, one hand pulling on his hair. I pulled him down for a kiss, moaning his name into his mouth. He kissed me back, tongue sweeping inside like he was desperate to memorize my taste. The stars in the night sky melded with the ones he made me see. Then he buried himself as deep as he could go and came, his release slamming through him in wave after blinding wave.

Jackson collapsed atop me, careful to keep his weight on his elbows, his forehead pressed to my shoulder. Our hearts hammered a wild, syncopated rhythm against each other's chests. The world came back in pieces—the scent of crushed clover, the cool of the evening air on his sweat-slicked skin, my body trembling as I came back to earth.

Slowly, he pulled out, disposing of the condom in the grass. He gathered me to him, turning us onto our sides, my back to his front. He wrapped his arms around my, holding me tight against the shivers that were now wracking my frame.

I was quiet for a long time. Then my hand found his where it rested on my stomach, and I laced my fingers through his. I brought our joined hands to my lips and pressed a kiss to his knuckles.

"What next?" I couldn't stop the words, and hated myself for speaking them aloud.

"We'll figure it out," he said into my hair, a lie we were both allowed to need.

"Yeah," I said, tracing a slow line over his ribs. "But you leave soon."

"Not tonight," he said, and kissed the crown of my head like a benediction. "Tonight, I'm right here."

The night kept on, indifferent to calendars. With my cheek pressed to the heartbeat I'd memorize until it hurt, I let the last of the old fear drain out of me and chose the thing that made me brave.

The orders came down two days later.

He didn't make a big deal out of it, just tossed the envelope onto the kitchen counter like it was any other piece of mail. But the way the whole clubhouse shifted—the looks, the silence that filled in around the noise—told me it was more than paper. It was the countdown.

Of course, the Saints weren't about to let one of their own leave without raising hell. By sundown, the clubhouse was packed. Beer flowed, music rattled the walls, and every brother found a way to clap Jackson on the back like they could anchor him here a little longer if they hit hard enough.

Dalton threw the first punch. Not literal, though I half expected one, but verbal. "Finally," he drawled, slinging an arm over my shoulder. "Peace and quiet. You know how long I've been waiting for him to get shipped out so I can breathe in this place?"

Jackson barked a laugh, snagging Dalton in a headlock as I ducked out of the way. "Peace and quiet? Brother, you wouldn't last an hour without me to clean up your dumbass messes."

Diego joined in, Jewel on his hip, Maria trailing after him with a casserole like the woman couldn't arrive anywhere empty-handed. They had literally just gotten back from Montana the day before. "Don't listen to either of them," he said, handing Jewel off to me. "We all know I'm the one keeping this place together."

"Sure," Dalton muttered, straightening his shirt after Jackson let him go. "That's why you almost set the county on fire last Christmas with that bonfire, right?"

The whole room cracked up. Even Mac cracked a grin, the soft one he reserved for rare moments. He leaned against the bar, arms crossed, watching his brothers with that steady weight of his. He didn't say much, but when Jackson met his eyes, it was like a whole conversation happened in the space of a look. I caught Hannah sniffling when she thought no one was looking, August a steady presence at her side that, for once, she leaned on heavily.

I pretended not to watch. Pretended not to notice the way Jackson moved through the room like gravity bent toward him. I let Jewel tug my hair and teased her about how much she'd grown in one summer. "She's practically ready for college," I complained, kissing her chubby cheek. Jewel squealed and Maria laughed, and it was easier to focus on that than the ticking clock in my head.

But every time Jackson's laugh cut through the noise, every time he crossed the room and brushed against me in passing, it gutted me a little more.

By the time the party wound down, the floor was sticky, the fire outside was nothing but glowing embers, and the clubhouse had thinned to the diehards and the drunks. Jackson found me in the kitchen, Jewel finally asleep in Maria's arms, Dalton losing a card game to Diego at the table. He didn't say a word, just jerked his chin toward the back hall.

I followed. Of course I did.

The room he pulled me into smelled like leather and cedar, quiet compared to the chaos outside. He leaned against the door once it shut, pulling me into him with an arm around my waist and running his hand through my hair. My throat was dry but I just stared into his eyes like I could memorize them.

Then he said it.

"I love you."

Just that. No build-up. No bravado. It landed between us like a grenade, and all I could do was force myself to breathe as my pulse ricocheted in my veins. My mouth opened. Nothing came out.

He saw it. The hesitation, the fear, the ghosts I still couldn't shake. His hand came up, cupped my cheek, thumb brushing a line under my eye. "Hey," he said softly. "It's all right. No rush. You don't have to say it back. I can wait for you, Malibu."

Relief and panic tangled in my chest. I leaned into his hand anyway, closing my eyes, letting the warmth of him brand itself into memory. Because he was leaving, and I didn't know how to hold onto him any other way.

Two mornings later, we drove to the airport. I let him drive, because him behind the wheel of Sally just felt right. One hand on the wheel and one hand on my thigh, we were quiet as we went down the highway. The radio crooned and I pretended like it was any other day.

The sky was that pale blue that didn't belong to night or morning, the kind that made the world feel like it was holding its breath. I couldn't go to the gate with him, no matter how badly I wanted to. So, we lingered in the drop off lane. Jackson was quiet beside me, his bag at his feet. Everything we had built this summer felt like it was threatening to dissolve under the weight of goodbye.

My chest clenched so tight I could barely breathe and before I could stop myself, I grabbed his sleeve, my voice breaking. "Promise me you'll come home."

He froze, eyes closing like I'd asked him to break a rule written into his bones. "Holly…"

"Promise me," I whispered, the words scraping raw.

When he opened his eyes, they were steady and full of the love he had given me these last few weeks. He kissed my forehead, lingering there like he could leave the shape of himself pressed into my skin. "I promise."

He held me for a few minutes as we leaned against the side of Sally. I willed myself to not cry, even as he turned to leave. He stopped before disappearing into the crowd. "Hey, Malibu?"

"Yeah?"

"Write me?"

I didn't hesitate before offering him a half-smile. "If you insist."

He winked at me. "Love you."

And then he was gone. Swallowed up by the crowd and the sky and the damn uniform that stole him from me. Before I could tell him I loved him too.

I stood there, alone with the echo of his heartbeat and a promise I prayed the universe wouldn't break.

Chapter Twenty-Three

↓ Holly ↓

Classes hadn't changed. Professors still droned on about syllabi, the cicadas still screamed like they owned every tree in Athens, and the football chants still spilled down Lumpkin Street on weeknights like the Dawgs were playing every damn day.

Everything was the same. Except me.

Summer had carved me open and stitched me back together, and I didn't quite fit in this place anymore. Not when every routine lecture and late-night study session felt small compared to lying on the hood of Sally with Jackson Morgan's heartbeat under my ear.

So I poured myself into Willow's Harbor. When I wasn't in class, I was hunched over my legal pad at Jittery Joe's, scribbling budgets, grant targets, and staffing notes until the ink smudged across my hand. Hannah and Mom still hovered, checking in with sharp questions and sharper encouragement. Hannah refused to let me slack; Mom and Dad refused to let me dream too small. Between them, Willow's Harbor wasn't just an idea anymore. It was a blueprint.

And then there was Dalton.

Somehow, the same man who spent his nights raising hell in a clubhouse was now a semi-celebrity on campus—UGA football's golden boy with half the freshman girls trailing him like ducklings. He pretended to hate it, but the bastard loved the attention.

"Blondie," he muttered, sliding into the seat next to me at Tate, his massive frame dwarfing the flimsy chair. "Tell me you're not still taking notes in purple gel pen. No linebacker is gonna take me seriously if my sister-in-law-slash-business-mogul is doodling hearts in Psych 101."

"It's Maria's favorite color," I shot back, not looking up from my notes and eyeing my purple pen with the fuzzy feathers on top. Totally not me, and 100% Maria.

"Yet you're the one using it out of all the pens in your bag." He stole a fry off my plate and grinned when I scowled. Some things never changed.

Maria called almost daily. Diego would shout something in the background, Jewel would laugh, and I'd cling to those calls like lifelines. Between Dalton's steady orbit and Maria's constant warmth, the Saints still felt close. But nothing filled the hollow where Jackson should've been.

That's why, when I opened my mailbox one Thursday evening, I froze.

It was just an envelope. Plain, a dirty off-white, nothing fancy. But the handwriting—crooked, rushed, familiar—hit me like a punch. My name. In Jackson's hand. I wasn't even sure how he got my address, come to think of it. But I didn't care.

The world went muffled. The hum of the soda machine, the slam of the stairwell door, the scuff of someone's shoes down the hall—all of it blurred until there was only me, the envelope, and my heart battering against my ribs like it wanted out.

I didn't even shut my mailbox. I clutched the letter to my chest and bolted upstairs, nearly tripping over my own feet. My backpack slid off my shoulder, textbooks threatening to scatter across the hallway floor. By the time I shoved through my apartment door, I was shaking so hard I could barely breathe.

I didn't make it to the couch. I sat right there on the carpet, legs folded under me, and ripped the envelope open with trembling fingers.

His voice spilled out in ink.

Malibu,

Writing this on my knee in the back of a Humvee, so if it looks like chicken scratch, too bad. Paper's bouncing everywhere and I think this pen's older than me.

Afghanistan's exactly what everyone said. Hot as hell in the day, cold enough at night to freeze your sweat. Dust in my boots, my gear, even my teeth. The Corps calls it character-building. I call it bullshit.

Chow's the same every day. Eggs that taste like rubber, MREs when we're too far out to get back. Some boot in my squad trades half his pack for the peanut butter packets—says they're gold. He might be onto something. Mostly it's hurry up and wait, drill till your legs go numb, then drill again.

Got a letter from Dalton last week—took its sweet time getting here. He sent a picture of himself holding that fire extinguisher like he just won MVP. Tell him when I get back, I'm choking him out until he taps.

Nights are the worst. Too damn quiet. That's when my head goes places. I close my eyes and try to be back on the hood of Sally with you. Georgia heat sticking to us instead of this dry oven air. You stealing my fries, your head on my chest, and for once I didn't feel like I had to be anything more than a guy who was whole because you were there.

Don't laugh, but sometimes I swear I catch the smell of your shampoo in my rack. Maybe I'm losing it. Or maybe it's the only thing keeping me sane.

Write me, Malibu. Mail's slow as hell out here, but I'll take whatever scrap of you I can get.

Love you,

Jackson

I read it once. Then again. And again. My hands pressed to my mouth, tears blurring the words, but I couldn't stop. Relief and panic and hope crashed through me all at once.

He loved me. He missed me. He was still out there—still mine. The letter shook in my hands. My chest felt too full, like my ribs couldn't hold it all in. I leaned back until I was flat on the carpet, the letter pressed to my chest, staring at the ceiling with wet eyes and a smile that wouldn't quit.

For the first time since he left, the silence of my apartment didn't feel

empty.
    It felt full of him.

Chapter Twenty-Four

✒ Jackson ✒

The desert didn't care if you were bone-tired. The sun still came up hot enough to cook you in your cammies, the dust still clawed into every seam of your gear, and the routine still chewed you up the same way it had the day before. Run. Drill. Chow. Wait. Do it all again.

By the time mail call rolled around, every single one of us were crowded around like eager puppies waiting on a treat. When the corporal shouted my name, my whole body went tight. The guys and Hannah wrote every now and then, but there was one letter I was still holding out for.

Then there it was. An envelope. Plain. Thin. A familiar swirling penmanship on the front.

I shoved it into my pocket before the guys could get a good look. Everyone was grinning, tearing into their boxes of cookies, letters, bad perfume-sprayed notes from girlfriends. I kept my face blank and waited until lights-out.

That's when I pulled it out. Sat back against my pack with a flashlight propped on my knee, hands almost shaking as I slit the edge. I swear I could hear her voice in every loop and curve.

And then something stiff slipped free—a photo. My throat closed up. Holly.

Perched on the hood of Sally, barefoot, clubhouse porch in the background. Sunlight in her hair, eyes on the camera but really on me. Like she'd carved out a moment from home and mailed it across the ocean just to remind me what I was fighting through all this shit for.

"Jesus," I muttered, pressing my thumb against the corner. For a second, the squad bay disappeared. It was just her and me and the Georgia heat clinging to our skin.

I read the letter three times before the words stopped blurring.

Jackson,

I'm sorry it took me so long to write. I didn't know what to say. Maria says I looked like an idiot pacing on the porch, chewing the end of my pen before I finally sat down. But you asked for me, so here I am.

Classes are the same. Professors talking like their words will change the world while half the room scrolls through their phones. Willow's Harbor is keeping me alive—I can hear Hannah's voice in my head every time I stall, and Mom's not far behind. Between the two of them, I don't have a chance to quit even if I wanted to.

Dalton's still playing big man on campus. He pretends he hates the attention, but I caught him signing someone's jersey last week. Don't let him tell you different. He still checks on me, though. Won't let me walk across Tate without trailing behind me, his herd of fan girls not too far behind. But I think he does it to remind me he's still watching.

The truth is, I miss you so bad it scares me. So I asked Maria to take a picture— me on Sally, the way you left me. If you hold it up to the sun, maybe it'll feel a little closer. Remember what you're missing out on.

Come back to me, Jackson.

Always,

Holly

By the end, my chest hurt worse than any hump pack ever had. I folded the letter slow, careful, like it might tear if I breathed wrong, and tucked it back in the envelope. Under "Always," she had written and erased "Love," but I would take it.

I kept the photo out, and the next morning, the squad noticed. They always notice. A couple of them grinned, and one whistled low. "Hey Morgan, damn—your girl back home, huh? Lucky bastard."

I didn't bother answering. Let them talk. Let them joke. None of it mattered.

That photo was taped above my rack before chow, so the first thing I saw when I opened my eyes wasn't desert or dust or another day in the suck—it was Holly. Barefoot, sunlight in her hair, smiling like she was mine. Whenever we went out on patrol, I tucked it under the band of my Kevlar. Whether she knew it or not, she was with me everywhere we went. And, when things got fucked, she kept me going.

Chapter Twenty-Five

Athens moved whether I kept up or not. Classes rolled forward, deadlines stacked, and the sidewalks around Sanford Stadium filled with red and black every weekend like the whole town had nothing else to live for. Some days it felt like I was living two lives—one on campus with professors who didn't know my name, and one just an hour down the road with a family who knew every piece of me but suddenly felt farther away than ever.

Willow's Harbor lived in the margins. Numbers scrawled beside bullet points in my notebook, grant deadlines crammed between exam dates in my planner. It was progress, sure, but it still felt like smoke and paper. Hannah swore it would stand on its own legs soon, that I'd see it, touch it. For now, all I had were scribbles, late-night calls, and the gnawing fear that the dream was running faster than I could keep up.

Friday afternoon, she proved me wrong.

We were at the clubhouse, Jewel babbling on Maria's hip and Dalton lugging grocery bags like he was competing for Strongman of the Year. Hannah caught me by the elbow before I could escape to the kitchen.

"Come with me," she ordered, and I followed her down a hallway I'd never bothered with because you don't argue with Hannah Mills. She stopped outside one of the storage rooms and pushed the door open.

It wasn't storage anymore.

The room had been remade into something small but soft—a twin bed with clean sheets, a dresser, a lamp casting warm light. A vase of plastic flowers sat stubbornly bright on the nightstand. It wasn't much.

But it was safe.

It was intentional.

"What is this?" My voice came out thinner than I meant it to.

"Insurance," Hannah said. "A place for anyone who needs to disappear for a while." She stepped inside like she was giving me the tour of a palace. "August signed off on converting all the spare rooms. We'll have half a dozen ready by the end of the month."

My heart swelled. And then…tightened.

"In the clubhouse?" I asked quietly.

Hannah didn't bristle. Didn't snap. She just looked at me. Waiting for me to speak my mind.

I stepped farther into the room, running my fingers along the dresser edge. "It's beautiful. It is. But…some women might not feel safe walking through a building full of men. Even good men. Even ours." I swallowed. "If they're running from someone who hurt them, the cuts, the noise, the bar…it might feel like another kind of threat."

Maria came up behind me, Jewel balanced on her hip. She didn't interrupt.

Hannah nodded slowly. "Good," she said.

I blinked. "Good?"

"Good that you noticed." Her mouth softened. "If you hadn't said it, I'd have worried."

"I'm grateful, I really am. I just don't want this to feel like charity," I continued, voice steadier now. "Or like they owe anyone here something just because the Saints gave them a bed."

"They won't," Hannah said firmly. Then gentler, "But you're right. We can do better."

She moved toward the window, thinking. "There's a side entrance we can convert. Separate lock. Separate access. No one needs to walk past the bar. We'll set strict boundaries with the boys—not because they're a problem, but because guests shouldn't have to wonder."

Maria nodded. "We can add signage that doesn't scream 'motorcycle club.' Make the entrance feel neutral."

"And we don't advertise it as the clubhouse," Hannah added. "We advertise Willow's Harbor. This is just the first harbor."

I let that settle.

"This isn't the final version," she said. "It's the bridge. Until we secure the property you want."

The knot in my chest loosened. "You're not upset?" I asked quietly.

Hannah snorted. "Holly McCarthy, if you're building something meant to protect women and you don't question every angle, I've failed you."

Maria smiled at me over Jewel's curls. "You're thinking like the woman who's going to run this."

I grabbed the doorframe, blinking hard. "You did this without telling me," I managed.

Hannah's lips twitched. "You would've tried to do it alone."

She wasn't wrong.

"You've got help," Maria said softly.

I stepped into the room again and touched the bedspread, really feeling it this time. It wasn't perfect. It wasn't the freestanding house with its own porch and quiet street. But it was movement. It was momentum. For the first time since Willow's Harbor had been scribbles and late-night calls, I didn't just believe in it.

I believed in us building it right.

Two days later, the envelope showed up.

I still hadn't figured out how mail worked halfway across the world. Some letters took weeks. Others slipped through faster, like the desert itself had carried them on the wind. I'd stopped trying to guess, but every trip to the mailroom still made my pulse jump.

And then there it was—my name in Jackson's hand, tucked in the little metal box under the buzz of the fluorescent lights.

This time I didn't fumble my keys or nearly trip over my own feet. I just grinned like an idiot the whole walk upstairs, the envelope clutched tight in my hand. My bag hit the floor the second I pushed through the door, forgotten. I slid down with my back to the wall, tore it open, and let his words pull me across the miles.

Malibu,

Got your letter. Got the picture. You trying to kill me? I opened it in the squad bay, and now every bastard in here knows I've got the prettiest girl in Georgia waiting on me. Half of them asked if you've got a sister. I told them no.

That photo wrecked me. I've got it taped inside my Kevlar so every time I throw it on, you're with me. The guys can razz me all they want—I don't care. I see you, sun in your hair, Sally under you, barefoot like the world can't touch you. That's mine. You're mine.

Life here's the same. Hump till your legs give out, chow that makes MREs taste five-star, dust everywhere it shouldn't be. But your letter cut through it.

Don't stop writing me, Malibu. Don't stop sending pictures. You're the only thing keeping me sane.

Love you,

Jackson

I leaned back against the wall, the paper warm from my hands, and read it again. "Humped until your legs give out?" I muttered, rolling my eyes at the page. "What the hell does that even mean?"

I caught myself tracing his words with my thumb, the corner of my mouth tugging up at the way he said "you're mine" like it was already settled. The ache was still there, sure, but it wasn't sharp anymore. It was steady. Bearable.

Chapter Twenty-Six

⚜

✒ Jackson ✒

Boots crunching gravel and the rasp of my own breath became the soundtrack to my life.

We were posted on the edge of a village, sun beating down so hard it felt like the air itself was pressing me into the dirt. Nothing moved except the heat shimmer, but that didn't mean nothing was out there. Out here, "nothing" was the best you could hope for.

By the time we rotated back through the wire that evening, my shoulders were screaming and my throat was dust. The squad was too cooked to talk much—just the usual bitching about chow and whether the showers would have water pressure tonight. Black humor kept us alive, but exhaustion kept us quiet.

Then the corporal barked for mail call, and suddenly every one of us was on our feet like kids at Christmas. When my name got shouted, I didn't even try to hide the way my pulse jumped.

Jackson,

Ok, we need to talk about this "hump until your legs give out" thing. Because I'm pretty sure you know exactly how that sounds, and if you don't, you better be glad Maria wasn't standing over my shoulder when I read it. She'd never let you live it down.

Also—five-star dining? With MREs? That's a war crime.

Dalton fell asleep in Psych again and snored so loud the professor threw an eraser at him. He called it a "tactical nap." Don't believe him. And it's too bad you're not here to tell your guard dog to "sit" and "stay"—he nearly mangled a guy on the field last weekend. Dalton swears it had nothing to do with the way the guy flirted with me before the game, but we both know better. Overprotective men, I swear.

Classes are the same. I should be paying attention, but mostly I end up doodling Willow's Harbor logos instead of taking notes. Don't tell Hannah. She'll ground me.

Maria says hi, and Jewel waved at me the other day like she knew something I didn't. She's going to grow up faster than either of us are ready for.

I'll send another picture soon. Don't expect me to top Sally, though—that was lightning in a bottle.

Stay safe, Jackson. Write me soon.

Holly

I laughed. Out loud, obnoxiously. Couldn't help it. A couple of guys cursed me for waking them, one threw a boot, but I was still grinning like an idiot.

Of course she'd latch onto the hump line. Leave it to my Malibu to make my legs-buckling misery sound like a damn sex joke. And she wasn't wrong—I'd never live that one down if Maria heard it.

I read it again, slower this time, letting every word sink in. The sass, the updates, the way she made me feel like we were still just two people lying under the summer stars together.

I folded the letter carefully and slid it under my pillow. Kept it close. Kept on letting it drive me forward, one step closer to going home.

Chapter Twenty-Seven

⊹ Holly ⊹

Spring slid over Athens like warm water—magnolia gloss on the air, students sprawled on the quad pretending finals didn't exist, red and black everywhere you looked. People talked about summer internships and lake weekends and road trips like the future was a line they could just step across. I went to class, I highlighted things that were apparently important, I ate french fries out of paper boats and told myself I was keeping it together.

Mostly, I was. Until Friday.

I was home for the weekend—one bag, a plan to raid the fridge and pass out face-first on the couch. But the house was empty so I got back into Sally and headed to my home away from home. I barely made it through the door before my mother clocked me like a heat-seeking missile. I froze, blinking at the unfamiliar sight of her and my father at the kitchen counter. I had expected them to be home, not *here*.

"There you are," she said, relief and steel she had learned from Hannah braided into one voice. "Good. She's waiting."

"Who's waiting? And waiting for what?" I asked, eyeing the casserole she or Hannah had set out like bait.

"For you," Hannah answered from the hallway, arms crossed, mouth set. "Come on."

"I—can it be after I eat?" I tried. "Or after a nap? Or after graduation?"

"Now," Mom said. Same tone. Same steel. Traitor. Hannah was waiting in the hall and smiled broadly when she saw me.

They flanked me—two small, immovable women—and steered me down the back corridor, past the rooms I used to ignore, past the one with the lamp I'd helped pick out, to a door I hadn't seen open. My stomach cinched upon seeing the light spill out from the open door.

"I'm not ready," I said, because fear had a way of making you a kid again, hands shaking in a crowded room and trying to make yourself small enough to survive. "Hannah, I'm not—"

"You are," she said, and laid a hand between my shoulder blades. It felt like a blessing and a shove. "Breathe. Then go in."

Mom squeezed my wrist. "You don't have to fix anything," she said, eyes fierce. "You just have to show up."

My hand found the doorknob. Cold metal. One breath, then another. I stepped inside.

She was younger than I'd expected. Early twenties, maybe. Hollowed-out eyes, lip split and eye blooming purple, an oversized hoodie swallowing her frame. A little girl pressed into her side so tight it looked like she was trying to climb back into her mother's body. The child's hair was damp with sweat; a cheap plastic bracelet dug into her wrist.

"Hi," I said, and my voice came out steady, which felt like a miracle.

Neither answered. The room hummed with their fear. Lamp light, fresh sheets, a clean towel folded on the dresser—little things that said safe without promising the impossible.

I sank to the floor so I wasn't towering over them. I set my elbows on my knees and kept my hands where they could see them. "Hello, my name is Holly. Welcome to Willow's Harbor."

The little girl's eyes—big and dark—tracked my every move. The woman swallowed.

"I'm Mara," she said finally. The name scraped like it hurt. "This is Bean." The girl pressed harder into her side. "Her name's Lila," Mara amended, a tiny apology tucked into the words. "Bean's what I call her."

"Bean is a good name," I said solemnly. "Lila too. Do you want to keep both? Lots of people have two names."

Lila's fingers flexed against her mother's sweatshirt. A nod that was almost nothing.

"Can I sit here?" I asked, gesturing to the wall a few feet away from the bed.

Mara nodded. Her eyes were rimmed red; the skin along her throat was mottled with finger-shaped bruises. A flash—Maria years ago, clutching Jewel to her chest, the look of a person who hadn't slept in months. Me, on a porch in a town that suddenly became foreign, jumping out of my skin when anyone raised their voice.

I settled on the floor, my legs crossed as I leaned against the wall. Mara watched me cautiously, arms protectively around Lila, but the little girl wouldn't meet my eye. "We can talk, or not talk," I said. "You can sleep. You can shower. We've got spare clothes and toothbrushes. We've got locks that don't have his key. Whatever feels best right now."

Mara's throat worked. "What's the cost?" she asked, and shame bled through the words until I wanted to kill the very word. "There's always a cost."

"Not here," I said. "You owe us nothing." I tipped my head toward the hall. "Some of us owe the universe, though. This is how we pay it back."

Silence. The kind in which you didn't want to breathe too hard in case it broke.

"What happens if—" She stopped. The question was a cliff.

"If he comes?" I said. "Then you're in the safest place in this county." I didn't say the next part—*and the men who run this place will make sure he regrets it.* I didn't have to. The walls said it for me.

Lila shifted, the bracelet cutting deeper into her wrist. I held out my hand, palm up. "May I?"

She stared at it. At me. Her chin lifted a fraction, fragile and brave. She gave me her wrist.

"Do you want to keep this? Or I could get you a kit to make a brand new one?" I asked, sliding the bracelet off gently and laying it on the nightstand, before rubbing at the red mark from the too-tight band. "Sometimes it helps to pick one thing to control today. This could be the thing."

Another almost-nod before she looked up at her mom and back at me. "Mine's too small."

"Well, we'll just have to fix that then," I said, like it was a secret. "If you want, I'll get you some markers and you can draw what you want it to look like."

The smallest sliver of a smile, gone as quick as it came.

We sat like that awhile. Mara's breathing slowly came down out of panic pitch. Lila's gaze drifted to the bracelet, to the door, and back to me. I told Bean about my ridiculous purple pen with the feathers on top and how it made me look unserious in lectures. I told Mara there was a shower at the end of the hall with new shampoo still in the plastic and a towel she didn't have to give back. When Mara's hands started to shake, I showed her how I counted my breath on my fingers—one to five, then five to one—until the shaking eased.

A knock landed soft against the doorframe. Maria slipped in, Jewel's old stuffed rabbit tucked under her arm, her mouth gentle. "I thought someone might like a friend."

Lila's eyes widened. She reached without thinking, then snatched her hand back like she'd done something wrong.

"For you," Maria said, and set the rabbit on the bed like a ritual. She tapped the rabbit's worn ear. "Her name is Poppy. She's very brave. And she is great at keeping secrets."

Lila reached again. This time she kept the rabbit.

Something uncoiled in my chest.

Hours blurred. Hannah drifted in and out, quiet and efficient, dropping a phone on the dresser that no one else had the number to, a Ziploc with travel-sized soap and lotion, sweats in two sizes. Mom appeared with soup and crackers and that look that could hold a drowning person up by force of will. August knocked once—respectful—and told Mara his name like a promise. My dad came by with a tote of stuff the hospital had donated to Willow's Harbor. I tried like hell not to cry. Not in front of them, at least.

By dusk, Mara had showered. Lila had drawn a small lopsided star on my wrist. I pretended it hurt and she pretended not to laugh. I helped Mara braid her damp hair because my hands needed something to do and because sometimes the only thing that said "you are safe" was a stranger's fingers moving gently through your hair without taking anything.

"Why are you doing this?" Mara asked, when the braid was done. Not suspicion anymore. Simple confusion. "You don't even know us."

I thought the way my skin sometimes remembered hands that weren't careful. About Maria's hands shaking while she warmed a bottle and Diego pretending not to see. About Jackson's palm on my knee under a table—the way I jolted, the way he backed off slow, the way I dragged his hand back because my fearful heart recognized him as safety.

"Because someone did it for me," I said. "And because I know what it's like to believe you're not worth saving. You are."

Mara's mouth trembled. For a second I thought she'd shatter. She didn't. She nodded. "Thank you," she whispered, like the words were a foreign language. We looked at each other, and I swear I saw myself reflected in her eyes. One survivor to another.

"Sleep," I said, and stood before I cried. "I'll be right outside."

I found Hannah in the hall, back to the wall, eyes soft and sharp at the same time.

"I didn't break them," I whispered, shaky laugh lodged in my throat.

"You won't," she said. "You'll make mistakes. You'll say the wrong thing sometimes. We all do. But you won't break them." She nudged my shoulder with hers, small and solid. "Welcome to your first intake, Harbor Holly."

"Don't call me that," I muttered, but the smile crawled up anyway.

Monday morning, Athens sparkled like a postcard and I drove back in for a study group I was definitely not prepared for. When I cut across campus, Dalton was pretending not to hold court in front of the dining hall, hood up, signing a jersey like he hated it.

"Don't start," he warned when he saw my grin.

"Wouldn't dream of it," I said. "How much are you charging per autograph these days? I'm keeping a ledger."

He groaned. "My life is misery."

Chapter Twenty-Seven

"Uh-huh. You love it."

He fell into step with me, tugging my tote higher on my shoulder like I wasn't carrying half the library. "You good?"

It was the way he asked that did me in—throwaway tone, eyes doing a full scan. But for once, I could say yes without lying. I nodded.

"Good," he said. "Because I'm not. That econ prof is trying to kill me."

"You should read the syllabus."

"I did. Burned my retinas."

"You're hopeless."

"You love me."

"Unfortunately."

He bumped my elbow with his. I let him.

By Friday evening the pull toward the clubhouse was a rope under my ribs. I drove back as the sun bled into the tree line, the road memorized under my hands. Maria was on the porch when I arrived, rocking lazily, Jewel's old rabbit now tucked into Lila's elbow as the two young girls colored at her feet. Lila was patiently trying to teach Jewel how to stay within the lines. Lila looked up, checked the door, relaxed when she saw me. That tiny, instinctive act hit me harder than anything had all day.

Inside, August was building a shelf like a man negotiating peace with stubborn wood. Mom argued with Hannah about whether aloe plants counted as decor or hazard. I bet Dad was starting to think his wife had been kidnapped and laughed a little. Mac passed through with a grease rag and a nod. I breathed. The spaced smelled like coffee and leather and life.

Night thickened. I was sitting in a rocking chair outside, a notebook open, trying to outline a process for intake that didn't feel like triage scribbled on diner napkins, when headlights swung into the lot and blasted my bones with cold. Mara scooped up Lila and rushed inside.

The car door slammed. A man got out like a problem. I knew his face— everyone in two counties did. He sold pills behind a laundromat and thought women were inventory. He sauntered like the world owed him. He watched Mara disappear behind the closed door and his mouth curled.

"You think you can hide here?" he called, loud enough to rattle the walls.

"You're mine. You and the kid."

Every part of me went ice and fire. I stood. My fingers found my phone without thinking. My tongue set itself to knife. I didn't need it.

The door behind me opened with a whisper and then the yard was full of bodies and leather. Mac first—calm like a loaded gun laid gentle on a table. Diego at his shoulder, jaw ticking, hands loose and ready. Dalton with that lazy grin that never reached his eyes, like he was already bored of how this would go. August, old power wrapped in a battered flannel. And August's best friend Silas—shadow first, smile second, the kind that said most people walked away from him because something in them understood they should.

The man's swagger faltered. He covered it with a sneer. "She owes me. You gonna pay up for her time?"

"Walk," Mac said, voice not much above a breath. It carried anyway. "Now."

The man laughed, wrong and high. "Or what?"

Dalton took one step down the porch. The boards protested. "Or we make you."

Diego tipped his head, a question and a promise. "Your call."

Silas smiled wider. It showed teeth. He didn't say a word. He didn't have to. That dude was creepy enough but the look on his face sent goosebumps along my spine.

The man took in the line of cuts and bruisers and history in black leather. Even more people had made their way into the yard. Rodney. Clint. Johnny and Dan. Names I had learned over the last couple of years. It was ten to one. Twenty, if you counted the shapes moving inside. This low-life had courage, I'd give him that. He also had a survival instinct that finally kicked in.

"Yeah," he muttered, backing up, hands spread. "She ain't worth it."

"You're wrong." I called, my voice carrying across the yard. "She's worth ten of you. And it's time for you to go. Shoo."

He sneered at me, and the guys shifted until they were between him and me. I lifted my chin, looking down my nose and sneering right back. The man swore vehemently then turned on his heel and went back to his car. Tires spat gravel. Taillights vanished. The cicadas screamed like the world had just exhaled.

No one moved for a count of five. Ten. Twenty. Then Dalton blew out a breath, turned, and grinned at me.

"Guard dogs," he said, winking like this was homecoming and not a line someone had almost tried to cross. "We sit. We stay. We heel."

I laughed then, sharp and bright and helpless. The sound came out like relief.

Inside, Mara sobbed once—a single ragged sound that ripped and stitched at the same time. Maria was already there, arms around her.

I sat down again, hands shaking now that it was over. Hannah lowered herself in the rocking chair beside me with a small grunt.

"Look at you," she said.

"Ummm..." I said, eyebrows up, not really sure where she was going with that.

"It was perfect," she said. "You didn't fight the fire. You held the door."

I tipped my head onto her shoulder for a second the way I never did, because if I looked at her face I'd cry.

Later, when the clubhouse had settled into its habitual midnight hum, I headed home and slipped into the quiet of the guesthouse before pulling out a postcard I'd been saving. A picture of the Arch downtown, all wrought iron and superstition. I flipped it over and wrote small.

J—

Lila smiled today. It felt like sunlight after weeks of rain. A new mom and her girl are safe here tonight. You would've hated the guy who came looking for them. He left fast. The Saints saw to it.

I don't know how mail works where you are. The letters wander. But on the off chance this one finds you quick—hurry home, handsome. We've got work to do.

—H

I set the card on the stack by my keys so I couldn't forget to mail it in the morning. Then I lay back and stared at the ceiling while the night breathed around me. In another world, in a life I barely remembered, I wouldn't have had anything to offer a woman like Mara except pity. Now I had a room with clean sheets. A phone no one else could ring. A line of men in black leather who would put their bodies between her and whatever hell tried to reach for her. And a dream with a name that finally felt like it fit.

Willow's Harbor. A place to land. A place to leave from, different.

The ache for Jackson rolled through me, slow and tidal. I let it. I folded it beside the pride and the exhaustion and the thousand logistics I'd spend tomorrow untangling. Then I closed my eyes and slept like I belonged to the future I was building.

In the morning there would be coffee and a grant to finish and a meeting with a city clerk who owed my mother three favors. There would be Lila's rabbit propped on a folding chair and August swearing at a tape measure and Hannah pretending she didn't cry when nobody was looking.

There would be my pen smudging ink across the side of my hand and good trouble to make.

And somewhere across an ocean of sand, there would be a man with my photo tucked under the band of his Kevlar, reading a crooked postcard that told him the truth:

I was not waiting. I was readying the ground.

Come home. We've got work to do.

Chapter Twenty-Eight

✒ **Jackson** ✒

We were shaving miles with our soles. That's how you made the heat bearable; break the day into feet and yards and the next patch of shade that never showed up. Dust climbed our legs and became second skin that you couldn't scrub off. Rifles rode that groove in the shoulder the Corps had carved into us. Radios hissed. No one wasted breath.

Back through the wire, sun sliding down, the only things that kept me going were water and ten minutes alone with the postcard I kept in my sleeve pocket. The Arch, her handwriting on the back: *Hurry home, handsome. We've got work to do.* Her last letter had been full of the work she was doing with Willow's Harbor. My girl was doing so good. She was making a difference. Like I always knew she would. Her letters were my lifeline.

"Bird inbound," Johnson yelled. "Saddle up!" He was a couple years older than I was and took a lot of the guys under his wing. He was the one our sergeant relied on to get shit done.

Orders came like a hammer strike—clean, unavoidable. Quick brief off the hood of a Humvee followed by kit checks because systems keep you alive. I slapped plates, tugged straps, got the same in return. Johnson smacked me on the shoulder. "Let's go, Morgan." The squad jogged for the LZ as we had done so many times before.

The helo dropped in hard, rotors chewing the sky, hot wash slapping grit into our eyes. JP-8 burned in my nose, sweet and rotten. Brownout turned the world to a moving wall. The crew chief was a shape in the storm, headset on, glove chopping: *move, move, move.*

We moved. Knees to knees on the bench, helmets knocking, gear scraping. I slid in, boots planted, clipped the strap for the guy beside me because his hands were shaking. Patterson, I think—he joined a few months after I did. He nodded, thanks swallowed by turbine scream. I tugged my Kevlar lower out of habit; the photo under the band was there, edge curling—Holly barefoot on Sally, sun in her hair. My chest loosened a notch. Johnson shouted a barely heard joke but we all smiled. The camaraderie was what kept us alive.

Lift. Bank. The crew chief walked the line, slapping shoulders—one, two, three—bracing on the bulkhead like he could hold the whole bird steady with a palm.

We were maybe two minutes off the deck when the call hit the headset. One word, ripped and flat: "Rocket!"

I barely had time to process the word. The look Johnson and Sarge shared. Then the world turned a searing, blinding white.

A streak—there and gone—like someone had drawn a line across the sky. Impact punched the air out of my lungs and then stole my soul itself. Light went to shard and heat; metal screamed like an animal. We weren't flying anymore; we were a can full of men getting shaken by a fist we couldn't see.

Weight tripled. Then it vanished. Then it came back mean.

The bird rolled. The floor became a wall. Something pitched across the cabin and slammed into Patterson who went completely limp. Straps tore. A boot came down on my hand; I didn't feel it until later. We hit once, bounced, hit harder. Rotors bit dirt and shredded themselves to knives. Some of us managed to stay strapped in; the rest got tossed like rag dolls in a game we hadn't realized we were playing.

Silence didn't come. It was replaced by a higher noise—tinnitus, the kind that eats your head from the inside. I moaned, tried to move, surprised myself when that moan turned into a scream of pain. Fuck. Fuck, I couldn't breathe. Smoke crawled down my throat. Hydraulics bled that sick-sweet smell. Somehow I had ended up behind the tail, or the tail had ended up in front of me. I wasn't sure which. I tried to move again and swore vehemently when my body failed me.

Somewhere, someone was screaming "Doc!" in a voice that had already given up on help getting there in time. I glanced over and wished I hadn't. Johnson had crawled to the mic, his leg mangled. His face was set to grim determination as he reached for the little box that was our lifeline now.

"We're hit! We're down. This is Eagle Two, repeat, Eagle Two down. Need medevac, coordinates—fuck, we're—"

Gunfire snapped outside. Not warning shots. Not at distance. Close. Clean. Finishing. Johnson's body jerked and then went still. A voice on the radio demanded answers, a location, anything but…Johnson wasn't going to be answering anytime soon.

A seat frame had my thigh pinned. I tried to move and got a hard answer back from pain. My fingers found the edge of my sleeve pocket and the corner of the postcard—paper soft with her touch and mine, and now soaked in red—and then they went numb.

Another burst tore through the skin of the hull and stitched the air over our heads. Shouts—ours, then not ours. Boots on gravel. A language I couldn't make out through the ringing. Somebody across from me tried to stand and a second burst made sure he didn't try again.

"Stay down," a voice rasped near my ear, calm in a way that made me listen because it had been calm other times that mattered. Sergeant Hale. He crawled into my view like the wreck itself had birthed him—sooty, bleeding from the scalp, eyes bright and pissed. He took one look at me, at the seat frame across my leg, at the bloody photo curled under my helmet band, and then he took in the wreckage around him. Most of the guys were…fuck. I didn't want to think about it. My eyes flicked to Johnson and Hale's gaze followed mine. When he looked back at me, he had this look in his eyes that I knew would haunt my nightmares.

His glove tapped the edge of the picture I clutched. Just once. Not soft. Not hard. Like a knock to a door I'd better answer. "Get back home, kid," he said. Voice low. No time for anything else.

He got a shoulder under a torn panel and hauled. Metal shrieked. The weight on my thigh shifted enough for me to suck in a new kind of pain. He didn't try to drag me—smart. Wrong move and I'd bleed out here without anyone able to help. Instead, he yanked it and flipped it over me, shoved a duffel and a box of God-knows-what against it until the shape read as wreckage and not a man. His hand landed on my chest, flat, pinning me a little harder than I could pin myself. *Don't move* without saying it. I couldn't if I tried.

Footsteps—three, then more. A shadow paused inches from the slit of daylight at my cheek. I tasted dust and metal and swallowed them both.

Hale slid away like smoke. He didn't look back. "Over here!" I heard him shout, and I assumed it was him that fired two rounds that cracked so close the report slapped my face. Screaming now. Then angry noise. Then the kind of quiet that's just between volleys.

They worked down the wreck. You could hear what they were doing if you let yourself. Checking. Deciding. Finishing. A body thumped the dirt and didn't complain. I could hear Hale leading them away, his thick New York accent unmistakable as he taunted them. Whoever they were answered in a language I didn't know but took the bait. I strained to hear anything but eventually, a round of gunfire interrupted Hale in one of his rants. And I didn't hear him again.

I pressed my tongue against the iron taste and tried to make my breath smaller than my ribs. The postcard in my pocket burned like a coal. The panel over me lurched—someone's boot on it, testing. A pause. My entire body screamed in protest and I went rigid as a white hot pain consumed me. The weight shifted off, but the pain never did. The boot moved on.

Something hot splashed my cheek through the seam and I didn't think about what it was. I didn't think at all. I counted. Because counting was the only math I had left. One, two, three—like steps—four, five, six—heel, toe, heel, toe—until numbers weren't numbers anymore and were just a rope I held in my teeth.

The ringing got louder. The world narrowed to burnt plastic and fuel and the weight across my leg and the thud of boots getting bored.

Then boots left. Voices bled away. The wreck creaked to itself, metal cooling. Somewhere a piece of rotor ticked as it spun down to a stop.

I tried to move again. My body said no. I curled my fist around that picture like it might keep me alive.

Darkness opened like a door again, patient this time.

I let it take me, the postcard under my fingers and the knock of his glove still landing against the picture under my Kevlar, repeating without sound:

Get back home, kid.

Got to get home. Holly.

But this time… I didn't think I was going to be able to keep my promise. I whispered an apology that I prayed made it back to her. "I'm sorry, Malibu."

Then my entire world went to black.

Chapter Twenty-Nine

◆ **Hannah** ◆

Julia Morgan's apartment always smelled like old vodka and lemon cleaner that had lost the fight hours ago. I cracked the windows anyway. Habit. Trash first—bottles clinking into the contractor bag like bones— then dishes, then the ring in the sink that never stayed gone. I set a pot of chicken and rice on low and lined up her pills by the sink where she'd actually see them. Check the mail. Switch the laundry she'd forgotten she started. Make sure the smoke alarms still had batteries. The list lived in my head, same order every week. Sixteen years of it. Long enough for muscle memory to be a religion.

She'd fallen asleep in her chair, robe slipping off one shoulder, breath thick and wet. I tugged the robe up and tied it, tucked the blanket around her and checked her pulse with two fingers like I always did. Steady. Skin warm. Alive. Still alive.

"Hey, Julia," I said, loud enough to thread into the fog. "Food in an hour. Your favorite. Try and eat today."

Her eyes cracked open, all broken glass and defiance. "You're bossy," she slurred.

"Good thing," I said. "The alternative is you dead."

She huffed, closed her eyes again. I set a glass of water where her hand would find it and poured the vodka down the drain. It wouldn't stop her.

It never did. But it slowed her down. Sometimes slowing was all you could manage.

Sixteen years of this. Not because she deserved it. Because a boy with dirty knuckles and a jaw set too hard for his age had stumbled through my door one August afternoon and tried to barter work for food with a spine that refused to bend. Ten years old, maybe eleven, too thin for his boots, eyes already learned on how to read a room for danger. "My mom's…busy," he'd said. And I'd looked at him and known: somebody had to be not-busy for this kid or he wouldn't make it.

I kept him coming back. August put tools in his hands and a sandwich in his pocket and the number to the clubhouse on a scrap of paper he pretended not to keep. He showed him how to swing a hammer and how to tell the truth without telling everything. I put my own number on every school emergency form I could slide past a secretary. And once a week, I came here and made sure the problem that birthed him didn't swallow him whole.

Some days the anger still bubbled up stupid and hot. Did she know where he was? What he'd signed himself up to? Did she have any idea what kind of man he'd been building himself into while she built a shrine out of empty bottles?

I beat the anger back with a wooden spoon. I wasn't here for her. I was here for the kid with his name stitched over his heart and a promise in his eyes he hadn't even known he was making.

The knock startled me hard enough I almost dropped the spoon. No one knocked here. The mailman barely knocked. In sixteen years, if I wasn't the one at the door, it was the landlord or a neighbor asking if the noise meant paramedics again.

I wiped my hands on a dish towel and went to the door. Habit had me look through the peephole. Habit had me go cold.

Dress blues. Two of them. And a third man in black—chaplain collar bright against a tired face.

No. No, no, *no*.

When I opened the door, it was all I could do to keep from trembling.

"Afternoon, ma'am," the taller one said. Young. They were always too young for this job. The brim of his cover shadowed eyes that had done this before. "We're looking for Julia Morgan."

"She's in the chair," I said. My voice didn't belong to me. It was too calm. It sounded like Mac when he was about to end a fight. "She's…not sober. Don't expect poetry."

"May we come in?"

I stepped aside. The chaplain's gaze cut to me and sat there like a hand on my shoulder I didn't want and needed anyway. I led them through the kitchen. Julia blinked up at them, confused. The shorter Marine took his cover off, tucked it under his arm, and knelt. He did it like a man who'd practiced in a mirror to get it right. Hands where she could see them.

"Ma'am," he said, voice soft in a way that made my teeth hurt. "I'm Gunnery Sergeant Lawson. This is Captain Rivera. We're here on behalf of the United States Marine Corps."

I stood behind the couch and gripped the back until my fingers went white. The chaplain stood opposite me, his eyes occasionally flicking to Julia but mostly staying on me.

Julia squinted at Lawson's mouth like the words might be a trick. "What for?" Defensive, because defense was all she had left.

Lawson didn't blink. "Ma'am, we regret to inform you that your son, Lance Corporal Jackson Morgan, has been listed Missing in Action, presumed deceased, following a helicopter incident during operations overseas on—" He gave the date, clean as a blade. "Recovery operations are ongoing. We have searched extensively. At this time, we have to list him MIA, presumed KIA."

The words didn't echo. They just landed and sat there, heavy as a man on your chest.

Julia stared. She looked at the window, then the kitchen, then me. She tried to stand and didn't make it. "No," she said, baffled, like she'd misplaced a set of keys. "No, he was just here. He—he just left. I made eggs. He said— he said he'd be back for Thanksgiving. What does this mean?" She looked to me like I could correct the Marines for getting the wrong boy.

"It means they don't have him," I said. The rocks in my throat turned to knives. "They've looked. They're still looking. But they…they have to put it in the book this way."

"The book," she repeated, and rage and grief picked a direction and then neither one could stand. "What book? He's my boy."

The chaplain watched me, measuring breakage. I kept my spine straight as steel. In his eyes was a sort of tired sadness that came from delivering the worst kind of news over and over. But there was a steadfastness too. I wouldn't look at him. I wouldn't crumble. Not yet.

Rivera stepped forward, steady. "Ma'am, a casualty assistance officer will contact you—help with logistics, communication, any questions. We will remain in contact." He set a folder on the coffee table with a card on top. Names. Numbers. Promises that might be kept. "Is there anyone we can call for you?"

Julia's mouth opened and closed. Her hand went blindly left. I moved first, slid the water glass into it. She drank and choked and drank again. "Hannah," she said, as if I wasn't already there. "Call Hannah."

"I'm here," I said.

Lawson's eyes flicked to me. "Are you family, ma'am?"

"Yes," I said, and then, because the truth has more than one edge, "Well, no. But I might as well be."

He nodded like that was an answer he'd heard before. "We're deeply sorry." He sounded like a man who meant it. Meaning didn't fix a damn thing.

They went through the rest like they had done it a million times. Which I was sure they had. Next-of-kin confirmation. Contact updates. The script human beings wrote to carry other human beings through impossible minutes. Julia cried that quiet, stunned cry that didn't involve tears yet because the body was still deciding whether to shut down or explode. I stood there and let the chaplain look at me and did not sway.

When they left, Julia fell asleep in the same chair, clutching the folder to her chest like if she let go he'd disappear a second time. I tucked the blanket tighter. I turned the stove off. I left a note the way I always did: *Eat. Drink water. I'll be back.*

I don't remember the drive. One minute I was on her sidewalk. The next I was turning into the yard at the clubhouse, gravel spitting under my tires, the sun already lower than it had any right to be.

August was in the garage, tape measure across his neck like a second, less patient priest's collar, arguing with a shelf that had disrespected him by being crooked. I walked straight past the bike in pieces and the tools, straight up to him, grabbed a fistful of his shirt, and dragged him toward the back office.

He came without asking why. He only started to ask when I shut the door and put my back to it like I could keep the world out if I just wanted it enough.

"Baby?" he said.

I shook my head once. The words felt like glass. "They came."

Everything in his face changed. The soft went away. The old soldier stood up inside the man I married. He did not ask who. He did not make me say it twice. He crossed the room in three steps and put his hands on my shoulders like he was bracing a beam. "What?"

"MIA," I said, and the syllables knocked the breath out of me. "Presumed KIA. Bird down. They've looked and looked."

My mouth kept trying to be strong. My body was done taking orders. The floor tilted. August caught me as gravity won. I didn't fold. Not in front of anyone. I folded then. All the way down, like a building that'd been waiting for the right charge.

He went with me, slow, big hands careful, until we were both on the ugly carpet I'd threatened to replace for seven years. He tucked me into him and I hated how much I needed it, and I let it happen anyway. His chest was a wall. I rested my forehead against it and finally, finally shook. Then I began to sob.

The door wasn't locked. It opened because it always did when you needed it not to. Mac stepped in, wiping grease off his fingers with a rag. Diego was a step behind him, grin half-formed on his mouth like he'd been mid-story.

They stopped like they'd hit a tripwire.

Nobody said Jackson's name. Nobody had to. It was in the way August had me crushed against him, in the way my hands were fisted in his shirt, in the thing sitting in the room we couldn't see and could feel anyway.

Mac closed the door with two fingers, careful like noise might shatter something that was still holding by a thread. He came to his knees on my side, then slowly leaned into me and his father. The three of us sat there, trying to keep each other whole.

Diego swore under his breath in Spanish, a prayer and a curse. He braced his shoulder against the filing cabinet and pressed his fist hard against his mouth like it could hold back the hurt leaking out of him.

For a long time nobody spoke. The Saints were loud men. They were also very good at silence when it counted.

Finally, when my lungs remembered how to work, I picked my head up and met Mac's eyes. "We don't tell Holly until we know what we're telling her," I said. My voice came back sounding like I could still put steel in other people's spines, even if mine had gone soft for the minute. "Dalton doesn't hear it from a rumor. Maria either. We do this right."

Mac nodded once. "We do it right."

Diego scrubbed a hand over his face. "I'll lock the yard down," he muttered, already halfway to motion.

August's thumb moved at the base of my neck, slow circles, pulling me back into my body. "We go see Julia tomorrow," he said, not a question. "Together."

"Yes," I said. "She won't remember half of it when she wakes up. We put eyes on her. We make sure she eats." He kissed my hair like he remembered how it made me melt twenty years ago. It still did. But this time, the familiar gesture couldn't put back the pieces of my heart.

I wiped my face with the heel of my hand and stood. My legs held. Barely. Good enough.

Jackson Morgan was not my blood. He was mine anyway. I'd kept his mother alive for sixteen years out of love and spite and stubbornness, and I would keep doing it whether she deserved it or not. I'd keep Holly upright. I'd keep the Saints pointed outward. I'd keep breathing until a phone rang with an answer that wasn't a sentence written without emotion.

Across an ocean, a boy I'd raised had vanished into the kind of dark you couldn't light with a lamp.

Three weeks was a long time to hold your breath.

We locked the yard down, kept the phone charged, learned to live with the sound of it not ringing. Lawson called when he could, said all the words he was allowed to say and none that mattered.

"Ongoing efforts."

"No updates at this time."

"We will notify."

I scrubbed Julia's kitchen twice a week now, fed her, watched her read the same line of his casualty folder over and over until the ink should've worn off. Sometimes she woke up clawing at the air and called his name like she could hook him back from wherever the Marines had filed him. I still tucked blankets. I still took out the bottles. I still left notes.

Maria knew by the second day. I told her behind the bar with the dishwasher humming so loud it covered the first sound that ripped out of her. She put a hand over her mouth and then over her heart and then over Jewel's head like she could shield her from a story she wouldn't remember and never, ever needed to live. Diego took her home. She came back the next morning with food and a determination that frightened me more than her tears.

Holly and Dalton were still in Athens, chewing through finals and texting updates when they remembered to breathe. I watched their bubbles appear and disappear and wanted to put my hands around the world's throat for not understanding timing. We agreed that we wouldn't tell her in the middle of a test in a town that wasn't home. We would not teach her to fear every phone vibration for the rest of her life.

I had never been at a loss. Not on a job site, not in a meeting, not in a hospital corridor. I couldn't find language for this. I tried to rehearse it and the words stuck like dry bread. How did you tell the girl you loved like the daughter you never had that the boy she gave her heart to was a line in a book written in careful navy blue?

So I went to Ruth. I had never been to Holly's home but it was just down the road.

She opened the door before I knocked. Mothers did that. She looked fine—pearls, pressed blouse, a list in her hand. David sat at the island, a massive marble thing that was too beautiful to bare witness to the news I was bringing.

Ruth set the list down and missed the counter. Paper slid to the floor. Her mouth opened, then closed, then trembled the way a dam trembled when it already was feeling the cracks. David came around the side and held onto as her legs threatened to give out.

"No," she said softly, as if politeness could bargain with the world. "No, he…Hannah, he just left." She blinked hard, like she could blink the sentence away. "He was at my table. He said Thanksgiving."

"I know," I said, and because there was nothing else to offer, "We're going to do this right."

She nodded, a small, helpless motion, then pressed a linen napkin flat with both palms until the blue stitching left marks on her skin.

David rested his chin on top her head, and looked between us. "When?"

"After finals. When they come home." The word scraped on the way out. "At the clubhouse."

She took a few wobbly steps towards me, putting a hand on my wrist like she might fall without it and then pulled herself up straight, the way women did when they decided the only way out was through. "We'll be ready."

I sincerely doubted that.

⸸ **Holly** ⸸

We murdered our last blue books and sprinted for Sally like she was a lifeboat. Dalton folded himself into the passenger seat with the grace of a moose on roller skates.

"Your car was built for dolls," he groaned, knees practically in his throat. "I've been living like a sardine all season and this is still a hate crime."

"Cry more," I said, patting the faded black dash. "Sally's a lady. She doesn't accommodate linebackers or egos."

"My spine is going to resemble a question mark."

"You're a student athlete," I said cheerfully. "Work on your flexibility."

He fiddled with the vent like he could command the air to cool faster. "She has the suspension of a shopping cart."

"Say that again and I'll strand you on 316 with your thumb out."

He snorted. "Joke's on you—this face stops traffic." It was a joke he had made a million times, and each time the fucker thought it was as funny as the last.

Sally answered for me, the engine dropping into that low, smug purr that made the road behave. Athens peeled off behind us in brick and azalea and leftover exam panic. Wind shoved our hair everywhere. My playlist thumped the kind of songs that made summer feel possible.

"First order of business," Dalton declared, digging through my tote even though I smacked his hand, "is me sleeping sixteen hours and then letting Mom feed me until I cry. If your mom's on dinner, I'm fleeing to Waffle House."

"Rude," I said, laughing. "Mom can cook."

"Yeah," he said, "Dry chicken and unseasoned green beans that taste like a torture device."

His words were without heat and I shook my head. "Pretty sure Hannah's running the kitchen tonight. Last year, she did steaks to celebrate another year of surviving finals, remember?"

"Then I live," he said, satisfied.

We rolled past the farm stands on the edge of town—strawberries piled like jewels, teenagers waving crooked signs, a puppy loafed in the shade with its tongue out like a greeting. Dalton tried to barter my last granola bar. I kept it and offered him gum. He looked personally betrayed.

"Psych prof posted grades already," he said, scrolling. "You're a monster."

"That's one way to pronounce 'A-minus.'"

"I got a C." He kicked the glovebox like it had done it to him. "Con Law ate me alive."

"You chose Criminal Justice and Con Law because your advisor said 'try

Chapter Twenty-Nine

General Studies' and you wanted to be difficult."

"Correction: I wanted to be right." He tucked his phone away. "They see 'football' and think 'dummy.' So I picked the thing with court opinions and footnotes. Turns out I like reading why power gets away with things. Don't tell anyone—I have a brand."

"Your brand is 'golden retriever who sues the county.'"

He pointed. "Put that on a shirt."

He went quiet for a mile, then: "You good?"

I shrugged and gave him the easy truth. "Tired. Excited. Harbor's going to eat me alive this summer. Can't wait for Thanksgiving."

"Yeah," he said. "Jackson's coming home on leave then, right? Or supposed to?"

I nodded and urged Sally down the road, going a little faster than I should in my eagerness to be home.

I honked the horn as I drove past my house, heading straight for the clubhouse. By the time the Saints' gates rose, my shoulders had loosened without asking. Home wasn't just a place—it was a noise: gravel under Sally's tires, the soft clank of the chain as the gate swings back, two bikers laughing at each other as the leaned against the side of the building.

Except…it was quiet. Not dead. Just…neat. No radio. No Mac cussing at a carburetor. The air sat too politely on my skin.

August stood on the porch like a statue deciding whether to fall. He didn't say hi. He hooked two fingers in Dalton's hoodie and nudged him sideways. No words. Dalton went without a wisecrack, which was how you know something was off.

I tried to laugh it into normal. "What'd you do? Steal his tape measure again?"

Dalton didn't look back.

Inside, the kitchen was wrong. The kitchen here hummed; even silence usually clinked. This one held its breath.

Mom and Hannah sat at the table like the beginning of a conspiracy. My brain filed it under *Willow's Harbor meeting*. They were probably ready to bully me about line items and "deliverables," and to pretend they didn't like my latest overly-bossy memo. Hannah had a folder. Mom had a cup of tea that wasn't steaming anymore.

"Ok," I said brightly, sliding my tote onto the chair before heading for the fridge. "If this is about the intake draft, I can explain my notes on trauma-informed language, but I'm not apologizing—"

"Holly," Mom said.

She didn't say my name like that. It was soft and careful, like the word itself had edges. The part of me that grew up reading rooms went very still.

Hannah didn't stand. Hannah always stood. She kept her palms flat on the table, tendons tight, like she was keeping something from sliding off the edge. The manila folder lay between them.

I pulled a smile on like armor. "If you tell me the city denied our permit, I'm going to—"

"Sit down, baby," Hannah said.

I sat.

Maria came in, but she didn't have Jewel. My mind started to race to a place I had brought it back from years ago and nearly forgotten. I looked over at my best friend, and her lip trembled like she was fighting to keep it steady. Hannah's eyes looked like something had ripped her open from the inside and left her hollow. The kind of look no one ever came back from.

My throat closed up. "What—what's going on? Is everything ok?"

Maria's hand fluttered toward me, then pulled back like touching me might break something.

Hannah swallowed hard. Her voice cracked. "Holly…"

She told me then. A crash. An abandoned search. A soldier who would never come home.

I didn't even hear the words. Just the weight of them. Heavy. Final. Crushing. My head shook before I even realized it. "No."

Maria's eyes blurred with tears.

"*No.*" My voice cracked, raw. I stood, and my mom reached for me as I backed away from them, from their faces, from the truth pressing in around me. "Don't you—don't you dare. Don't you say it."

But I already knew.

I knew because he hadn't written. I knew because they were standing here instead of him. I knew because the world had a way of taking everything good from me, and this time it had taken him.

The walls tilted. My chest shattered. My hands fisted in my hair as if I could hold myself together by sheer force, but the sob tore out anyway—jagged, violent, unstoppable.

Mom caught me before I hit the floor. She was whispering in my ear, but I couldn't make out the words. Maria's arms wrapped around me, strong and desperate, even as her own body shook with grief. I could feel their tears on my skin, could hear their voices whispering my name, telling me they had me, they weren't going to let me go. Hannah knelt on the ground, unable to hug me. That space was taken by the two women already trying to keep me together. So she just wrapped a hand around my ankle and held on. She too whispered words I couldn't hear.

But the one voice I needed—the only one that mattered—was gone.

And my world broke clean in half.

When the day came, it came like thunder.

Momma Laverne closed the restaurant down. The high school held a memorial. And on a too-beautiful Saturday, the Saints lined the lane, leather and chrome catching the pale light. Bikes rolled in nose-to-tail until engines idled low, a heartbeat you could feel through the soles of your boots in an otherwise quiet cemetery. When they killed the motors, the silence hurt my ears.

Across from us, Marines formed a rigid line, dress blues so sharp the brass flashed like broken stars. The air smelled like cut grass and the faint metallic tang of rain that hadn't yet decided to fall. It smelled like everything I'd been trying not to breathe for weeks.

I wore black because that's what people put on for funerals. My dress felt too big, a costume for a grief I didn't recognize. Maria stood on my left, fingers crushing mine; the mask she'd worn for weeks was fraying at the edges. My mother sat on my right, hands folded in her lap, eyes rimmed red from holding herself together for show. Dad sat next to her, and every now and then he would place a loving hand on her knee. Hannah was a wall at my back; August a steady post at her shoulder. Dalton and Mac and Diego hovered like shadows, anchors in leather.

The ritual moved like we were all actors in someone else's play. A bugler stepped forward. The rifle party took position. The chaplain's words floated like ash—*honor, service, sacrifice*—and should have landed like balm. They sounded far away, like I was underwater.

There was no casket. There was a photograph on an easel, a small table with his name, and—because the Saints insisted—boots and helmet on a rifle stand, the battlefield cross set just off to the side, and his bike parked next to it all. It felt obscene and precise all at once.

They folded the flag with machine attention—hand to hand, crease to crease—until those white stars disappeared and the blue became a tight, perfect wedge that could fit in two hands. The presenting officer stepped forward.

Julia was led down the line. She moved like someone walking in a dream. For a beat I thought she wouldn't take it. Then her trembling hands reached. He placed the triangle in her arms and said the sentence that unthreaded people: *"On behalf of the President of the United States, the Commandant of the Marine Corps, and a grateful Nation..."* She clutched the flag to her chest as if fabric alone could keep him safe.

Hannah stepped to her—not to claim anything, just to hold what could be held. One hand on Julia's elbow. The mother who'd given him life and the woman who had raised him stood raw beside each other. Julia's eyes went glassy, then wet; the first sound she made was small and broken.

I watched them through a face scraped smooth. I had cried until I had nothing left. My chest felt as if someone had removed the part that held breath. Tears were coins I'd already spent weeks ago. When Julia sobbed, it should have opened something in me—some crack where two people met and mended.

I stared instead.

How could she finally sob now, after all the missed chances? She hadn't even noticed he was gone.

The rifle party fired. Three volleys split the sky like hammers. The first ripped through my ribs. At the second I whimpered, a sound I didn't recognize as mine. At the third, time slowed. The blaze in my ears, the ache in my jaw, the way that flag looked impossibly small in hands that had not been there the way Hannah's had.

Taps followed. The notes crawled under my skin and burned a map I didn't want.

Then the living did the small mechanical kindnesses we do when we can't do anything real. Heads bowed, leather creaked, uniforms rustled. Saints filed past with palms folded—prayer or oath, I couldn't tell. Marines posted crisp salutes. People touched shoulders. *I'm sorry.* Tissues. Nods.

I should have moved with them. I should have let my knees bend and go with the stream, let people close around me like a net.

I didn't.

The photo, the folded flag, the battlefield cross—the choreography of it—was too final, too neat. I stood frozen, a statue in a ritual I rejected.

Dalton eased an arm around my shoulders and tried to steer me. "C'mon, blondie," he said, voice low and wrecked. "We gotta go."

I pulled back. "I'm not leaving." My voice was small but iron. My knees shook; I planted them anyway.

"Holly—" He tried soft.

"No." The word came out raw. "I'm not leaving him."

He tried reason—sleep, home, not falling apart in public. I didn't hear a word. My hands were fists. My throat was rope.

The sound bubbled up—anger, grief, animal and human and infinite— and I let it. It scraped out of me and then tore free, a scream that split the afternoon. I said his name like I could pull him back through the air. I said it because naming him felt like holding him for one more heartbeat. I turned and hit Dalton's chest with both fists.

Why are you making me leave?

Why don't you understand?

He promised.

He wouldn't just break that promise.

People turned. Momma Laverne held onto Maria who held onto her daughter, and I saw the way Diego angled his body around theirs. Mothers set hands on small shoulders. Mac's voice came from behind, stern and impossible and kind. August's face went heavy and furious and, somehow, tender.

Dalton's hand tightened on my elbow. He tried to walk me. I wrenched free. "I am not leaving," I sobbed. "I am not leaving him. I will not leave what's left."

My legs quit, and I fell into Hannah. She caught me without thinking, one arm around my waist, the other smoothing my hair like I was a child. My father slid in at my side; my mother flanked me. August took the flag from Julia—no, not *took*, *lifted*, reverent as a relic—and carried it to the car like a second procession inside the first.

And I thought, wild and useless: *I will never get to tell him just how strong it is. How strong I am because of it. My love for him.*

Saints started their engines then, a low, guttural choir that filled the place with sound—a howled acknowledgment, not celebration. With every rev they told the world Jackson Morgan had been theirs too.

I didn't move. My face stayed in Hannah's shoulder, stealing her warmth and steel because there was nowhere else to land. The bugle faded. The bikes bled into the road. People left in small clusters, their condolences shaped like kind lies.

When the taillights finally blinked away and the silence settled, it was loud enough to hear my own blood. The flag would be placed. The papers would run. Letters would be written. Rituals would stitch themselves to the calendar.

On that damp grass, under a sky that hadn't decided whether to cry, I mourned everything that could've been.

Chapter Thirty

↓ **Holly** ↓

At some point, somehow, I found myself back at the clubhouse. I sat at the table, clutching a cup of coffee. Someone had shoved it into my hands, but I couldn't find it in me to take a sip. So, I sat. Staring at it. The steam rose from the cup, and the smell…my mind went back to the first time Dalton had brought me a coffee at school. When he had shoved a mountain of a blended, caffeinated goodness into my hands and permanently planted himself in my life. Becoming my friend. Because Jackson had asked him to. Suddenly, the coffee repulsed me and I shoved it away angrily.

Maria came up behind me, claiming the seat to my right and pushing a plate of lasagna into the spot the coffee had vacated. I frowned at it. Why did the entire fucking world seem to think casseroles and lasagnas were the funeral blues cure-all?

"*Hermana*, you have to eat." She pushed the lasagna closer.

I curled my lip at it, "I'm not hungry."

Movement on my left, and Mom took up residence in that chair. A hand on my shoulder and the distinct smell of magnolias told me Hannah was behind me. Great. It was the lasagna brigade. Mom reached for me, and I recoiled at the hand she placed on my arm. "Honey, Maria is right. You need to eat something."

Hannah squeezed my shoulder. "If not lasagna, then what? I will make you anything you want."

Momma Laverne extracted herself from the throng of well-wishers and stopped in front of me. "How about some country fried steak, honey?"

Seriously? Could they just *not*?

"I'm not hungry." The thought of food made me sick. My stomach rebelled at the idea of anything in it. And I resented the effort.

I looked up, desperate to focus on *anything* but the four women closing in around me. Unfortunately, that meant catching the eyes of the others. Rodney. Clint. Hell, even that weirdo Silas. Their pity hit harder than any blow.

The room started shrinking—air thinning, sound dimming—until I couldn't breathe. I shoved my chair back. It scraped loud against the floor before toppling. Hannah stumbled out of the way as it clattered to the ground.

Too much.

The sympathy.

The coffee.

The fucking lasagna.

I bolted.

Out the door, into the sharp air. My lips tingled, that first kiss replaying like a cruel trick. On the porch, I could still hear his laugh. By the time I hit the yard, I was drowning in memories. The snowball fight. His jacket draped over my shoulders. The way he'd smelled—pine, motor oil. Home.

He smelled like home.

I couldn't breathe in that air anymore. God, I had to get out of there. Without a second thought, I turned toward the road. If my legs would carry me, I'd walk home. Anywhere but here. I heard Maria shouting for me, but I pretended not to hear her. The quick tap tap of heels on pavement gave my mother away as she hurried to catch up with me.

"Holly, honey. Let's just get in the car, and we can go home."

"I want to walk."

She hesitated and I chanced a glance at her. Her eyes were red from crying, and she was gnawing at her bottom lip, a habit she'd tried for years to break. When she made no move to walk away but instead kept pace with me, I reiterated, "Alone, Mom. I want to walk alone."

"Oh." For a second, I was sure she was going to protest, but instead she slowly dropped back. I didn't even glance behind me.

I was determined to find a moment of peace, so when I got to the end of the Saints' driveway, I frowned when a shadow cut through the afternoon sun's rays. Dalton didn't say anything, but his long legs didn't have to work hard to keep up with me. He didn't even look at me. "I said I want to be alone."

"I know what you said."

His tone was not the light, carefree one I had grown so used to. This was the kind of weary that came from a grief so deep it settled in your bones like a cancer. I knew the feeling. I felt like someone had carved my heart out with a rusty spoon. So, while I wanted to protest, I kept my mouth shut. We walked in silence for the twenty or so minutes it took us to get to my house. My eyes strayed to the guest house, the wide expanse of lawn where I had spent many a summer night. In his arms. Skin to skin. I stumbled on the even ground, and Dalton caught my elbow. At my door, he stopped and sighed. He turned, staring at Sally where she gleamed in the driveway. He was a million miles away, so I headed inside without a goodbye.

His voice stopped me just as I crossed the threshold. "He was my brother, you know."

"What?"

"You're allowed to hurt, Holly. But you're not the only feeling like they are drowning. You're not alone. Don't…don't push us away, ok?"

I gaped at him, and I blinked furiously, trying to banish the unshed tears. He gave me a tight-lipped smile before turning around walking back the way he came. I stood there for a minute, before closing the door behind me and bolting up the stairs.

In the doorway of my bedroom, I looked at the little box on my desk. I wasn't sure why I had brought them. They usually stayed at my apartment. But I made my way to them on shaky knees, like the little box called to me. I couldn't stop the trembling of my hands as I took off the lid and set it carefully to the side. Inside was a pile of letters. His familiar scrawl stared back at me. I had teased him so many times about his awful handwriting. Picking up the little bundle, I sat on the floor and thumbed through them, the ache in my chest growing sharper with each memory.

Hey Malibu

Dear Malibu

My Malibu

I had hated that nickname. Until I didn't. What I would *give* to hear it just one more time.

"Please," I whispered, not really sure to whom I was pleading. "Please, don't take him from me." I hugged the letters to my chest, "Please. Just let him come home. I need him home."

The tears came then. Sudden, fat drops. I had thought I had cried myself dry but the sobs that began to wrack my body proved otherwise. One of the drops fell onto the papers in my hand, smearing the ink and I threw them in a panic, desperate to not ruin the last piece of him I had. The letters scattered around me. The one that landed nearest to me just so happened to be the last one I had gotten.

Chapter Thirty-One

⸸ Holly ⸸

Everyone told me to take time off.

"Don't push yourself."

"School can wait."

Take time off. Try yoga. Try journaling. Grief isn't meant to make sense.

Yeah, well. We could at least agree on that last bit.

One night, I was on the phone with Mom. Back at my apartment, staring at the ceiling, and ignoring the textbooks beside me.

"Honey, your dad and I have been talking. There is this really great therapist-"

"No. No shrinks."

"It might help."

"It won't."

She didn't argue further, just changed the subject and I did my best to play along until she hung up the phone. I stared at the dark screen. Therapy? The thought of sitting in some dull room while a stranger dissected my pain made me want to throw up. I'd done that dance before. Years ago, after the thing I never spoke about. The mandatory counseling sessions. The clipboard. The pitying looks that said *poor broken girl*.

Never again.

So I went back to school. Because movement meant survival, and stillness meant remembering.

The first week was fine. I showed up. Turned things in. Slept when I could. My professors treated me like I might burst into tears mid-sentence. Everyone around me overcompensated with awkward cheer. People I barely knew came up to me with murmured apologies. I was going to launch myself off Rooker Hall if they kept this shit up. But I learned to smile and say, "I'm ok," until the words stopped meaning anything. Dalton was a constant, steady presence and eventually stepped into his role as a natural buffer. Everything was fine. I was fine.

Then the fog hit. I found myself staring at the same paragraph until it blurred. My brain wouldn't focus; my heart wouldn't stop racing. I willed my eyes to focus. To just get to the end of one sentence. But my body wouldn't obey. I felt trapped in my own skin.

Some guy in my study group offered me an Adderall. "It helps me lock in," he said.

I hesitated but took it back to my apartment with me. Maria texted me. A cute picture of Jewel, concern disguised in what was supposed to be a carefree message. Wishing me luck on my next test. The study guide for said test taunted me, and I eyed the Adderall. Just to help me focus, just this once. I swallowed it dry.

It worked.

The noise in my head straightened out. The ache dulled. I cleaned the apartment at 3 a.m. and finished three essays I barely remembered writing. I didn't cry once.

Progress, right?

I passed that test with flying colors. My professor looked at me with more than a little surprise. It felt good doing something wrong, proving someone wrong. The next night, I took another.

Then two.

Dalton noticed before anyone else. "You look wired," he said one morning, holding out my usual coffee like it was peace.

"I'm fine," I scoffed.

He arched a brow. "You say that a lot."

"Because it's true."

"It's bullshit."

"Don't start, Dalton."

He didn't. But he also didn't leave. He started showing up more. At my door, in the library, outside my classes. Always with food or coffee. Always pretending he wasn't watching me unravel. Watching me like if he could just catch the fraying threads of my soul he could tie me back together.

Weeks blurred. I ran on caffeine and pills and pure willpower. If I stopped, the memories came crawling back. The funeral, the flag, the way I'd felt frozen while everyone else moved on. And beneath that, older ghosts. The ones I'd buried so deep I thought they were gone.

Therapists back then had called it *repressed trauma*.

I called it surviving when I downed a Xanax to shut the voices up.

I was sixteen. The world had been rough hands and a locked door. They'd told me talking would help, but all it did was make me watch their faces twist with sympathy. I hated that look. I still did. So no, I didn't need therapy. I needed quiet. Control.

The pills gave me both.

By midterms, I wasn't sleeping. My body buzzed like a live wire. One weekend when I was home, I found an old bottle of hydrocodone in my mother's drawer. A pain killer from a long ago surgery. She didn't notice its absence.

One to wake up.

One to slow down.

One to survive another day of pretending.

Dalton found me in the kitchen of my apartment one night, staring at a pill bottle like it might blink first. I'd given him a key a long time ago, something I was seriously regretting now.

"Don't," he said quietly, eyes flicking between me and the little yellow bottle like someone rubbernecking a car crash. Couldn't look away even if he wanted to.

"It's prescribed."

"Not for this."

"You're not my babysitter."

His jaw flexed, voice sharpening. "No. But I promised your boyfriend I'd look out for you, and I'm not breaking that promise just because you're trying to disappear."

The word *boyfriend* hit like a slap.

"He's gone, Dalton. Gone. He's not coming back. He left me."

"I know," he said. "It sucks, but he knew the risks. He signed up for this."

"Yeah, well. I didn't."

"And you think I did?!"

I flinched. I'd never heard him yell before. His voice cracked, ragged with something more than anger.

"You're not the only one hurting here, Holly," he went on, breath coming fast. "Mom cries all the damn time. Dad and Mac take turns drinking themselves stupid. Everybody's trying to pretend they're fine, like if we just fake it long enough, it'll stop hurting."

He dragged a hand through his hair, eyes glassy with exhaustion. "It'd be really fucking nice if, for once, someone just *didn't* hide it."

Silence. The only sound was the hum of the fridge and my heartbeat pounding in my ears. He waited for me to say something. I didn't. Finally, he turned, muttered something under his breath, and walked out.

The next morning, there was a note taped to my door: *He would want us to get through this together. Sorry for yelling.*

But I was still alone. That was the problem.

The pills worked until they didn't. Then I chased them with whatever I could find—caffeine, leftover painkillers, anything to level out the crash.

Maria texted constantly.

Mom called almost every night, except for when I could find an excuse for her to leave me alone. Big test coming up. A headache. Busy. Anything.

Hannah threatened to drag me home if I didn't bring myself. So, some weekends, I would find myself back there, pretending I was coping while the memories threatened to eat me alive.

Then I would go back to my apartment in Athens. Repeat the cycle. My friends and family were safe in Atlanta. They couldn't see me unraveling one dose at a time.

Dalton could. And he wouldn't look away.

He'd stop by uninvited, bringing food I wouldn't eat, talking until I stopped pretending I didn't hear him. Sometimes I'd lash out just to make him leave. He never did.

"Why do you care so damn much?" I snapped once.

He met my glare without blinking. "Because he did."

That shut me up.

The night before finals, everything caved in.

I'd been awake for three days, papers due, heart hammering like it wanted out. My hands

wouldn't stop shaking. The mirror showed a stranger. Pale, bruised under the eyes, hair

matted.

I swallowed another Adderall. Then half a Xanax to smooth the edge. The math made sense at the time.

When the world started tilting, I tried to sit down. The floor hit back. The tiles were cold. I liked that part. They cooled the fire under my skin. Somewhere far away, my phone was buzzing.

Oh, right.

Maria.

She was coming over for…dinner. Or something.

I blinked at it when it buzzed again. Reached for it. But my arms felt so heavy. And I was so tired. I yawned and curled in on myself. Suddenly, I was very cold. Distantly, I wondered who had turned on the AC. Maria's name kept lighting up the screen, then it was Dalton's.

I was half asleep, and then I heard Dalton's voice outside the bathroom door. I tried to tell him to go away. I was trying to sleep. But the words were like sandpaper on my tongue.

"Holly? Open up." A pause. Louder. "Holly!"

"*Hermana*! You need to open this door. Now! Please, open the door!"

Oh, Maria was here. Why was Maria in Athens? I struggled to remember. I could hear them arguing in the hallway, and I wanted to tell them I couldn't think with all the arguing. Then the crash of wood splintering. Hands on my face. Her voice breaking. Dalton on his knees, pulling me into his lap as Maria grabbed her phone from her purse and cursed when she dropped it. She was crying, and I couldn't understand what she was saying. I wanted to tell her not to cry. I felt fine. I just wanted to sleep.

Dalton started smacking my cheeks, and I turned my attention back to him. "Hey, come on, breathe, don't you fucking do this!" He shook me none to gently, and for a second, I could've sworn I saw Jackson. Right there. He was right there.

"Is it you?" The words dragged, thick and broken. Dalton's brow furrowed, but Jackson understood.

He knelt beside me, his hand running down my face. "I'm here, Malibu."

I tried to smile. Maria was still crying.

Then nothing.

When I woke up, it was to beeping and white light. My throat burned. My body felt hollow. Frantically, I scanned the room.

Dalton sat in the corner, head bowed, blood dried on his knuckles. He looked up when I moved. "Hey," he said hoarsely. "You scared the shit out of me."

"Jackson?" I glanced around the room again and licked my cracked lips. But Jackson…I could've sworn I had heard him.

He looked at the floor, then back at me. And that was answer enough. My lip trembled, and I closed my eyes. It had been so real.

Dalton leaned forward, brushed hair out of my face. "You're ok. Just breathe."

A nurse told me later that if he hadn't broken down the door when he did, I'd be gone.

When I was moved from ICU, the room filled with too much love for one girl who'd nearly thrown her life away.

Flowers on every surface. A card from Clint that said, *Those boys would go soft without you.* Maria had left a stuffed bear from Jewel, tucked against my pillow. Someone had written *Steel Saints don't quit* across the top of the whiteboard in permanent marker.

Mom and Dad came every day. They brought food I couldn't eat and guilt I couldn't swallow. When I opened my eyes one morning and saw Mom holding my hand, she was crying so hard she didn't even notice I was awake until I squeezed back.

"Holly," she gasped. "Oh, my sweet, beautiful, brave baby girl." She kissed my forehead over and over, whispering prayers that didn't reach the ceiling. Dad just stood at the foot of the bed, staring at me like he was trying to make sure I never left again.

Later, when they thought I was asleep, I heard Hannah's voice from the hallway—sharp, brittle. "You saw her doing all this and didn't tell us?"

Dalton's voice cracked back, raw from too many sleepless nights. "I was *trying*, Mom! You think I didn't notice? You think I didn't try to stop her? You were there, but you weren't. None of you were. You were all grieving him, and I was trying to keep *her* alive!"

Silence fell like a dropped weight. Then the sound of Hannah breaking. I saw her shadow embrace him, reaching for the son who towered over her. Watched him melt into her arms like he had been carrying a weight that wasn't his for too long. And, truth was, he had.

"I am so sorry," she said softly. "I'm here now, baby."

When I opened my eyes again, Dalton was back in the chair by my bed, elbows on his knees. He didn't say anything. Just watched me like if he blinked, we would be back on the bathroom floor.

Rehab came next. Voluntary, technically. I signed the papers anyway.

Dalton drove me. We didn't talk much. The hum of the tires filled the silence between us. When he parked, he left the engine running and just stared out the windshield, jaw tight.

"Why are you doing this?" My voice cracked more than I wanted it to.

He didn't look at me. "Because he asked me to."

That used to work, that excuse, that invisible line back to Jackson, but not anymore. I shook my head, the motion small and sharp. "That's bullshit, Dalton. He's gone."

He sighed, rubbing a hand over his face, the sound somewhere between exhaustion and surrender. "Yeah," he said quietly. "He is."

Finally, he turned to look at me. "You're like the sister I never had, Holly. You're smart, and funny, and you've got this huge heart that never stops trying to fix people who are already in pieces." His throat bobbed as he swallowed hard. "And you made a guy who was like a brother to me happier than I've ever seen him."

The words hit harder than he meant them to. I didn't know what to do with them, with the truth in his voice, or the ache sitting heavy behind it.

"Thank you," I whispered.

He winked at me. "Anytime, blondie."

My heart ached at the sadness in his blue eyes, and I wondered how long it would be before they were bright again.

In case anyone was wondering, rehab was hell. Beige walls. Weak coffee. Counselors with kind eyes that made me nauseous.

Every time they asked me to "share," I shut down. They wanted to talk about grief. I wanted to burn it.

Day three, I shook so bad I thought my bones would break. They called it detox. I called it penance.

Maria came once. Cried. Said she wanted to bring Jewel but didn't want her to see Aunt Holly like this. A piece of my heart fractured. The thing about addiction was…it was a greedy monster. It took and took until there was nothing left but shame and skin. You thought you were numbing the pain, but you were really feeding it. One pill, one drink, one lie at a time. And the cruelest part? It didn't just eat you alive. It ate everyone who dared to love you, too.

One Tuesday, I was sitting by a window in the common room. An aide came over to let me know I had visitors, and I turned to see Hannah in her leather jacket and Mom in her red-soled heels making their way to me.

Hannah didn't bother sitting down. Mom stared at me in a way I was sure she meant to be intimidating.

"We're keeping Willow's Harbor afloat," Hannah said. "Barely. But it's *your* dream, Holly. You started this. There are women and kids depending on you. On *your* name. On what you built."

Mom folded her arms, voice softer but no less sharp. "We heard you weren't cooperating in therapy. So, you can sit here and feel sorry for yourself, or you can get back to work. You wanted to give people a second chance. Start by giving yourself one."

I stared at them, still shaking from withdrawal, still trying to believe I was worth the air I was breathing.

Hannah leaned forward, eyes fierce. "You survived hell. Now prove it meant something."

I stared at them, jaw nearly on the floor. Mom slid a piece of paper over to me. Numbers. From Willow's Harbor. How many had been saved. How many had been given a new life. How many had a future now…because of us. I glanced from it to them. The pain was still there. It probably always would be. A love like that was not the kind you forget. But it could be the kind that kept you going on the bad days. If you let it.

I looked up at them. "Ok."

Mom frowned. "Ok?"

Hannah must have seen the look in my eyes change and she put a hand on mom's shoulder. "Good."

That night, and every night after, before I nodded off to sleep, I whispered the only words that ever made sense anymore. *Got to get home.*

When they finally released me, the air outside felt different. Lighter somehow.

I threw myself into school the way I used to throw myself into running from the past, from pain. Full throttle, teeth gritted, head held high. Late nights, lots of coffee, and notepads full of ideas that felt like redemption. I was behind, so I worked twice as hard.

I learned to lean. On Dalton when the nights got too loud. On Maria when the guilt crept in like smoke. On Mom and Hannah when I forgot why I started this in the first place. It turned out failure wasn't weakness. It wasn't shoring up your defense and closing yourself off when things got tough. Sometimes opening up the gates, letting people in…that was the real strength.

Willow's Harbor grew beyond my wildest dreams. Women came in shaking and left with jobs, apartments, laughter. Kids started school for the first time without fear in their eyes. The men of the Steel Saints had became a unit. Deadly, precise. They weren't just a motorcycle club anymore. They were protectors. Silas sneered when he thought I wasn't looking. Said we were going soft. But a hard look from Hannah or August always silenced him. I didn't let it bother me.

I gave my first speech at a conference, palms sweating, heart hammering, and looked out over a sea of faces that reminded me what survival looked like when it turned into purpose. Someone asked how I was supposed to help others when I could barely help myself. Others around them squashed him, admonished him for the harsh question, but I took it in stride. I smiled and told him, "One day at a time. That's all you can do."

I still went to meetings. I still counted days.

And I still thought of him. Every time I passed the Harbor sign, every time a new mom walked through our doors, every time I caught a sunrise and remembered what it meant to make it through the night.

I used to think moving on meant forgetting.

Now I knew better.

You honor the ones you lose by living the life you promised them you would.

Chapter Thirty-Two

✦

✍ Jackson ✍

I lost whole pieces of time. Woke up once with the sun burning through a hole in the fuselage, again with night already full of stars. Each blackout was longer than the last until the dark felt permanent.

Then hands clawed at the wreckage. Someone shouting in a language I didn't know. Metal screamed, and I was dragged out into air that smelled of smoke, dust, and goat hide. I blinked, fighting to stay conscious. To adjust to the wave of pain the sudden movement cost me. Faces closed in, only frightened, dark eyes visible underneath thick head coverings. Children hovered behind them, staring like I was a ghost they didn't believe in. I wanted to tell them to go. To let me rot here with the others. But my tongue was thick and swollen, my mouth full of blood.

A boy crept close, tugged at my boot and tugged again when it didn't come free. It wasn't my bad leg but shit still hurt. Instinct moved before thought.

"Hey...don't do that."

The sound came out dry and broken but it was enough to startle him. The boy bolted. Someone shouted before pulling him closer, and the dark rushed back in.

When I woke again, I was somewhere small. Smoke-stained beams above me, dirt packed tight under my back. A single blanket over me—coarse

301

wool, smelling of animals and sweat. My leg was wrapped in sticks and rope, already swelling around the binding. My ribs hurt to breathe; every inhale scraped. My entire body screamed, each thump of my heart sending a wave of pain that ended with a pulsing in my head.

I coughed, and then swore. I had never had broken ribs before but I was willing to bet this was what they felt like. The air tasted like smoke and something boiled too long. A woman crouched near the doorway, her scarf pulled low. She wouldn't meet my eyes. Poured tea into a tin cup, slid it across the floor. Her hands trembled just once. I drank. It was bitter and sharp, but it was wet. Movement behind her, a tall man that had me trying to sit up. To do what, I wasn't sure. Defend myself? If they had wanted to kill me they would've already. A boy peeked around her skirts. The woman, his mother I assumed, snapped a word and they both vanished.

They fed me thin lentils, hard bread, goat's milk gone sour. Each mouthful took effort. Still, I lived. Hazel eyes danced in my mind every time I closed my own.

Time blurred. I measured it by the color of the light that slipped through the cracks in the wall. Pale gray meant morning. Orange meant I'd made it another day.

Then the fever came. I floated through nights slick with sweat, the world burning through my skin. Someone pressed cool cloths to my head; another voice hummed low and sad. Once, when I thrashed too hard, rough hands pinned me down until the shaking stopped. My skin, my bones…everything was on fire. But slowly, even that began to fade.

When guests came, I was yanked from the cot and dropped into a pit beneath the floor. They covered me with boards and a blanket that smelled of goats. I lay still, afraid to breathe too loud. Boots thudded overhead, voices trading short, sharp words. One of them laughed. Then the door creaked and silence poured in.

The woman lifted the boards. Her eyes were wide, white in the dark. She touched her chest, then mine. "Shhh."

I wanted to thank her, but the words stuck in my throat. All I managed was to catch her hand before she pulled away. Her skin was calloused, warm.

For a heartbeat, we just stayed like that. No words. No need for them. Just two people who'd seen too much of what the world could take and still reached out anyway.

Kindred spirits. Survival stripped down to touch and breath. We spoke the same language, even if neither of us could say it.

The days folded into each other. The man mended tools in the yard. The children chased goats through dust that never settled. The smell of smoke never left my skin. When I could finally stand, they bound a stick to my arm as a crutch. I hobbled circles inside the tiny room, ribs aching, leg screaming, but movement felt like proof that I still existed.

I learned the sounds of their language—the rise of laughter, the sharp hiss of warning, the soft murmur used for prayer. I never learned the words.

At night, I lay awake listening to wind slide over the roof. Sometimes a child laughed in her sleep, and it sounded just enough like Holly that my chest cracked open.

"Got to get home," I'd whisper into the dark. "Got to get home."

By the third month my beard had gone wild, my hair matted. The woman combed through it once with gentle fingers, muttering, half scolding, half pity. I didn't stop her.

When strangers came through the village—fighters, traders, it didn't matter—they hid me again. I'd lie in the pit breathing the heat of the earth, counting heartbeats, thinking of the postcard folded against my chest.

Got to get home.

One morning the man woke me before sunrise. He pressed the stick into my hand, slung a goatskin of water across my shoulders, tucked two rounds of bread and a thin blanket under my arm. He said something low and pointed toward the horizon—mountains smudged purple against the sky. The woman said something soft in a language I didn't know. The kids just stared. I nodded, because there was nothing else to do. Then I limped into the dark. The first step hurt like hell. The second proved I was still alive.

The air cooled fast once the sun dropped, thin and sharp enough to sting my lungs. I followed the faint thread of a dry riverbed east, the moon bright enough to paint the stones silver. It was marked by a scraggly line on my map. I followed it dutifully, 'cause what the fuck else was I going to do? The wood splint on my leg creaked with every step. Each breath whistled through cracked ribs. Every sound carried for miles, so I learned to move in bursts—thirty paces, stop, listen.

Daylight was the enemy. By dawn, I'd dig myself into whatever shadow I could find, under a shelf of rock, behind a dead bush, and wait out the heat. Sleep came in snatches, shallow and mean. Flies, thirst, fever dreams. Sometimes I'd wake convinced I was still in the wreckage, smell burning metal, hear Sarge yelling my name. Then I'd remember the map scrawled on the back of a rice sack and whisper my only prayer. *Got to get home.*

The second night I saw lights far off—tiny, trembling, maybe a village. It wasn't on the map, so I skirted wide around them, afraid of what kind of eyes might be waiting. My canteen was half-empty. My lips split when I swallowed. I chewed the last of the goat jerky until it turned to dust. Swore I would never eat anything goat related ever again. If I could just make it back.

By the third night I was done. My damn leg had swollen twice its size, and the fever was back. I moved because stopping meant dying right there in the dirt. But damn if I didn't fall from time to time and want to stay down. One night, I chewed on some berries I had found that curbed the hunger in my stomach without making me hurl my guts. When the sun started to bleed up over the ridge, I caught the faint scent of smoke—cooking fire, not burning fuel—and forced my body toward it.

The village appeared like a mirage: ten mud-brick houses crouched in the dust, goats tied to posts, laundry rippling in a wind that smelled faintly of cumin. I crawled behind a low wall and stayed there all day, hidden. A boy spotted me once. He froze, eyes wide as moons, then ran. My hair was long, and through the dirt, the blonde peeked through. So I wrapped the ragged bundle that had been my blanket over my head, covering the truth. If I stuck to the shadows, no one glanced at me twice.

I waited until the next dusk before moving again. That's when I heard it. Voices carried on the wind, the click of metal against metal, a burst of laughter that didn't belong here. English. I limped toward the sound, every instinct screaming that this could be a trap. But the words were right. Accents I knew. *American.*

I stepped from the shadows with my hands raised. "Don't shoot! U.S. Marine! Lance Corporal Jackson Morgan! DOD ID five-three-one-seven-seven—" My voice broke. "Please...please don't shoot."

Three figures turned, rifles snapping up. For a moment, the world held its breath.

"Hands where I can see them!" one barked.

"I'm American," I gasped. "Crash—three months ago. I—"

They glanced at each other, then at me. The one who seemed to be in charge took a step forward, "Name again!"

"Jackson Morgan." My knees gave out. I hit the dirt, pain lighting up my leg like fire. "Lance Corporal. U.S. Marines. I just want to go home." I reached slowly for tags still hanging from my neck and held them aloft. They watched, rifles aimed at me as I slowly removed the blanket from my head.

Silence. Then the leader lowered his rifle an inch. "Holy shit...we thought you were dead."

"Me too."

Hands were on me—steady, practiced. Someone gave me water, someone else covered my shoulders with a blanket though the night was still warm. They loaded me into the Humvee. The seat felt too clean, too real. The desert blurred past as the village vanished behind us. Every bump in the road had me gritting my teeth.

At the edge of the valley, floodlights glared over a landing zone. The chop of rotor blades filled the air, low and rhythmic. My chest clenched. The smell of fuel and dust hit like a fist.

"Easy, Corporal," a medic said, guiding me forward.

"No," I croaked. "Not that. Not again." I stumbled back from the too-familiar beast in front of me.

"Only way to base, kid."

The rotors spun faster, the noise swelling until it became the same scream that had haunted my sleep. I stumbled back, shaking my head, hands pressed to my ears.

"He's panicking—get him on board!"

They half-dragged me inside. I fought, uselessly, until the harness bit my shoulders. The world narrowed to sound and memory—fire, falling, Johnson's body as it jerked with each shot. A sting in my arm. Cold fire. The edges softened. Someone shouted, "You're safe now, kid! You're safe!" I didn't believe them. But the sedative dragged me under before I could argue. The last thing I saw was the desert falling away beneath the helo's lights, the night swallowing the mountains whole.

And through the blur, the same thought burned steady as a flare: *Got to get home.*

I woke to light so white it burned. A ceiling fan turned slowly above me. The air smelled like antiseptic and jet fuel. Somewhere close, a monitor beeped steady and smug—proof I hadn't died yet.

"Easy, Lance Corporal. You're safe."

The voice was female, American. A medic leaned over me, eyes bright and kind. "You're at Forward Operating Base Argon. You made it back, Marine."

I tried to speak. Only a croak came out.

"Water," she said, slipping a straw to my lips. "Small sips."

The water tasted like metal, but it might as well have been holy.

They started questioning me before the IV bags were half-empty. Two intel officers—one young, one carved from stone—sat beside my cot with a recorder. "Lance Corporal Morgan, you were listed KIA on June eleventh. Tell us where you've been."

I told them everything I remembered: the crash, the family that found me, the map drawn on a rice sack, the trek by night. When I got to the part about the villagers, the older man cut me off. "You're sure they weren't Taliban?"

"They were the reason I'm alive," I rasped. "They are good. Kind. Leave them be. They are *innocent*."

He didn't answer. He and the other guy exchanged a look. Then he just clicked his pen and said, "Understood."

They re-set my leg two days later. I remember the morphine hitting and the world bending sideways. When I woke, there was a new cast, metal pins, and an entire spool of gauze covering various parts of me.

Physical therapy came next—parallel bars, rubber bands, endless sweat. The nurse joked I was trying to sprint out of there. She wasn't wrong.

A chaplain started visiting in the afternoons. Lieutenant Reeves. Army, mid-forties, voice like a gentle creek. Easy, peaceful. Soothing. He didn't start with prayers. He started with silence.

Finally he said, "When you were in the mountains, what kept you moving?"

"Home," I told him. "A promise."

He nodded. "That's good. Promises are lighter than guilt."

We talked about my unit. My sergeant who dragged wreckage over me, Johnson's last desperate attempt to help his men. Poor Patterson who didn't even stand a chance. Reeves listened like the words were scripture. Late one night, I admitted the guilt that wore me down more than the injuries. They had been good men, kind men. They hadn't deserved it. Why them and why not me? When I broke mid-sentence, he didn't reach for a Bible—just passed me a tissue and said, "You don't have to earn being alive, son. You just honor this second chance, and them, by giving your next shot your all."

I wanted to call her. Hell, it was the first thing I thought of when they handed me back a uniform. But command still had me on ice—debriefs, psych evals, a goddamn mountain of paperwork. They said I couldn't make contact until the official notice went out. So I sat there staring at the phone on the wall like I could will the rules to bend.

Weeks blurred into a routine—meds, PT, debriefs, more questions. I gained weight, got a haircut. One morning, Reeves appeared with paperwork in his hand. "You're cleared, Lance Corporal Morgan. Stateside transfer. Time to go home."

Home. *Finally.*

They drove me to the airstrip at dawn. The plane waited on the tarmac like a mechanical beast daring me to climb aboard. My palms went slick.

The smell of jet fuel twisted my stomach.

"You all right?" the escort asked.

I swallowed hard. "Not yet."

He handed me headphones. "These can help block out the noise."

I hesitated but eventually took them. The engines roared, the plane lifted, and for a heartbeat, the panic almost won. But through it I heard Reeves's voice, calm and sure: *You don't have to earn it.*

When I woke again, the sky outside the window was softer, humid—the kind of air you could taste. Stateside. The escort helped me through the terminal, into a government SUV, and an hour later I was standing on a porch I barely recognized.

The door opened slowly. My mother blinked at me through a haze of last night's whiskey, makeup smeared, hair a mess. For a second I thought she might slam the door, like maybe I was just another hallucination.

Then she laughed. Or maybe she sobbed. Hard to tell the difference. "You're not real," she said, voice small and cracked. "They brought me a flag. They said you were gone."

"I got lost," I managed.

Her eyes filled, and she reached for me with shaking hands. The hug was clumsy, half-hearted, like muscle memory instead of love. Behind her, the house smelled of liquor and lemon cleaner, the mix of a woman trying to drown one scent with another.

The escort gave me a nod, climbed back into the SUV, and drove off. The silence that followed felt heavier than gunfire.

I stood there a minute, letting her talk—rambling about neighbors, the VA, some check she never cashed. I looked at the photos on the wall: me in uniform, her younger and sober, people I didn't remember. Everything frozen in time.

The quiet pressed too close. The air felt stale. My chest started to ache again. Home, but not home.

The place I needed to be was still a few miles south. An old clubhouse, engines rumbling, laughter spilling through open doors, a girl with fire in her eyes who once made me promise I'd come back. I set my pack down beside the couch, stared at my hands, and whispered the same words that had carried me across three months of hell.

Got to get home.

Chapter Thirty-Three

I spent a grand total of maybe six hours with my mom before I was crawling out of my skin. She eventually fell asleep on the couch and I snuck out the door. I suddenly hated the rickety old steps as they wobbled under my weight. But eventually, I found myself in front of the little shed back behind the house. I wasn't sure who groaned louder, me or the door, but eventually, I got the damn thing open.

Inside, my bike waited. Someone had cleaned it. The chrome caught the morning light, tank full, chain oiled. Diego's handiwork, no doubt. The sight hit me harder than the desert sun ever had. I gripped the handlebar, felt the smooth leather under my fingers, the faint tremor in my leg screaming *don't even think about it.*

"Yeah, not today," I muttered, but still, I leaned the cane against the workbench and propped myself carefully up next to the familiar machine. The silence pressed in. I hadn't realized until that moment that I didn't even own a phone anymore. No wallet, no car. I was a ghost trying to rejoin the living. I was sure they had sent Mom my things, but the chances of her having any idea where she had stashed it was slim to none.

So I did the only thing that made sense—I grabbed my cane and hobbled across the gravel to knock on the neighbor's door.

Old man Carter opened the door, wearing a fishing hat and an expression somewhere between heart attack and ghost sighting. "Jackson?"

"Hey, Mr. Carter. Sorry to bother you. Can I borrow your phone?"

Carter blinked. "They said—you were—"

"Yeah," I said quietly. "I know."

The man finally stepped aside. "Phone's on the counter."

I ordered an Uber to the only address that mattered. When he handed the phone back, Carter was still staring. "Thanks," I muttered, not meeting his wide eyes.

"Anytime," came out on autopilot, the man still frozen in the doorway as I limped back down the steps.

Back outside, the air smelled like honeysuckle and rain. I eased myself down onto the front step, cane across my lap, and waited. The Uber driver pulled up in a dented Camry, chewing gum and glancing at me in the mirror every few seconds like she was afraid I was a ghost she had picked up and was trying to make sure I didn't vanish.

When the car turned into the long gravel drive, my throat went dry. The Steel Saints sign stood proud on the siding, weathered but unbroken. The main bay door was half open; sunlight spilled across concrete scarred by years of oil and tread marks.

I paid, stepped out, and let the smell hit me—gasoline, sweat, motor oil, and home. The gravel shifted under my boots as I crossed the lot. The cane clicked against stone, steady as a heartbeat. Beyond the open garage door, the familiar chaos waited: a dismantled engine on a lift, toolboxes stacked like fortresses, a couple of couches shoved into a corner.

Every conversation in the garage stuttered out.

Rodney was elbow-deep in a carburetor. Clint leaned against a workbench, mid-story, grinning until he saw the figure in the doorway. The wrench slipped from Rodney's hand, clattering loud enough to echo.

"Holy shit," someone whispered.

"Impossible," another muttered.

I didn't stop. The click of my cane and the uneven drag of my step were the only sounds as I crossed the concrete. I didn't look left or right. I just kept moving, through the maze of dismantled engines, straight toward the small door that led to the kitchen.

One mission left. Get home.

The kitchen smelled like frying onions and fresh coffee. Laughter. Real, easy laughter. Dalton's low rumble, Maria's quick tongue, Hannah's sharper one. They didn't notice me at first so I leaned against the doorframe, letting the sight soak in—family alive, whole, moving on.

Maria swatted Dalton with a towel. Diego was telling some story that had Hannah actually smiling. And Jewel, God, she was taller now. She sat on the counter swinging her legs, clutching a juice pouch like it was contraband. My chest burned. I didn't trust my voice, so I said nothing. Then Jewel froze mid-sip. Her eyes, so similar to her mother's, met mine. Her mouth formed a perfect O. I smiled, but I think it came out as more of a grimace.

"Stranger danger!" she shrieked.

Everything stopped.

Dalton turned first, towel still in his hand. Maria's spatula dropped into the skillet with a hiss. Hannah's smile vanished.

For a second, no one moved.

Then Dalton whispered, "No way…" He took two stumbling steps before nearly running, and then he was across the kitchen, arms wrapping around me so hard my cane went skittering across the tile.

Pain shot up my leg, sharp enough to blur my vision, but I didn't let go.

"You son of a bitch," he rasped, voice cracking. "You're supposed to be dead."

I offered up a broken grin, "Yeah. Didn't take."

Maria made a broken sound—half laugh, half sob—and then she was there too, Jewel on her hip. Tears streaked down her cheeks as she reached out, her fingers trembling before she pressed her palm against my face.

"*Mi Dios*…Jackson. It's really you."

I swallowed hard. My throat burned. "Yeah. It's me."

Jewel peeked out from behind her mom's shoulder, eyes wide, frowning like she was trying to solve a puzzle. "You're not a stranger?"

The sound that came out of me almost didn't feel real—a laugh choked through too much ache. "Not anymore, kiddo."

Hannah hadn't moved. She just stood there, hand pressed to her chest, eyes shining like she was afraid to blink. When she finally came forward, it was slow, deliberate—like one wrong move might wake her from a dream. She stopped in front of me and reached up, fingertips brushing the stubble on my jaw. "You came home," she whispered.

I nodded once, my voice low. "Guess I did."

For a few heartbeats, everything blurred together—voices, tears, the weight of too much love, too much loss. The walls started to close in. The clang of a pan from the stove made me flinch. My chest tightened.

"I'm fine," I said when Mac's hand found my shoulder.

He didn't buy it. "You look like hell."

I forced a grin. "Hell looks worse."

Maria wiped her face, trying to steady her voice. "Somebody needs to tell Holly," she said softly.

The name hit me like a live round. My chest locked up. I turned to her. "Where is she? How is she?"

Maria hesitated, glancing toward Hannah. "She's alive. Stronger now. Out of town for a conference. She'll be back soon."

I nodded, but my throat felt like sandpaper. Of course she was out of town. The disappointment threatened to settle deep in my bones. Dalton glanced at me.

"I just need some air," I muttered as I headed towards the porch.

Outside, the late afternoon light spilled gold across the gravel lot. The bikes gleamed in neat rows, dust glowing in the beams from the open garage. Somewhere out back, a wrench clanked against metal, steady and familiar. I made it as far as the porch before my leg started screaming. I eased myself down onto the step, elbows resting on my knees, the cane balanced across them like a lifeline.

The screen door creaked behind me. Dalton stepped out, two beers in hand. He didn't say anything—just dropped one beside me and sat down. For a while, neither of us spoke. The cicadas filled the silence. The wind moved slow through the pines.

"You look good. All things considered."

I glanced at him, eyebrow raised. I looked like shit and knew it. It would take a few more months of eating something that wasn't jerky and naan to get me back into shape. "That's generous."

"Maybe. But it's good to have you back."

I tipped my head back, watching clouds drift slow across the tree line. "Feels weird. Like I'm visiting my own life."

"It'll pass," he said. After a moment, quieter, he added, "She's not the same, you know."

I didn't need to ask who.

Dalton rubbed the back of his neck, eyes on the gravel. "She went through hell after you were gone. It's not my story to tell, but…she's a hell of a woman. She's like a sister to me."

My throat tightened. "I always knew she was special."

He laughed. "Yeah. The way she eviscerated you in that parking lot all those years ago must have been a dead giveaway."

I laughed then too, a genuine sound that sounded foreign. We settled into a comfortable silence and I stared down at my hands—scarred, shaking, *real.* A few minutes later, Diego and Mac joined us on the porch. For a few moments, I remembered us as kids. Freshman year. Then sophomore year, dominating the football field. The carefree, natural we had worked together as a team even after Mac graduated.

"Didn't think I'd ever get back here." The admission surprised even me.

Diego nudged my shoulder. "You made it. That's all that matters."

We sat there until the sun dipped low, painting everything in orange and shadow. Inside, the clubhouse started to hum again. I was finally home. But home was still missing its heart.

My heart.

⸸ **Holly** ⸸

The terminal still buzzed with end-of-conference adrenaline—rolling suitcases, clacking heels, and the smell of too much coffee and cheap perfume.

My tote bounced against my hip, the conference badge still swinging from my neck: *Young Entrepreneurs Summit—Detroit.* Three days of panels and speeches. Three days of smiling until my cheeks ached. Three days proving that I could stand on my own, that I wasn't just the girl who almost broke and stayed broken.

The keynote went perfectly. Willow's Harbor picked up two new donors. I even had people asking for advice afterward—me, the girl who used to live off caffeine and panic attacks.

I was exhausted. Proud. *Alive.*

Then I saw them.

Maria. Hannah. My mom.

They were standing by baggage claim like a wall of silence.

I smiled, lifted a hand, tried to play it off. "You all came to pick me up? What, did I win something?"

Maria smiled back, but it didn't reach her eyes. Hannah's jaw was locked tight. Mom's hands twisted the strap of her purse so hard her fingers went pale.

The smile dropped right off my face. "Ok...what's going on?"

They all started talking at once—Maria's words tumbling over Mom's, her Spanish bleeding into mom's English:

"We didn't know how to—"

"Es un milagro—"

"He's alive—"

"Alive! No está muerto—"

I blinked between them, my pulse pounding in my ears. "What? Who's alive?"

Hannah's voice cut through, steady and sharp. "Let's find a place to sit."

We ended up in one of those half-dead airport restaurants, the kind that smells like stale fries and burnt coffee. The TV above the bar was tuned to the news, but the sound was off. They slid into a booth across from me. Hannah reached across the table and wrapped her hands around mine. Hers were warm; mine were ice. That look in her eyes turned my stomach. It was the same look people wore when they were about to tell you someone had died.

I swallowed hard. "Who?"

Hannah exhaled slowly. "Honey…it's not who you think. Or what you think." She hesitated, then said it anyway. "It's Jackson."

I stared at her. The name didn't fit in my ears. It was a sound that didn't belong here, didn't belong *anywhere.*

I shook my head. "What are you talking about? What about Jackson? Did they find his…his body?"

Mom's eyes swam, and she swayed like she was slightly drunk.

Maria leaned forward, eyes glassy. "He's alive, Holly."

I felt the air punch out of me. "That's not funny."

Mom's voice wavered. "It's not a joke, sweetheart. He's home."

I laughed, sharp and hollow. "Home? That's impossible. I saw—"

The words jammed in my throat. The funeral. The flag. The sound of rifles and Dalton's broken voice reading his brother's eulogy.

Maria reached for my arm, tears slipping free. "They found him. He made it out. He's alive."

Alive. I looked at Hannah for confirmation, and she gave me a watery smile before nodding.

The words didn't land; they just spun around my head until everything started to tilt. My chair scraped back. The sound of it felt miles away. The whole restaurant blurred. I couldn't breathe. The air was too thin.

Maria was crying openly now, voice rising. Hannah was suddenly beside me, one arm around my shoulders, steering me out of the booth. "Come on, baby. Breathe."

I tried, but the breath came jagged and shallow. I wasn't sure if I was moving or if she was just dragging me. The lights smeared into streaks, the hum of the crowd turning into a roar in my ears. Someone bumped into me. Someone apologized. My body didn't react. My brain was locked between *he's dead* and *he's alive,* and neither version made sense.

By the time we made it to the car, I didn't remember crossing the parking lot.

Maria opened the passenger door, her voice thick and shaking. "He's at the clubhouse. You want to go there or…?"

I nodded because my mouth wouldn't work. Maria didn't ask for clarification; she understood. I got in, buckled my seatbelt, and stared out the window like I was watching someone else's life roll by.

The car started. The world moved. I didn't. The hum of the tires filled the silence, steady and relentless. Maria sniffled softly beside me, her hand on mine where it rested rigid on my knee. Hannah's hands were tight on the wheel and Mom stole glances at me from where she sat in the passenger seat.

I pressed my palms to my knees to stop them from shaking. It didn't work.

Finally, Mom spoke, her voice quiet and careful. "He looks different. Thinner. Hurt. But he's alive, Holly. You'll see."

Alive.

I wanted to believe it. I wanted to let that word be real. But my body remembered too much—the folded flag, the empty bed, the echo of his voice in my head long after it was gone.

I turned toward the window. The city blurred into streaks of gold and rain alight. My reflection looked older, harder. The kind of woman who'd learned to keep going even when it hurt. Maria's warm, soft hand stayed on mine and her fingers brushed the back of my hand.

We drove in silence. The city gave way to fields, fields to pine woods, and soon the familiar backroads unfurled like old scars. The smell of damp earth crept in through the cracked window.

Every mile closer made it harder to breathe. I pressed my forehead against the glass, feeling the vibration of the road hum through my skull. When the first flicker of the Steel Saints MC neon sign appeared through the trees, my pulse went wild. Hannah slowed the car as the gravel lot opened up before us. The roll-up garage door stood wide, light spilling onto the dirt like a beacon.

Dalton's truck. Maria's minivan. A neat line of bikes glinting under the floodlight. I stared at them, frozen. It looked like any other night. Like nothing monumental waited inside. Hannah parked and killed the engine.

The sudden silence roared in my ears. Mom turned in her seat, eyes soft and steady. "Take your time, honey. He's just through there."

Maria got out first, walking around to open my door. Cool night air rushed in, beckoning me out of the car but I couldn't move. They waited patiently for me. My mom and Hannah shared a look, and Maria and I shared a long look. The kind of look between friends that didn't need words.

Ok," I whispered. "Ok."

I stepped out. My heels clicked on gravel, quick and uneven. Each sound from inside, laughter, the clang of tools, Dalton's unmistakable voice, felt like an ache I couldn't name. Dalton's laugh was different. I hadn't heard him sound like that in a very long time.

I followed the voices toward the garage, one breath at a time. The light grew brighter, spilling out onto the lot.

Through the open door, I saw a group of Saints huddled in the open bay. People I knew by name. People who turned to me and stepped back from a central figure. Tall. Thin. Leaning on a cane.

My breath stopped.

The shape was all wrong and exactly right.

He turned at the sound of my footsteps.

The world narrowed to him.

And then—

Our eyes locked.

And the world stopped.

No breath. No heartbeat. Just *him.*

For a split second, my brain refused to believe what my eyes were seeing. His hair was longer, sun-bleached to sand. His face was leaner, sharper around the edges, with a beard that didn't quite hide the hollows beneath his cheekbones. There was a scar slicing through his eyebrow I didn't remember. He leaned heavily on the cane, like it was the only thing tethering him to the floor.

But his eyes—God, his eyes were the same. Gray and wild and so damn *alive.*

My knees went weak. The sound that ripped out of me wasn't a word—it was raw, broken air.

He moved first, or maybe I did. It didn't matter.

He stumbled forward, half limping, half falling, and I was already running, fast enough that my shoes skidded on the concrete.

We collided in the middle of the room, the force of it nearly knocking him off balance. His arms came around me—tight, desperate, shaking. I clutched the back of his shirt, my fingers curling into the thin fabric like if I let go, he'd vanish.

He smelled so different but underneath the scent of somewhere far away, of too much pain, was a smell that frequented my dreams. Pine. Smoke. *Home.*

"I'm sorry," he whispered. Over and over. The words cracked with every breath. "I'm so sorry, Malibu. I'm sorry. I'm sorry."

I didn't realize I was crying until I felt it—hot tears sliding down my face, soaking into his shoulder. I didn't care. I couldn't stop. Then I pulled back, just enough to see him. To really *see* him. Tears blurred everything, but I forced my eyes to focus, to memorize every scar, every line, every impossible detail of him standing there in front of me.

His hands came up, rough and calloused, cupping my face so gently it broke me all over again. His thumbs brushed tears from my cheeks like he could wipe away the time we had lost.

My breath came out in ragged pieces. "Please tell me this is real," I managed. "Please, Jackson. Please tell me this isn't another dream."

His forehead rested against mine, breath hitching. "I'm here," he rasped. "I swear to God, Malibu, I'm here."

And just like that, the floor came out from under me.

I sobbed—ugly, shaking, loud—and he held on tighter. He was crying too; I could feel it in the tremor of his chest, the uneven way he breathed.

Around us, the crowd dispersed. A firm word from Hannah had everyone scurrying to the kitchen. But none of it mattered. I paid them no mind. It was just us. Me and him.

My fingers threaded through the hair at the back of his neck, the texture grounding me. He trembled against me, one hand clutching the back of my jacket like he couldn't believe I was real either.

He pulled back again, just enough to look at me. His voice cracked. "You cut your hair."

I laughed, or maybe it came out more like a gasp. "You grew a beard."

His lips quirked—barely. "It's terrible, isn't it?"

"Awful," I said, and the sound that escaped me was half a sob, half a laugh. Then I kissed him.

It wasn't graceful or cinematic. It was frantic and messy and too hard. The kind of kiss that didn't know whether to beg or to blame. He caught my face between his palms like he couldn't decide if he should pull me closer or apologize again. But I felt the moment he gave in. Sitting there on the concrete floor, he wrapped one arm around me as he pulled me closer. When I opened to him, he groaned and slipped a hand under the bottom of my shirt, his rough palm on the small of my back and I whimpered, desperate for this to be real. Not wanting to wake up if it wasn't.

When we finally broke apart, my whole body was shaking. I pressed my forehead to his chest and listened to the wild rhythm of his heartbeat.

"Don't you ever do that to me again," I whispered.

His breath hitched above me. "Wasn't part of the plan."

I pulled back, just enough to look up at him again. "You're really here."

He nodded. His jaw trembled when he said it. "I'm home."

That word cracked something deep in me—something I didn't even realize I'd been holding together.

I didn't know how long we sat like that, or how many tears I shed into the front of his shirt. All I knew was the feel of his arms around me, the weight of his body against mine, the sound of his uneven breathing and the smell of the man I'd already mourned once.

I'd thought seeing him would bring relief, joy, closure. But it didn't. It just hurt. Beautiful, unbearable hurt. Because to feel him meant remembering what it was like to lose him.

He pressed a kiss to my forehead, soft and lingering. "You ok?"

I shook my head, laughing through the tears. "Not even close."

He smiled—small, crooked, so heartbreakingly *him.* "Me neither."

I leaned into him again, closing my eyes. For the first time in months, I let myself believe.

Chapter Thirty-Four

⸙ **Holly** ⸙

I hadn't expected it to feel so strange having him here. I'd always imagined this moment. The first night together, the sound of his voice echoing down a hallway, the way his eyes found mine in a crowded room. In my head it had always been cinematic. But real life was quieter. Softer. Awkward in the way grief never warned me about.

Jackson stood in the doorway of my apartment in Athens with his duffel slung over one shoulder, ready to retreat if I so much as blinked wrong. The air in my apartment felt too polite for him. No oil, no leather, no trace of the world he came from. His boots squeaked against the hardwood, loud in the stillness. He winced at the noise, like he was breaking something sacred. I stood frozen in the hallway, just staring at him. Part of me wanted to bolt; another part wanted to drag him inside and never let him leave again.

I didn't even know what made me say it that night. We had been sitting outside the clubhouse when he admitted he couldn't go back to that single-wide trailer with the ghost of a woman who'd forgotten him. Something in me wanted to revolt at the lost look in his eyes. Eyes that, before, had always been sharp as steel. Warm, cold. Kind, angry. But never lost. The words had come out before I could stop them.

"Move in with me."

He'd stared at me like I'd spoken another language. "What?"

"Come live with me."

"Malibu…you don't have to do that."

"I know."

"You sure?"

"Yes."

My tone was firm, confident. Somehow I managed to keep that one word from shaking. But it had been a lie. I wasn't sure. Not even a little. In fact, I was strongly considering getting my head checked. But as I sat there with him…I'd just known the thought of him going back there made my chest cave in.

He'd opened his mouth to argue, to tell me it was a bad idea, but I'd kept talking because if I stopped, I'd lose my nerve. "You said you don't have a home anymore. Well, I've got one. Big enough for both of us."

He'd looked at the ground, thumb rubbing the edge of his cane. "Malibu…"

"I'm not saying you have to," I'd said. "I just…it makes sense."

The silence afterward had felt like standing on a cliff, waiting to see if he'd jump too. Then he'd nodded once—barely—and said, "Ok."

Now he was actually here, and the air hummed with everything unspoken. Everything in my apartment was neat. Books lined up by color, candles never lit, throw pillows sitting just right. Maria teased me that she was going to have to give Jewel a pack of donuts and then just let her loose in here. To make it feel real, lived in. But I liked it like this. It looked calm, curated. The exact opposite of how I felt, especially in that moment.

Jackson set his duffel down and glanced around like Dorothy in Oz. "Is it always this sterile, or did you just hide the body?"

I arched a brow. "Wouldn't you like to know."

A ghost of a grin crossed his face then he cleared his throat. "I can take the couch."

I blinked at him, my head going in a million different places, none of them good. The fucking couch? "You can't be serious."

"I just figured you'd want space. After—"

"I've had space," I cut in. "Too much of it. You're not sleeping on my couch, Jackson."

I need you next to me, damn it. I couldn't say it. But I didn't have to.

He nodded, surrendering, and followed me down the short hallway. My bedroom was as spotless as the rest of the apartment—pale curtains, soft lamp light, a bed that took up half the room. His gaze moved around the room, landing on the framed photos on the dresser: Maria, Jewel, and Diego, the girls at Willows Harbor, a snapshot of me, Mom and Hannah from last Christmas. There was guilt in his eyes, like he was trespassing on something good.

"You sure about this?" he asked, fingers tightening around his cane.

"Jackson." I tilted my head toward the bed. "It's late. Get in."

He hesitated, then dropped the duffel and eased down onto the mattress like it might explode. I shut the bedroom door, and the silence stretched long enough for me to hear every heartbeat in the room.

I went into the bathroom to get changed. Safe behind the recently replaced door, I slid onto the floor. Dalton and Maria had found me here so close to death. That felt like ages ago. And now…where the fuck did we go from here? I took a few steadying breaths, dug the six months sobriety coin out of my pocket, said a prayer to a god I didn't always believe in, and got dressed before crawling into bed next to him.

He watched me as I slid under the sheets, his eyes widening as I passed through the dim light of the window. "Hey," he said, voice rough. "That's mine."

I glanced down at the faded red jersey hanging off my shoulders. It went down to mid-thigh and I always wore it to bed; I hadn't thought twice before putting it on. "Yeah. I know."

"Where'd you even—" He stopped himself. "I haven't seen that thing since…"

"Diego gave it to me," I said softly. "After your funeral." The word hung heavy between us. His jaw flexed. "I sleep in it," I added, wincing at the obvious statement. "It helped me feel like you were still here."

His breath caught. Those gray eyes I had missed so much met my hazel ones. "It looks better on you anyway."

I didn't have words, so I moved closer until my head rested against his chest. His heartbeat thudded steady beneath my ear. Proof that the universe had given me back something I had never expected it to.

"You're really here," I whispered.

"Yeah," he murmured. "Guess I am."

We fell asleep like that—two people who'd already buried each other once, clinging like maybe this time the world would let us keep what was left. I woke once in the middle of the night to find our legs tangled together. His arm had slipped around my waist, hand resting against the curve of my hip like muscle memory.

For a second, I forgot how to breathe. The room was dark, quiet except for his heartbeat under my ear and the faint rasp of his breathing.

I told myself not to move. Not to ruin it.

But his fingers twitched, and then he murmured my name in his sleep—soft, almost reverent—and every piece of me that had been frozen since that ten-gun salute thawed just a little.

The next morning he was unpacking his bag, a task I'd assumed would take five minutes and a single drawer. I'd already cleared out space for him in the closet. Half an afternoon of reorganizing, folding, and cursing myself for caring what my hangers looked like.

"Don't say I never gave you anything," I said, leaning against the doorframe. "You should feel blessed. That closet was sacred territory."

He shot me a look over his shoulder. "Malibu, the inch of emptiness in that closet isn't space. It's a hostage negotiation."

"Hey, I made room."

"Barely." He smirked. "Good thing I don't own much."

The banter made the apartment feel alive again. Like old times, before loss became the only language we spoke. I grinned, shaking my head as I went to grab a drink from the kitchen.

When I came back, the laughter died before it hit my throat.

Three prescription bottles sat neatly on my dresser. Their white labels caught the light, names I didn't need to read. Oxycodone. Cyclobenzaprine.

Lorazepam.

He was bent over his duffel, pulling out a folded T-shirt, completely unaware that my world had just narrowed to those orange bottles. For a second, I couldn't breathe. My vision tunneled. I was on my bathroom floor again. Back before rehab, before the nights spent chasing numb. My palms went clammy, heartbeat turning jagged.

"Jackson." My voice came out too sharp.

He looked up, brow furrowed. "What?"

"Why are those on my dresser?"

He glanced over, confusion flickering into realization. "Oh. The meds. They were in my bag. I figured I'd keep them where I can reach them."

"Yeah, well, I can reach them too."

That pulled his eyes to mine—steady, cautious, like he was piecing together something dangerous. "Yeah?"

I crossed my arms. "They can't stay here."

"I need them, babe," he said quietly. "They're prescribed. For pain."

I knew that. God, I knew that. The logical part of me understood he needed them. His leg still ached, his ribs were a mess, his sleep habits were probably worse than mine, but logic had nothing on the flood that hit when I saw those bottles.

"I don't care what they're for. I just—" I stopped, forcing air into my lungs. Forcing myself to see past the haze of panic in my mind. "You can't leave them out like that."

His expression softened instantly. "Ok, no problem."

"I went…it got bad. I just, please. Put them somewhere else."

He set the shirt down and limped over, moving slow, careful not to startle me. "Malibu," he said gently, "it's ok. You don't have to explain. I got you."

"It's not—" I bit the inside of my cheek. "It's not about trust or even about you. It's about…temptation. And me. One bad day, one sleepless night, and it's right there."

He nodded once, no argument, no pride. Just quiet understanding. Then he reached for the bottles, screwed the caps tight, and held them out. "Where do you want them?"

I pointed to the bathroom. "Top shelf. And I want a lock."

He didn't hesitate. "Deal."

When the click of the cabinet latch finally sounded, I could breathe again—but barely. He turned back, leaning on the doorframe, watching me like he wasn't sure if he should reach out or give me space. "You ok?"

I nodded, even though I wasn't. "I'm sorry."

"Don't apologize. You *never* have to apologize to me."

For a long time, neither of us moved. The space between us was full of ghosts, but at least this time, they weren't winning.

The first week was a minefield. He tiptoed around like a houseguest. Asked if he could open the fridge. Asked if he could order food to the house for us. Folded his blanket every morning and stacked it neatly on the edge of the bed like he was checking out of a motel.

By day three, I snapped. "You live here," I said, standing in the doorway with my coffee. "You don't have to act like a guest."

He flashed that crooked grin that made my ribs ache. "Just trying not to mess it up."

I wanted to tell him I'd been trying not to mess it up too—but that would have meant admitting how much he mattered. So I just rolled my eyes and handed him the extra mug I had poured for him.

Our mornings became a quiet rhythm. He used the last bit of cereal; I scowled and stole the bowl when he wasn't looking. Sunlight filtered through the blinds, painting stripes across his face. The smell of caffeine and clean laundry filled the space between us, and for a few breaths, it felt like peace.

But the ghosts didn't stay gone for long.

Sometimes I woke before him and found him sitting at the edge of the bed, cane leaning against his knee, staring at nothing. His shoulders were tense, jaw set.

"You ok?" I'd ask. I already knew the answer but I asked anyways.

"Yeah," he'd say without looking at me. "Just… "

I knew that tone. The one people used when silence felt like punishment. I reached for him, running my hand down his back. "Nightmares fucking suck."

His laugh was dry but he lay back down and held me like I was the only thing keeping him afloat.

By the second week, we started bumping into each other's habits.

He left his boots by the door—mud tracks and oil mixed on his soles and tracked across my rug. My cute rug that changed with the seasons and holidays. I bit my tongue, then spent an hour scrubbing when he wasn't looking. He insisted on fixing the leaky faucet himself; I came home to a half-disassembled sink and water pooling on the floor.

We argued over small, stupid things but underneath the frustration, there was laughter trying to find a way out.

Little by little, we started fitting together again.

He'd started using my bathroom like it was his own, which shouldn't have bothered me, except one morning he walked out with steam curling around him and nothing but a towel slung low on his hips.

I was sitting on the bed, cup of coffee in one hand and an invoice in the other. I looked up at him, forgot how to breathe, and brought the invoice to my lips like I was going to drink it. I hadn't realized what I had done until he gave me a crooked grin.

He was still thinner than I remembered, scars fading but not gone, his hair damp and curling at the edges. But it wasn't the body that stopped me—it was the look on his face when he realized I was staring. A flicker of the boy he used to be, the cockiness. The sexy smirk.

"What?" he said, voice still rough from sleep.

"Nothing," I muttered, eyes definitely not on the towel. "Just…you missed a spot."

He chuckled, winking at me. "Wanna help me get it?"

I sputtered, then pretended to be very interested in my mug while my pulse did stupid things.

He worked part-time at the garage, came home smelling like motor oil and exhaustion. I worked late on Willows Harbor paperwork. We orbited each other—close enough to touch, cautious enough not to burn.

Sometimes, when I was typing at my desk, I felt his eyes on me. Not in a way that trapped me—just quiet awe. Like he couldn't quite believe I was real.

One night he leaned against the doorframe, watching me finish a donor call. "You know you're amazing, right?"

I blinked. "Excuse me?"

"The way you walk into a room and just…own it." He scratched the back of his neck. "Makes the rest of us look like we're standing still."

"You flirting with me, Morgan?" I teased.

"You would know if I was," he said, voice low. "But no. It's just the truth."

My cheeks warmed. I typed another line I wouldn't remember later. He walked off down the hallway and I tried to pay attention to the rest of the meeting. But my body was remembering what it was like to want and I had a feeling we were both happily marching to the edge of a cliff. So, the question wasn't *what if*… but when.

Jackson

The soft glow of the television painted shifting blue shadows across Holly's face. Some forgettable comedy movie played on, scenes I had long since ceased to pay attention to. A month. A month of shared coffee, of folded laundry, of her scent on my pillow. A month of a peace so profound it felt like a held breath. A month of watching her move through our shared space, a ghost of the girl I'd left, now a woman whose every curve and sigh was a geography I was desperate to map.

My hand, resting on the couch cushion between us, twitched. The domestic rhythm was a sweet torture. All I could think about was our last night under the stars. The feel of her under me, her breathy little moans. A memory worn smooth by ages of lonely, desperate recollection. Now, the reality of her was here. The vanilla-and-cinnamon scent of her skin. The soft sound of her breathing. The way her lower lip caught between her teeth when she was concentrating on whatever task was at hand.

The craving was a physical ache, a wire pulled taut from my sternum to my groin. I couldn't wait another second. I turned, the leather of the couch creaking under me. She glanced over, a small, curious smile on her lips.

That curiosity turned to the old, familiar fire when she saw the look on my face. An unspoken challenge. My expression must have been raw, stripped bare. I saw the flicker of understanding in her eyes, then the shadow of old fear.

"Can I help you, Marine?"

I didn't speak. Words were sand in my mouth. I just reached for her, my hand cradling the back of her neck, my thumb stroking the frantic pulse under her jaw. I leaned in, stopping a breath away. Letting her see the want, the near-violent need, before I gave in to it. My mouth found hers. It wasn't a gentle kiss. It was a claiming. A release of over a year's worth of hunger. She gasped against my lips, her hands flying up to my shoulders, not pushing away, but clutching. Anchoring. I tasted the wine she'd had with dinner, the unique, sweet flavor that was just *her*. A groan tore from my chest, and I deepened the kiss, my tongue sweeping into her mouth, learning her all over again.

When I broke for air, we were both panting. Her eyes were wide, dark pools in the dim light. "Holly," I rasped, my voice unrecognizable. "I need...I need to taste you. I need to hear you. I need *everything*."

I saw the war in her eyes. The history. The man who'd taken something from her that I'd spent years trying to help her rebuild. My heart hammered against my ribs. *I should stop. I should pull back.*

But then she spoke, her voice trembling but clear. "I want to know what it's like," she whispered. "To be craved like that. Don't be gentle, Jackson. Not tonight. Use me. Show me what it's like to be yours so completely it burns."

Her words were a detonation. Any last shred of hesitation incinerated. I stood, pulling her up with me, and in one motion, swept her into my arms. My damn leg protested but I paid it no mind. She let out a small, surprised sound, her arms looping around my neck. I carried her the short distance to our bedroom, the movie's soundtrack fading into meaningless noise.

I laid her on the bed, following her down, my body covering hers. My mouth was everywhere. Trailing hot, open-mouthed kisses down her throat, nipping at her collarbone, laving the swell of her breasts above her t-shirt.

I pulled the soft cotton up and over her head, tossing it aside. Her bra followed. I took one tight, pink nipple into my mouth, sucking hard, my tongue circling the peak. She cried out, her back arching off the mattress, her fingers tangling in my hair.

"If you need to stop," I growled against her damp skin, my hand sliding down her stomach to the waistband of her sleep shorts. "Any second. Just say the word. Any word. And I stop. Do you understand?"

"Yes," she breathed, her hips lifting to help me peel the shorts and her panties down her legs. "I'm good. Promise. Show me what you've got."

God, I had missed her. That wicked tongue, that sharp mind. I kissed my way down her quivering stomach, over the gentle curve of her hip, along the sensitive skin of her inner thigh. Her scent, musky and sweet, filled my senses. I'd dreamed of this. I settled between her legs, my hands spreading her wide for me. She was already glistening, flushed and beautiful. I didn't tease. I lowered my mouth and licked a long, slow stripe from her entrance to her clit.

Her whole body jerked. A sharp, broken moan ripped from her throat. *Music.* I did it again, flattening my tongue, savoring her taste—tangy, addictive, *Holly.* I found her clit with the tip of my tongue and circled it, slowly, deliberately. Her thighs trembled against my ears. Her hands fisted in the sheets.

"Jackson… oh, god…"

I built her up with relentless focus. My tongue flicked and pressed, my lips sucked. I slid two fingers inside her, curling them, finding that spot that made her shriek. Her hips began to buck in a ragged rhythm, her breathing coming in sharp, desperate gasps. I could feel her tightening around my fingers, her body coiling like a spring. She was close. So close. I pulled my mouth away.

She made some sort of noise that was almost a growl, a sound of pure, frustrated need. Her eyes flew open, glazed with pleasure. "Wha… why did you stop?"

I looked up her body, meeting her heated gaze. "Not yet," I said, my voice rough. I lowered my head and licked her again, a slow, torturous pass, but avoided her clit. I worked her with my fingers, driving her to the edge again, listening to her pleas and curses, feeling her body beg for release. And again, just as her muscles began to flutter and seize, I withdrew my mouth, leaving her gasping on the precipice.

I did it a third time. Her cries were raw now, tears of frustration and overwhelming sensation leaking from the corners of her eyes. *"Please,"* she sobbed. "Jackson, please, I need to come. I need it."

Fuck me. Hearing this wildfire of a woman beg for me? I would never get enough. Not to my dying day.

"You'll come when I'm inside you," I promised, my own control hanging by a thread. I was painfully hard, straining against my jeans. I rose up on my knees, fumbling with my belt. "Condom," I muttered, turning toward the nightstand.

Her hand shot out, gripping my wrist. Her touch was electric. "No."

I froze. "Holly…"

"I want to feel you," she said, her voice fierce. "All of you. *Bare.* I'm on the pill. I want…I want to feel it."

That undid me. The last of my sanity shattered. I shoved my jeans and boxers down, freeing myself. I was thick, aching, the tip already slick. I positioned myself at her entrance, using my hand to guide myself, rubbing the head through her wetness. She was so hot, so ready.

I looked into her eyes, holding her gaze.

"Mine," I said, a low growl.

"Yours," she echoed.

I pushed inside. The feeling was obliterating. Hot, silken, impossibly tight wetness sheathing me. A groan was torn from the depths of my soul. I buried myself to the hilt in one long, slow, inexorable thrust, feeling her body stretch to accommodate me, hearing her choked cry of pleasure-pain. I held there, embedded fully, letting us both feel the shocking, complete connection. Then I moved.

I pulled out almost all the way and slammed back in. No gentle rhythm. No careful pace. This was a claiming. A fucking. Each thrust was deep, hard, driving the breath from her lungs. The bed rocked against the wall with a solid, rhythmic thump. Her legs wrapped around my waist, her heels digging into my back, urging me on.

"Yes! Like that! God, just like that!" she screamed, her head thrashing on the pillow.

I fucked her with a ruthless, pounding intensity, each stroke aimed to bury myself as deep as I could go. The sounds were obscene and beautiful: the slap of skin, her ragged cries, my own guttural grunts. I could feel her inner walls beginning to flutter again, that delicious, rapid clenching. She was right back on the edge I'd denied her.

"Now," I commanded, pistoning into her. "Come for me, Malibu. Come on my cock."

Her climax hit her like a seizure. Her body arched violently, a raw, shattered scream tearing from her throat as she convulsed around me. The feeling of her pulsing, milking tightness was too much. My own release detonated, a white-hot torrent flooding into her as I drove in one last, deep time, my shout muffled against her neck. I collapsed on top of her, spent, both of us slick with sweat and trembling.

After a long moment, I shifted my weight, but didn't pull out. I couldn't. I was still semi-hard inside her, the aftershocks of my orgasm still rippling through me. I nuzzled her throat, tasting salt. "Holly?" I murmured.

She turned her head, her eyes hazy and sated. A slow, wicked smile touched her swollen lips. Her hips gave a subtle, testing roll beneath mine, and I felt myself stir in response inside her still-clenching heat. "You're not done," she whispered, her voice hoarse. "Are you?"

I could only smile before pulling her on top of me.

Over the next few weeks, we got very reacquainted with each other's bodies. Very. The counter. The bed. The shower. The bath. The couch. On the couch so frequently, in fact, that when Dalton teased about bringing a black light over we practically tripped over each in our hurry to dissuade him from doing just that. Which, of course, was the opposite of subtle. In between Dalton's roaring laugh, Maria's deep blush, and the look we shared over their heads…we started to find ourselves again.

Things weren't perfect. Hell, what did I expect? We'd never been the soft, easy kind of couple. We were gasoline and a match, two alley cats in a room full of fireworks, always one spark away from lighting the whole place up.

The first real fight hit a few months in.

I'd pushed too hard at PT that day. Told myself I could handle it. Told myself pain meant progress. By the time I made it up the stairs to our apartment, my leg felt like it had a live wire wrapped around it. Sweat soaked through my shirt, and every step sent a warning up my spine.

She was waiting on the balcony. Dinner was set on the table inside. Candles lit. The kind of domestic scene that still startled me sometimes— like I'd walked into someone else's life by accident. I tried slipping past her.

"You overdid it," she said.

"I'm fine," I tossed over my shoulder, already angling for the bedroom where I could collapse without an audience.

"You're not."

I dropped my keys harder than I meant to. The clatter echoed down the hallway. "You gonna start bubble-wrapping me too? Dalton already tried."

Her jaw tightened. "I'm trying to keep you from ending up back in a hospital bed."

"Newsflash, Malibu—I'm not broken."

The second the word left my mouth, I wanted it back.

She stepped closer, and I saw it then. The anger. But underneath…fear.

"We buried you, Jackson," she said, voice shaking in a way that cut deeper than shouting ever could. "And doing that almost had our friends burying me. Don't you dare snap at me."

That knocked the air out of me. I stared at her, breathing hard, leg throbbing, pride flaring uselessly in my chest. I hated that she saw weakness. Hated that she worried. Hated that I couldn't give her a clean, unscarred version of myself. But underneath all of that was something worse.

Guilt.

"I know," I said quietly.

Because she was right. They had buried me. Folded a flag. Said goodbye. And she'd unraveled in the wreckage of it. Silence stretched between us.

She moved first. Pressed her forehead to my chest like she was anchoring herself. Or maybe anchoring me. I felt the tension drain out of me in a rush I didn't expect. I swallowed hard, lifted her chin until I could see her eyes, and kissed her.

Soft. Careful. Like something breakable.

"Guess we're both still learning how to do this," I murmured.

"Yeah," she whispered. "But we're learning together."

That was the part that scared me the most. Together meant I could fail her in real time.

Slowly but surely, we found a rhythm. Not perfect. Just ours.

We cooked together most nights. I handled the knife work—hands steady, movements precise. It felt good to be good at something again. She hovered like I might slice myself open at any second, pretending she wasn't watching.

We ate on the couch. Watched the news. Made fun of terrible commercials. I stole her socks because she wore the thick ones and mine were always disappearing. She stole my hoodie and never gave it back. We discovered several new uses for her massive shower.

Balance.

At night, my body betrayed me. Sometimes I'd jolt awake before I even knew I'd fallen asleep, lungs burning, heart racing like I was still under metal and smoke. Sometimes I'd hear rotor blades in the hum of the ceiling fan. Sometimes I'd see fire when I closed my eyes.

She never panicked. She'd press her palm flat against my chest, right over my heartbeat. "You're home," she'd whisper. "You're safe."

Home.

Safe.

Two words that still felt foreign in my mouth.

"I just had to get home," I'd murmur sometimes, half stuck in whatever dream had dragged me under.

She never asked what that meant. She knew. Some nights, when I was drifting but not fully gone, I felt her tracing the scars on my arm. Light touches. Like she was memorizing them. Counting proof that I'd made it back. I never said anything. I just shifted closer until our foreheads touched. That closeness weighed more than any kiss. More than any promise. Eventually the apartment stopped feeling temporary. My boots stayed by the door. My toothbrush sat next to hers. My coffee mug—stained beyond redemption—claimed permanent territory on the counter. The air smelled like motor oil and her favorite candle. It shouldn't have worked.

It did.

It wasn't some fairytale version of survival. It wasn't clean or shiny or Instagram-worthy.

It was real.

One night after dinner, we sat out on the balcony. The city hummed below us, lights scattered like someone had dropped a handful of stars. Rain hung heavy in the air. She leaned into me, head on my shoulder. We'd just showered together. My skin was still warm. For once, my head was quiet. No crash. No sand. No rotors.

Just breathing.

"You ever think we might actually be okay?" she asked.

I thought about it longer than I should've.

"Maybe," I said finally. "Still feels like a second chance I didn't earn. Like I'm living somebody else's tomorrow."

It was the truth.

Men better than me didn't make it out of that valley.

Why did I?

Her head snapped up.

"Don't you dare say you didn't earn it," she said, sharper than she meant. "You bled for this life. You clawed your way back. You get to have a tomorrow, Jackson."

I kissed the top of her head. "Yes ma'am."

She grumbled and tucked herself closer like she was claiming territory.

Later, in bed, when she fell asleep beside me, I stayed awake a little longer. Watched the streetlight glow crawl across the ceiling. Felt her weight against me. Her breath warm against my neck. For months, I'd whispered one sentence into the dark.

Got to get home.

Chapter Thirty-Four

Now I was here.

Her arm was draped across my ribs, careful without realizing it. My leg throbbed in a dull, familiar way. My scars pulled when I shifted. But the ghosts were quieter.

For the first time since I crawled out of that wreckage, I wasn't bracing for the dark to swallow me whole.

It just…settled.

Most nights, that was enough. On the ones it wasn't, I'd lie there staring at the ceiling until the shadows started moving again. Counting breaths. Counting seconds. Counting the ways I didn't deserve to still be here. Sometimes I'd slip out of bed and pour a finger of something amber into a glass. Just enough to quiet the hum under my skin. Just enough to take the edge off the memories without waking her.

It wasn't about getting drunk. It was about turning the volume down.

I'd stand at the kitchen counter in the dark, swallow slow, wait for the burn to chase the ghosts back into whatever hole they'd crawled out of.

Then I'd go back to bed, trying not to wake her as I tried forcing myself to believe I was allowed this.

It didn't always work.

<h1 style="text-align:center">Chapter Thirty-Five</h1>

⁂

I woke to the sound of his cane tapping once against the bedroom wall and the soft scrape of a mug on the counter. Sunlight striped the floor. The apartment smelled like coffee and the citrus candle I forgotten to blow out last night. For a minute I let myself sink into it—the ordinary hum I'd prayed for. Just the two of us breathing.

He was at the stove when I walked in, hair rumpled, T-shirt crooked on one shoulder. He glanced back and smiled like the sun had finally done its job.

"Morning Malibu," he said.

"Barely," I said. "That clock has to be lying."

He poured coffee into my mug and slid it across the counter. When I reached for the creamer, I watched him reach for the little bar cart I kept in the corner of the kitchen, mostly for shits and giggles because I wasn't much of a drinker. He uncapped the small flask we had kept from some gift basket and tipped a bit into his mug. The sound was nothing—no louder than a drip from a faucet. But the movement was almost familiar. Like he had done this before, and I somehow hadn't noticed. My heart changed tempo.

He saw me looking and raised a brow. "Breakfast of champions."

"Classy," I said, too light. My laugh came out bright and hollow. "You

338

gonna garnish it with a cherry, too?"

He grinned, then took a sip. "Don't tempt me."

It was nothing. People did this all the time. A splash after a long night, a nightcap after a long week, a champagne toast at a wedding didn't make anyone a villain. I told myself that once, then again. It's fine. A drink every now and again is fine.

We sat at the table with our mugs and our separate to-do lists. I circled a few names for Willows Harbor. He drew a little wrench next to the name of an old man who swore his carburetor was possessed. I watched his hand while he wrote; the knuckles were still rough. I liked the look of those hands around a mug. The strong veins that ran along the back. My eyes slid back to the bar cart anyway.

It's fine.

He left a glass half-full on the counter when he headed for the garage. I put it in the sink, rinsed it, ran the water until the smell was gone. A normal morning. Nothing to see here but a woman washing a glass that didn't belong on the counter.

We got through the day. We got through the next. The house kept doing what houses do while I moved in quiet circles, picking up after us both like I could tidy the air, like control was the same thing as safety.

On Thursday I cleaned the bookcase, dusted the frames on the dresser. The picture of me, Mom, and Hannah was a little crooked. I straightened it. I opened the drawer where I kept my coin and shut it again without touching it.

In the living room I found a second glass on the coffee table. Not half full. Empty. I took it to the sink, washed it, and set it beside the first one. Two empty mouths facing up. No sound but the careful clink of glass on porcelain. *It's fine. People have drinks.*

On Friday, I emptied the small trash can we kept by the bar cart. The bag was heavier than I expected.

It happened the way a body moved when it was hot and the stove was near—you didn't think about not touching it. You just didn't. It was late, and I was cleaning up after dinner. He went to the bathroom, the whiskey and Cokes he'd had running through him. One second, I was eyeing the bottle of Jack on the counter. The next, the bottle was in my hand. I froze, and when I twisted the cap, the little click sounded exactly like a the pop of a pill bottle opening.

The whiskey hit the basin in a steady brown line and smelled like somebody else's idea of comfort. My mouth tasted metallic, like I'd bitten my tongue and didn't want to check for blood.

"What are you doing?" His voice came from the hall. I didn't turn around, just kept pouring. The stream thinned. I tipped the bottle higher. "Hey." Closer now, confused, already wounded. "That's mine."

"Not anymore." The words were flat, automatic. I set the empty bottle beside the sink like evidence. "I don't want alcohol in my house anymore." The word hung there like I'd thrown it. I wanted to catch it and shove it back in my mouth before it hit him. He blinked once like I'd actually done it.

"Got it," he said, voice low. "Your house."

"That's not—Jackson, that's not what I meant."

"Sure," he said, but the sure wasn't agreement. It was a door closing.

He walked past me and the smell of whiskey and motor oil trailed after him. He shut himself in the bedroom like a polite guest who didn't know where else to go. I stayed in the kitchen with an empty bottle in the sink and the certainty that I had both saved and ruined something in the same breath. Then I emptied every bottle on that damn cart.

A few nights later, we sat on the couch with the news talking to itself in the corner. Rain tapped the balcony rail. He leaned back the way he always did, head tipped, eyes half-closed, and his body looked like it had finally found a shape that didn't hurt. My foot rested against his leg. The space between us felt lived-in. I almost relaxed.

The news anchor smiled that anchor smile and shifted to a local story about a ceremony downtown. Something about honoring service members. Neither of us were paying attention.

Then the man said his name.

I heard it as sound first, not meaning. Then his name was followed by other names. Quick, efficient, like reading groceries, and all at once the air got thin.

Jackson's eyes flew open. I watched the muscle in his jaw go taut and stay there. The anchor kept talking, the chyron kept rolling, and the room became a tunnel. Bryan Johnson. Miles Hale. Kyle Patterson. Ryley Donato. A few others that I missed because I was watching him. The way a piece of him visibly fractured right in front of me with each name. When the channel went to commercial, at first neither one of us moved.

"That's not how it happened," he said, and his voice didn't sound like his voice. It sounded like a radio that couldn't find the station.

"Jackson—" I reached for him.

He stood up too fast. The glass fell off the couch arm and shattered, sharp and clean. He didn't look down. The door opened and closed. No slam. The quiet kind of exit that meant it was already too late.

I picked up the pieces with my fingers wrapped in a dish towel and bled anyway. It was a small cut. I kept pressure on it and watched the door like it could explain itself.

The next week dissolved. Dinners went cold on the stove. His boots multiplied near the door like he was coming home and taking a different pair off each time. The laundry gathered itself into careless little shrines around the hamper. My coffee mug gathered a permanent ring I could not scrub out.

He answered when I called, until he didn't. He said he'd be home by nine, until ten arrived and it was eleven. Sometimes his voice sounded like he was standing in a field with no buildings around. Sometimes it sounded like a bathroom. Sometimes like a bar. I asked how his leg was. He said fine. I asked if he'd eaten. He made a joke about the world's worst diner and changed the subject. I laughed, because that's what you do when the person you love hands you a lighter while you're standing in a gas station.

I hid the other bottles. He found two, didn't find three, brought home replacements that didn't hide. I told myself: if he cut back by the weekend, it was fine. If he ate dinner twice this week, it was fine. If he slept, it was fine. If I can smell coffee on his breath in the morning, not bourbon, it was fine.

I called Dalton at the garage and pretended I had a reason. "Sally," I said. "She's making that sound again."

"What sound?" he asked.

"The one like it's making a sound."

"Blondie," he said softly. "What's going on?"

"I don't know."

"He won't talk to me."

"Me either."

I cornered Diego behind the shop and asked him not to let Jackson drive if he looked wrong. Diego's eyes were the only kind of gentle that didn't make me want to scream. "I'll try," he said.

Trying didn't latch a seatbelt. Trying didn't pour a bottle down a sink. Trying didn't hide the keys.

It was a Tuesday night when trying stopped being enough. It started with a phone call I didn't want to answer and ended with me standing under a flickering neon sign that said "Cold Beer, Hot Wings."

Jackson was exactly where I didn't want him to be—at the bar, a glass in front of him and a girl hanging off his arm like she'd claimed a prize. Her laughter was too high-pitched, too eager. The kind of sound that made my teeth hurt.

I didn't say a word. I just walked up, placed my hand on his shoulder, and gave her a look that could have burned a hole through drywall. She went pale and vanished without protest.

He looked up, bleary-eyed, that crooked grin trying to save him. "Malibu," he said, all slow vowels and whiskey breath. "You came."

"Yeah," I said, voice flat. "Guess I did."

He tried to stand. His barstool wobbled. He caught himself on my arm, muttered something about driving, and I almost laughed. Almost. I hooked his arm over my shoulder and half dragged him toward the door, ignoring the bartender's look.

Outside, the night air hit him, and the last bit of strength he had went out like a bad lightbulb. He slumped against me, heavy and useless.

Sally sat a few spaces away. Her custom leather interior that was cleaner than sin. My girl. My one constant. I stared at her and muttered, "If you throw up in my car, I might leave you on the side of the highway."

He mumbled something unintelligible, leaning heavier into me. I caught a whiff of whiskey and cheap perfume. My stomach turned.

Then my gaze flicked to the trunk.

No.

Absolutely not.

I shouldn't.

The bar door swung open. The bimbo from earlier leaned out, waving her phone like a drunk lighthouse keeper. "Call me!" she yelled, all fake giggles and audacity.

My jaw flexed. "Yeah," I said under my breath. "Trunk it is."

I popped the latch. The trunk opened with a satisfying click. I stepped aside and let gravity do its job. He slid right in, a deadweight tangle of limbs and regret. One solid thud. I didn't even flinch.

"Stay," I told him, like he was a misbehaving dog.

He made a noise—half protest, half snore. Good enough. I shut the trunk.

By the time the sky went from black to gray, I was sitting on my balcony with a mug of coffee. The world was quiet except for the sound of a far-off truck and the hum of my neighbor's AC unit. From here, I could see Sally parked below. Pretty and patient as ever.

Headlights swung into the lot. Dalton's truck. Right on time.

He climbed out, stretched, and started walking toward Sally. He slowed when he heard it. Thuds, muffled curses, a very familiar voice shouting something that sounded a lot like my name. Dalton froze. Looked up. I met his eyes over the balcony rail.

I didn't say a word. Just picked up the keys from the table beside my coffee and pressed the button. The trunk popped open.

Jackson sat up like a devil resurrected, wild-eyed and furious. "What the hell—"

He stopped when he saw Dalton. When it dawned on him where he was and why. The fight drained out of him in one slow exhale.

Dalton blinked, rubbed a hand over his face. His voice carried up to me. "Dude, you've fucked up bad this time." I didn't hear Jackson's muttered response but they both glanced up at me.

"Take him back to the clubhouse," I said, standing and speaking loudly enough they could both hear me. "Keep him there until he sobers up. I don't want to see him tonight."

Dalton didn't argue. He just nodded, grabbed Jackson by the shoulder, and steered him toward the truck. Jackson glanced back at me. I held my chin high, pretending he wasn't wrecking me as I watched him walk away. I raised my mug in a mock toast and went inside before I could second-guess it.

The next time I walked into that bar, the air tasted like damp wood and bad decisions. The bartender recognized me by my posture, standing up too straight to look small. He opened his mouth to say whatever they said to women who come looking for their men. I set my palms on the bar and leaned in.

"If he comes in here again," I said, "don't serve him."

"We can't—"

"You can," I said, and the calm in my voice surprised both of us. "You will. Tell your boss the same thing. Tell your night shift the Saints asked nicely."

He stared at my face long enough to realize I wasn't bluffing. The nod he gave me was quick.

I went to two more bars. Three. I learned the smell each one left on my clothes. I sat in my car with my forehead on the steering wheel and let one sob out like a cough so I could be done with it. Then I wiped my face with the back of my hand and went home like a person who wasn't actively losing.

The next morning, I left when the sun was barely up. I didn't tell Jackson where I was going. If he asked, I would've lied.

The bell above Momma Laverne's door chimed like it always had. Grease, coffee, sugar—comfort in scent form. I slid into the booth across from Dad without a word. He took one look at me and reached for my hand. My lip trembled and I bit the inside of it so hard, I tasted iron.

Momma Laverne made her way over and poured coffee I didn't touch then set a plate of biscuits in front of me. "Well," she said mildly, "you look like you're about to punch somebody."

"I already did," I muttered. "Just not with my fists."

Dad's brow twitched. "What happened?"

"I went to the bars last night," I said. "All of them. Told them if they serve him, they answer to me. And the Saints."

Momma Laverne let out a slow breath through her nose. Not impressed. Not shocked either. "Honey," she said carefully, "that's a bold move."

"I don't do subtle."

Dad leaned back, arms folding across his chest. "And how did Jackson take it?"

"He hasn't found out yet."

That silence? That one had weight.

I stared at the cracked vinyl table instead of either of them.

"I buried him," I said flatly. "I stood there while they handed his mother a flag. I clawed my way out of a bottle of pills because I couldn't survive losing him."

My voice sharpened, heat creeping up my spine.

"I did rehab. I did the shaking and the sweating and the 'share your feelings' bullshit. I've got a sobriety pin in my jewelry box that I fought like hell to earn."

Dad's jaw tightened at that.

"And now he's standing in our kitchen every night pouring whiskey like it's medicine."

The words cracked on the last syllable. I was shaking now, and tucked my hands under the table while they pretended to not notice.

"I know what that looks like," I went on. "I know what that slope feels like under your feet. First it's just to sleep. Then it's to quiet your head. Then it's because you don't know how to exist without it."

Momma Laverne slid into the booth across from me. "And you're scared," she said.

"I am pissed," I shot back.

She held my gaze. "And scared."

My shoulders sagged just a fraction. I focused on a broken chair shoved into the corner, my throat tightening as I blinked furiously before turning my attention back to them. "Yes," I snapped. "I'm scared."

Dad reached across the table, steady as ever, and held his hand out. Flat on the table, palm up. Not a demand. Just an offering. An anchor if I decided I wanted one. I hesitated before taking it.

"I cannot go back there," I said, lower now. "I won't."

"Back where?" he asked gently.

"To being the girl who needed a pill to survive her own brain." My voice didn't waver. "I built Willow's Harbor out of that wreckage. Women walk through those doors every week because I didn't give up. I cannot drown because he doesn't want to face his ghosts."

Momma Laverne nodded slowly. "You love him," she said.

"With everything I've got."

"And you don't want to leave."

"There is nothing," I said, leaning forward now, "*nothing* I want less than to walk away from him. I would fight God himself before I gave up on Jackson Morgan."

Dad's mouth twitched despite himself.

"But," I continued, breath catching, "if staying means I start justifying one glass of wine…one bad night…one 'it's not a big deal'…then what?"

The question hung there. "What if I lose myself trying to save him?"

Dad squeezed my hand once. "Holly," he said, voice like granite, "you can't rescue a man who doesn't want rescuing."

"I know."

"You can love him."

"I do."

"You can draw a line."

I swallowed. "And if he crosses it?" I asked.

Momma Laverne's eyes softened, but her voice didn't. "Then you let him fall," she said. "And you don't fall with him."

That hurt worse than anything else she could've said. I sat back hard against the booth. "I hate that answer."

"I know," Dad said.

A tear slid down my cheek, and I swiped angrily at it. "I am so tired of being strong," I muttered.

Momma Laverne huffed, her own eyes watering now. Dad leaned forward again, eyes steady on mine.

"You don't have to carry him," he said. "You just have to stand steady. Let him see what staying sober looks like. Let him choose."

"And if he doesn't?"

"Then you protect the life you built," he said. "And you don't apologize for it."

The diner hummed around us. Plates clinked. Someone argued about pie at the counter. The world kept moving. I stared at that same broken chair. I didn't want to leave Jackson.

But I would not disappear again.

Not for love.

Not for grief.

Not for anything.

"Okay," I said finally.

Dad squeezed my hand.

Momma Laverne stood up and pointed at the biscuits.

"Eat," she ordered. "You make better decisions when you're not running on caffeine and rage."

That almost made me smile. And for the first time since the bottle showed up between us, I felt something other than panic. Not peace. But clarity. And that was just going to have to be enough.

Over the next couple of weeks, it just got worse.

Some nights I thought I heard his key in the lock and it was only the neighbor on the floor above us. Some nights he came home and was almost normal. Tired, quiet, the edges of him sanded down. Those nights I made eggs at midnight and watched him eat because chewing was proof he was still here. I touched his shoulder, light, like static might jump between us. He reached up and squeezed my fingers and I wanted to believe that squeeze contained everything I needed to know.

If I'd been a different woman, I would have prayed. Instead, I folded laundry. I wrote down groceries we didn't need. I polished the faucet he'd tried to fix last month and hadn't finished because the part was wrong. My hands needed something to do besides hold my head.

When the door opened, it was three in the morning. I was half asleep on the couch, the bed having felt too empty. Too cold. I startled awake because I hadn't been expecting him home. His shoulder bumped the jamb. Keys hit the wall and bounced. He took two steps in and stopped like he'd lost the next instruction. I could smell the alcohol from half way across the room.

"You drove," I said. No hello. No where were you. "You drove like this."

He looked at me. His eyes were glassy and old in the same moment. "It's fine."

"You could have killed someone. Could've killed yourself."

"Tried that already. Devil gave me back." He said it like a fact, like the weather or a broken light bulb.

"Don't you dare," I said, and my voice broke like a plate. "Don't you dare make that the story."

He swayed a little. I reached out and took his arm because that's what you did when someone was falling. I steered him toward the couch and sat him down hard enough that he grunted.

"Shoes," I said. He didn't move. I dropped to a knee and untied them because rage and love are apparently cousins. The laces were wet. Mud flaked and stuck to my fingers. He watched my hands like they belonged to someone else. "You don't get to do this to me," I whispered when I got the second boot off. The words fell out like a secret I didn't want to keep.

He didn't seem to hear me, just tapped his forehead. Hard enough to leave a red mark on the skin. "I can't turn them off," he said.

I think I heard my heart shatter on the floor. I was losing a good man to his demons. And I couldn't do a damn thing to stop it. You couldn't stop a soul hellbent on its own destruction.

I covered him with the throw blanket we kept at the edge of the couch and started to walk away. But when I glanced behind me and saw him watching me, I couldn't stop myself.

"You used to tell me you wouldn't be like her. You promised yourself you wouldn't end up like your mother. You fought every day of your life to prove you were stronger than that."

Even in the dim light, I saw him tense. When he spoke next, his words sounded terrifyingly sober. "Don't go there, Holly."

"I didn't," I shot back. "You did."

"You don't get it."

A laugh ripped out of me. Broken. Sharp.

"Really? I don't get it?" I stepped closer. "After they found him not guilty all those years ago, I swore I would never let a man touch me again. Ever. Then you showed up."

My voice wavered but I didn't let it fall.

"I tried so hard not to love you. So fucking hard. But you climbed every wall I built. Letters and stolen kisses and promises."

I swallowed.

"Then I buried you. I mourned you. I let that grief almost kill me. So don't stand there and tell me I don't get it."

"Malibu—"

"You survived a war," I cut him off. "You survived a crash. You dragged yourself across a desert to get home."

My throat tightened.

"And now you're in our home with the same glassy eyes she had."

I paused, swallowing and clenching my jaw so hard it hurt.

"I am not going to sit here and watch you disappear one drink at a time," I said. "I love you too much for that."

I turned and forced myself toward the bedroom without looking back. I didn't sleep. Not then. Eventually I went back out into the living room and sat on the floor with my back against the wall until my legs went numb and my lower back throbbed. I watched him. I watched his chest for the rise and fall. And realized this was almost as bad as watching them fold that flag over an empty grave.

The rain kept at the balcony. The clock did its job.

Around dawn, the apartment turned the color of dish water. Every surface went from sharp to smudged as the morning rays fought their way through the closed curtains. His face looked younger when he slept and I hated it for a second because it made me want to forgive him faster than was good for either of us. I stood and walked to the kitchen. I had left my sobriety coin on the counter and I palmed it, running my fingers over the familiar edges around the rim. I couldn't go back there.

When I went back to the living room, he'd turned on his side and curled a little like his ribs remembered something his mind refused to. I touched his shoulder and he startled, then settled. "Jackson," I said.

He didn't open his eyes.

"If you won't fight for yourself," I said, and the steadiness in my voice came from someone I didn't recognize, "I can't keep fighting for both of us."

He made a small sound that wasn't a word. I waited. A tiny, silly part of me hoped he would wake up. Beg for forgiveness. Promise to change. Something. But his breath just evened out again. I watched his fingers twitch and thought of the first night he'd slept in my bed like it might explode under him. I thought about the fire he'd ignited under my skin when he touched me. I fought back the tears as I remembered the way he'd said my name like a promise. About how he'd made me feel safe, loveable, and cherished when I thought that part of me had been broken forever.

I went to the bedroom and pulled out his duffel, putting clothes in it without folding them. I put his toothbrush in the pocket with the dog tag he never wore, and then I took the dog tag out and set it on the table beside my coin. They looked wrong together and exactly right.

My phone was on the charger. Hannah's name sat near the top of recent calls because fate had a sense of humor. I tapped it. The line rang twice.

"Morning, darling."

"Hannah." The word came out half sob, half question.

"It's ok," she said. Not a question. She knew. "I'm coming."

The sun climbed a half inch. The rain stopped like someone remembered to turn off the hose. He slept through the knock that wasn't a knock, just the handle turning because she still had a spare key.

Hannah came in with her hair pulled back and the expression of a woman who had already buried too much and refused to do it again. She looked at me first, not him. I handed her the bag. She took it without looking inside. "Do you want me to wake him?"

"I don't think I can hear his voice right now," I said, and that was the truest thing I'd said all week.

"I've got him." She put a hand on my arm in a way that didn't ask me to crumble. "I'll call when—" She changed her mind about the sentence and let it end there.

She went to the couch and crouched. She touched his shoulder the way I had, light but enough to carry meaning. He flinched and then sat up with the guilty look of a kid caught sleeping in church. He saw her, and confusion washed over his face before the other thing did—the thing like a weather front. Understanding. Resignation. Shame.

"What did I do?" he started.

"Enough," Hannah said. "Get your shoes."

He looked at me. I stared at the window and counted the streaks the rain had left on the glass. He stood, didn't meet my eyes. Hannah picked up the duffel and didn't say anything else because there was nothing left in the room that language could fix.

At the door, he paused like he'd forgotten his wallet. I knew if I turned, I would undo whatever resolve I had managed to build in the last hour. I stared at the table instead. My nostrils flared. My jaw clenched. My eyes burned. *Don't you dare cry.* My coin shone a little in the watery light. The dog tag didn't.

The door opened. Closed. The hallway gave back the sound of their footsteps, then swallowed it. The truck outside coughed and settled. A second later it backed out. The tires made that wet hiss as they rolled over the last of the rain.

The roof held. The couch sat in the same place it always sat. The cups waited on the counter. The light on the ceiling shifted and didn't mean anything yet. I sat down at the table and put both hands flat on the wood. I didn't touch the coin or the tag. I didn't call anyone. I didn't cry. I listened to the quiet until it wasn't quiet anymore, just a thing with weight. I'd buried him once and walked away with a folded flag and a hole that didn't understand geometry. Now I stared at a shut door and felt the same ache rearrange my lungs.

No sirens. No speeches. Just the sound of a car that had already turned the corner, and a room that remembered how to be empty.

Chapter Thirty-Six

Hannah didn't say a word the whole way back. Morning light came in low and gray over the fields, turning the frost on the ditch weeds into cheap glitter. Her old Suburban rattled like it had loose change somewhere under the dash. She drove the limit, both hands on the wheel, jaw set. I started to speak once—something small and defensive and pathetic like *it's not what it looked like*—and she cut me off without turning her head.

We pulled into the gravel lot and the clubhouse came up out of the cold like a freight ship—blocky, stubborn, familiar. The sign over the door needed paint. The flag needed the wind. A couple bikes were already lined along the front like dogs at a back door, chrome dull under the morning cloud cover. She parked. I reached for the handle. Her voice, finally softer, found me before I got out.

"You smell like whiskey and regret," she said. "Go shower."

That was it. No lecture. No pity. Inside, the bar still held onto last night—fried food and bleach, a lemon wedge turned brown on a saucer, the jukebox quiet like it had been scolded. I kept my eyes down, moved fast through the hall to the back showers, and let the hottest water the plumbing could manage burn me clean. The stink of cheap liquor came off my skin like a confession. When I was done I stood there with my head against the tile until the water started to cool, counted to thirty on my breath, and made a choice. I got out before it could turn cold enough to feel like punishment.

By the time I came back to the main room in a clean shirt and my hair still damp, Hannah was at the stove, making breakfast. Maria was behind the bar with a coffee pot like a weapon. Her sweater sleeves were shoved to her elbows, the small gold cross at her throat catching light from the neon beer sign that never turned off. She saw me. She didn't blink.

"Coffee?" she asked, neutral as a judge.

"Sure," I said. My voice sounded better wet—less gravel, more man. I came close enough to take the mug, and that was when her hand flashed.

She slapped me. No windup, no drama, a clean crack that snapped my head a fraction and lit fire across my cheek. I didn't step back. Hannah didn't move. Diego looked up from where he sat at the table.

"I can't believe you," she said quietly. It was worse than a shout ever could be.

"I didn't—" The explanation died on my tongue.

"She is my best friend," Maria said. "In the whole world. She is the strongest, most selfless, bravest person I know." She didn't give me a beat to recover.

"And do you know what color she turned in that bathroom?" she asked, voice shaking now, not with fear—with rage that loved this much. "You know what sound came out of Dalton when the door finally gave out and she didn't get up? He held her while I dialed 911."

"I watched her rebuild herself one day at a time. I watched her put vitamins in a stupid little organizer like a ninety-year-old woman because it made each morning more doable. I watched her talk to a therapist and tell the truth even when it made her gag. I watched hope come back into her eyes by millimeters. Then you walked in from the dead and it went brighter than I've ever seen. And now—"

Her voice shook, finally. "Now you throw all that in the trash. You make me watch her watch you drown so she can decide whether to follow. I watched hope crawl back behind her eyes—" she stabbed a finger toward my face "—and you are stealing that from her, you selfish son of a bitch."

She stepped towards me like she wanted to hit me again but Diego was there, sliding in behind her like a catcher snagging a wild pitch. He wrapped his arms around her waist and hauled her back as she came forward for another round. "Baby, no," he said into her hair, steady and low. "You said what needed saying."

Diego's jaw worked. He looked at me over her shoulder with something that wasn't hate. God, I kind of wished it was. It was worse. Pity. Fury. Fear. A mirror held up to my wreckage. He pulled her closer and let her tremble against his chest, and that nearly buckled my knees.

Hannah didn't say a word. She wiped the bar with one perfect swipe like she was clearing a surgical field, before fixing each of us with a stern look. "Enough," she said. "We've got work to do."

Maria's eyes stayed on me until Diego moved her toward the door. She didn't say another thing. She didn't have to. The look she left in the space between us kept speaking.

I stood there with my cheek stinging and every muscle in my back tight enough to hum. The hunger that rose in my gut felt like anger, but beneath it was something uglier—shame. The kind that made you want to turn yourself inside out and run. "Eat your breakfast," Hannah said like we hadn't all just watched a bomb go off. "Then go make yourself useful."

I ate even though the food was like sawdust in my mouth. The bacon chewy. The eggs were over medium because she knew I hated runny. Coffee, black. The only way I should've been drinking it these past few months.

The garage drew me like a magnet drew filings. Metal and noise. The holy smell of oil and cut steel. Men who didn't say things until they have to. Mac had the top half of a Panhead open like a book. Dalton sorted parts on a rag towel with that quiet precision he got when he didn't trust his temper. Diego came in a few minutes after me, jaw hard, eyes blown out and black, hands still shaking from holding his woman back.

They all looked at me. The world tilted the smallest measurable amount. Dalton continued his task and he didn't look up at me when he spoke.

"Do you love her?"

"I—"

He set a part down harder than necessary. Metal rang against concrete.

"No. None of that. Do. You. Love. Her?"

I glanced at the three guys I'd grown up with. The only ones who'd seen every version of me. "Yeah," I said. "I do."

Mac shook his head once. "You've got a real shitty way of showing it lately."

My jaw tightened. "Y'all don't get it."

Dalton huffed a dry laugh. "Nope. Sure don't. Never been dead. Never crawled out of a hole we shouldn't have walked away from." He stepped closer. "But you got a second chance."

He held my stare.

"And if it were me? I wouldn't be pissing it away."

"It's not that easy."

Diego finally looked up. Calm. Too calm. "Do I need to bring Maria back in here?"

I winced.

"I watched Holly fight it," Dalton went on. "So I know it ain't easy." His jaw ticked. "But she made a choice."

Silence.

"And now you have to."

Diego folded his arms. "You don't get to keep the whiskey and her."

Mac nodded. "Pick one."

"Personally?" Dalton said. "I'd choose her."

Mac pushed off the tool chest, brushing his hands on his jeans. "We can help you face your demons," he said. "But—"

Dalton smirked, "—but when it comes to a certain five-foot-tall blonde menace…you're on your own, brother."

That got a real laugh—from me, from all of us. The kind that didn't erase the pain but proved we're still standing in it together. For the first time all day, I could breathe. .

I found a broom and started to sweep. Something, anything, to keep my hands busy. The sound of bristles on concrete filled my head where whiskey wanted to live. A discarded washer, a cigarette butt, random bits of metal. I pushed them into a dustpan like a man collecting tiny wrongs. My hands steadied. I didn't feel better. But it was better than doing nothing.

Hours knocked by. Prospects drifted. A couple regulars came through for coffee and gossip. The sun got tired of all of us and started down. Hannah reappeared with food from time to time. The next three days went by just like that.

One evening, Hannah found me on the back steps, elbows on knees, staring at gravel like it might spell an answer if I read it long enough. She set a coffee beside me and sat with the kind of sigh that belied her age.

"You already know what to do," she said. No preamble. No parable. "You keep waiting for someone else to tell you it's time, so I'll say it: it's time."

My eyes burned. "I don't have the right words."

"That's the thing about honesty. It doesn't have to be perfect or right. It just has to be real." She nudged the cup toward me with a knuckle. "You've got everything you need. Keys. Jacket. Backbone."

"Backbone's on order," I joked half-heartedly.

She almost smiled. "Expedited shipping. Go to her. And remember, you both deserve this."

I stood. The lot air cut clean lines through the fog in my head. My cut still smelled like rain and the kind of trouble you survived by choosing not to be the guy you were when you bought it. I grabbed my keys. My hand didn't shake until I put them in the ignition. Then they did. I drove anyway.

Holly's building sat square and ordinary and holy. The front light put a cheap halo on the brick. The ficus in the lobby looked healthier than I did. I took the elevator 'cause I'm pretty sure my knees wouldn't have made it up those damn stairs. My knuckles hovered over the door like they were checking for heat.

I knocked.

Footsteps. A pause. Then the chain slid. Deadbolt. The door came three inches, four, stopped.

She looked like the longest night and the reason you waited for dawn. Hair twisted up with a pen stabbed through it. Old sweatshirt. Bare face. Eyes swollen and furious and wounded all at once. God. I had never wanted to kneel so badly in my life.

"Hey," I said. It sounded useless.

She didn't open the door wider.

"I'm done," I said, and my voice shook before I could stop it. "I'm done."

"With what?" she asked.

"With hurting you. With making you look at me like you're already planning the funeral."

Her jaw tightened.

"I didn't drink," I said quickly. "I wanted to. I stood there with it in my hand. I could feel it burning in my throat before it even touched my lips. And I thought about you."

She didn't soften.

"I thought about you in that VA hospital room when I couldn't remember my own name but I remembered yours," I said, voice breaking now. "I thought about you reading my letters like they were oxygen. I thought about you standing at a grave with my name on it."

Her breath caught. She did that thing where she clenched her jaw, raising her chin like she was bracing for a hit. My Malibu.

"And I thought if I drink this, I lose you for real."

My chest felt tight. Too tight.

"I can survive a lot," I said. "I have survived a lot. But I won't survive you walking away."

Her eyes went glassy.

"I've loved you since we were seventeen," I said. "Since you told me I was arrogant and you hated my stupid bike."

A flicker of something moved in her expression.

"I don't want to numb you out," I said. "I don't want to forget your face just to quiet my head. I don't want to be a man you have to survive."

Her fingers tightened on the edge of the door.

"You are the only thing I've ever chosen that made me better instead of smaller. I don't need you to forgive me tonight," I said. "I don't need you to say it's okay."

My throat burned.

"I just need you to believe that I am fighting for you."

Her eyes filled. She blinked hard.

"I packed your bag because I won't go back there again," she said.

"I know." I nodded immediately. "And if I ever put you there again, you don't wait. You leave. You hear me? You leave."

She recoiled, and I hate myself for it. But it needed said.

"I am not asking you to save me," I said. "I am asking you not to give up on me while I learn how to save myself."

The chain on the door rattled softly.

"I choose you," I said again, but this time it wasn't a declaration. It was a plea. "I choose you over the noise. I choose you over the bottle. I choose you over the easy way out."

Her breath trembled.

"I want to deserve you," I whispered. "I don't just want to love you. I want to deserve you."

She stepped into the hallway. "I'm angry," she said. "I'm hurt."

"I know."

"I don't forgive you."

"You shouldn't."

"I won't be your rehab."

"I won't make you be."

A beat.

"If you walk away from this again," she said quietly, "I won't survive it."

I reached for her and stopped myself because I wasn't sure I had that right.

"I am not walking away from you again," I said, and for the first time there was no shake in it. "You are it for me. You always have been."

She crossed the space between us. Her hands grabbed my face like she was afraid I'd disappear. The kiss wasn't gentle. It was furious and terrified and desperate. When she pulled back, her forehead pressed to mine.

"Go," she whispered. "Go fight for us."

I nodded, not trusting words. She kissed me again, and then I drove to the meeting with my hands steadier than they had been in a long time. I sat in a circle of ugly chairs and worse coffee and said my name and my voice didn't break. I listened to men and one woman talk about who they were when the bottle held the leash and who they were learning to be now that their hands were empty. I didn't feel fixed. But I was going to try. For her. For them. For me.

Outside, the air was cold and honest. I texted her to let her know I was headed back to Atlanta. Driving to the clubhouse, my leg ached with the vibration of the bike under me. The lot lights threw long cones on the gravel. Through the front window I saw Hannah closing up, moving like the personification of a heart that refused to quit. In the garage, Dalton and Mac argued about a shim that didn't exist and would have to be made. Somewhere, Maria and Diego were probably at home tucking Jewel into bed.

I stood by my bike and breathed until the shake in my hands dropped to a hum. I thought about whiskey. How it lied like a good salesman. How it told me I could hold fire and not smell like it. How many times I'd let it make me smaller, just so the voices in my head weren't quite as loud. I thought about Holly's eyes tonight. Not pleading. Not even hopeful. Just watching to see if I was a man who could hold eye contact with the truth.

She was better than any whiskey. A math problem with only one right answer.

I went inside. Hannah didn't say anything. She didn't have to. She slid a Tupperware at me and then headed home to August.

In my room, I sat on the edge of the bed and set my phone on the nightstand face-up like a man waiting for orders. I typed, erased, typed again. Settled on the only thing that didn't taste like a commercial.

Me: I love you, Malibu. Always have. Always will.

The dots came and went.

Malibu: You better. Goodnight, handsome.

I lay back. My phone pinged again.

Malibu: And for the record... I love you too.

I smiled when I set the phone back down. The ceiling didn't spin. The ghosts in the corners kept their voices to themselves for once. I closed my eyes on the image of a door half-open, a chain that would come off when it was supposed to, and a woman with a pen in her hair who had already done the hardest thing and might let me try.

I slept without dreaming.

361

Epilogue – One Year Later

⁜ **Holly** ⁜

The wind carried the smell of cut grass and rain, the kind that clung to headstones long after the storm was gone. I knelt in front of the grave, tracing my thumb over the carved name, though I didn't read it aloud. My lips moved anyway—habit, not prayer. There were flowers from half the city tucked into the brass vase: grocery-store lilies, roses from somebody's yard, one plastic sunflower a kid must've insisted on. The wind moved through the cemetery trees with a long, low hush, like the world trying to quiet a crying child.

Behind me, footsteps crunched in the gravel. I didn't have to look. Jackson's boots had a rhythm I could pick out of a thousand others. Slow. Heavy. Present. My eyes never left the headstone. "I don't know how to keep going without her."

He exhaled—that long, quiet sigh that meant he was steadying himself before he spoke. "I think that's the trick of it," he said softly. "You don't keep going *without* her. You keep going *because* of her. She didn't teach us how to quit, Malibu. She taught us how to live messy and love loud."

He took my hand and pulled me up until I leaned against him. My head found that spot beneath his jaw where the world had always made sense.

I pressed my forehead against his shoulder. "I miss her laugh."

He smiled faintly, brushing his thumb along my jaw. "Yeah but she's probably up there giving God pointers by now. Poor bastard."

That earned a wet laugh from me. He always knew when to break the heaviness before it drowned me. I let myself breathe him in. He had become my safe place, one that smelled like soap and leather and the man who had chosen me in a thousand small ways over the last year.

He'd stopped drinking one day at a time until those days stacked into something solid. Meetings. Calls. The ugly chairs and bad coffee, the texts with pictures of coin-colored tokens in his palm when he felt brave, and pictures of empty chairs when he didn't. He still shook sometimes. He told me when the dark got loud. He put his hands where I could see them. We had learned how to be not-ok together and still get up in the morning.

It had been two months without her, and every morning I still expected to hear her at the clubhouse door, hollering about somebody's muddy boots or the price of eggs. Instead we had casseroles from women who couldn't think what else to do, and a chair at the big table no one would sit in, and the memory that the city had swallowed her in the middle of an ordinary day.

A drive-by, they said. Random, they implied. No, we all thought, even if we didn't say it. Not random. Nothing about Hannah was ever random. The story of it still lived in my muscles: the phone vibrating on the counter, Dalton's voice stripped to bone, the way the clubhouse turned into a church and a hospital and a town hall without anyone calling for it. The grieving that never seemed to stop. The after. God, the after.

The sky had that swollen look it got before it opened. He slid his fingers through mine. The ring he'd put there in front of the whole damn club flashed when a weak strip of sun broke free. It was simple and solid and heavier than it looked. Like us.

"Ready?" he asked.

"No," I said, honest. "But let's go anyway."

We took the long path back to the truck, past names that belonged to people we'd fed and fought for and forgiven. The family plot wasn't far from the clubhouse—a short drive, a lifetime away.

August didn't have a stone yet. He still slept in the little back room where

Hannah used to fold napkins and organize men, his breath thinner every day, his eyes always turned toward the door. He'd started talking to her like she was just in the next room. We all knew her absence was killing him and none of us knew how much longer he would hold out for.

On the ride back, Jackson kept his hand on my knee. Wind lifted the edge of my hair where the window was cracked. The city slipped by in fragments—bodegas, girls in school uniforms dragging their feet, a mechanic rolling out from under a car just in time to wave as we went by. Atlanta didn't stop grieving on your schedule. It just kept moving around you, giving you something to push against so you didn't float away.

The clubhouse came into view like a ship that had lost its figurehead. Same old sign, same ugly angel over the door with chipped wings, same bikes lined up like good soldiers. But the hum under the skin was off. We all knew who the heart of the place was.

Dalton stood on the porch, coffee in one hand, his other hand cupped around the rim like he could keep the heat from escaping. He looked like a man trying to hold three different roofs up with his shoulders. When he saw us, his mouth softened. He tipped his chin. No big show. Just, *I see you.* Tired blue eyes that always tried to hide the hurt.

Inside, the place smelled like coffee and lemon oil and a hundred meals Hannah had taught the surfaces to remember. Someone had tried to put things in order. The bulletin board was newly pinned and squared. The sink was empty, miracle of miracles. Her coffee cup still sat by the pot, a relic no one was willing to touch.

Maria's voice floated from the hallway.

"—no, you're not lifting that, Diego. Your job is to admire me and pass me things when I ask you to."

Jackson smiled into his cup. "She's nesting."

"She's always nesting," I said.

We followed the sound and found her on a step stool, rearranging framed photos on the hallway wall like she was conducting a symphony. Diego hovered behind her with a dish towel over his shoulder and the expression of a man who would fistfight gravity if it looked at her wrong.

"You two look like sin and trouble," Maria called the second we stepped in. "Hannah's probably yelling at you from Heaven to take your shoes off before you track mud through her clean floors."

Jackson smirked. "We'll risk it."

Maria clicked her tongue. "Disrespectful."

She stepped down carefully and smoothed her skirt, surveying the wall. The hallway had been slowly transforming under her command. Fresh paint in warm tones. New curtains. Little touches Hannah would've approved of, even if she'd pretended not to.

"You're redecorating again?" I asked.

"I am reclaiming," Maria corrected. "There's a difference. Grief likes to sit in corners. I'm moving the furniture so it has nowhere comfortable to stay."

Diego kissed the top of her head. "She's been on a rampage."

"Organized rampage," she snapped. "Willow's Harbor deserves to feel alive. So does this place."

Jackson nodded once. "Hannah would've liked that."

"She would've micromanaged it," Maria said. "But yes. Let me get this room finished. I'm going for a meadow theme. Then I will make us all some lunch." Maria had been themeing each room. Oceans. Planets. And now meadows. The guests of Willow's Harbor seemed to enjoy it, and it made her happy. So, we just let her do it.

Eventually, we all made our way to the kitchen. Dalton drifted in and took the opposite stool, hunch loosening a notch in the kitchen light. Mac followed a beat later, a clipboard tucked under his arm like he has been in the middle of something important.. He looked older—grief carving a new set of lines around his mouth, a new steadiness behind his eyes. He wasn't trying to be August. He was trying to be the man the club needed now. Those aren't the same thing. He was learning.

"You two coming to the run tonight?" Mac asked, flipping a page. "Short one. Just to… say goodbye."

Jackson nodded. "Yeah."

"We'll be there," I said.

Maria slid a plate in front of Jackson first because she liked him best, and then one in front of me because she loved me more. Diego handed out water bottles like a man on a mission.

"You eat?" he asked.

"Not yet."

"You will," Maria said firmly. "Hannah didn't raise us to starve while we're sad."

Dalton snorted. "She'd haunt you personally."

"She already is," Maria said, glancing toward the hallway. "Every time someone leaves a coffee mug in the sink too long, I feel judged."

Mac almost smiled.

The room felt fuller for a second. Not healed. Just held.

Footsteps sounded at the hallway door. Silas paused in the threshold like a man who'd learned doorways were power. Tailored shirt, cuffs unbuttoned just so. Hair too neat for this building. He carried a stack of folders and an expression that practiced concern in the mirror. If charisma had a smell, it would've been his cologne—expensive and a little oily.

"Morning," he said, voice warm enough to melt butter. "Brought the vendor bids for the fundraiser, Mac. And I got the city to expedite the permit for the street closure. Should be in by end of day."

Mac's relief was visible enough to make me feel petty. "Good," he said, clapping Silas on the shoulder like a man thanking a neighbor for bringing in the trash cans. "Appreciate it."

"Always," Silas said, holding his hands up like *don't mind me, just helping*. He took the seat at the edge of the table—that sly not-in-the-center, not-too-far-away spot that let you hear everything and be seen as little or as much as you wanted. He had a way of appearing exactly where the empty space was. The day Hannah died, he'd been there with paper plates and a schedule and the names of three different pastors on his phone, and nobody asked how he knew what we needed. You didn't judge a man for handing you a life jacket while you were drowning. You took it and breathed, and the questions came later when your lungs stopped burning.

I didn't have proof of anything. Not even a shape to my unease. Just a small prickle along the back of my neck when his eyes landed on me and slid away, like he saw me as part of a calculation, not a person. He'd always been around the edges—August's oldest friend, the uncle who brought good cigars and bad advice. I had never paid him attention because men like Silas assumed women like me were standing too far back to matter. That's how they miss us noticing.

"Meeting at three," Mac said, flipping pages. "We'll nail down the route and the press."

Silas smiled. "I can invite Councilman Reyes—he loved Hannah. It'd be a good look."

Maria's jaw went tight. "It's not a look."

Silas spread his hands, apologetic. "You know what I mean."

"I do," she said, and went back to her plate like cutting a man open with a fork was beneath her. I could tell Maria at least shared my sentiments.

Jackson's knee pressed into mine under the table. A small, careful question. *You good?* I nodded once. *Good enough.*

The day moved the way days do when there's too much to do and not enough of the right person to do it. People came by with envelopes and hugs and a hundred stories that started with "You know what she said to me once?" Men who had never cried wiped at their eyes, angry about it. Women who had never been welcomed anywhere but here sat at Hannah's table and ate second helpings and laughed too loud because here they could. Kids ran through the side yard and got yelled at by three different bikers who then handed them popsicles.

August slept through most of it. When he woke, he asked for her like she'd gone to the store, and we told him the truth again, soft as we could. He nodded and stared at the ceiling and whispered something that made Dalton swallow hard and leave the room. One of us would tuck the blanket around August's thinning shoulders and kissed the top of his head and pretended not to see how bones were winning.

Sometime after lunch, rain finally spat once and gave up. The heat came back angrier for having been interrupted. Jackson found me on the back steps, elbows on my knees, watching a line of ants transfer an entire feast crumb by crumb. He sat behind me and bracketed me with his legs, his chest to my back, his chin on my shoulder. I leaned into him like I'd been built for that angle.

"You holding?" he asked.

"Like cheap tape," I said.

"Still works if you double it."

He smelled like soap and road. His heart thudded steady against my spine. I could feel his breathing change when his thoughts did. He had tells now. He let me have mine.

"Meeting tonight?" I asked.

"Yeah. After the run. My sponsor wants me to share." He huffed. "I hate sharing."

"You're good at it," I said. "You make the hard parts sound survivable." I turned my head so my mouth brushed his stubble.

He kissed the spot under my ear, a promise more than anything.

We stayed quiet until the shadows lengthened and the mosquitoes got cocky. Out front, engines rumbled and died in waves. The club gathered like weather. By dusk, the bikes were lined two deep, chromed bones catching the porch light. Men hugged like they were bad at it and pounded backs like they weren't. The women settled into chairs with fans and secrets. Dalton stood on the porch and talked numbers and safety and respect into the air until it felt like a benediction. Mac added logistics. Silas drifted just close enough to place a hand on Mac's shoulder at the end, like the punctuation mark a sentence didn't strictly need.

The run was short and bitter sweet. A loop past the hospital where we'd waited for news that didn't come. My father knew the surgeon who had tried to save her. I heard him tell Mom one night that the whole surgery team went quiet when the machines told them it was too late. Past the church with the hand-painted sign that said "Love is a verb," and meant it. Past two storefronts Hannah had nagged into donating to every coat drive since forever. Past Momma Laverne's who had shut down the restaurant for a week, opting to send plate after plate to the clubhouse. Her way of trying to fill the hole in everyone's hearts. The air tasted like cut grass and gasoline. I rode behind Jackson, arms around him, forehead to his spine, the way we'd learned to breathe together when nothing else made sense.

People on sidewalks lifted their phones and their hands. Some put palms over hearts. Some cried. Every hat taken off and held over saddened hearts that mourned a woman who had changed this community so thoroughly.

Back at the clubhouse, someone put out food without being asked. Someone else lit the hanging bulbs Hannah had insisted on stringing across the yard because joy should be visible at night. The world softened at the edges. Maria held court on the porch with her feet up on a spare chair, telling exaggerated stories about Hannah teaching her how to stretch a dollar and feed twenty people with one skillet.

"She'd haunt your pantry if you wasted food," Maria declared, waving a fork like a baton.

"Terrifying," Dalton muttered.

"She was terrifying," Maria corrected, softening. "And generous. And loud. And impossible to ignore."

When it got late, the crowd thinned. The mechanics stayed to argue about a part only they cared about. The mothers left in clumps, calling threats and blessings over their shoulders. Silas shook hands on his way to his car, smiling that soft, unearned smile. He bent toward me when he passed, the way men did when they thought getting lower made them less threatening. "Beautiful turnout," he said. "You did Hannah proud."

"We all did," I said. Her funeral felt like forever ago but tonight, it felt like Hannah was still with us.

His gaze flicked over my shoulder toward Jackson and back to me, calculating something I didn't get to see the end of. "Of course," he said, and walked away with a little wave that suggested we were friends. I couldn't keep my lip from curling.

"*Cabron*," Maria muttered at my elbow.

"You don't even like that word," I said.

"I'm expanding my vocabulary."

Jackson came up behind me then and slid his arm around my waist, palm flat over my stomach like a claim. He nodded toward the far end of the lot where the sky had gathered itself into something darker. Heat lightning flared along the line of trees like someone taking pictures of us without permission.

"What's on your mind, love?" he asked, low.

"I don't know," I said. "I keep thinking about…everything. How fast it all shifted. How August looks past me when I stand right in front of him. How Mac talks like he's reading a map he didn't draw. How Dalton holds his shoulders like they're carrying a roof."

I was rambling, but he listened the way he always listened now—entirely, without complaint. "It shifted," he said. "You're not wrong. We'll keep shifting with it."

"I don't trust him," I said before I could talk myself out of it, eyes still on the tree line where lightning kept flashing without thunder. "Silas. I know that sounds…I don't know. Petty? Paranoid? He's always around when there's a gap, with the exact right fix. He smiles too much. My gut doesn't like it."

Jackson's thumb stroked absent circles against my hip. "I've learned to trust your gut."

"I never paid attention to him before," I said, which was its own confession. "He was just August's friend. I assumed the men had their male things and I'd stay out of it. But I see him now. I see how he positions himself. How he watches. I don't know what that means."

"It means we keep our eyes open," Jackson said. "And we don't borrow trouble. If it's coming, it'll get here on its own."

"Comforting," I said, dry.

He smiled into my hair. "I can do better." He angled me toward him so I had to look at his mouth, his eyes, the scar that softened when he was dead serious. "I fought my war. I know what my ghosts look like in daylight now. If another war shows up—club politics, city snakes, whatever—then we fight the one in front of us. Together. I don't care if the sky cracks. You hear me?"

I did. I heard the weight of every meeting coin in his pocket, the creak of every chair in every circle where he'd said his name and then said it again. I heard August breathing thin and Maria laughing and Dalton's jaw grinding and Mac quietly redrawing maps. I heard Hannah's voice in every corner: *Feed them. Love them. Tell the truth.* I heard my own heart, stubborn and sore and still beating.

"I hear you," I said. "And just so we're clear? If the sky cracks, I'm throwing the first punch."

"Malibu," he said, smiling that smile he only smiled for me. "I'd pay to see it."

Thunder finally grumbled from far off, late to the party. The air went more still, like everything knew to make space. The porch bulbs glowed soft. Somebody inside turned off the radio and left the lights. The clubhouse hummed like a tired thing still willing to work.

We stood there and watching the horizon, his hands on me, my hands on him, two people who had screwed up and learned and kept choosing anyway. Grief didn't shrink. It stretched and made room for the rest of your life to fit beside it. Maybe that was the trick Hannah had known all along—love big enough to hold sorrow without letting it drown the table.

Out past the trees, the sky flickered again—silver behind black. You could smell the rain coming the way you sometimes smell trouble: mineral and electric, metallic on the tongue.

A storm was coming.

I didn't know its name yet or how it would break or who would be standing where when it did. I just knew this: whatever it was, whatever tried to tear through what we'd built, we'd face it together.

From the Author

Hello you,

You made it to the end.

Which means you survived the chaos, the heartbreak, the second chances, and probably at least one scene that had you staring at the ceiling afterward.

Thank you for riding this out with me.

Stories like this are written in stolen hours, fueled by stubborn hope and characters who refuse to behave. The fact that you opened this book—and stayed—means everything.

If you have a moment, leaving a review is one of the most powerful ways you can support an author. And if you're not ready to say goodbye to this world just yet, there's more coming.

Buckle up.

— Sarah

About the Author

Sarah Mason writes emotionally charged contemporary romance where love is rarely easy and redemption is hard-won. Her stories explore trauma, loyalty, and the messy beauty of second chances within the Steel Saints MC universe.

Based in Missouri, Sarah draws from small-town culture, close-knit communities, and complicated family dynamics to create immersive worlds filled with flawed heroes and fiercely resilient heroines.

Her debut novel, *Riding the Line*, marks the beginning of an expanding interconnected series.

You can connect with me on:

- https://sarahkmasonauthor.com
- https://www.facebook.com/profile.php?id=61583190391422
- https://www.instagram.com/sarahkmason_author
- https://www.tiktok.com/@sarahkmason_author

Subscribe to my newsletter:

- https://dl.bookfunnel.com/v25pok6r6e

Riding the Line (Steel Saints MC)
In this steamy, heart-wrenching motorcycle-club romance, a cop must make a choice—her heart or her badge.

Detective Kaitlyn McGrady has trained for every situation imaginable—but nothing prepares her for life undercover as Nicole Moore, a hardened woman with a fake rap sheet and a chip on her shoulder. Her mission: infiltrate the Steel Saints Motorcycle Club and get close to the DiAngelo crime family.

Her rules are simple: don't break character, don't trust anyone, and definitely don't fall in love.

Then she meets *them*—Dalton and Maverick. Two brothers. One's all Southern charm and quiet strength; the other is pure fire and fury. Both see straight through her walls, and both threaten to burn down everything she's built to protect.

As the lines between right and wrong blur, Katie's torn between duty and desire, justice and family. The deeper she falls, the harder it will be to walk away… and the more dangerous the mission becomes.

Caught in the Crossfire

After a night of heat and bad decisions, they never expected to see each other again—until a case throws them back together in the harsh light of day.

Sergeant Owen Bishop likes things simple: one case, one glass of bourbon, one empty bed. Divorced and burned out, he's long made peace with being the department's resident cynic. But when he's called into his captain's office and told he's getting a new partner, the last person he expects to walk through the door is her—the woman who left the sheets a mess and his thoughts even worse.

Sergeant Casey Chambers is twenty-eight, ambitious, and the youngest officer ever to lead the Vice unit's field team. She clawed her way through the old boys' club to earn her stripes, and she refuses to let one brooding homicide veteran slow her down—especially not the man she swore she'd never see again.

When young women start turning up dead with track marks and no history of addiction, Owen and Casey are forced to join forces. Between long nights, blurred lines, and secrets that cut too deep, their chemistry becomes as dangerous as the case they're chasing.